Did something go bum
Square residence?

Nate pushed open the double doors to the library. If only he didn't have to attend any damnable ton balls or soirees. God, the idea of courting a simpering debutante like Lady Penelope Purcell was enough to turn his stomach—

A decidedly feminine gasp and a dull thud stopped him dead in his tracks.

What the deuce?

Behind his father's desk stood a raven-haired angel. A beautiful young woman wearing nothing but a pale blue shawl over a thin white night rail, and an expression of sheer terror.

"Lord Malverne. Oh, heavens. Oh, my goodness." The angel's shocked, wide-eyed gaze dropped to the desk, and then, much to his amusement, he was certain she muttered something not so angelic like *blast* beneath her breath.

Nate's gaze followed hers. *Blast indeed.* His father's cut crystal inkwell was on its side, and a black pool of ink was rapidly spreading across the dark red blotter, heading inexorably toward the young woman's pristine nightgown. In the next instant, as he strode toward the desk to offer assistance, she whipped off her shawl and pressed it against the inky puddle.

"I'm so, so sorry. What will your father think of me? I only meant to borrow a little ink. I didn't think he'd mind." Her words came out in a breathless rush as she began to dab furiously at the blotter. "And now I've ruined some of his papers. Oh, Lord, I hope they're not too important." She nodded at a dark splash marring the top of a document that looked a lot like a draft parliamentary bill. "What a disaster."

HOW TO CATCH A WICKED VISCOUNT

AMY ROSE BENNETT

JOVE
New York

A JOVE BOOK
Published by Berkley
An imprint of Penguin Random House LLC
1745 Broadway, New York, NY 10019

Copyright © 2019 by Amy Rose Bennett
Excerpt from *How to Catch an Errant Earl* copyright © 2019 by Amy Rose Bennett
Penguin Random House supports copyright. Copyright fuels creativity, encourages
diverse voices, promotes free speech, and creates a vibrant culture. Thank you for buying
an authorized edition of this book and for complying with copyright laws by not
reproducing, scanning, or distributing any part of it in any form without permission.
You are supporting writers and allowing Penguin Random House to continue to
publish books for every reader.

A JOVE BOOK, BERKLEY, and the BERKLEY & B colophon
are registered trademarks of Penguin Random House LLC.

ISBN: 9781984803924

First Edition: August 2019

Printed in the United States of America
1   3   5   7   9   10   8   6   4   2

Cover art by Aleta Rafton
Book design by George Towne

*To Richard,
the love of my life
and my very own hero,
you are the reason I write romance novels.*

ACKNOWLEDGMENTS

A heartfelt thank-you must go to my wonderful agent, Jessica Alvarez. Your insight and support have been invaluable.

I'm also extremely grateful to Cindy Hwang at Berkley Publishing for believing in my story. And of course, I must thank my fabulous editor, Kristine Swartz, for her expertise, and all the team at Berkley who've worked so very hard to make my book the very best it can be.

And last but not least, I want to thank my amazing husband and two beautiful daughters for their endless love and unwavering belief in me. I wouldn't have achieved my dream without you.

CHAPTER 1

Disreputable Debutantes in the making!

A shocking scandal of epic proportions at a certain London school for "Young Ladies of Good Character" shakes the ton.

Does your genteel daughter attend such a den of iniquity? Read on to discover ten things one should consider when choosing a reputable academy . . .

The Beau Monde Mirror: The Society Page

Mrs. Rathbone's Academy for Young Ladies of Good Character, Knightsbridge, London

Midnight, February 3, 1815

Heavens. Take care, Charlie." Sophie Brightwell winced as her friend entered her bedroom and carelessly pushed the door shut with her slippered foot. The resultant bang was decidedly too loud in the relative silence of the dormitory wing of the Hans Place town house. "You'll wake Mrs. Rathbone for sure. If she finds out what we're up to . . ." Sophie couldn't suppress a shiver.

Lady Charlotte Hastings—or Charlie to her friends—threw her a disarming smile as she deposited a large band-box of contraband and a battered leather satchel on the end of the single bed. "Don't worry so, darling Sophie," she said as she untied the black satin ribbon securing the box's lid with a flourish. "I just passed her bedchamber and she was snoring like a hold full of drunken sailors."

Arabella Jardine, who was perched on the edge of a bed-side armchair, pushed her honey-gold curls behind her ears and then smoothed her robe over her night rail. "Aye, 'tis true, Sophie," she agreed in her soft Scots burr. "I suspect she's been into the sherry again."

Sophie pressed her lips together to suppress a small sigh. Even though she loved Charlie like a sister, the earl's daughter didn't have as much to lose as she did, or indeed their other two partners in crime this night—Olivia de Vere and Arabella—if they were caught flouting the young ladies' academy's strict rules. So while it was quite true that Mrs. Agatha Rathbone, the apparently upstanding, middle-aged headmistress of her eponymous boarding school, was fond of a tipple—or ten—on Friday evenings, and nothing short of an earthquake or a herd of rampaging elephants was likely to rouse her, Sophie was still anxious about the whole idea of a midnight gathering—especially because it was oc-curring in the room she shared with Olivia.

Sophie's pulse leapt once more as the door opened again, this time admitting her roommate, bearing a tray of mis-matched china teacups.

"Ah, perfect timing, Miss de Vere," Charlie remarked as she lifted two dark glass bottles from the bandbox and bran-dished them in the air. "So what poison will you choose, my lovelies?" she asked, her topaz brown eyes dancing with merriment. "French brandy or port?"

Olivia carefully placed the tray on the cherrywood bed-side table then tossed her dark braid over one slender shoul-der. "Wh-what do you r-recommend? I h-haven't tried either one." Her manner of speech was an unusual combination of the lyrical and the discordant, her tone low and melodious with an appealing smokiness. Yet it was her stammer that drew attention; Sophie knew it tended to emerge when Ol-ivia was nervous or extremely fatigued.

"My grandfather let me try a wee sherry at Christmas," added Arabella. "But I've never tasted brandy or port wine."

"Hmm. The port is probably a little smoother for unsea-soned drinkers. But I've heard my brother Nate say French brandy is excellent. Perhaps we should all begin with that."

Charlie turned her bright gaze on Sophie. "Wouldn't you agree?"

"Yes." A burst of curiosity overcoming her trepidation, Sophie leaned across the quilted counterpane to examine the jumbled contents of the box. "So, what else have you smuggled in here?"

An enigmatic smile tugged at the corner of Charlie's mouth. "Oh, this and that," she said as she passed the bottle of brandy to Olivia to dispense. "All will be revealed after we raise our glasses—or I should say cups?—in a toast."

"A toast to what?" Arabella asked as she took her brimming teacup from Olivia. Beneath her gold-rimmed glasses, her pretty nose wrinkled when she sniffed at the amber liquid. "You are being altogether too mysterious, Charlie."

"To us, of course. And our new society."

Sophie arched an eyebrow. "And does this society have a name?"

"It certainly does." Charlie handed a teacup to Sophie and then beamed as she added, "Right, my darling girls. From this night on, we four shall henceforth be known as the Society for Enlightened Young Women, a society that will aim to provide its members with a stimulating education in all manner of worldly matters not included in this academy's current curriculum. Such knowledge will, of course, be invaluable when each of us leaves here and is subsequently obliged to embark on a quest to secure an advantageous match during the coming Season. And as we all know how cutthroat the marriage mart can be, I, as head monitor, feel it is my incumbent duty to begin your supplementary tutelage sooner rather than later." Her gaze touched each one of them. "If we are all in agreeance . . ."

Olivia nodded, Arabella murmured yes, and Sophie's brow knit into a suspicious frown. "What worldly matters in particular?" she asked.

Charlie cast her a knowing smile. "Why, matters that all men, young and old, know about, but we, as the fairer, weaker sex, are supposed to remain ignorant of until we are wed. But by that time, I rather suspect it is too late. To my way of thinking, it would be much better to enter into marriage with one's eyes wide open. And dare I say it, perhaps *we* might have a little fun along the way too?"

"Are . . . are you referring to sexual c-congress?" whispered Olivia, her doe brown eyes widening with shock.

"Yes, I am. Among other things. The art of flirting is also an essential skill any wise debutante should have in her arsenal, and naturally, it is a precursor to any activity of an amorous nature." Charlie turned to Sophie and raised a quizzical brow; her eyes glowed with anticipation. "What say you, my friend? You haven't responded yet."

Sophie worried at her lower lip as she considered Charlie's proposal. Even though she hailed from Suffolk and possessed a rudimentary knowledge of "sexual congress"—as it pertained to the mating rituals of farmyard animals, at least—there was still much she did not know about the ways of the world—and the male of the species—compared to Charlie.

Indeed, Lady Charlotte Hastings was the only one in their close-knit group who had several brothers—one of whom was a well-known rakehell. And she also had a bluestocking aunt who was purported to be a "liberal thinker" and "a woman ahead of her time." For these reasons, Sophie didn't doubt for a moment that Charlie possessed unique insights into the male mind and a singular knowledge of taboo topics.

Unlike her confident, highborn friend, Sophie was not a member of the *haut ton*. But if Charlie was prepared to equip her with the skills and knowledge of a sophisticated debutante, she would be an avid pupil. She'd much rather possess a modicum of self-assurance attending ton social events when the Season began in earnest. Heaven forbid that she should come across as a naive and nervous bumpkin who blushed and stammered whenever an eligible gentleman asked her to dance or even cast a glance in her direction. "Your idea has some merit," she at last conceded with a smile. "After all, forewarned is forearmed. How often will we meet?"

"Oh, once a week I expect," said Charlie with a wave of one elegant hand. "And only when we are certain Rathbone is as drunk as a wheelbarrow. Which always seems to be on a Friday."

Sophie inclined her head. "Then I agree too."

"Excellent." A spark of mischief lit Charlie's eyes. "Now, if we were male students, at this point we'd no doubt plight our troths by doing something dreadful like expectorating across the room or slicing open our palms to make a blood oath, or at the very least we'd all expel some kind of foul air from an orifice we shall not speak of."

A delighted bubble of laughter escaped Arabella. "Oh, Charlie. I suspect you are quite right. But I think your original suggestion of a toast will suffice."

"Yes indeed," agreed Sophie.

Charlie's smile widened as she moved to the center of the worn hearthrug. The firelight limned her unruly chestnut hair in gold, and in that moment, Sophie couldn't help but think her friend bore more than a passing resemblance to a fiery Valkyrie or Artemis, the huntress—she was a determined young woman on a mission and she would not be thwarted.

Lifting her chipped Spode china teacup, Charlie caught all of their gazes and led the toast. "Well then, without further ado, let us all raise our cups and drink to the Society for Enlightened Young Women. Long may we prosper. And may we all find happiness wherever life takes us."

Sophie, Olivia, and Arabella raised their cups and in unison proclaimed, "Hear, hear," before they each took a sip of brandy. Then Olivia coughed, Arabella gasped, Sophie's eyes watered, and Charlie laughed.

"Oh, girls. It's not all that bad, is it?" she asked, rubbing Olivia's back.

"Where did you get this . . . this fire water?" Sophie wiped her eyes with the sleeve of her flannel night rail.

Charlie took another sip before replying. "My father's study here in London. He won't miss it. And even if he does, he'll probably assume Nate took it. He's such a devil."

Nate—or Nathaniel Hastings, Viscount Malverne—was Charlie's older brother and, as the eldest son of the family, heir to the earldom of Westhampton. Sophie had met him in passing two months ago in Hyde Park while out walking with Charlie, so she could certainly attest to the fact that he was wickedly handsome—a man who could easily make females blush just by casting a sinful smile their way. Indeed, Sophie rather suspected she resembled a boiled lobster when Charlie had made the introductions.

Of course, Charlie had warned her, Olivia, and Arabella on numerous occasions that Nate was a rogue to his very bones, and exactly the sort of man they should be wary of when they made their debuts. He seduced women regularly, without care or regard for their feelings or their ruined reputations. He was definitely *not* the sort of man who wished to marry anytime soon.

But despite Charlie's warnings, a small part of Sophie had always thrilled to the idea of capturing the attention of a man like Nate, even if it was just for a little while. What was it about wicked rakes that lured her—and perhaps other women—like a candle flame lured the hapless moth? The glint of mischief in Lord Malverne's dark eyes had seemed to contain a promise as his gaze traveled over her that cold winter's day: *Come with me and I will show you sensual delights. Forbidden things both bright and burning. Secret things that are inherently dangerous yet irresistible.* No wonder she still blushed at the memory. The heat in her cheeks had nothing to do with the brandy she sipped . . .

The sound of Arabella calling her name pulled Sophie from her ruminations, and she approached her bed to examine the other illicit items Charlie had brought with her to supplement their "education." Aside from a jar of sugared almonds and one of barley sugar sweets, there were several leather-bound volumes, a slender silver box, and a folio, which Charlie had just pulled from the leather satchel.

Sophie put down her cup, picked up one of the books, and then gasped. *Memoirs of a Woman of Pleasure*, volume one.

"Charlie," she breathed. "Where on earth did you get this? You know it's banned, don't you? That the author was arrested?" She once overheard two older women at the circulating library discussing it in excited whispers behind one of the standing shelves when they'd come across another not-quite-so-scandalous book entitled *Pamela; or, Virtue Rewarded.*

"Of course, I do," replied Charlie. "And to answer your first question, I found it in my father's library, along with volume two, and these . . ." She fanned a sheaf of sketches and drawings across the counterpane that put Olivia to the blush and sent Arabella into a paroxysm of laughter.

Sophie leaned closer, and her eyebrows shot up when she saw the erotic nature of each picture. "Oh, my Lord," she whispered, picking one up with shaking fingers as heat crawled over her face. "*What*, in heaven's name, is he doing to her?"

Charlie grinned. "That, my dear Sophie, is one of the many things you'll become enlightened about."

Behind her glasses, Arabella's gaze sharpened with interest as she picked up the ornate silver box, unfastened the clasp, and lifted the lid. "Cheroots, Charlie? Are these for us to try?"

"If you like," she said, taking one of the slender, quite feminine-looking cigars from the box. "My aunt Tabitha calls them *cigarrillos*. Her tobacconist makes them especially for her using a tobacco blend from Seville."

Olivia also picked up one of the cigars and gave it a small sniff. "My g-goodness. Perhaps we should call ourselves the Society for Scandalous Young Women."

"Well, we will only be deemed scandalous if we are caught," Charlie remarked as she plucked a taper from the spill vase on the carved wooden mantelpiece. She dipped it in the flame of a candle and touched it to the end of her *cigarrillo* until the tip caught alight. Then, after inhaling a small breath, she expertly puffed out a delicate cloud of smoke. The earthy yet sweet scent of burning tobacco filled the room.

"Ha, it's clear you've done this before," declared Arabella. Following Charlie's example, she used a taper to light her *cigarrillo* before placing it between her lips. She drew a breath and then promptly burst into a fit of coughing so violent, her glasses were dislodged.

Charlie's brow dipped into a concerned frown. "Gently, gently. Don't breathe in too deeply."

"Oh . . . that's . . . that's truly awful," gasped Arabella. Her face had turned a sickly shade of green. "I'm sure my lungs will never be the same again." Wrinkling her nose, she held the smoking cigar away from her like one might hold a dead mouse by the tail. "I'm sorry, Charlie. I don't think I want any more."

"That's quite all right." Charlie took it from her, then glanced between Olivia and Sophie. "Would either of you like to try?"

Olivia shook her head and Sophie crossed to the window, drawing back the dull blue utilitarian curtains. "No thank you, Charlie. And I think we should let some fresh air in. If Mrs. Rathbone notices the smell—"

"Mrs. Rathbone *has* noticed the smell. And the raucous laughter and chatter."

Oh no. Oh no, no, no. Her heart vaulting into the vicinity of her throat, Sophie whirled around then nearly fainted. In the open doorway, her plump arms folded over her ample chest, stood a glowering Mrs. Rathbone. Even though she only wore a rumpled night rail, a coarse woolen shawl, and a linen cap that was askew, her informal attire didn't diminish her gravitas or the seriousness of the moment in the least. From beneath heavy gray brows, her pale blue eyes skewered them all in turn. Arabella's countenance was green again, Olivia was as white as the bedsheets, and Sophie wondered how she continued to remain upright when her knees felt as though they were made of blancmange.

Charlie, on the other hand, looked remarkably unperturbed. She tossed both of the *cigarrillos* into the fire and lifted her chin. "Our apologies for disturbing your sleep, Mrs. Rathbone. We shall, of course, retire immediately. If you would just give me a moment to gather my things—"

Charlie had barely taken a step across the rug when Mrs. Rathbone raised a hand. "Stop right there, my gel," she barked. Her glare swept over Sophie's bedside table and bed, and then her fleshy face turned an alarming shade of crimson when she took in the nature of the scattered sketches. "What. Are. Those?" she demanded in a shaking voice. When no one responded, she raised a quivering hand to her equally quivering jowls. "And what have you all been drinking? Brandy? Is that brandy I see in your cups? And what's that other bottle on the bed?"

"Port," replied Charlie without batting an eyelid. She started to add, "They're for medicinal pur—" but Mrs. Rathbone jabbed a finger in her direction.

"Not another word out of you, Lady Charlotte." The headmistress all but charged across the room and snatched up both bottles. Although her expression still bordered on furious, Sophie thought she detected a covetous glimmer in the woman's eyes. "This behavior is outrageous," she continued as she tucked both bottles into the crook of one arm. "Beyond the pale. Smoking? Imbibing alcohol? Studying lewd material? And all in the middle of the night! I can scarcely believe it. In all my years as the headmistress of this establishment, I have never, *ever* encountered such shocking conduct from young ladies. You should all be ashamed of yourselves. Just wait till the school's patrons and your parents hear about it!"

Charlie inclined her head. "Yes, it is shameful," she agreed in a contrite tone that *almost* sounded sincere to Sophie's ears. "And although you forbade me to speak, Mrs. Rathbone, I feel compelled to confess that everything you see on the bed—the books, the sketches, the cheroot cigars—*and* the bottles of port and brandy, all of it belongs to me. I alone bear the blame. Miss Brightwell, Miss Jardine, and Miss de Vere are innocent of any wrongdoing."

Mrs. Rathbone narrowed her eyes. "Yet all of these proscribed items are in Miss Brightwell's and Miss de Vere's bedchamber. And"—her gaze darted about the room—"I spy *four* teacups of brandy." She gave an inelegant sniff and looked down her flushed nose at them all. "As far as I can see, each one of you is guilty of unladylike conduct in the extreme and, subsequently, you are not fit to remain within this academy's walls. In the morning, I shall send word to your families and begin the process of having you all expelled."

Arabella sucked in a startled breath, Olivia wrung her hands, and Sophie felt as though a massive weight had just crushed her chest, driving all the air from her lungs. *Oh, dear God, no. This can't be happening.* What would her family say? Her mother? Her stepfather?

The ton?

But it *was* happening. Even Charlie's face was ashen.

As Sophie struggled to drag in enough air to breathe, Mrs. Rathbone issued instructions to Charlie and Arabella to gather up all of the offending items off the bed, and Olivia was ordered to tip the contents of the teacups out of the window into the frosty garden bed below.

"I'm sorry," mouthed Charlie as she picked up her bandbox and followed a tearful Arabella and a righteously indignant Rathbone out of the room.

As soon as the door clicked shut, Sophie sank onto her bed and hugged a pillow against her chest. Hot tears of mortification and despair scalded her eyelids.

There was sure to be a scandal of monumental proportions. *Thrown out of a young ladies' academy.* Her reputation and that of all of her friends would be ruined. There would be no invitations to Almack's. No invitations to anywhere at all. Only stares and whispers, closed doors and censure wherever she went.

Her parents would be livid, her younger sisters heartbroken.

She was only eighteen, but she would be forever branded as a woman of loose character and questionable morals. A hussy.

A slut.

Sophie swallowed, attempting to dislodge the gathering ache in her throat. How on earth was she to meet her love match now? She'd never make a socially and financially advantageous union as her family had hoped she would; indeed, without such a marriage, there was a very real chance her stepfather might lose Nettlefield Grange and the accompanying estate. How shocking that her dreams and her family's livelihood could be crushed to dust because of her folly.

The weight on her chest was back, and her heart felt as though it might crack beneath the strain.

"Do . . . do you think there's any chance Rathbone m-might try to hush things up? To preserve her own and the school's reputation?" murmured Olivia in a voice husky with tears.

Sophie dashed away her own tears with shaking fingers. "I expect she might try to, but word is bound to get out. Who doesn't love a juicy piece of gossip? And besides Charlie, none of us has any social connections that would hold sway with Rathbone. I really don't think there is anything we can do to stop our expulsion."

Olivia's eyes glimmered with fresh tears. "We'll be socially destroyed then."

Sophie's heart broke just that little bit more at witnessing her sweet friend's distress. She cast aside her pillow and crossed to the other bed. "Yes, Olivia," she whispered as she enveloped the trembling girl in a hug. "I'm afraid we will."

CHAPTER 2

∂℃

The great drawers caper!

    What sort of gentleman would wager another to procure a pair of a certain noblewoman's drawers? Surely not a respectable one, but then some might say boys will be boys, especially when the boys in question are the ton's most notorious rakehells. Read on to discover what happened last night at one of London's most prestigious addresses . . .

The Beau Monde Mirror: The Society Page

Astley House, Cavendish Square, London

Midnight, March 5, 1818

Bloody hell, Nate," growled Gabriel Holmes-Fitzgerald, Lord Langdale. "How in the devil's name are you going to climb up there?" He gestured at the second floor of the elegant white brick town house. "You'll break your neck."

Nate Hastings, Lord Malverne, grinned as he shrugged out of his dark blue superfine evening jacket and tossed it to Hamish MacQueen, Lord Sleat. The marquess had agreed to stand guard with Maximilian Devereux, the Duke of Exmoor, while he fulfilled the dare they'd challenged him to earlier in the evening. At stake was a wager of four hundred pounds, and he was determined to win. "Maybe. But aren't you coming with me, Gabriel? If I'm to pilfer a pair of the infamous Countess of Astley's drawers, I'll need someone to witness that they're actually hers, don't you think, and not a guest's or even the housekeeper's?"

Gabriel grimaced and ran a hand through his disheveled black hair. "God damn you. All right." He blew out a resigned sigh before throwing his own jacket to a scowling MacQueen.

Nate suspected the burly Scot, who looked more like a pirate than a Highlander because of his eye patch, hadn't reckoned on playing the part of valet during their alcohol-fueled escapade.

Oblivious to MacQueen's glowering stare, Gabriel circled his shoulders and cracked his knuckles as he added, "Might I suggest we scale the iron fence and then try to find a way in around the back?"

"My thoughts too," drawled Max. He dropped the stub of his cheroot onto the pavement and ground it out with the toe of his glossy black Hessian boot. "Only, why don't I pick the lock on the gate to minimize the spectacle of several men illegally entering Lord and Lady Astley's town house in the dead of night. I don't know about you, but I don't fancy spending the rest of the evening explaining myself to the Runners if a passerby or a neighborly good Samaritan notices us."

"Good point," agreed Nate. He stepped aside to give the duke room to work his magic on the gate's lock. Within moments, the gate swung open on well-oiled hinges and then all four of them ducked down the side path that led to the enclosed courtyard garden at the back of the house.

Rubbing his hands together—the night was devilishly cold—Nate craned his neck and examined the upper floors at the back of the house. Subdued light filtered out of a central second-floor window—probably the casement window above the main staircase—and through the filmy curtains hanging in another window farther along to the right. The windows and French doors on the ground floor that led onto a flagged terrace were completely dark. "Have any of you been inside before?"

MacQueen gave a soft huff of laughter. "Aye. At Covent Garden a few years back. Lady Astley and I shared a theater box. But a gentleman isn't supposed to kiss and tell, is he?"

"I meant the town house, you dog. Not the countess."

"I have," said Max. "I attended a ball here a while ago, but from memory, the main bedrooms are on the second floor on the eastern side." He nodded toward the window on the right.

"It's a dashed nuisance that there's no trellis to scale or even a nearby garden wall to climb," murmured Nate. He turned to Max. "Do you think you could pick the lock to the French doors?" He was still well liquored after spending the last six hours drinking at White's, and he didn't really want to crack his head open over a scandalous countess's drawers. Skulking about the inside of the Astley town house, while risky, was a far less dangerous prospect than attempting to scale unclimbable walls with only the pitiful light of a thin crescent moon to see by. He might be foxed but he wasn't stupid.

Max shrugged a wide shoulder. "Probably. But it will cost you."

"Go on. Name your price then."

Max's white teeth gleamed in the darkness. "Your bottle of Renaud and Dualle cognac. The ninety-five vintage."

Bastard. Nate heaved a sigh. "Very well. Agreed."

Max withdrew a penknife from the inner breast pocket of his black evening jacket and proceeded to prize open the second lock with a few deft slides and twists of the knife's small, thin blade. He carefully pushed open the door and stepped aside with an exaggerated flourish. "Gentlemen . . ."

MacQueen chuckled softly from behind them. "Don't do anything I wouldn't do."

Cheeky sod. As if he'd even think about seducing one of the Scot's former conquests. Nate cast a sideways glance at Gabriel as he followed him through the door. He wouldn't put it past the Earl of Langdale though. He was the randiest devil out of the lot of them.

The room they'd entered appeared to be the library; the glowing coals in the banked fire gave off enough light for

Nate to make out floor-to-ceiling bookcases, the bulky form of a large desk, and several wingchairs by the fireside.

Praying his new leather Hessian boots wouldn't squeak, Nate quickly traversed the room, then cracked open the door. The hall beyond was softly lit by several wall sconces, and halfway along he could see a wide staircase with ornate iron balustrades. Thankfully, there was also no one in sight. Apparently, Lady Astley liked to retire early. Or perhaps she wasn't even here at all, a circumstance that would be most fortuitous considering Nate had to steal into her chambers.

"We're sure Astley is away, aren't we?" Gabriel murmured from behind him.

"Yes. Max overheard him chatting at Gentleman Jackson's two days ago. He's returned to his Gloucestershire estate for a week or two."

"Excellent."

Nate slipped through the door and walked as swiftly and silently as he could to the marble staircase. At least it wouldn't creak. Gabriel trailing close behind, they slunk up the stairs until they reached the dark gallery. Again, the area was deserted and silent as the grave save for the ticking of a nearby longcase clock; its gold face gleamed in a ray of pale moonlight that had penetrated the casement window above the staircase landing.

"God only knows which room is Lady Astley's," whispered Gabriel as they started down the hall. The thick Turkish runner deadened their footfalls as they passed potted palms, marble busts, and several closed doors.

"There." Nate stopped and pointed to a strip of light edging the bottom of one of the doors. "I suspect this might be it. It's worth a try at any rate."

Gabriel cursed beneath his breath. "Christ. I hope she's asleep."

"Me too."

Inhaling a bracing breath, his pulse pounding like a battle drum, Nate tried the brass handle. When the lock clicked, he grimaced. *Shit*.

He waited for the space of a breath. And then another, but nothing happened. Expelling a measured sigh, he pushed the door open a fraction and peered into the softly lit chamber beyond. The glow from the fire and several low burning candles revealed a sitting room with decidedly feminine furnishings: the overstuffed armchairs were upholstered in pale blue and gold brocade, the window was festooned with frothy lace curtains, and a floral Aubusson rug carpeted the floor before an elegant fireplace of white marble.

But best of all, the room was empty of occupants.

Nate slid inside and Gabriel followed.

"Hopefully the countess has a dressing room apart from her bedchamber," Gabriel whispered.

Nate nodded and pointed toward a door that stood ajar on the other side of the room. If Lady Astley was actually asleep, perhaps he just might pull off this prank and win the wager after all. He hoped to God the rumors were true that the notorious countess did indeed wear drawers. Perhaps he should have asked MacQueen a bit more about his amorous encounter with the woman.

He'd made it halfway across the sitting room when all hell broke loose. A yapping terrier, no bigger than a sewer rat, charged from the open doorway and launched itself at Nate's ankles.

Fuck. Nate stooped down to pick the dog up in the hopes of muzzling it, but it latched onto the cambric sleeve of his shirt. Snarling, its beady black eyes glimmering with hellfire, its tiny fangs bared, it threw its small weight backward, yanking and tugging in a series of rhythmic jerks. The distinctive sound of fabric tearing filled the room.

"Do something," growled Nate over his shoulder at Gabriel, but his friend's attention was focused on the door from whence the terrier had come.

Bloody, bloody hell.

"Bexley!"

Nate straightened and his gaze locked with that of a very attractive, very scantily clad woman. Her flaxen locks tumbled over one pale, slender shoulder, and her silk and lace night rail was so flimsy, it was practically transparent. Indeed, Nate was certain he could see the dusky pink of her jutting nipples. The triangular shadow at the apex of her thighs . . .

He swallowed and summoned his most charming, lop-sided smile. "Lady Astley," he said as smoothly as he could with a small bow—a maneuver that was no mean feat considering Bexley was still attempting to chew through his left boot as though on a mission to sever his Achilles tendon. "My sincerest apologies for invading your rooms and disturbing you at this late hour. But please allow me to introduce myself. I am Nathaniel Hastings, Lord Malverne. And my companion"—he gestured over his shoulder—"is Gabriel Holmes-Fitzgerald, the Earl of Langdale."

Lady Astley crossed her arms, an action that pushed up the creamy mounds of her round, tempting breasts. She arched an eyebrow. "I know who you both are," she drawled in a voice husky with sleep. "Why are you here? What do you want?"

I want you to call your vicious rat of a dog off my ankle, was Nate's first thought, but instead he simply donned his rake's smile once more. "I'm afraid it's rather an inane and innocuous reason, really. I was dared by my friends to filch a pair of your famous drawers."

He didn't see the point in lying to the woman. And anything else he could come up with on the spur of the moment would sound equally as bad.

She threw back her head and laughed, a sinful, throaty sound that curled around his spine and made his balls twitch. "You know, I'm inclined to believe you, Lord Malverne," she said, her eyes dancing with amusement. Her gaze dropped to the ravaging terrier and she clicked her fingers. "Hush, Bexley. Come."

The dog at last let go of his boot, and with a disdainful shake of its curling tail, it trotted over to its mistress.

Lady Astley crooked her finger and beckoned. "This way, Lord Malverne and Lord Langdale. I wouldn't want you to go away empty-handed considering the trouble you have already gone to."

Nate traded glances with Gabriel, and his friend shrugged as if to say, *Why not?*

Bemused, Nate followed the countess into her lavishly appointed bedchamber. An enormous four-poster bed, its sheets and blue silk counterpane rumpled, dominated the center of the room. Bexley leapt into a bedside armchair, turned around three times, then plopped down with a censorious huff.

"Over here," called Lady Astley as she padded through to her dressing room. The doors of a large satinwood armoire stood open, and the countess was rifling through a pile of filmy and silky undergarments when Nate entered.

With a flourish, she held up two pairs of drawers, one of dark crimson silk embroidered with white roses, and the other a rich cream satin. Her mouth curved into a seductive smile. "You can each have a pair if you like. They're French. All I require is a kiss . . . from both of you. Also in the French style."

Holy hell. Nate ran a hand through his hair. He'd heard the Countess of Astley was a sexually brazen woman, but he hadn't realized *how* brazen until now.

Gabriel cleared his throat. "As much as we're flattered by your offer, Lady Astley, I'm afraid the dare only required Lord Malverne to procure *one* pair of drawers."

"Please, call me Camilla," she purred, approaching them both. She rubbed the crimson drawers against her flushed cheek. "Perhaps I could model them for both of you? Then you can decide which pair you like best."

Nate's cock jerked. While his body would appreciate the show, his head told him to beware. The woman was clearly propositioning both of them, but he wasn't going anywhere near her unless he was wearing a sheath. And, fool that he was, he hadn't brought a single one with him.

Gabriel could do what he liked, of course.

"I'd be happy to take the crimson pair, Lady Astley," Nate murmured in a voice that was clearly graveled with lust. Stepping forward, he tilted up her small chin. "For your original price of a kiss."

The countess pouted prettily for a moment, then licked

her lips. "Very well," she whispered. As she closed her eyes, she pressed her body against his. With the crimson drawers still in hand, she cupped his half-hard length.

Nate groaned. The woman was sin personified. Best he get this over with before he began thinking with his cock instead of his brain. He bent his head and claimed her mouth in a brief but thorough kiss. When he pulled away, Lady Astley was smiling.

"Oh, that was wonderful, Lord Malverne," she breathed as her eyes fluttered open. She pushed her drawers into Nate's hand, then turned her desire-glazed gaze to Gabriel. "Would you like a kiss, too, Lord Langdale? I wouldn't want you to feel left out."

Gabriel gave her a wolfish smile. "Why thank you, Camilla." One of his hands slid around the countess's slender waist and he pulled her against him. "That's most considerate of you."

Nate quietly exited the room. While he had indulged in a sexual threesome on the odd occasion, it had never been with another man's wife. Or another man, for that matter.

Besides, he achieved his aim for the night; he had procured a pair of Lady Astley's drawers.

Ignoring the low growl that emanated from the bedside chair, Nate headed for the hall and the stairs. When he gained the terrace, Max and MacQueen emerged from the shadows.

"What the deuce happened up there?" whispered Max. "We heard a dog yapping. And where's Gabriel?"

Nate brandished the crimson drawers in the air. "Everything is all right," he said. "Lady Astley is a most . . . amenable woman, even if her bloody terrier isn't."

A snort of laughter escaped MacQueen. "Isn't she just? If the recent rumors I've heard about her are true, I'm surprised she didn't proposition both you *and* Langdale."

"She did. But I thought I'd leave Gabriel to it," admitted Nate. "I got what I came for, and it seems you all owe me four hundred pounds."

"Good God," breathed Max, ignoring the fact that Nate had won the bet. Staring up at the second-floor window where the light still shone, he continued, "Now I'm regretting the fact that *I* didn't offer to go up with you."

MacQueen handed Nate his evening jacket. "You could always take Langdale's coat up to him," he said to Max. "And then see what happens."

"I wouldn't unless you had some prophylactic sheaths on you," warned Nate.

Max grinned and patted his pocket. "I always come prepared."

MacQueen slapped him on the back. "Well, what are you waiting for, Your Grace?"

Max tossed Gabriel's jacket over his arm and headed for the French doors.

"Just watch out for the terrier," called Nate after his retreating back. "It might be small but it's a nasty piece of work."

"Shall we call it a night then?" asked MacQueen when they stepped out onto Cavendish Square. Somewhere in the distance, a clock struck the half hour.

Nate sighed. His head was clearer than it had been earlier on, but annoyingly, lust still fizzed through his veins. He knew he wouldn't sleep unless he did something about it. So he could either drink more or slake his desire elsewhere. Both seemed like good options. Although he'd lived with nightmares for years, they were much worse since Waterloo. Not just for him but for his fellow brothers-in-arms: Max, Gabriel, and MacQueen. They'd all been there, and each of them still wrestled with the mental aftermath. Especially MacQueen—although the scarred Scot would probably stake his heart with his dirk if he ever suspected Nate knew his emotional wounds were worse than anyone else's.

"It's early yet. Why don't we stop by the Pandora Club?" he suggested. It had been at least a week since he last paid a visit to the exclusive "gentlemen's club," an establishment that was both a gaming hell and high-class brothel in St. James's. It was also quite conveniently located; just a hop, skip, and a ten-minute stagger away from his bachelor's residence, Malverne House.

MacQueen grinned. "An excellent idea. And if you need a sheath"—he pointed to his breast pocket—"I have several."

"Brilliant." As Nate watched the Scot hail a hackney cab, he grimly acknowledged, not for the first time, that the life he and his friends led was more than a little unhealthy. It could certainly be diverting, but there were moments, like now, when a bleak hollowness spread through his chest. A bone-deep emptiness. Sometimes he believed his father, Lord Westhampton, might actually be right: that he was a good-for-nothing scoundrel who would never amount to much.

Christ, he needed a drink and a woman. Perhaps two.

And sleep. Most of all he needed dreamless sleep.

Perhaps he'd achieve that blissful state by dawn.

CHAPTER 3

❧

A Disgraced Debutante may just get her Season.
Has the tide turned for Miss B. of M. G. . . . ?

The Suffolk County Chronicle:
Vignettes of Village Life

Nettlefield Grange, Monkton Green, Suffolk

March 6, 1818

*T*he End.

Sophie put down her goose feather quill on her small beechwood writing table and scattered sand over the page to set the ink.

Her mouth lifted into a smile as the warm glow of accomplishment filled her. She couldn't quite believe it, but she'd done it!

It took her over half a year, but at last she'd completed her first ever manuscript. A children's novel. All the short stories she'd written years ago to help her youngest sister Jane learn to read had evolved into *The Diary of a Determined Young Country Miss; or, a Young Lady of Consequence.*

Indeed, Sophie had never experienced such heady elation. It fizzed through her veins like the champagne she'd tasted last Christmastide. She fancied that even the dust motes glimmering in the shaft of morning sunlight spilling through her bedroom window were dancing. Considering how stultifying her existence had been since her expulsion from Mrs. Rathbone's academy, feeling joy of any kind was a rare occurrence.

But then her happiness dimmed as she realized it would be useless sharing her good news with her mother and step-father; they always dismissed her writing as fanciful scrib-bling and nothing more than a waste of time. Although, they might begin to think differently if her book were pub-lished and brought in income to help replenish the family's almost empty coffers . . .

Of course, her parents' lack of support wasn't the only obstacle she had to contend with. It would also take some time to scrape together the funds to send her manuscript to one of her preferred publishers. The postage to London would be exorbitant. A despondent sigh escaped Sophie as she capped her inkwell. It seemed there would be no quick fix to improve her family's lot in life . . .

At a knock on her bedroom door, Sophie hurriedly lifted the hinged lid on her writing slope, and heedless of the sand scattering everywhere, she slipped the barely dry page of her manuscript inside. Turning in her seat, she called, "Come in," and was more than a little surprised to discover it was her mother.

Oh, dear. Her mother *never* visited her room. This didn't auger well at all. If Lydia Debenham wanted something, she usually sent the housemaid or one of Sophie's half sis-ters to fetch her.

Pushing her ink-stained fingers into the folds of her workaday pinafore—her mother was always lamenting the fact that Sophie didn't possess pale-as-milk ladylike hands—she began, "What is it, Mama? If you're worried that I haven't finished the accounts for Father, well, I have. They're all up to date." She'd recently begun keeping the ledgers for her stepfather's estate so he no longer needed to employ a steward. If she couldn't marry well, she'd do whatever she could to help alleviate the financial pressure on her family. It was the least she could do under the circumstances.

To her further astonishment, the corners of her mother's blue eyes, so like her own, crinkled with an emotion akin to sympathy as she crossed the faded floral carpet and sat on the edge of Sophie's narrow bed. "Now, there's no need to sound so beleaguered, Sophie. I'm not here because something is wrong. Quite the contrary . . ." Her mother's round cheeks split with a smile so bright, Sophie was quite dazzled. "I have news that will no doubt please you. Very much."

It was then that Sophie noticed her mother was holding a sheet of very fine ivory parchment, and hope swelled within her breast. "Has the post arrived? Is it a letter from one of my friends?" Even though she hadn't seen Charlie, Olivia, or Arabella since that fateful night at the academy, she was grateful that she could still correspond with them.

"It's even better than that." Still smiling, her mother passed her the page. "The Earl of Westhampton has extended a most kind invitation. You've been asked to stay after Easter so that you might be a companion for his daughter, Lady Charlotte, while the family resides in London for the Season. And after speaking with Mr. Debenham just now, we are both inclined to consent."

"Oh, my goodness." Sophie's hand rose to her throat, where her pulse fluttered erratically. Tears misted her vision so much, she could barely make out the earl's handwriting as she scanned the letter. She could scarcely believe that she'd been granted such a gift considering how dreadful the past three years had been. Three long, tedious years in which she'd spent most of her time confined to Nettlefield Grange.

Since the academy incident, and the ensuing humiliation of being labeled "loose" and "unprincipled" far and wide, disgrace was the cross she'd had to bear. Shunned by the other genteel families of Monkton Green and surrounding villages, banned from attending any social events other than a weekly visit to St. Mary Magdalene Church for the Sunday service, Sophie had endured it all, telling herself that eventually another, more salacious piece of gossip would catch the attention of the lower gentry matrons and tabbies. That, in time, she would be forgiven her transgressions and invited to tea, or card parties, or dinner, or even a ball.

Unfortunately for Sophie, no other scandal had come close to supplanting her own, and her notoriety as "that Brightwell girl"—the one who liked to illicitly imbibe alcohol, smoke, and peruse obscene books and pictures—continued unabated. Indeed, the whole family had been held to account because of her youthful foolhardiness. Sadly, seventeen-year-old Alice and fifteen-year-old Jane were never invited anywhere. And late last year, Sophie was denied a teaching position at the local charity school because she was deemed an unsuitable role model. Even though the vicar of St. Mary Magdalene's had been most apologetic, it hadn't really lessened the sting of rejection or the disappointment of not being able to bring in a little more income.

But now . . . perhaps now Sophie's fortunes and that of her sisters might be reversed. If she could somehow repair her reputation in the eyes of the ton, then surely the folk of Monkton Green would see her, and therefore her sisters, in a different light.

And maybe her stepfather wouldn't keep pushing her in the direction of their ghastly neighbor, the portly, middle-aged baron, Wilbur Northam, Lord Buxton. Wouldn't that be wonderful? Despite the fact that her stepfather still owed Lord Buxton a good deal of money, the baron was a regular visitor to Nettlefield Grange, particularly on a Saturday when Mama served her lovely roast luncheon. Sophie supposed Lord Buxton came because he was a widower and he might be lonely. She didn't wish to be unkind, but there was something about the way he looked at her with an anticipatory gleam in his eyes that made her feel decidedly uncomfortable, as if she were one of the courses about to be served. A sacrificial-lamb-in-waiting.

Barely suppressing a shudder, Sophie handed the invitation back to her mother and asked, "I'm curious. Why have you and Mr. Debenham been persuaded to accept Lord Westhampton's offer?"

Her mother's gaze softened. "I know you've had the most horrible time of late, and it worries me how much it has affected you. You're not the bright, smiling Sophie you used to be. And Alice and Jane are pining away too. Mr. Debenham took a little convincing—I think he's worried something else untoward might happen considering Lady Charlotte's prominent role in your expulsion—but there's nothing more powerful than a title to help open doors. And Lady Charlotte's aunt, the Dowager Marchioness of Chelmsford, will be your chaperone. While I'm not certain you'll be able to acquire a voucher to Almack's, I'm confident that under Lady Chelmsford's care, you might gain admittance to at least some ton social events. And who knows . . ." Her mother leaned forward and patted her knee. "Perhaps you'll meet an eligible gentleman of means."

An eligible gentleman of means. The weight of expectation was suddenly very heavy indeed. It was clear her mama and stepfather still harbored high hopes that she'd make an advantageous match. But how many wealthy gentlemen would be willing to overlook her tainted reputation? Well, aside from Lord Buxton.

An image of Charlie's older brother popped into Sophie's mind's eye, and her heart gave an odd flutter. She'd tried not to think of Lord Malverne—or Nate, as Charlie called him—and their fleeting encounter in Hyde Park over three years ago. He was certainly eminently eligible in her eyes, but according to Charlie still too entrenched in his rakish bachelor ways, particularly after returning from Waterloo. Charlie occasionally recounted some of his wilder exploits in her letters, and while certainly wicked, they always made Sophie laugh. If only she wasn't "a shy country miss of no consequence," then perhaps he might be tempted to consider her.

One thing she knew for certain: she'd sooner stick a hatpin in her eye than become the next Lady Buxton.

Realizing her mother was waiting for her to respond, Sophie pushed her foolish thoughts about her friend's much-too-handsome viscount brother and the odious baron from her mind—surely they weren't the only eligible gentlemen of means in the world—and summoned a smile. "One never knows, Mama. And nothing ventured, nothing gained. Perhaps I will find someone."

Hastings House, Berkeley Square, Mayfair

March 6, 1818

"Explain yourself!" Lord Westhampton slammed a newspaper down on his polished mahogany desk. "And don't bother to deny you weren't involved. I *know* you were. You and your equally dissolute friends."

Nate winced as he took in the first line of the society page in the latest edition of the *Beau Monde Mirror*. *The great drawers caper!*

Bugger. Nate ran a hand down his face before looking up at his father; his scowl was thunderous as he stood over him. At this particular moment, the Earl of Westhampton was even more imposing than the towering oak bookcases that lined the walls of Hastings House's library.

"Yes, I took part." With a deep sigh, Nate leaned back in his leather wing chair and silently wished the scandalmongers who contributed such dross to the *Beau Monde Mirror*, and all the other gossip rags for that matter, to hell. "But surely it's not as bad as you think. It looks as though our names have been kept out—"

"Really?" His father cocked a sardonic brow before retreating to the other side of his desk. "You can't be that naive. Lord M., Lord L., Lord S., and 'the Duke'? Everyone knows the four of you are as thick as thieves. Good God, Nathaniel. I swear you'll be the death of me."

Lord Westhampton snatched up the crystal brandy decanter at the edge of his desk, sloshed a decent amount of the amber liquid into a tumbler, and then took a large swig. "This"—he jabbed a finger at the paper—"has *got* to stop. Your name has appeared in newspapers too many times over the past year. And I've had enough. It's not even noon and look at me." He waved the brandy glass in the air before taking another sizable gulp, draining it. "You're driving me to drink."

Ordinarily, Nate would have asked for a brandy as well, but now didn't seem quite the right time. Besides, it probably wouldn't mix well with the guilt beginning to gnaw at his gut. Even though his father was clearly overreacting, it seemed an apology was in order. He sat forward and schooled his features into a suitably contrite expression. "Look, I'm sorry, Father. Truly I am. But honestly, no real harm has been done. We're not the first ton bucks to engage in a bit of harmless horseplay."

"Harmless horseplay? It's outrageous debauchery, that's what it is. Aside from publicly cuckolding Lord Astley—and yes, everyone knows it's his wife's drawers you intended to steal—you've essentially committed burglary. How am I supposed to walk into the House of Lords with my dignity torn to shreds? Having to deal with Charlotte's scandal three years ago was bad enough. And now this?" He gestured at the paper again. "I'm fast becoming the resident laughing-stock of Parliament! What would your mother say—God rest her soul—if she were still here?"

Ouch. Nate grimaced as a sharp stab of guilt sliced through his heart. His mother would have been both mortified and ashamed of him. "I'm certain it will blow over soon enough," he offered. *Hopefully.*

"Until next time." Lord Westhampton poured himself another brandy. His narrowed gaze was as hard and cold as the crystal of the decanter as it met Nate's. "But there won't be a next time. Of that I can assure you."

Foreboding pricked its way along Nate's nape. "What do you mean?"

His father sipped his drink before flipping out his coat-tails and taking a seat behind his desk. "If you can't be trusted to behave as any decent gentleman should, I'm going to have to put measures in place to make sure that you do."

Nate swallowed, his mouth suddenly as dry as the Arabian Desert in midsummer. "What measures?"

His father placed his tumbler very carefully on the

burgundy red leather blotter before pinning him with another fulminating glare. "You have until the end of the Season to mend your libertine ways. Not only will you stay out of the scandal rags, you're going to begin taking responsibility for Deerhurst Park instead of leaving it up to your long-suffering steward and me to manage."

Nate inclined his head. "Of course, sir." His father had gifted Nate the estate on his twenty-fifth birthday, after he'd returned from Waterloo. It was true he didn't visit often enough. Or take as much interest as he should. Even though his father knew why, it seemed his forbearance had at long last run out. And Nate only had himself to blame.

"But that's not all."

Damn. Nate inwardly cringed. This couldn't be good.

"During the Season proper," his father continued, his tone as cutting as any lash, "you will begin attending respectable ton events with a view to finding a suitable wife. The Duke of Stafford's daughter, Lady Penelope Purcell, springs to mind. I know you're reluctant to marry, but it's high time you at least made *some* effort. As my heir, it is your duty. And while I don't expect you to forgo all amorous pursuits such as keeping a mistress or visiting certain clubs, you'll do so discreetly. Profligate behavior such as this"—he gestured at the *Beau Monde Mirror* again—"will *not* be tolerated. Not anymore."

Double damn. But it could be worse; at least his father hadn't demanded he actually propose to Lady Penelope or any other young chit by the end of the Season. Drawing a fortifying breath, Nate braced to receive the final blow he knew was coming. "And if I don't comply?"

His father's steely-eyed glare was unwavering. "I'll take back Deerhurst Park and cut off your funds. Come to think of it, I'm also going to close up Malverne House. You'll move back here—today in fact—so I can keep an eye on you. And once a week, we shall meet for dinner. Whether it's here at Hastings House or at White's, I don't much care. But I *must* see that you are taking your responsibilities seriously, as well as keeping your nose out of trouble. Do I make myself clear?"

"Yes, perfectly." Nate rose and bowed. "If there's nothing else, I shall see you anon. I take it dinner is still at seven?"

"Yes. I look forward to it. And I know your sister will be pleased to see you too. She misses you."

Nate's hand was on the brass door handle when his father spoke. "Son, these demands seem harsh, and I know how difficult things have been for you, especially since Waterloo . . ."

Nate turned back; his father had risen from his seat, and instead of censure, concern creased his brow. "I appreciate your understanding."

"It's just . . ." Lord Westhampton took a deep breath before continuing. "If you could just direct your considerable energy into things that *really* matter instead of living each day as though it were your last, I would worry less about you and your future. And if you won't do it for yourself, do it for me. And Charlotte and your younger brothers. God knows"—the earl ran a hand across his face, his expression suddenly gray with weariness—"we don't want to lose you too."

Nate dredged up a smile, even as dark remorse threatened to drag him under. A failure he might be, but despite that, he could see his father still loved him. Strangely, that knowledge hurt him more than believing his father no longer cared. But he couldn't put all that into words, so aloud he simply said, "You won't, Father. I promise you I'll make an effort. And that I'll be all right," even if he feared that last statement might be a lie.

CHAPTER 4

❧

When will the wicked Lord M. return to London
for the Season?

Most ladies of the ton would agree: town just
isn't the same without him . . .

The Beau Monde Mirror: The Society Page

Hastings House, Berkeley Square, Mayfair

April 1, 1818

"Sophie!" Charlie enveloped her in a warm hug as soon as
she crossed the threshold of Hastings House. "It's been
far too long, my darling friend."

"Indeed it has." Stepping out of Charlie's embrace, Sophie pulled off her slightly askew bonnet—during her enthusiastic greeting, her friend had knocked it a little
sideways.

Charlie, on the other hand, was the picture of refinement
and self-assurance. Her bright chestnut locks had been
tamed into an elegant Grecian-style arrangement of cascad-
ing curls, and her exquisite day gown of pale lemon silk and
Belgian lace looked like a design plucked straight from the
pages of the latest issue of *Ackermann's Repository*.

After Sophie handed her bonnet and gloves to the waiting
liveried footman, Charlie helped her out of her traveling pelisse, then exclaimed, "My goodness, Sophie. Just look at you.

You are quite the elegant beauty now. All of the ton gentlemen will flock around you as soon as we set foot outside."

Sophie promptly blushed at the well-meant praise even
though she doubted the veracity of her friend's assertion. Her
plain traveling gown of navy blue worsted wool had definitely seen better days, her hair was escaping its pins, and
she was certain her left cheek bore crease marks from snoozing too long against the squabs. "I suspect you might need
spectacles, Charlie. My mama thinks I'm far too thin."

"Well"—Charlie linked an arm through Sophie's and led
her across the perfectly polished black and white parquetry
tiles of the vestibule—"I don't agree. But in any case, a few
visits to Gunter's Tea Shop on the other side of the square
will soon rectify that. In fact, why don't we go tomorrow? I'll
send an invitation to Arabella and Olivia straightaway."

"Oh, how wonderful! I didn't know they would both be
here in town as well."

Charlie's smile slipped a fraction as they paused at the bottom of a sweeping mahogany staircase covered with the plush-
est carpet Sophie had ever seen. "Yes . . . Olivia's guardians
have recently rented a town house in Grosvenor Square, but
I'm afraid they can be quite—how shall I put it?—difficult
when it comes to letting Olivia get out and about. As for Arabella, her family is whisking her off to the Continent for a
grand tour in a day or two, so our Society for Enlightened
Young Women will be short one member for most of this Season. But I'm sure she'll have a brilliant time. I must admit"—
Charlie leaned a trifle closer in that conspiratorial fashion of
hers that Sophie had almost forgotten but loved—"I'm a trifle
jealous. But I digress. Let me show you around the house
while your luggage is taken up to your room. It's right next to
mine, by the way. It used to be Nate's."

"Oh"—Sophie's brow knit with a frown—"I hope I
haven't caused your brother any inconvenience."

"Not at all." Charlie patted her hand and led her toward
a set of double mahogany doors with impossibly bright
brass handles. "It's a guest room now. Besides, Nate's away
at the moment, tending to matters at his Gloucestershire
estate. Actually, he used to reside at Malverne House in

St. James's and only moved back recently. He muttered something about renovations needing to be done. At any rate, he's taken the room at the far end of our hall and he's hardly ever in. I suspect we shan't see much of him at all."

Sophie tried to ignore the sinking feeling in her chest. But she didn't have time to dwell on her disappointment for long because Charlie was opening the doors to reveal the room beyond. And it took her breath away.

It was a library, the likes of which she had never seen.

Enormous oak bookcases filled with fine leather-bound volumes lined every wall. A richly carved mahogany desk dominated the center of the room, while off to one side, an arrangement of leather wing chairs and a velvet chaise longue graced a luxurious Persian hearthrug of deep reds and blues. Firelight glinted off the silver candelabra, cabinet knobs of brass, and the gilded edges of wall sconces and chair legs. Even the arrangement of snow white lilies in a porcelain vase seemed to gleam.

"Oh, my goodness."

Charlie smiled. "I knew you would love it. And you must feel free to explore and borrow as many books as you like at any time. Father does use it on occasion"—she gestured toward the imposing desk—"but don't let that stop you."

Sophie advanced into the room, praying her boots weren't crusted with mud. "It's . . . it's so quiet. I feel as though I'm in a church," she whispered.

Charlie laughed. "Well, yes. It is quiet. Jonathon, Daniel, and Benjamin—my younger brothers—are away at Eton. And my father is . . ." She waved an expansive hand. "He's currently off doing whatever it is he does."

After Charlie had introduced Sophie to the housekeeper and butler and showed her the location of Hastings House's equally elegant drawing room, morning room, and dining room, she escorted her upstairs to her bedchamber. Charlie's young maid, Molly, was already busily unpacking Sophie's traveling trunk and valise.

"I suspect you might like to rest after your journey," Charlie said as she perched in the window seat, "but if you're not too tired, I propose a visit to Hatchards in Piccadilly. It's not far but if you'd prefer not to walk, I can have the carriage brought around. Father has an account so we can purchase whatever books or magazines we'd like. Oh, and Father would very much like us to join him and my aunt, Lady Chelmsford, for dinner. I believe Cook has prepared four courses."

Sophie's head was spinning. The life Charlie led was so different from her own; the extravagance was astounding. Nevertheless, a walk to the bookstore to clear her head, as well as sharing dinner with her magnanimous sponsors, sounded perfect, and she said as much to Charlie.

The excursion would also afford her the opportunity to see the range of titles currently available in the children's section of Hatchards—she assumed there was such a thing—and if there were any books like hers; she liked to think her idea was original, but one couldn't be sure. And as soon as she had the opportunity, she'd pay a visit to a publisher or two about town. She hadn't quite decided who that might be, but perhaps the visit to Hatchards would help.

In the meantime, Sophie was certain Charlie would keep her so busy, she wouldn't have time to fret about how her book would be received. And hopefully she wouldn't think too much about the wild and elusive Lord Malverne. Glancing at the four-poster bed, and its rich blue counterpane and hangings, she couldn't help but blush. Hadn't Charlie mentioned this room used to be his?

As her friend left to change into her walking gown, she paused in the doorway and remarked with a luminous smile, "Even if we don't get invited to any social events, or fail to meet our perfect love matches, Sophie, I know we are going to have a splendid time."

And Sophie, her heart at long last brimming with the promise of bright possibility, didn't doubt her pronouncement for a moment.

D amn and blast." The unladylike expletives escaped Sophie as she tipped up her traveling inkpot and gave it a shake over her sloped writing box. It was empty. Practically bone dry.

At least there was no one to hear her swear at this late hour; the gilt clock on the white marble mantel in her bedroom proclaimed the time to be half past eleven. And Charlie, in the chamber next door, was likely to be sound asleep.

Unlike herself. Sophie sighed. Unaccustomed to her new surroundings—and her mind abuzz with all sorts of thoughts about the coming Season—she'd at last given up tossing and turning in favor of putting quill to paper.

Lady Chelmsford was partly to blame for her unsettled state. During dinner, the marchioness—who proved to be as delightful as Charlie had said she would be—was so impressed to hear Sophie had written a children's book, she'd immediately declared her personal secretary would be at Sophie's disposal to collect the manuscript tomorrow morning and deliver it to any publishing house she wanted. And so Sophie had decided the only way to quiet her overactive mind was to write the covering letter that would accompany *The Diary of a Determined Young Country Miss; or, a Young Lady of Consequence.*

But now she'd run out of ink, which was most bothersome; a perfectly phrased sentence hovered in her mind, and she didn't want to lose it before she'd written it down. Unfortunately, her only pencil was broken and she'd left her penknife at Nettlefield Grange, so she couldn't sharpen it. Of course, Charlie might have some ink or a pencil in the sitting room adjacent to her bedchamber, but Sophie didn't wish to disturb her by creeping in and rummaging about.

There was simply no avoiding it; she was going to have to go in search of something to write with in the library. Surely Lord Westhampton wouldn't mind if she borrowed a *teeny* bit of ink. From what she had seen of him during dinner, he didn't seem to be the stingy sort. And after all, it was in aid of a worthwhile cause.

Putting aside her writing box—she'd carefully propped it on a pillow on her lap while she sat in bed—Sophie slipped out from beneath the covers and donned her slippers and a plain woolen shawl. She supposed she could have thrown on a gown, but that seemed like too much bother.

Lord Westhampton had already retired for the night, and besides, she'd be back in her room in a jiffy.

G ood evening, my lord."
    Nate acknowledged the night footman's greeting with a quick nod as he wearily stepped into the vestibule of Hastings House. He'd set out from Deerhurst Park well before dawn, and while in hindsight he probably shouldn't have stopped by White's on his way home, he hadn't been able to resist the urge to catch up with Gabriel, Max, and MacQueen. After all, it had been over three weeks since he last saw his friends. It had also given him the opportunity to nip a new scandal in the bud. In his absence, MacQueen had somehow procured four vouchers to Almack's. Once inside the assembly rooms, the Scot had proposed they all change into kilts, thus shocking all and sundry, and hopefully generating another monumental scandal.

A grin tugged at Nate's mouth as he pulled off his gloves and handed them and his beaver hat to the footman. He could see the *Beau Monde Mirror* now: *The great kilt caper!*

Wouldn't *that* impress his father? Of course, Nate had declined to take part, and with a chorus of good-natured ribbing that questioned his manhood ringing in his ears, he'd bidden his friends good night.

After passing his garrick coat to the footman, Nate crossed the hall, heading for the library. Although he was dog tired and had already imbibed a considerable amount of very good claret during the evening, he rather fancied a nip of his father's fine French brandy before retiring. It would also give his valet time to fuss about with unpacking his trunk before he collapsed into bed.

At least he'd be able to rest easy tonight knowing he'd played his part in ensuring his estate was running smoothly. And according to his friends, his name had appeared only once in the *Beau Monde Mirror* during the last month, a rather weak piece lamenting his absence from town. Surely his father couldn't blame him for that.

Nate pushed open the double doors to the library. If only he didn't have to attend any damnable ton balls or soirees. God, the idea of courting a simpering debutante like Lady Penelope Purcell was enough to turn his stomach—

A decidedly feminine gasp and a dull thud stopped him dead in his tracks.

What the deuce?

Behind his father's desk stood a raven-haired angel. A beautiful young woman wearing nothing but a pale blue shawl over a thin white night rail, and an expression of sheer terror.

"Lord Malverne. Oh, heavens. Oh, my goodness." The angel's shocked, wide-eyed gaze dropped to the desk, and then, much to his amusement, he was certain she muttered something not so angelic like *blast* beneath her breath.

Nate's gaze followed hers. *Blast indeed.* His father's cut crystal inkwell was on its side, and a black pool of ink was rapidly spreading across the dark red blotter, heading inexorably toward the young woman's pristine nightgown. In the next instant, as he strode toward the desk to offer assistance, she whipped off her shawl and pressed it against the inky puddle.

"I'm so, so sorry. What will your father think of me? I only meant to borrow a little ink. I didn't think he'd mind." Her words came out in a breathless rush as she began to dab furiously at the blotter. "And now I've ruined some of his papers. Oh, Lord, I hope they're not too important." She nodded at a dark splash marring the top of a document that looked a lot like a draft parliamentary bill. "What a disaster."

Her long black braid had fallen forward over her slender shoulder and it swayed with her movements, caressing the swell of one pert breast. A breast covered by nothing but threadbare cotton. It was cold in the room and her nipple pressed quite impudently against the fabric.

Holy hell. Nate swallowed as his body tightened with longing. The sight was so distracting, he had to force himself to lift his eyes back to the girl's.

"I'm not sure it's as bad as all that," he lied. His father would be livid. On an impulse, he laid a hand atop the angel's slender, ink-stained fingers to stop her frantic attempts to contain the mess. She stilled instantly, her breath hitching. And when she looked up at him, Nate's breath caught too.

At these close quarters, the lamplight illuminated the girl's lovely face. Her eyes, as clear and blue as a midsummer sky, were ringed with a darker liquid navy and fringed by impossibly long, black lashes. When she dropped her gaze to his hand lying atop both of hers, they fanned across her cheeks where a bright red blush was beginning to spread almost as rapidly as the ink had. God, she was an innocent and he was behaving like a cad, but he was thoroughly enchanted and couldn't seem to help himself.

His voice, when it emerged, was embarrassingly unsteady. "You seem to know me, but I'm not sure that I know you, Miss . . ."

"Brightwell. Sophie Brightwell," she supplied in a voice that was also oddly husky. She clearly felt the sizzle of attraction between them too.

"Sophie Brightwell," he repeated, savoring the feel of her name on his lips. It suited her perfectly. The girl was about the same age as his sister, and a distant memory stirred. A cold winter's day in Hyde Park. Three years ago. This was the awkwardly shy but pretty schoolroom chit that Charlie had introduced him to. "You're Charlie's friend. From the academy."

"Yes." Miss Sophie Brightwell slid a hand from beneath his and pushed a loose strand of hair away from her flushed cheek. "Your father and Charlie . . . I mean, Lady Charlotte, have invited me to stay. For the Season. I know this looks terrible, my skulking about the library at the dead of night, but I couldn't sleep. You know how it is in a strange bed. Honestly, I only meant to borrow a little ink."

"Yes, you said that before. But then I barged in and I startled you, no doubt. So this accidental spill"—he couldn't resist lightly squeezing her hand—"is entirely my fault. And I shall tell my father so." His father would believe him. It wasn't as though this was the first mess he'd ever made.

"No." Miss Brightwell shook her head. "No, I can't let you do that, Lord Malverne."

"I insist." Removing his hand from hers, Nate pulled a silk kerchief from his coat pocket, then, rake that he was, he leaned closer. The heady scent of warm female laced with something delicate and floral—perhaps it was the soap she used—teased him, enticing him to do something unthinkable, like burying his face in her sweet neck. To inhale deeply and run his lips along her collarbone. To taste the silken flesh where her pulse fluttered at the base of her throat . . .

Jesus Christ and all his saints, what was he thinking? Less than a month of abstaining from sexual congress had clearly addled his brain.

He couldn't seduce Charlie's friend no matter the desire thrumming through his veins. She was a young woman alone with a known rake, late at night. The situation was highly compromising to say the least.

Dangerous.

Nate cleared his throat and said what he meant to before he'd been struck with the insane and completely inappropriate urge to kiss this intriguing girl. "I also must insist that you allow me to help you clean up."

Miss Brightwell eyed him with suspicion, as well she ought. She drew a breath and parted her full, sweet lips as though to speak—perhaps to declare that she could manage well enough on her own—but instead, all that emerged was a tantalizing gasp when he captured her chin with gentle fingers. Turning her face ever so slightly toward the lamplight, he then carefully wiped a black streak from her smooth-as-alabaster cheek before releasing her. "If you are to have a Season, Miss Brightwell, you can't very well go about with an ink stain upon your pretty face."

She swallowed and another furious blush flooded her cheeks. "Th-thank you, my lord," she stammered and took a step back. Lifting her ruined shawl, she grimaced. "At least the blotter will be all right. I can't say the same about your father's papers."

Nate righted his father's inkwell and, with his kerchief, wiped the ink from Miss Brightwell's small pewter inkpot.

"If you don't mind my asking, why were you down here looking for ink at such a late hour?" He waggled his eyebrows. "Not writing an illicit love letter, are you?"

Miss Brightwell nibbled on her lower lip as though debating whether she should share a confidence with him or not. She reached for a horribly stained piece of parchment that lay to one side of the blotter and pushed it beneath her shawl. "No, nothing like that."

Nate quirked a brow. "Then why won't you show me?"

"It's . . ." She gave a resigned sigh and withdrew the piece of paper, offering it to him. "It's just a letter outlining the details of my manuscript."

"Manuscript?" Nate took it and propped his hip on the edge of the desk as he frowned at the neatly written script at the top the page. "Is it a diary of some sort?" He glanced back at her face. "Your diary?" *Now wouldn't that make for interesting reading?*

But Miss Brightwell was shaking her head. "No." She raised her chin and crossed her arms across her chest in a defensive stance. "It's a children's book. The first in a series. Well, at least I hope there will be more books. I'm not certain if I'll retain the title, *The Diary of a Determined Young Country Miss*, though. It all depends on what the publisher thinks. If I can find a publisher, that is . . ."

"I don't see why you wouldn't. It sounds like an awfully clever idea to me. A series, you say?"

"Yes." She blushed, perhaps in response to his enthusiastic praise. "Actually, your aunt has kindly made arrangements to have my manuscript delivered to a publishing house tomorrow. Minerva Press. I don't know if you've heard of it. Although I imagine it will be some time before I hear an answer. Anyway, I thought to write a letter to the proprietor of Minerva Press, to accompany my submission. But then I ran out of ink . . . I'm sorry." She sighed and rubbed ink-splotched fingers across her brow. "I'm rambling and I'm sure I must be boring you."

"No, of course not. I think what you're doing is marvelous, Miss Brightwell. In fact, I'm in awe of your talent. You've written a whole book, whereas I can barely scrawl my name half the time. I had no idea Charlie had such an accomplished friend."

"That's very kind of you to say so." She took back her piece of paper and folded it in half. "I can only hope Mr. A. K. Newman—he's the publisher—feels the same way."

There was something about Sophie Brightwell's downcast expression that made Nate think she wasn't used to receiving compliments. She clearly doubted his heartfelt praise, and for some reason he really didn't wish to examine, the thought saddened him.

Gathering up her shawl, inkwell, and quill, Miss Brightwell pressed them and the soiled page of her manuscript close to her chest. "At any rate, I probably should retire. Good night, Lord Malverne. Thank you for . . ." She broke off, blushing again, and Nate had the distinct impression she was recalling the moment he'd held her face in his hand and wiped away the ink. "Thank you for your assistance."

"You're very welcome."

When she was almost at the door, Nate called after her, "I meant what I said before. I will tell my father that I'm to blame for this mishap."

She turned around, and when her blue eyes met his, he was struck by her incandescent beauty all over again. "Are you certain? It doesn't seem right."

Somehow Nate suppressed the urge to laugh. Good God, the girl felt guilty about a bit of spilled ink. What a breath of fresh air she was. "Trust me, it will be better this way. We'll make it our little secret."

She inclined her head. "Very well. Our little secret. Thank you again. And good night."

As the door shut, Nate blew out a sigh. *Bloody hell.* How inconvenient that Charlie's friend was so damn divine. He'd been planning on a good night's sleep, but now he rather thought he might be plagued by inappropriate dreams that involved seducing a black-haired, blue-eyed angel.

He reached for his father's brandy decanter. He'd best have a double nip. Then hopefully he wouldn't dream at all.

CHAPTER 5

❧

Four Disreputable Debutantes are spotted at a most prestigious tea shop famous for its pots of pineapple ices . . .

They might be out and about, but will the ton forgive them?

Or will they continue to receive the cold shoulder?

The Beau Monde Mirror: The Society Page

Berkeley Square, Mayfair, London

April 2, 1818

M y goodness, it certainly is teeming down now, isn't it?" observed Charlie as she and Sophie stood beneath the portico of Hastings House, contemplating the sheets of spring rain turning Berkeley Square into a lake. "One can barely see the plane trees in the park, let alone Gunter's, from here."

Sophie worried her lower lip with her teeth as she peered up at the leaden sky; it didn't look as though the rain would abate anytime soon. At least Lady Chelmsford's secretary had arrived well before the showers had begun, so she knew her manuscript would have made it safely to the Minerva Press office.

However, it was unlikely they would make it to the tea shop across the square unscathed. Even though they had umbrellas, they would both be soaked within a half a minute. "Do you think Olivia and Arabella will venture out?"

Charlie secured the very top button of her smart, caramel brown pelisse of fine wool before pulling on her cream kid gloves. "They both sent word this morning that they'd love to join us. They are both dying to see you. And I believe Arabella is collecting Olivia on the way."

Sophie pulled on her black leather gloves as well, hoping that no one would notice the worn patches at the knuckles and near the heels of both hands. Unlike Charlie, she only wore a plain blue wool spencer over her muslin walking gown; her travel-stained pelisse was not fit to be seen. But then, what did fashion matter at a time like this? Darling Olivia and Arabella wouldn't give a fig about what she wore.

But first they had to make it across Berkeley Square.

"Ladies, you aren't seriously thinking of crossing the square in this downpour, are you? You'll need a boat."

A deep male voice wound around Sophie, making her cheeks heat and her breath quicken. Lord Malverne was standing right behind her. She dared not turn around. She didn't want him to know he'd put her to the blush. *Again.*

She always turned into a peagoose in the presence of handsome men. Actually, if she were honest with herself, it was only this man in particular who reduced her to a state of breathless, flustered idiocy. Thank heavens Charlie never teased her about her silly tendre, an affliction that had only grown worse. Well, ever since that unexpected and altogether disconcerting encounter with Lord Malverne in the library last night.

It was their little secret.

Had he really covered her hands with his and gently wiped ink from her cheek?

She'd tried to tell herself it meant nothing, that Lord Malverne was a notorious libertine who flirted with women all the time. But even so, she couldn't deny he'd been chivalrous when he offered to take the blame for the ink accident.

And his flattery—not only had he remarked she was

pretty, he appeared genuinely impressed by her writing—
made her feel hot all over and more than a little giddy
whenever she allowed herself to recall those strangely intimate moments.

Indeed, right at this particular moment, she was certain
her face was bright red and she had to remind herself to
breathe. As she battled to control her physical reactions to
Lord Malverne's overwhelming presence, Charlie simply
snorted. "The weather isn't *that* bad, Nate. Besides, we've
promised to meet someone at Gunter's."

Lord Malverne—or Nate—stepped forward, and from
the shelter of her bonnet, Sophie chanced a glance at him.
As always, he was dressed in an exquisitely tailored ensemble. His unfastened black wool garrick coat did nothing
to hide his athletic physique. Gleaming black Hessians and
buff pantaloons seemed to be molded to his muscular legs,
a waistcoat of burgundy red satin was buttoned up neatly
over his trim torso, and at his throat was a perfectly tied
ivory silk cravat. In hand, he carried a matching beaver hat
and a pair of dark brown leather gloves. Not a seam was out
of place, nor a speck of lint visible. Not a splotch of ink
upon his well-manicured fingers.

Perhaps in an effort to provide a foil to such sartorial
perfection, his too-long chestnut hair was artfully disheveled. Indeed, a tousled wing perpetually flopped over one
eye, only serving to enhance his overtly rakish air, especially when he tossed his head back or ran a hand through
his thick locks to clear his vision.

At that precise moment, as if he'd read her thoughts, the
wickedly handsome viscount did just that, raked his fingers
through his hair, pushing it back from his high, noble forehead. As a whimper of helpless longing threatened to escape her throat, Sophie promptly bit her lip again and
whipped her gaze back to the rain-soaked square.

Good heavens. She needed to build up some sort of re-
sistance to this man's charms, or she was sure to melt into
a pitiful puddle at his feet. And to think she'd once harbored dreams of developing the demeanor of a sophisticated young woman . . .

Out of the corner of her eye, Sophie noticed Lord Malverne putting on his hat and gloves, and then to her consternation, he moved to her side, his arm touching hers, the scent of his spicy cologne teasing her. "Well, if you are both set on this course of action, you must allow me to escort you. Miss Brightwell"—his large hand slid around the handle of her umbrella, and when his gloved fingers brushed hers, Sophie swore a jolt of electricity sizzled through her—"might I suggest I hold this for you so that you may pick up your skirts? To keep them out of the pond that was once Berkeley Square."

Inhaling a fortifying breath, Sophie forced herself to meet Lord Malverne's dark brown eyes. "Of course you may, my lord," she murmured. "Thank you."

Charlie shot her brother a narrow-eyed look. "That's very gallant. And very unlike you, Nathaniel Hastings."

Lord Malverne opened the umbrella and held it above Sophie's head. "I'm just trying to save your friend from a potential near drowning, dearest sister."

Charlie rolled her eyes as she put up her own umbrella. "Good Lord. Please don't tell me you have designs on my friend. Because if you do, I'll be forced to tell Papa about the article that appeared in the *Beau Monde Mirror* this morning. You know, the one that mentioned your return to town along with a detailed account of all your past escapades?"

"All lies, I assure you, Miss Brightwell," said Lord Malverne, his dark eyes twinkling with mischief. "Everyone knows most of the salacious rumors that appear in those gossip rags are utter rubbish. I never read them myself."

Sophie cleared her throat, praying that when she spoke, her voice would sound relatively normal. "Yes. Of course. Absolute garbage." Lord Malverne undoubtedly knew about her "escapade" three years ago with Charlie. He clearly didn't think any less of his sister because of the scandal. But given his reputation as a rakehell, perhaps scandal rolled off him like water off a duck's back. She suddenly wondered if he thought any less of her . . .

Charlie's suspicious gaze settled on Sophie, so she forced

herself to adopt a carefree smile. "I'm ready if you are, Charlie and Lord Malverne," she said, picking up the skirts of her periwinkle blue gown with one hand.

"Let us away then." Lord Malverne's smile was dazzling as he offered his arm. Ignoring Charlie's frown, Sophie took it, and then they all descended the stairs into the deluge.

Lord Malverne was the perfect gentleman and held the umbrella over Sophie steadily as they made their way around the square at a brisk pace, skirting the worst puddles on the pavement and steering clear of the splashes sent up by the wheels of passing hackney coaches. Within the space of a few minutes, they'd gained the shelter of Gunter's Tea Shop.

To Sophie's mortification, she discovered her blue muslin skirts were soaked through and were now quite scandalously plastered against her legs, leaving nothing about her figure to the imagination. She prayed no one within Gunter's would notice. She could see the salacious article in her mind's eye now . . .

> Miss B., the notorious chit with a penchant for hard liquor, tobacco, and erotica, arrives at Mayfair's most lauded tea shop, scantily clad in wet, all-but-transparent skirts. Once a hussy, always a hussy it seems . . .

Protected by her wool pelisse, the skirts of Charlie's dark russet silk promenade gown had fared much better, and it was impossible to detect any muddy splashes on her neat black kid boots.

Lord Malverne, despite the fact that he'd not taken shelter beneath her umbrella, seemed to be hardly affected by the rain at all. Shrugging out of his garrick, he revealed a set of impossibly wide shoulders that seemed to ripple beneath his perfectly cut tailcoat of chocolate brown wool with lapels and cuffs of black velvet.

He grinned when he caught Sophie staring. "We survived the flood," he declared as he handed his coat, hat, gloves, and the wet umbrella to a hovering attendant at the door.

"Heavens, and they say women are prone to exaggeration," countered Charlie, removing her gloves and bonnet. Her rich, red brown curls had clustered into tighter ringlets around her damp cheeks. "Are you going to join us, dear brother, or do you have better things to do?"

Lord Malverne kept his gaze on Sophie as she self-consciously untied her own bonnet and smoothed her hair; it seemed a wayward strand had become plastered to her cheek, and she fancied the viscount's eyes lingered on her face as she pushed it behind her ear. "I'd love to," he said after Sophie dropped her own gaze to the toes of his boots. "Unless I'm intruding. You said you were meeting someone?"

"Yes. Arabella Jardine and Olivia de Vere." Charlie caught the eye of one of the waiters and asked him to show them to their reserved table.

"Ah, the other two sisters from your Society for Enlightened Young Women," Lord Malverne remarked as they followed the liveried waiter past a counter laden with an eye-catching array of decadent cakes, desserts, and mouth-watering pastries and then into the surprisingly crowded tearoom. Despite the inclement weather, the shop was brimming with well-heeled patrons.

Sophie's forehead knit into a frown as the import of what the viscount had just said sank in. "You know about our group?" she asked. She'd had no idea that Charlie and her brother were so close.

Lord Malverne's dark eyes glimmered with amusement again, but it was Charlie who responded. "I hope you don't mind that he does." Touching Sophie's arm, a shadow of guilt flitted across her face. "After 'the incident,' shall we say, I felt compelled to explain the situation to my father and Nate."

"You know *all* your secrets are safe with me," murmured Lord Malverne near Sophie's ear, making her heart stutter. However, as he pulled out an elegantly turned wooden chair for her at their table, he deftly steered the conversation in a different direction by adding, "I swear Charlie will kill me if I don't stay silent about your society. I'm sure you know how fearsome she can be."

Sophie smiled as she sat. Her friend *could* be fearsome. But she was also lively and loyal to a fault, and during their time at Mrs. Rathbone's academy, she'd grown to love her like a sister.

Charlie, who'd taken a seat across from her, must have heard her brother as she arched an elegant brow. "Yes, you'd best not forget that, Nathaniel Hastings," she warned. Although Sophie noticed her wide mouth twitched with a smile.

Lord Malverne flipped out his coattails in preparation to sit down, when Olivia and Arabella appeared at their table.

"I . . . I'm so s-s-sorry we're late, everyone," Olivia stammered breathlessly, her cheeks as pink as her well-cut gown. "It's m-my fault entirely. My aunt was being . . . well, her usual self." Her dark liquid eyes flitted from Lord Malverne to Charlie and then to Sophie.

"Sophie!" she cried. Ignoring the usual dictates of decorum, she gathered her into a warm hug. Arabella, who appeared to be her usual unflustered self, offered Sophie a gentle kiss on the cheek.

Charlie laughed. "We just put it down to the abysmal weather."

Lord Malverne offered an elegant bow when Charlie introduced him. "Miss de Vere, Miss Jardine, your timing is perfect," he said with a smooth smile. "We've only just arrived, too, so you're not late at all."

"Olivia, darling," Charlie declared as they all took their seats. "I'm so glad you were able to come. I must confess I was a tad worried your aunt and uncle wouldn't let you join us."

"Truth to tell, a wee bit of skullduggery was involved," said Arabella with a sly grin. After pulling a cotton handkerchief from her rather sturdy leather satchel, she then removed her spectacles and set about wiping the rain spots away. "I informed Olivia's aunt Edith that her niece would be accompanying me on a tour of the Foundling Hospital, a most worthwhile charitable concern, so she could hardly complain about the nature of the outing. And that my aunt Flora, our supposed chaperone, was waiting in the hackney because of the rain."

"Yes and as Aunt Edith's rheumatism was playing up, she let me go without the usual interrogation," added Olivia. "Thankfully my uncle Reginald was out of the house, too, so it all worked out quite nicely."

Sophie's heart clenched. It appeared Olivia's guardians had started to treat her like a felon since "the academy incident." Five years ago, Olivia's life was torn asunder when her parents were both killed in a tragic carriage accident. Ever since that time, she'd been under the care of her uncle and aunt, who seemed to only value their niece for her large inheritance, which was currently held in a trust fund. Naturally, Olivia couldn't wait for the day when she could cut ties with them completely—either by marrying a man of her choosing after she turned twenty-one, or when she turned twenty-five, the age at which she could claim her entire inheritance.

"You poor thing, Olivia," she murmured, reaching for her friend's hand. "It sounds like you've been having a hard time of it. But I'm so happy to see you. I've missed you so much." She cast a misty-eyed smile at Arabella. "Both of you."

"Me, too, dear Sophie," responded Arabella. Without her glasses on, it was easy to see her hazel eyes were suspiciously damp as well.

"Oh fie, you three," said Charlie with a mock frown. "You'll make me cry, too, at this rate. And you know how dreadful I look when I do."

"Yes you do. Utterly frightful," agreed Nate, and Charlie poked her tongue out at him, which set them all laughing. A waiter approached, and after he'd distributed menus, Nate continued, "Ladies. I say it's high time we celebrated your reunion. My treat."

Charlie grinned at them all. "In that case, let's all order something quite wicked. *And* expensive."

Sophie was running her gaze over the delightful fare on offer when Lord Malverne leaned closer, his leg bumping hers. She supposed it was an accidental nudge as the chairs were quite small and delicate, and he was a tall man; his long muscular legs barely fit beneath the table. "What do you recommend, Miss Brightwell?" he asked in a low voice. "I must confess, this is the first time I've been to Gunter's. And while I do enjoy wicked things, I wouldn't know where to begin."

Sophie's eyebrows shot up. *Everyone* visited Gunter's. It was the crème de la crème of tea shops. Her mama even brought her, Alice, and Jane here whenever they visited London. "You cannot be serious," she said, unable to keep the note of surprise from her voice. "You only live on the other side of the square."

Lord Malverne's mouth tilted into a rakish smile. "Indeed, I am perfectly serious. Sweet things usually aren't to my taste." His gaze dipped to her mouth for a brief moment before returning to her eyes. "But I'm always willing to try something new."

Oh, my goodness. A blush heating her cheeks, Sophie glanced at Charlie to see if her friend had noticed Lord Malverne's overt flirting, but she was listening to one of the waiters as he listed the puddings of the day.

"I . . . well . . ." She dropped her attention to the menu again. Anything to avoid Lord Malverne's devilishly twinkling brown eyes and knowing smile. "If you have more of a savory palate, there are dishes like salmon and asparagus tartlets, and stilton and fig pastries. There's even a variety of savory ices. See here." She pointed to the list. "I've never tried it, but there's a frozen *fromage de Parmesan* spiced with cloves and cinnamon, and there's an artichoke ice cream. And then there's always the tarter, citrus sorbets. I quite like lemon verbena, but there's also one flavored with bergamot. And of course, there's Gunter's signature pineapple ice, but perhaps that's a bit too sweet for your taste. Then again, maybe you think it's too cold today for an iced confection . . ." Oh, dear Lord, she was babbling, so she pressed her lips together to make herself stop.

Lord Malverne didn't seem to mind her nervous blathering, though, as he continued to smile at her. "Hmm. They all sound tempting. And I have no doubt you are quite the connoisseur." He ran a finger along his full lower lip as though weighing the options. "Tell me, Miss Brightwell. What are *you* going to have?"

Sophie smiled. "Well, that's an easy question to answer. I usually have the strawberry ice cream."

"That sounds wonderful." Lord Malverne turned his attention to the waiter who had been hovering nearby. "Two goblets of your strawberry ice cream, thank you."

The waiter bowed. "*Bien sûr*, sir."

As much as Sophie would have liked to continue her discourse with Lord Malverne—she was just starting to feel more at ease in his company—Olivia claimed her attention by asking her about her family and the recent goings-on in Monkton Green. Sophie quite happily filled her in on all the details—as pedestrian as they were—before the discussion moved onto Arabella's upcoming trip abroad.

"We will miss you terribly," remarked Charlie. "So you must promise to write to us about all your adventures. And often."

It appeared to Sophie that Arabella's smile seemed forced rather than genuine when she agreed. "What is it, Arabella?" she asked. "Is everything all right?"

Arabella gave a short laugh, and there was a note of bitterness in her voice when she responded. "Is it dreadful to say I'd much rather stay here in London with you all, or even return to Edinburgh, so I can get on with my charity work? But it seems my aunt Flora is determined that I curb my 'unnatural bluestocking tendencies.'" She let out a derisive huff. "She thinks a trip to the Continent will somehow cure me— that visiting castles and châteaux and endless churches will somehow turn me into a romantic, biddable creature rather than a practical, disagreeable one. Of course it won't. But it seems I have little choice in the matter."

As long as Sophie had known Arabella, she'd always professed a desire to follow in her dearly departed grandfather's footsteps. He was a Scottish physician of renown in some quarters, and Arabella had always wanted to continue his crusade of improving the health and living conditions of the working poor, institutionalized infants and children, much to the horror of her aunt Flora. Like Olivia, Arabella was an orphan too. Since her grandfather's passing a year ago, she'd been obliged to live with her aunt and, much to her chagrin, had become little more than a companion to her and her cousin, Lilias, Flora's recently wedded daughter.

"On the other hand, as much as I wish to wed and have my own family one day, at least she won't be trying to drag me to Almack's." Arabella shuddered. "As you all know, I cannot dance, so at least I am saved from that particular hell."

Lord Malverne grinned. "Miss Jardine, it seems you and I are of a similar mind. Almack's is indeed a most singular hell."

When their ices and puddings arrived, Charlie and Lord Malverne regaled them with amusing on-dits about various members of the ton. Despite his assertion that he never read the scandal rags, it seemed Lord Malverne was quite familiar with all of the latest gossip.

Sophie was just finishing off her dish of ice cream when she noticed Lord Malverne had stopped eating his. She was about to ask him if the dessert wasn't to his taste when she followed the direction of his gaze; he was looking toward the front door, where another small party had just stepped in from the rain.

"Oh look, Nate," Charlie murmured, "Lady Penelope Perfect has just arrived. Perhaps you'd best slide beneath the table."

Nate grimaced and focused on his ice cream again. "Believe me, I wish I'd fit."

Sophie threw her friend a quizzical look. "Lady Penelope Perfect?"

"The young blond woman in the pink gown who rather resembles a Meissen figurine. Her real name is Lady Penelope Purcell and her father is the Duke of Stafford. But it just so happens that *our* father wishes Nate would court her this Season. She recently made her debut, and it's universally acknowledged she'd be quite the catch."

"I don't wish to pay anyone court, paragon of perfection or not," grumbled Nate.

Charlie smirked. "Don't worry, dear brother. Viscount or no, I'm sure she's too picky to give you more than a passing glance."

"I'm counting on it."

As Sophie watched the beautiful Lady Penelope cross the room—even her walk was elegant—she couldn't help but breathe a small inward sigh of relief. At least Lord Malverne didn't seem in the least bit smitten with the debutante.

Talk soon turned to what all of their plans would be for the rest of the Season.

Charlie's eyes sparkled with mischief. "I see no reason to stop us from reconvening the Society for Enlightened Young Women now that we are all together once more," she declared as she scooped up the last of her *mousse au chocolat*. "After all, whether we grace Almack's or not, we still have similar aims in life, don't we? To make suitable matches—not just because our families and society expect it—but because we desire wedded bliss also? However"—she punctuated her point by jabbing her spoon in the air—"the *only* way we can make truly informed decisions about the men we may encounter, men who *may* propose marriage, is to improve our knowledge of the other sex."

"I don't know if I should be listening to this," murmured Lord Malverne. His expression was decidedly pained.

Charlie cast him an amused look. "We could always make you an honorable member, Nate. I'm sure you'd be able to offer your own unique perspective on how we should best go about finding, and then ensnaring, husbands. Perhaps you could even suggest a few eligible male specimens."

"Good Lord, please don't mention my name and anything to do with marriage in the same breath," muttered Lord Malverne. He raked his hand through his hair, then got to his feet. "Ladies." He bowed to Olivia, Arabella, and then Sophie. "While it's been a pleasure to spend time in your company—and Miss Brightwell, I truly enjoyed the strawberry ice cream—I'm afraid I have other pressing business I must attend to. And Charlotte . . ." He pinned his sister with a narrow-eyed stare and lowered his voice. "Some brotherly words of advice. Please be cautious. I know I am not a paragon of exemplary behavior, so I cannot cast stones, but you really do not wish to end up in hot water again, do you?"

Charlie frowned back at him. "Of course I'll be careful, Nate. Do not worry. It's just . . . harmless girlish talk."

"As long as it's *discreet* talk and nothing else." Lord Malverne inclined his head in farewell. "Ladies."

Sophie watched his retreating back with a sigh. If only Viscount Malverne were an eligible male specimen. When she turned her attention back to the table, Charlie gave her another one of her assessing looks.

"Why do you keep looking at me like that?" she asked, even though she knew very well why. Olivia and Arabella were casting her curious looks too.

"I've seen you making calf's eyes at my brother, Sophie. I'll admit he is charming and handsome, but you heard it straight from his mouth. The institution of marriage is anathema to him."

A scalding blush crept up Sophie's neck and across her face. "I . . . he's . . . it's not . . . I'm not . . ."

Olivia smiled and touched her hand. "Dear Sophie. You are beginning to sound like me. But don't be embarrassed. Lord Malverne makes me blush too. As Charlie said, he *is* very handsome."

Sophie sighed. "I was hoping no one would notice my silly infatuation."

"It's all right," Charlie said. "I suspected he was flirting with you when he asked you to recommend something for him to try."

"You heard that?"

Charlie's eyes softened with compassion. "Yes. I'm sorry he's been acting like a cad, but it's just the way he is. You really should try to ignore him. He has a good heart, but he is as inconstant as the moon or the ocean tide. As much as my father wishes Nate would court a respectable young woman and settle down, I really don't think he ever will."

Olivia pushed her unfinished plate of crème caramel away. "What is it about rakehells that make them so appealing? They are wicked and can only be bad for us, yet we seem to crave them. A bit like everything on the menu here at Gunter's, don't you think?"

Sophie gave a weak smile. "Yes. I think that analogy works very well. I feel a little better now knowing I'm not the only one who feels this way."

"Hmmm." Charlie looked thoughtful as she turned her empty glass dish of mousse this way and that. "You know, the more I think on it, the more I'm convinced rakehells are exactly the sort of men we should be targeting in our quest to wed."

Sophie frowned. "I'm confused. You just said I should ignore my tendre for your brother."

"Yes, simply because I know Nate and what he's truly like. But there must be other rakehells who aren't *quite* so bad," replied Charlie. "They can't all be as shy of marriage as Nate."

Arabella's forehead creased in consternation. "Be that as it may, I'm not convinced this is a sound or indeed safe strategy."

"I admit it's unorthodox, but it might be the only feasible strategy we have," countered Charlie. "Think on it. Three years ago, we were all thrown out of Mrs. Rathbone's academy and gossiped about to no end. Called all kinds of terrible names. Even though I believe the scandal surrounding us *has* faded to a degree, we will still be regarded with disdain by many within the ton. But Nate just said that he can't really throw stones at us. So what if other gentlemen with rakish tendencies are of a similar opinion? From what I know of Nate's conquests—which isn't a great deal, mind you—he prefers women who aren't so demure and virtuous. In fact, I think he finds prim and proper debutantes, like Lady Penelope, to be quite boring and bland."

Olivia's brow had also knit into a deep frown. "But, Charlie, don't you think it's risky for us to be actively pursuing rakes? I know everyone might think we are immoral hussies, but we're not really. What if these men expect certain things from us? Things that really will result in our ruin?"

Charlie shrugged. "While I concede we will need to be careful, I also firmly believe not all rakes are out-and-out scoundrels. According to my aunt Tabitha, rakes sometimes turn into the very best husbands, simply because they've become jaded with the endless carousing and general shallowness of their lives. She maintains that when the right woman comes along, some are quite ready to settle down.

And some even fall in love. I, for one, will only marry if it's a true love match."

"Something tells me your aunt Tabitha must have wedded a reformed rake," observed Sophie.

"Yes. She did. And very happily too. For thirty-five years."

Sophie pressed her lips together. "Like Olivia, I'm still not sure, Charlie. It sounds dangerous. We could be playing with fire."

Charlie's mouth lifted into a beguiling smile. "Well, *I* think it sounds like fun. Besides, what else have we got to lose?"

"All right," agreed Sophie. "If we all concede your logic is sound, how are we to go about luring these not-so-wicked rakes into the parson's mousetrap?"

"Well, we shall just have to make them fall in love with us," said Charlie with an enigmatic smile. "I never said it would be easy, but I think it's worth a try, don't you?"

Chapter 6

❧

The husband-hunting Season is well and truly open, but how is a debutante to stand out in today's crowded marriage mart? Read on to discover essential tidbits of advice that will ensure your Season is a successful one . . .

The Beau Monde Mirror:
The Essential Style and Etiquette Guide

Well, we shall just have to make them fall in love with us.

At Charlie's words, Sophie's thoughts immediately strayed to Lord Malverne again.

Nate. Even saying his first name in her head made her heart trip wildly. She barely knew him, but she couldn't deny the attraction she felt for him. And it wasn't just his handsome looks that drew her. It was his devil-may-care charm and his heart-stopping smile—a well-practiced smile no doubt, but it was dangerously appealing all the same. And then there was his infectious sense of humor. And his gentlemanly manners, which she knew were probably all for show, but still . . . She shouldn't really be thinking of trying to win his affection, let alone his love. It would surely be an impossible feat.

She sighed and stared out of Gunter's front bow window onto the dull and rainy afternoon and the sodden park. Why would Lord Malverne even be interested in someone like her to begin with? She was but a poor country mouse with limited prospects. A ninnyhammer who blathered and blushed like a silly chit straight out of the schoolroom—which she practically was anyway. If someone like Lady Penelope couldn't capture Lord Malverne's attention, what hope did she—shy, bookish, practically impoverished Sophie Brightwell—have? It was a sobering thought indeed.

"Sophie." Charlie touched her arm. "You're woolgathering. Do you agree my idea has some merit?"

Sophie blinked. "I . . . I suppose so. Only, I'm still not clear on where we will find these not-so-wicked rakes. And how do we *make* them fall in love with us? I mean, I cannot claim to possess even the most rudimentary flirting skills." She lowered her voice. "I certainly don't know how to kiss."

Charlie's smile was wry. "I'm sure they would be happy to teach any one of us how to flirt, at least. It's in their natures."

Arabella's expression grew thoughtful behind her spectacles. "While I won't be here to take part, I do believe you should approach husband hunting scientifically if you are set on such a course. Let logic guide you," she said. Reaching for her satchel, she pulled out a pencil. "Does anyone have something to make notes on?"

"I do. And I like your suggestion. Very much." Charlie passed her one of Gunter's menus. "Here, write on the back of this."

"Are you sure?" asked Olivia, her expression doubtful as Arabella turned the piece of parchment over to the blank side.

Charlie waved a hand. "I'll just add it to my father's account if anyone complains, which I doubt they will."

Arabella nodded. "Very well." She tapped the end of the pencil against the small space between her front teeth before adding, "I think you should break your plan into steps. Things you can actually do that might aid you in your quest."

Charlie's brown eyes shone with enthusiasm. "I like it. A battle plan of sorts. And I don't know about you, but I think we should order tea to fortify ourselves for the task. Something hot and bracing like souchong."

After Charlie had placed the order, Sophie ventured, "It

might be useful to make a list of the rakes we should think about targeting."

"Yes, that should be our first step," agreed Arabella as she jotted down, *Step One: Rakes of Interest*. She looked up at Charlie. "I'm sure you would have some gentlemen in mind considering your brother's circle of friends and acquaintances, even if he isn't willing to make any suggestions."

Charlie nodded. "Yes . . . I'm thinking we need to consider rakes who not only make our hearts flutter because of their dashing good looks, but who have other notable qualities such as loyalty, courage, honor, intelligence, and most importantly, who are capable of caring and showing respect toward women. And men who show compassion and kindness to others."

Sophie's eyebrows shot up. "Heavens, a loyal rake who cares about and respects women *and* shows kindness to others. That sort of man sounds rarer than a unicorn."

Charlie laughed. "Not really. I can think of quite a few rakish gentlemen who certainly care about their mothers and sisters. Or are involved in notable philanthropic endeavors. And many rakes that I know of have served in the military at one time or another, so they would clearly be capable of demonstrating loyalty and acting with honor. Men we *don't* want on our list would be bounders who have a reputation for being mean and selfish. Men who've been deliberately callous or cruel. Men who cannot keep their promises. Men who drink and gamble to excess. Men on the brink of financial ruin who are on the hunt for an heiress." She gestured at Olivia before lowering her voice to a whisper and adding, "Men with the pox."

Arabella nodded sagely. "The pox is particularly nasty. A disease to be avoided at all costs."

Olivia blushed. "Goodness me. However would one know if a man is so afflicted?"

Charlie laughed. "There are rumors and Nate is sure to know; he'd tell me in no uncertain terms if a creature like that began to court any one of us. And Aunt Tabitha is a veritable fount of knowledge. I can always seek her opinion on our list of candidates if we think we need it."

The tea service arrived, and once they were all armed with steaming cups of fragrant souchong, Arabella picked up her pencil again. "Very well then," she said, pencil poised. "Whom do you suggest I add to the list, Charlie?"

"My first thoughts go to my brother's friends," she said. "They might be a bit wild, but I do know that Nate couldn't abide anyone who was a true blackguard."

"How do you think your brother will react to the fact that we are targeting his friends?" asked Sophie with a worried frown. "I can't imagine he'll be pleased."

"We shan't tell him," said Charlie simply. "What he doesn't know can't hurt him." She sipped her hot tea gingerly, then said to Arabella, "All right. The first candidate who springs to mind is Maximilian Devereux, the Duke of Exmoor."

Sophie's eyebrows shot up. "A duke? You cannot seriously think a duke would consider someone like me."

"Or me," added Arabella after she'd dutifully recorded his name at the top of the list.

"Fiddlesticks," declared Charlie. "Any of the men I suggest would be fortunate indeed to have women like you as wives. And as for the Duke of Exmoor, I believe he'd make any one of us a wonderful husband. He's as rich as Solomon, as handsome as an Adonis, *and* he served under Wellington, alongside Nate."

"Who else then?" Sophie wasn't able to hide the note of skepticism in her voice. A duke would never be interested in marrying a nobody like herself. He might consider Olivia; she was an heiress after all. And Arabella's family was quite well-connected within the ranks of the lower gentry and wasn't without means. Charlie, on the other hand, was the daughter of an earl, so she would definitely fit the bill of prospective duchess.

Charlie took another sip of her tea, then added, "Hamish MacQueen, the Marquess of Sleat."

Olivia sucked in a small, startled breath as Arabella added his name.

"You know him?" asked Sophie.

"*Of* him . . ." A deep blush had washed over Olivia's

cheeks. "He . . . he resides next door to us in Grosvenor Square. He's certainly a man with a good deal of . . . presence. Not that I've seen him all that much. He keeps to himself."

"Oh, I didn't know he was your neighbor," remarked Charlie. "I know he looks quite formidable with his eye patch, like a cross between a wicked pirate and a wounded Highland warrior of old. And even though he often wears a scowl and sounds gruff when he speaks, don't let that put you off."

"So he's another of your brother's friends?" asked Sophie before she took a sip of her tea.

"Yes. He was injured horribly during the Battle of Waterloo, hence the eye patch. But from what I've heard, that hasn't diminished his appeal with the ladies of the ton."

"Well then, who else would you suggest?" asked Sophie. It seemed shy Olivia might already harbor a tendre for the piratical Scottish lord, so she'd best not look in that direction.

"Gabriel Holmes-Fitzgerald, the Earl of Langdale," said Charlie with a decided nod. "He's probably the most notorious of all Nate's friends. He's . . ." Charlie paused as though she was trying to choose her next words carefully. "He is the sort of man who exudes a certain type of potent charm. When he enters a room, he draws the eye of almost every woman. It's not just because he's handsome. He's . . . magnetic. I can't think of another way to describe him."

"Goodness, he sounds quite delicious, Charlie. Even to me," said Arabella as she wrote down his name. When she looked up to find everyone was smiling at her, a rosy blush colored her cheeks. "What?" she demanded stiffly. "Just because I'm a bluestocking and I don't plan on looking for a husband in London's ballrooms this Season, it doesn't mean I don't appreciate attractive men."

Sophie smiled over the rim of her teacup. "I think he sounds quite delicious too. They all do."

"Now"—Charlie replenished her tea from the silver teapot—"the only other candidates that spring to mind for the moment are Matthew Ellis, Viscount Claremont, and Timothy Beaumont, Baron Edgerton. They aren't as close to Nate as the other gentlemen I mentioned, but they have solid reputations."

"Despite the fact that they're considered rakes," said Sophie with a wry smile.

"Yes, indeed. I've even heard Lord Claremont is actively looking for a wife this Season. Nate was laughing about the fact that bets were being taken at White's on the date he would announce his betrothal. I believe his father is pressuring him to find a suitable match."

"Hmmm. He might have someone in his sights already then," observed Olivia.

"Perhaps. Perhaps not. I wouldn't discount Lord Claremont just yet," said Charlie.

Sophie blew out a sigh. "All right then. We have five potential eligible men we can pursue with *relative* safety. What is the next step in our plan? I for one, have no idea how to capture anyone's eye, let alone a rakehell's."

"Nor me," remarked Arabella with a despondent sigh. "Much to my family's annoyance, there are some days I'm not even sure I want to marry anymore. Not unless I can find a gentleman willing to put up with my singular ways." She tucked an unruly blond curl behind her ear. "Or someone whose vision is as impaired as mine."

"What nonsense, you two. You are both underestimating your charms," said Charlie with a dismissive wave of her hand. "Aside from the fact that all of you are sweet and kind, unswervingly loyal and intelligent, you're all pictures of loveliness. There are at least half a dozen gentlemen in Gunter's who have been sending interested looks our way the entire time we've been here. And I truly believe getting their attention is half the battle."

Sophie snorted. "I'm sure it's you, Arabella, and Olivia they are stealing glances at." *If they're looking at me, it's only because my skirts are see-through.*

And then she recalled the intimate way Lord Malverne had wiped the ink from her cheek. The smoldering look in his dark gaze. He might think her pretty, clever, and even a little desirable, but that clearly wasn't enough to capture the heart of Lord Malverne.

"Oh, pish. You two both need to give yourselves more credit," admonished Charlie with a mock frown. "Now, weren't we up to formulating 'Step Two' of our plan? Does anyone have any suggestions?"

"I still think you should continue to use a methodical, scientific approach," observed Arabella. She tapped the pencil against her teeth again, then added, "Perhaps you need to find out more about these gentlemen. Do some more research into their backgrounds, discover their likes and dislikes, their interests. The sorts of females they may have been attracted to in the past. Their natural habitats."

"Yes, I think finding out a little more about their past histories is a very good idea," remarked Charlie. "And in doing so, we might also discover their weaknesses. The chinks in their armor. Rakes are notorious for guarding their hearts, so it would be useful to know how to break down their defenses."

"Goodness gracious, I don't wish to be a naysayer, but that sounds like an almost impossible feat," murmured Sophie.

Charlie shrugged. "I can try to gather some more information from Nate and Aunt Tabitha. And then we can always study the newspapers for the latest rumors. Discover something about any females who have caught their attention of late. For instance, do they prefer blond women? Do they like women with a penchant for the arts, or the sciences?" She nodded at Arabella. "Or do they prefer women who enjoy more active pursuits such as riding and archery, like me? There's sure to be some tidbits of information floating about that might prove useful. One never knows."

"I rather suspect they like women who enjoy amorous pursuits," remarked Sophie.

"Very true. Which reminds me, I must share a particular set of illicit memoirs with you so you have an idea of the sorts of amorous activities that exist in the world." Charlie lowered her voice. "All the things we are not supposed to know about before we get married, even though we really should."

Sophie guessed that Charlie was alluding to *The Memoirs of a Woman of Pleasure*. "Mrs. Rathbone didn't confiscate them?"

Charlie's eyes danced with mischief. "She tried to. Just like she tried to purloin the port and brandy. But my father demanded them back, claiming the items were all his. He really can be rather sweet, although Nate will tell you otherwise."

Sophie was certain there must be more behind such a statement, but it wasn't her place to pry. Instead she said, "I'm not sure what else we can add to our list of steps other than trying to think of how we might make the acquaintance of any or all of these candidates. As you said, Charlie, many in the ton may not be willing to welcome us into their drawing rooms, dining rooms, or ballrooms. Meeting some of them could prove difficult."

"True. But rakes often avoid the more respectable marriage mart venues such as Almack's like the plague. So that's where research into their 'natural habitats,' as Arabella put it, will be so important. For instance, do they frequent public places like the theater, Hyde Park, and Vauxhall on a regular basis? Or perhaps even a place like the Foundling Hospital if they or someone close to them has a philanthropic bent. It would be easy enough to arrange excursions to any of these. And at a pinch, my father or Aunt Tabitha could always host an event or two. A soiree or, at the very least, a dinner." Charlie cast Olivia a sly smile as she added, "And then, of course, our lucky Miss de Vere lives right next door to the mysterious Scottish marquess. It's a pity you don't have a dog or a cat prone to wandering into other people's gardens, Olivia."

Olivia's forehead plunged into an uncharacteristic scowl. "My aunt and uncle will not let me own a canary or even a goldfish. They can be such p-prigs sometimes. I cannot w-w-w-wait—" She broke off, her mouth twisting with emotion before she blew out a measured sigh. "I . . . I cannot wait until I have my independence."

"If you need me to, I shall buy a puppy and you can let it loose in Lord Sleat's garden," declared Charlie fiercely. The Valkyrie was back, and a bright spark of vengeance lit her eyes. "And then I shall take it into your aunt's and uncle's private chambers and let it chew up their shoes and lift its leg on their chairs, and generally let it do whatever else puppies are prone to do, in the middle of their sitting room rug."

Olivia let out an unladylike snort of laughter before clapping a hand over her mouth. "Oh, Charlie," she said eventually when the wave of mirth subsided. "I would love that."

Sophie sat back in her chair and sipped the last of her tea. "We seem to have the beginnings of a sound plan," she remarked when she put down her empty cup. "If your brother, father, and Aunt Tabitha can help us in our quest, I would be most grateful." For the sake of her sisters, Alice and Jane, she really hoped she could improve their family's social standing. And with any luck, perhaps she would find happiness for herself.

"I would too," agreed Olivia. "While I have no urgent need to wed, I have been concerned for a little while now that my aunt and uncle might try to arrange a marriage for me. A union that would be to their advantage, not mine. And then there is the threat of fortune hunters. At least I know that these men"—she touched their list—"will not want me for my wealth alone."

Compassion softened Charlie's gaze. "Oh, Olivia. As I said earlier, I will do whatever I can to help you. I hope you truly believe that."

"I do. And thank you," she murmured.

"Yes, thank you, Charlie," agreed Sophie around the lump forming in her throat. "If it weren't for you, I wouldn't be here right now."

Charlie's eyes suddenly grew bright with tears and she dipped her head, hiding her face. "I'm sorry," she whispered at length before lifting her gaze to meet theirs again. "It's my fault entirely that all of you never had the debuts you deserved. There's not a day that goes by that I don't rue my foolish actions. And I will make it up to you, I swear it."

Sophie's heart twisted at witnessing her friend's bone-deep remorse, her suffering. "Oh, Charlie, you mustn't blame yourself. We were all willing participants that night. We all agreed to become part of the Society for Enlightened Young Women. And we will all move on and lead wonderful, fulfilling lives, with or without rakish husbands." On an impulse she reached out and clasped Charlie's and Olivia's hands in her own. "Whatever else happens, we will always have each other."

Arabella placed a hand on Sophie's arm. "I couldn't wish for better friends."

"Hear, hear," said Olivia.

Plans were made to reconvene with Olivia in a week's time, and then after they bid Arabella a fond farewell and saw her and Olivia off in a hackney coach, Charlie and Sophie waded their way back across Berkeley Square to Hastings House.

An hour later, wrapped up in a cashmere blanket on the chaise longue in the library, Sophie put aside her favorite book, *Pride and Prejudice*, and fell to watching the flames dancing in the grate. By virtue of her birth, she'd never be like Lady Penelope. But then, hadn't Mr. Darcy fallen in love with Elizabeth Bennet even though she wasn't from his exalted social sphere? Perhaps the seemingly impossible *was* possible. She needed her very own battle plan to catch a rake.

She needed *enlightenment*.

Leaning toward Charlie, she said softly, "I'm sorry to interrupt your reading, but do you have those illicit memoirs about Fanny Hill at hand? If I *do* read those memoirs, as you suggested, perhaps I will feel less gauche when we begin husband hunting in earnest."

With a grin, Charlie put aside her book. "Of course. I'll find volume one right now."

"Thank you." Sophie idly traced the letters on the cover of *Pride and Prejudice* and smiled to herself. One thing she had a talent for was studying. She would learn what Nate and other men liked. Learn how to flirt and all about amorous pursuits—at least in theory. Become more worldly-minded. While she would never be a "paragon of perfection," she also didn't have to be quite so prim and proper, or worse, boring and bland.

Even though she mightn't win Nate's heart, that didn't mean she shouldn't try.

Capturing his full attention—or indeed any rake's— would certainly be a start.

Chapter 7

We all know scandal abounds behind closed doors—but which ones in particular?

Discover where the rakehells of the ton play in the wee small hours.

Editor's Note: This article is not for the faint-hearted. Read on if you dare . . .

The Beau Monde Mirror: The Society Page

The Pandora Club, St. James's, London

Midnight, April 4, 1818

Lord Malverne, can I get you anything? Anything at all?" purred a sultry female voice from the velvet shadows of a secluded corner of the exclusive gaming-hell-cum-brothel, the Pandora Club.

Nate put down his glass of cognac with deliberate care on the nearby polished kingwood table and tried to focus on the semiclad demimondaine before him. From what he could make out, she was a tall, slender blonde wearing a low-cut bejeweled bodice paired with some sort of voluminous trousers of a diaphanous fabric. With her bare midriff and kohl-lined eyes and a paste jewel adorning her pale forehead, her exotic costume brought to mind the Persian queen consort, Scheherazade.

Her heavy, musk-laden perfume wafted about him as she leaned closer and ran a slender finger along the line of his stubbled jaw. "I am at your disposal, my lord," she whispered. From this angle, Nate could see straight down her bodice. Her breasts as round and firm as ripe pomegranates with tight, dusky nipples beckoned to him, but he found that, for once, he had no appetite for what she was so clearly offering.

And it is all because of that chit, Sophie Brightwell.

He had no idea why, but he hadn't been able to stop thinking about the girl all night. And he really should. She was pretty, of that there was no doubt. And from what he'd seen, she was kindhearted with an amiable disposition and clearly an innocent despite the ridiculous scandal surrounding her expulsion from that priggish girls' academy. Charlie certainly thought the world of her. Which meant Charlie would be after him with her fencing foil if he ever dared lay a hand on her friend.

And he wouldn't blame her in the slightest. Reprobates like him shouldn't besmirch sweet young women like her.

The demirep was still waiting for him to respond to her blatant invitation, so he summoned a smile, hoping that would be sufficient to keep her happy. "Another cognac is all I require, m'dear," he drawled, or perhaps his words only sounded slurred because he'd had far too much to drink. Either way, the prostitute understood him. She fluttered her eyelashes coquettishly and murmured, "Of course, my lord," before brushing past a set of plum velvet curtains and disappearing into the softly lit chamber beyond.

With a groan, Nate slumped back into the pile of gold and rose silk cushions at his back and stretched his legs along the plush brocade settee. He didn't want to close his eyes, because whenever he did, the room began to spin. He hadn't been this foxed in a long time.

On the opposite side of the semisecluded alcove was the Duke of Exmoor. Coatless, with his silk waistcoat undone and his cravat in disarray, he, too, was sprawled across a settee; his gentle snores mingled with the muted chatter and ripples of laughter of other patrons and cyprians.

It seemed Max couldn't hold his drink tonight either.

As for MacQueen, Nate had no idea where the Scot had gone. The last time he'd seen him, he was at the hazard table. Or had it been faro? Although, by now, he also might be upstairs in one of the bedchambers, sampling the abundant feminine delights that could be had for the right price at the Pandora Club. He was vaguely surprised that Gabriel wasn't here. After they'd all been to Limner's to plan their next out-of-town boxing match excursion, the earl had disappeared. Although the horny devil could just have easily arranged another tryst with Lady Astley.

Forcing himself to sit up straight, Nate had to hold his head in his hands as the world tilted for a moment. Dear God, he was an idiot. Now that Malverne House was closed up, he'd have to drag himself all the way back to Berkeley Square. Which meant he'd also have to skulk into Hastings House via the servants' entrance because he didn't want the night footman to feel obliged to help him to his room or, worse still, summon his valet when he arrived home. Davenport, who was his batman when he'd served under Wellington, wouldn't dare say anything, of course. But Nate didn't wish to see the look of quiet disappointment in the man's eyes when he lost his balance as he undressed or he cast up his accounts; considering how heavily he'd drunk, both were possible outcomes.

The demirep returned with his cognac but Nate had no stomach for it. After she'd placed it on the table and departed, he surged to his feet and then woke up Max by nudging his trouser-clad calf. "Wake up, you dog. Time to head home."

Max's eyes flew open, then he blinked a few times before emitting a groan. Dragging himself into a sitting position, he scrubbed a hand up and down his face. "How long have I been out?" he mumbled from between his long fingers.

"About half an hour." Nate tossed his coat at him. "I have no idea where MacQueen is, but I'm ready for bed."

Max squinted up at him, his eyes bloodshot. "God, me too. We really need to stop doing this."

Nate had to agree.

They stumbled out to the street and Nate hailed a hackney. After he'd seen Max home to Grosvenor Square—both the duke and MacQueen resided in town houses at the same prestigious address—he directed the driver to take him to Berkeley Square. He'd contemplated walking the short distance from Max's town house to Hastings House—it had stopped raining in the early evening, and the fresh air may have cleared his head a little—but he had an awful feeling he might actually trip, and the last thing he wanted was to be the headline in tomorrow's *Times*. He could well imagine it:

VISCOUNT MALVERNE KILLED IN TRAGIC ACCIDENT!

RUN OVER BY A HACKNEY COACH ON MOUNT STREET.

After surviving Quatre Bras and Waterloo, what a pathetic way to die.

Better think of something else. As the hackney rolled along the quiet, rain-slick streets, Nate's thoughts turned to Miss Sophie Brightwell once more. And not in a remotely appropriate way. Rather in a wholly improper way. Indeed, all bloody night he'd been half-hard whenever he recalled the sight of her delectable mouth as she ate her strawberry ice cream at Gunter's this afternoon, the way her tongue had curled around her spoon and swiped the droplets of slick cream off her full lower lip. He wondered yet again if her nipples were the same pale hue of rose pink as the ice cream or a duskier shade. And would her skin be as pale and silky smooth as the dollop of cream that had adorned the iced confection before he'd dipped his spoon in?

There was something else he'd like to dip into. And it had nothing to do with ice cream or spoons, and everything to do with his tongue lapping at the warm, honey-sweet nectar between her—

The cab stopped and Nate swore. His groin was throbbing with arousal. But as he clambered from the carriage, he realized with a grimace that the reason he was in so much pain wasn't solely because he was sporting a fierce cockstand. He really should have used the water closet back at the Pandora Club.

Indeed, the need to relieve himself was so urgent, once he'd pushed through the side-gate to Hastings House, he was compelled to make use of a heavily shadowed corner by a high hedgerow, not far from the servants' entrance at the back.

Feeling slightly better in body, if not in mind—the world was still out of focus and his balance shot—he unlocked the door and then attempted to slink upstairs to the second floor where the bedchambers lay, as quietly as he could. He'd best not wake his father.

The upper gallery was dark save for a wash of weak moonlight filtering in through a tall window at the far end—the servants had obviously forgotten to draw the curtains. To muffle his footfalls, Nate trod with concentrated effort down the center of the thick Turkish hall runner—or as close to the center as possible; at one point, he nearly collected a potted fern when he veered off course.

The beginnings of a monumental headache had already started to throb in his right temple when he reached his bedroom door and pushed inside. The fire in the white marble fireplace was so low, he could barely see his hand in front of his face, but he didn't need much light to strip. Discarding his coat and waistcoat onto the carpeted floor, he clumsily tugged at his cravat. He couldn't wait to fall into bed.

I adore you, Sophie, my darling." Nate brushed his lips across her ear, making Sophie sigh and shiver in delicious anticipation. When his large hand slid to her breast, barely concealed by her almost transparent silk night rail, the place between her thighs began to ache in the most curious way. "And now that we are at long last wed," he continued in a voice that made her very bones melt, "I'm going to make you mine. Right here, right now . . ."

Curling her fingers into the rich satin of Nate's waistcoat, Sophie wantonly pressed herself against the man she loved. She wanted to touch him. Run her hands over his wide shoulders. Explore his marble-hard chest. Discover *every single thing about his glorious body. And to have him touch her in return.* "Yes . . . yes please, Nate."

In the velvet darkness something stirred beyond the bed hangings, and Sophie turned her head on the goose-down pillow. Was that a rustle of fabric? The whisper of a voice, low-pitched and decidedly male, breaking the quiet stillness of the night?

For a moment, she held her breath, listening. There it was again, but this time it was more like a muttered expletive, not fit for her ears.

It *was* Nate. But why on earth was he cursing? A moment ago he was about to make mad, passionate love to her in this very bed. Frowning in confusion, Sophie rolled over and reached for her lover, chasing after the threads of her blissful dream. But he wasn't there . . .

With an effort, she prized open heavy eyelids, and a sliver of awareness penetrated her foggy brain. Blast, it *was* only a dream. She was alone in the guest bed of Hastings House. The posset Charlie had given her to help her sleep was conjuring up the strangest erotic visions she'd ever had. Of course, it probably didn't help that she was avidly reading the salacious and quite shocking adventures of Miss Fanny Hill before she'd snuffed out her bedside candle. That, as she drifted asleep, her body had ached with a strange unsettled longing. A feeling of wet warmth in her most intimate parts—the same feeling she had now—had made her squirm with restless need. A need she was sure only one particular viscount would be able to satisfy . . .

Drowsiness tugged at Sophie's consciousness once more, enticing her back toward Nate and all the wicked and wonderful things they were about to do together. As her eyelids fluttered closed, she could just discern her newly wedded husband's magnificent body, a dark and hazy silhouette against the soft glow of the coals in the fireplace.

Sophie's mouth curved into a smile. How beautiful he was. An Adonis come to life. Her sleepy yet appreciative gaze drifted over his disheveled hair, broad shoulders, bare lean torso . . .

My goodness. Nate was in the process of removing his clothes. *Every single stitch.*

A sizzling bolt of desire seared through Sophie when he pushed his trousers down his powerful thighs and she caught a glimpse of his bare buttocks. The flash of firm, bunched muscles and sleek flesh made her breath quicken and her pulse race. Should she look away?

Don't be a prude, Sophie. Nate's about to introduce you to the exquisite delights of the marriage bed. Why shouldn't you look your fill? After all, it's only a dream.

Only it wasn't.

The realization that she wasn't asleep crashed over Sophie like a bucket of ice-cold water a moment later when Lord Malverne threw back the covers on the other side of the bed. Too stunned to scream or even call out his name, she could only gape as the viscount—apparently oblivious to her presence—flopped down beside her, burrowed his head into the pillow, and then emitted a soft snore.

Oh, my God! She might have been invisible to Lord Malverne, but the large, masculine, *naked* body stretched out beside her was most definitely real.

Sophie forced herself to swallow, to moisten her mouth so she could speak. To say something to wake Lord Malverne. To roundly scold him for this bizarre and inexplicable intrusion into her bedchamber.

But she didn't. Her voice refused to work, just as her body refused to move.

This couldn't be happening.

Shouldn't be happening.

And what did it say about her that she was doing nothing to stop Lord Malverne?

Not one single thing.

Even now, it was excitement fizzing through her veins, not terror, as he rolled toward her and one of his long muscular arms settled over her breasts. Clad only in her thin cotton night rail, Sophie's nipples hardened in a most alarming way, as though she were cold.

But she wasn't. Far from it. Wicked desire warmed her suddenly too-sensitive skin, and moist heat pooled low in her belly. Propriety demanded she throw Lord Malverne's arm off, pull away, and shriek at him to get out of her bed. She should flee from the room. But it seemed the only thing that had fled was every last shred of her common sense.

In the quiet of the night, all she could hear was the mad beating of her heart and Lord Malverne's slow, steady breathing. It was clear he was fast asleep. Practically insensible. If seduction had been on his mind when he'd entered the room, it certainly wasn't his intention now.

Long minutes passed in which Sophie tried very hard to stay as motionless as possible. She really couldn't afford to make a monumental fuss. Because if others came running— the servants or, worse, Lord Westhampton—and discovered she was alone with the viscount in her room, it could prove to be disastrous. Although she was physically attracted to Lord Malverne, that didn't mean she wanted to be forced to marry him because he'd compromised her. And rakehell that he was, he certainly wouldn't want that either. He was sure to resent her rather than love her. It was bound to be a marriage made in hell.

As Sophie continued to lie there, her mind awhirl yet her body frozen by indecision, another part of her was trying very hard to ignore the pleasant weight of Lord Malverne's arm across her chest, the heat of his body, and the tantalizing fragrance of his spicy cologne. Was it sandalwood and bergamot? Or citron? She noticed other scents, too, like male musk, cigar smoke, and something alcoholic like brandy.

Yes, she most definitely smelled brandy.

That was it! Lord Malverne was foxed. *Drunk.*

So drunk he'd come into the wrong bedchamber. That *had* to be the reason for his outrageous behavior.

Sophie let out a small sigh. She couldn't let the viscount sleep here all night, and neither could she stay. All things considered, she really had only two choices: she could either try to wake Lord Malverne and pray to God he didn't cause a hullaballoo given his inebriated state, or she could try to steal from the bed and enlist Charlie's aid in quietly ejecting him from the room. Sophie barely suppressed a shudder at the thought of her friend's reaction to all this.

She'd be livid with her brother. Despite her warnings that he was marriage averse, Charlie might insist he save her from ruin.

Dear Lord, Sophie hoped not. One thing was certain, the longer she stayed here with Lord Malverne, the greater the risk they'd be found together. She had to sneak out of bed. Now.

Not daring to breathe, Sophie began to slide away from the viscount. But she'd barely moved an inch when his hand tightened about her shoulder. And then the unthinkable happened: he began to nuzzle her neck. "Sweetheart," he groaned against her skin, making her traitorous body shiver in delight. "You taste like heaven. So fucking sweet. Like strawberries."

Oh, God. Did Lord Malverne really just say that?

It was depraved. It was lewd.

Yet it made her blood race faster and hotter. So hot . . .

Before Sophie could summon the urge to push him away, Lord Malverne dragged his lips across her jaw, then swirled the tip of his tongue around her ear. A firestorm of wild desire flared to life inside her body, and without thinking, she moaned.

But Lord Malverne didn't seem to mind. In fact, the small sound seemed to spur him on. His hot, wet mouth slid down her neck until he encountered the edge of her night rail, and then she felt his fingers pulling at the ribbon tie securing the neckline. Cool air washed over her bared breasts.

Stop him, Sophie Brightwell. Stop him right now.

But she didn't. *Couldn't.* In all her twenty-one years, she'd never experienced anything like this. The sensation of his fingers kneading her bare flesh, gently rolling her tight nipple, was delightfully wicked. Intoxicating like the sweetest, strongest wine imaginable.

She wanted to stroke Lord Malverne's naked skin as well but she didn't have the courage. Instead, she curled her fingers into the sheets and gripped them with all her might.

Perhaps I'm asleep too, she thought in desperation as good sense continued its war with burning want. *Perhaps this is all a sinful yet oh-so-pleasurable dream.*

But the press of Lord Malverne's body against her side,

the jut of something hard and decidedly male into the curve of her hip, the glide of his mouth, the rough scrape of his stubble across her collarbone and then lower, it all felt very, *very* real. And not at all unwelcome. Not one little bit.

She *had* to touch him. Turning toward him, she slid one trembling hand over his lean hip, her fingertips brushing hard bone and hot sleek flesh. As the rigid shaft of his manhood jerked against her belly, Lord Malverne flicked his tongue over her distended nipple.

Oh, dear Lord. Sophie gasped and her whole body bucked at the unexpected, entirely novel sensation.

And her dream lover froze.

Oh, no.

"What the bloody hell?" Lord Malverne jerked away and Sophie scrambled from the bed in such a hurry, her hip collided with the bedside table. She yelped and something crashed to the floor. At the same time, Lord Malverne leapt out of the other side of the bed, dragging the counterpane with him

"Who the hell are you? What are you doing in my bed?" he demanded in a voice rough with sleep and fury.

Before Sophie could even draw breath to answer, the bedchamber door burst open, revealing Charlie in her night rail with a candle in hand.

"Oh, my God," she breathed. Her topaz brown eyes were wide with shock as she took in the scene, her gaze darting from Sophie to her brother, then back to Sophie.

Then she swiftly stepped into the room and closed the door.

Her blazing gaze shifted to Nate again. "Nathaniel Hastings. You have a *lot* of explaining to do," she hissed before she addressed Sophie in a softer tone. "Are you all right?"

Her pulse racing, her mouth dry, Sophie moistened her lips. "It's . . . it's not what it looks like," she whispered, even though it was.

Charlie's eyebrows snapped into a frown. "Then why is your nightgown undone?"

Sophie gave a small squeal and yanked up the loosened bodice of her night rail. At the same time, Lord Malverne adjusted the blue silk counterpane so that it covered his lower half a little more adequately, although Sophie could still see the line of one lean hip bone and a fascinating trail of dark hair that arrowed downward from the viscount's navel toward his—

Don't even think about that part of him, Sophie Brightwell.

Charlie turned her ferocious gaze on her brother. "And why are you *stark naked* in my friend's bedroom?"

Lord Malverne scowled and raked a hand through his hair, a movement that only emphasized the bulging muscles in his upper arm and the impressive breadth of his wide chest. "What the deuce do you mean? This isn't Miss Brightwell's room. It's my—" The viscount's dark brown eyes swept over the chamber and then widened in dawning horror.

"Oh, God," he groaned before he took a few steps backward and collapsed into the bedside armchair. "Oh, no."

"Oh, no?" snapped Charlie, advancing toward her brother, her eyes spitting fire. "It's a good deal worse than 'oh no.' It's appalling, Nathaniel. You've compromised my very best friend!"

At that moment, a knock sounded at the door. "Lady Charlotte? Is that you? Are you all right?"

Charlie deposited her candle on the mantelpiece, then rushed over to the door. "Yes, it is, Molly," she said in a lighthearted voice as she gripped the door handle, possibly to prevent another intrusion. "And Miss Brightwell. We're perfectly fine."

Charlie's maid occupied a small chamber on the other side of her mistress's room. "But I heard a cry. And raised voices . . ."

Charlie squeezed her eyes shut as though praying for both patience and a miracle. "Miss Brightwell saw a mouse and took fright. But it scuttled away so all's well now."

"Well, if you're sure, my lady . . ."

"I am. And thank you, Molly. Good night."

"Good night, my lady."

Sophie expelled a shaky sigh of relief at the near miss. The fewer people who knew about this, the better.

Lord Malverne shook his head. "Dear God, what a mess." His expression was completely guilt-ridden as his sorrowful brown eyes settled on Sophie. "Miss Brightwell. I am so very sorry. This bedchamber was once mine."

"Yes, five years ago." Charlie's voice was sharp with accusation as she added, "You've had too much to drink, haven't you?"

To his credit, Lord Malverne didn't shy away from the truth. "Yes. I have. Much too much. I wasn't thinking. This has all been a terrible mistake, Miss Brightwell. Entirely my fault. But I will do the honorable thing—"

Charlie planted her fisted hands on her hips. "No, you bloody well won't, Nathanial Hastings. You will *not* propose to my friend. She deserves better than someone like you for a husband, and you know it."

"Ouch, Charlie." Lord Malverne winced. "But I won't disagree with you there. Nevertheless, honor compels me to make an offer." He turned his gaze—both solemn and pained in equal measure—toward Sophie. "Miss Brightwell—"

"No. No, honor doesn't compel you. You don't need to do anything." Sophie blurted out the words in a rush as panic flared. "I mean, nothing really happened. Honestly. My virtue might be a little smudged but I didn't lose . . . I mean we didn't . . ." A fiery blush stormed across her face as she struggled to articulate the fact that she was still a maid. "If no one else knows about this, surely it can be just our little secret. We can pretend this never happened. And no harm done."

Lord Malverne gave her a considering look as he rubbed his stubble-clad jaw; perhaps he was recalling their original little secret. But Charlie shook her head. "While I agree we need to keep this between ourselves, I do not think we can forget about it. For one thing, Nate needs to make amends."

Sophie's forehead knit into a suspicious frown. "But how? What are you proposing?"

Lord Malverne quirked a brow in skepticism too. "Yes, what do you have in mind, dear sister?"

Charlie crossed her arms, her expression deadly serious. "Nate, you are going to help Sophie find a husband. The man of her dreams. A love match. Or else I'll tell Father what you've done, and then you *will* have to marry her. And I don't think either of you wants that"—her gaze shifted between them—"do you?"

"Good God, Charlie." Lord Malverne wiped a hand down his face, but it didn't conceal his pained grimace. "That's a tall order."

Charlie's fierce gaze was implacable. "Nevertheless, it's one that you must fill."

Lord Malverne's wide shoulders lifted with a heavy sigh. "Yes . . ."

Charlie snorted. "Don't look so glum, Nate. You will benefit from this arrangement too."

He cocked a sardonic brow. "Oh, please do enlighten me."

"There's no need to be quite so sarcastic. You cannot deny that Father has not been happy with your behavior of late. And"—she gestured at his barely clad body—"this escapade is clearly a case in point."

Lord Malverne's mouth twisted. "Go on."

"When he sees you chaperoning Sophie and me about town, escorting us to respectable ton events, he'll believe you are at long last curbing your wild ways." Tapping her chin, she gave her brother a considering look. "In fact, if he happens to hear you are courting a debutante as a gentleman should, so much the better. All you have to do is dance with Lady Penelope a few times at a few balls—or anyone at all, really—and he will be ecstatic."

"Very well," Lord Malverne said with a deep sigh. "You've convinced me. I agree to the terms of the bargain." All at once, his expression changed. Even in the weak light of Charlie's candle, Sophie watched as the viscount's face turned a sickly shade of pale green and deep lines bracketed his down-turned mouth.

He lurched to his feet. "My apologies, ladies." With the counterpane still slung around his waist, Lord Malverne bolted toward the door that led to the adjoining dressing room. And then the unmistakable sound of retching filled the room.

"Oh, Nate." Charlie shook her head, her disgust and exasperation clearly written upon her face. She closed the dressing room door on him, then gestured to Sophie. "Come, my dear. I think it's best that we leave him to it. You can share my bed if you like."

As the sounds of violent vomiting continued, Sophie wasn't about to disagree.

She also tried not to dwell on the uncomfortable notion that perhaps just the thought of marrying her had indeed turned Lord Malverne's stomach. However, now there was also no doubt in her mind that he had well and truly been foxed to the eyeballs when he climbed into bed with her. When he did all of those wicked things.

Things I wanted him to do.

Hoping her blush didn't show in Charlie's dimly lit room, Sophie climbed into the enormous tester bed and pulled the sheets and pale gold counterpane up to her chin.

"He's not a bad man, you know," murmured Charlie, stroking her hair. "He's just . . . He tries to soothe past hurts in ways that are not entirely healthy or wise. I'm sorry he frightened you."

If you only knew the truth. "He startled me. At first. And I believe you. I don't know your brother all that well, but I sense he does have a good heart too."

As Charlie slid into sleep, Sophie stared at the dying fire, going over everything that had happened.

Charlie was effectively blackmailing her brother. And Sophie wasn't sure how she felt about that. It felt wrong somehow. And awkward.

On the bright side, she would be spending an inordinate amount of time in Lord Malverne's company. He would undoubtedly be able to open doors for her that had hitherto been shut. And considering he was acquainted with the who's who of society, he would be able to scrutinize the bachelors she encountered. Offer insights into their characters, their suitability, their trustworthiness.

And perhaps he could also quietly give her some advice

on flirting. And as Charlie had said at Gunter's, chasing rakes might even be fun. What did she have to lose?

Perhaps her friend's plan wasn't so mad after all.

The irony was, Sophie suspected that in her heart of hearts, the only man she really did want for a husband *was* Nathaniel Hastings. A man who didn't want her, or any woman, for a wife.

CHAPTER 8

What are the latest debutante fashions guaranteed
to turn his head this Season?

A list of Mayfair's top five modistes who will be
sure to make you shine whatever the occasion . . .

The Beau Monde Mirror:
The Essential Style and Etiquette Guide

Conduit Street, Mayfair

April 4, 1818

Madame Boucher, modiste extraordinaire, clucked her
tongue as her shrewd black eyes ran over Sophie's
attire. Sophie was sure the seamstress hadn't missed the
worn patches at the elbows of her red velvet spencer or that
she'd attempted to hide the slightly frayed hem of her
striped rose and ivory silk gown by adding a wide ruffle
that didn't quite match.

"Mademoiselle Sophie," she began in her heavy French
accent, "you are such a lovely young woman, yet your ap-
parel is . . ." She sighed heavily and gestured at Sophie's
gown. "Well, we shall fix this. You shall be the belle of
every ball, as they say."

Lady Chelmsford—Charlie's much-loved aunt Tabitha—
gave a nod of approval that sent the black ostrich feather
adorning her purple velvet turban bobbing. Ensconced on a
gilt-legged settee, she looked for all the world like a queen

holding court as she peered through her gold lorgnette at Sophie. "Excellent, Madame Boucher. Excellent," she said in her deep, distinctly nasal voice. "We shall put everything on my account. Spare no expense."

Charlie, who sat beside her aunt, threw Sophie a bright smile, whereas all Sophie could do was gape like a ninny.

"But, Lady Chelmsford," she said when she managed to find her voice, "you cannot . . . I mean, I never expected. I'm grateful for your generosity, but what you are offering, it is far too much."

Lady Chelmsford gave a gentle huff of disagreement as she waved her lorgnette in the air. "My dear gel, I have so much money set aside in Drummonds, I sometimes don't know what to do with it all. So if I want to spend it on a whole new wardrobe for my favorite niece's best friend, I shall do so."

Sophie blushed. "Of course, my lady. I did not mean to offend."

The marchioness's gaze softened. "And no offense has been taken, my dear Miss Brightwell. None at all. You gels need a little spoiling considering everything that you've all had to endure over the last few years."

"Yes," agreed Charlie. The smile playing about her lips was nothing but sly as she continued, "And don't forget, it won't be long before the gentlemen of the ton will be paying you court. In my opinion, a new wardrobe is essential."

Madame Boucher clapped her hands, and several young women appeared as if from nowhere. The main room—or *salon* as Madame Boucher called it on their arrival—was essentially a display room for clients. Decked out in ornate, overstuffed chairs and other luxurious furnishings, which included a thick Aubusson carpet, plush blue velvet curtains, and a wall of gilt-edged mirrors, it could pass for a fine French boudoir.

"Take Mademoiselle Sophie away to be measured," she ordered. "And, Marie, bring Lady Chelmsford and Lady Charlotte a tray of tea and petit fours, *tout de suite*."

Sophie was immediately ushered into a smaller but no less opulent room, stripped down to her shift, and after she'd been poked and prodded and measured, and spun around endless times by two of Madame Boucher's assistants who spoke in French so rapidly, Sophie could barely understand it, she was permitted to don her stays again.

As if by magic, Madame Boucher appeared. "*Très bon*, Mademoiselle Sophie. You have a beautiful figure." She ran her cool hands over Sophie's shoulders, down her arms, and then, after clasping her waist, turned her around again.

If she was spun around anymore, Sophie thought she might be ill.

When she'd completed her inspection, Madame Boucher declared, "Yvonne, fetch the shot silk ball gown in turquoise. And the one in azure satin *avec* the silver thread embroidery." She clasped Sophie's chin gently. "*Mon petit chou*, do not look so alarmed. This will be fun. I shall create the most spectacular ball gowns for you, all the young men of *le bon ton* will fall at your pretty feet. Just you wait and see."

Sophie exhaled slowly and tried to make herself relax. While she was excited at the thought of having a range of new clothes for the Season, she couldn't help but feel a trifle guilty about how much money Lady Chelmsford was about to spend.

And she also felt unaccountably nervous. She decided she disliked being the center of so much fuss and attention. How would she cope when she accompanied Lady Chelmsford, Lord Malverne, and Charlie out into society?

At least she would look as though she belonged, even if everyone whispered nasty things about her behind her back.

The young woman named Yvonne soon returned with the gowns Madame Boucher had requested, and Sophie gasped. They were exquisite. She'd never, ever seen such fine silk and satin, lace and ribbons, or such precise needlework.

Yvonne and the other assistant helped her to don the turquoise silk gown, and when Sophie looked in the full-length oval looking glass, she gasped again.

Was that really Sophie Brightwell staring back at her with bright eyes and flushed cheeks? The cut of the gown was perfect, accentuating her best features and minimizing her flaws. She looked slender as a willow, yet her small breasts swelled above the round neckline of the bodice, higher and plumper than she'd ever imagined possible. Earlier in the day, Charlie's maid, Molly, had arranged her black hair into an elaborate style that consisted of a large twisted coil at her crown and a cascade of tight glossy ringlets around her face. If she stepped into Almack's right now, she would not be out of place.

"*Superbe*," exclaimed Madame Boucher from behind her. "*Merveilleux*." She adjusted a seam and plucked at the puffed sleeves, then declared, "Come, you must show the marchioness and Lady Charlotte how beautiful you are."

Drawing a steadying breath, Sophie returned to the salon and was greeted by exclamations of delight from both Charlie and Lady Chelmsford.

"Spin around, Sophie darling," urged Charlie. "I want to see the ribbon work at the back and how the skirt flares when you turn."

Sophie smiled and complied with her friend's request. It seemed she was destined to be dizzy and light-headed all day.

"The color suits you perfectly, Miss Brightwell," declared Lady Chelmsford.

"Yes, it certainly does."

Sophie froze and her gaze snapped to the doorway. She knew that deep male voice.

Lord Malverne had arrived.

Dear God, what on earth was *he* doing here?

"Thank you, my lord," she said in a voice that somehow sounded relatively normal. Her cheeks grew warmer, but as they were already flushed with excitement, perhaps no one would notice that the viscount's appearance had affected her so much.

Well, perhaps no one except Charlie. But at least she knew why.

She glanced at Lady Chelmsford, but she was too busy crowing over the unexpected arrival of her nephew.

"Nathaniel. Fancy seeing you here. It's been an age, dear boy."

Lord Malverne crossed to his aunt and placed a brief kiss on the powdered apple of her cheek. "It has been too long, Aunt Tabitha. I hope you don't mind that I dropped by."

"Of course not. But how did you know we were here?"

"Charlotte mentioned she would be here with you and Miss Brightwell. And as I was nearby making some purchases on Bond Street, I thought I would take the opportunity to pay my respects to my favorite aunt."

"Well, I'm so glad that you did. Please, take a seat," she said, gesturing at a nearby bergère. "I'm organizing a new wardrobe for Miss Brightwell and she's modeling some of the choices available. I'm sure she wouldn't mind if you stayed to offer your opinion." The marchioness glanced at Sophie as she added, "Would you, Miss Brightwell?"

Oh, no. Lord Malverne is going to stay for the entire consultation? Sophie could think of nothing worse, but nevertheless she said, "No, of course not." Because what else could she say?

Lord Malverne's mouth tilted into an appealing smile, and he inclined his head in acknowledgment of her concession, such that it was, before claiming the seat his aunt had indicated. He folded his large frame into the elegant chair, his long, muscular legs negligently sprawled out before him. The figure-hugging fawn pantaloons he wore left little to the imagination, and Sophie caught herself blushing again. Had that wonderfully athletic body really been pressed against hers last night? Had that wide mouth really kissed her so intimately? And uttered such wicked words?

So fucking sweet. Like strawberries.

Lord Malverne's eyes met hers, and the heat she saw in their dark brown depths made her nipples tighten to hard, aching points. Made her belly flip. Was he recalling what had happened last night too? And their secret bargain?

She wanted to escape his hypnotic stare, but Madame Boucher's assistants began fussing around the hem of the gown, pinning up the fabric, thus preventing her retreat to the changing room.

Good Lord, how was she to survive the next few weeks, perhaps months, as Lord Malverne complied with his sister's request to help her find a husband? As they engaged in in-depth discussions about the merits of one man over another? When he discreetly coached her in the art of flirting. With her embarrassing tendency to blush bright red at the slightest provocation, she'd look like a beet for the entire Season.

How was she to endure it? Even now, anticipation and tension vibrated through her entire body, making her muscles tighten. Indeed, she had to consciously will her fingers to loosen their crushing grip on the skirts of the haute couture gown lest Madame Boucher rebuke her for ruining the exquisite silk.

One thing Sophie was certain of, she needed to become inured to Lord Malverne's presence, and quickly. She must bury the memory of what had happened last night. And somehow, some way, she needed to crush her silly infatuation altogether, because how could she possibly consider any other men when her heart only seemed to want Lord Malverne?

Nate accepted the cup of tea and a petit four from Aunt Tabitha, then settled back in his chair to enjoy the delightful show.

Good God, he was a cad. After his unforgivable behavior last night, he really shouldn't be ogling the poor girl. But then, how could he not?

Attired in an exquisite couture gown that highlighted her narrow torso and exposed a good deal of her creamy, pert breasts—breasts he'd fondled and had attempted to taste—Miss Sophie Brightwell practically took his breath away. He'd always thought her a pretty girl, but right at this moment, she was more than pretty. She was utterly delectable. Dangerously so.

So fucking sweet. Had he really whispered that into her ear as he'd mauled her neck? Did she remember?

Jesus Christ, he should be horsewhipped for what he'd said and done. In his defense—a defense he acknowledged was weak—he'd barely been awake. Indeed, he'd had no idea it was Sophie Brightwell sharing the bed he mistakenly believed was his. He thought she was simply the siren appearing in his very vivid, very erotic dream. A dream similar to the one he'd had after he first encountered Sophie in Hastings House's library. All things considered, he was getting off quite lightly given that he really should be on his way to visit the Archbishop of Canterbury to procure a special marriage license.

He took a large sip of the hot, sweet tea and grimaced as it scalded the roof of his mouth. *Sweet.* He wasn't wrong about how sweet Miss Brightwell had smelled and tasted. Even though he'd been drunk, that was one detail he did remember clearly. That and the fact that she hadn't protested when he began to kiss her. Which was interesting indeed.

When he eventually returned to his own bed last night, as he tried to go to sleep, he was initially terrified by the idea that he might have forced himself on Sophie—not that he'd ever behaved that way before, but he *had* been riproaringly drunk. The thought of a man taking a woman by force was abhorrent to him.

Sophie would have been well within her rights to take a candlestick or a poker to him last night, but she hadn't. When he'd kissed her, she released a small throaty moan of desire and curled one of her small hands over his naked hip.

She'd rolled closer.

Sweet, prim and proper Miss Sophie Brightwell had been aroused.

Nate's cock stirred at the thought, and he crossed one ankle over his other knee in the hope of hiding his wayward physical responses from everyone in the room. The last thing he needed was to grow an erection in front of his aunt and sister. Or Miss Brightwell, no matter how receptive she'd been last night.

Sophie disappeared—probably to change into another gown—and Nate permitted himself a small sigh of relief. He really should focus on the guilt that lurked beneath his lust. Yes, hopefully guilt over his appalling conduct last night would dampen his wholly inappropriate and damnably inconvenient desire for his sister's friend.

No, it was more than that—it was a dangerous desire.

Of course it would be much easier to rein in his fierce attraction if he could also maintain his distance. But that would be well nigh impossible now that he was compelled to squire Sophie about town. Damn Charlie and her wicked bargain—

". . . don't you think that would be best, Nathaniel?"

Nate blinked. "Yes. Of course. I trust your judgment implicitly, Aunt Tabitha." What the hell had his aunt and Charlie been talking about? He took another sip of tea and glanced at Charlie over the rim of his cup. She quirked an eyebrow at him, her eyes gleaming with amusement, and he scowled back. She must know he was frightfully hungover—his head ached and his stomach was delicate—so her instruction to attend the appointment at the modiste's this afternoon was clearly part of his punishment for almost ruining her friend. The meddling minx.

She really was too good at this blackmailing caper.

As Nate reached for another petit four, his attention was claimed by Sophie's reemergence from the changing room.

Good Lord she was divine. This time she wore a gown of sky blue satin, and he could see even more of her lovely décolletage. With her looking like that, he had no doubt that it wouldn't be long before half the ton's bachelors would be chasing after her; hopefully one of the more suitable bucks would sweep her off her feet just as she dreamed before the end of the Season.

Yes, with any luck, this trial would soon be over and he could return to his carefree bachelor existence, doing whatever he wanted, whenever he wanted, with whomever he wanted—and that "whomever" wasn't his father's choice of a prospective bride, Lady Penelope Purcell, or Miss Brightwell, no matter how delicious she was.

Popping the petit four into his mouth, Nate tried not to think about how sweet it or anything else in the room tasted.

* * *

After an hour and a half, Sophie was exhausted and entirely overwhelmed by emotion. Lady Chelmsford,
aided and abetted by Charlie *and* Lord Malverne, had insisted on purchasing so many clothes for her, she rather
thought she could change her attire several times a day for
a whole week and there would still be unworn garments in
her wardrobe.

Madame Boucher and her seamstresses would create
five ball gowns especially for her, seven morning dresses
with matching spencers, three promenade gowns, two
carriage gowns, a blue velvet riding habit, several pelisses,
and a smart wool redingote, as well as several fine evening gowns suitable for wearing to dinner parties and
soirees.

In addition to these garments, three day dresses and a
promenade gown had been carefully wrapped up so that
she might take them with her straightaway. It was enough
to make Sophie's head spin.

"Lady Chelmsford, words can simply not express how
grateful I am," began Sophie as they prepared to quit Madame Boucher's salon.

"Think nothing of it, my dear gel," replied the marchioness, touching her cheek with a gnarled hand. "Besides,
we've only just begun."

Sophie frowned in confusion as she accepted her worn
red spencer from one of the salon's assistants. "I don't quite
take your meaning, my lady."

"Well, we have suitable gowns aplenty for you now," replied Lady Chelmsford as Nate helped her into her black
velvet redingote. "But what of bonnets, shoes, fans, reticules,
and gloves, et cetera?"

Oh, my goodness. "I'm sure all those things are not
necessary, my lady."

"Of course they are," said Charlie as she tied the emerald
green ribbon of her poke bonnet beneath her chin. "Matching accessories are an absolute necessity. Don't you think
so, brother dear?"

Lord Malverne cocked an eyebrow. "You're asking me to comment on women's fashions, Charlie? I know nothing about them."

"Well, that's funny," murmured Charlie as they headed toward the salon's vestibule, "because you seemed to have quite an opinion on whatever Miss Brightwell was modeling this afternoon. You couldn't take your eyes off her."

Color rose along Lord Malverne's high cheekbones, and Sophie blinked in surprise. Was the viscount actually blushing?

Rather than respond to his sister's gibe, Lord Malverne offered his arm to his aunt and escorted her out of the salon's door onto Conduit Street.

"I don't think your brother actually *was* all that interested in what I was wearing," Sophie remarked as she and Charlie followed Lord Malverne and Lady Chelmsford out into the street. One of the marchioness's footmen, laden with packages, trailed behind them. Charlie's brother *might* have appeared to be staring at her with avid attention throughout the appointment, but surely he was just being polite.

"Oh, believe me, he was most interested in your appearance," her friend replied with a grin. "And his reaction to what you were modeling was an excellent way to gauge how other rakes might respond when they see you all dressed up in your new finery. Also"—Charlie leaned closer to murmur in her ear—"I couldn't resist torturing him a bit, to punish him for his atrocious behavior last night. I knew he'd feel frightful today and wouldn't want to get out of bed unless I insisted he help you in your quest straightaway. Aside from that, I wanted to let him know I'm watching him. He is *not* to misbehave around you."

Sophie bit her lip. What Charlie didn't know was that it wasn't only her brother who was guilty of misbehaving last night. If she learned the truth of the matter, what would she think?

The footman piled the packages into Lady Chelmsford's waiting carriage, but the marchioness decided that they should continue on foot to her favorite milliner's shop as it was on Mill Street, only a little farther along in the direction of Savile Row.

Charlie threaded her arm through Sophie's as they followed her aunt and brother. "When we return home," she began, "I'll have the servants prepare you a warm bath so that you can have a nice long soak. After last night, you must be exhaust—"

"Miss Brightwell? My word, is that you?"

Sophie froze and grimaced. *Oh, no.* She knew that gruff voice that reminded her of something being dragged over gravel.

Plastering an amiable smile on her face, she turned around to find Wilbur, Lord Buxton, but a few feet away. *Damn and blast!* How unlucky could she be?

"Lord Buxton, I had not expected to see you here in London," she said with forced politeness. As usual, the portly baron was wearing an ill-fitting coat and waistcoat that stretched in a most disconcerting way across his middle, and his ivory pantaloons appeared to be padded around the thigh area as though he was attempting to make his spindly legs look more muscular than they actually were.

Lord Buxton's lascivious gaze traveled over Charlie, who was regarding the baron with a look that could only be described as chilly.

Even though she didn't want to, Sophie offered the required introductions. "Lady Charlotte, may I introduce Baron Buxton? Lord Buxton, this is Lady Charlotte Hastings, daughter of the Earl of Westhampton."

Lord Buxton looked as though he'd like to kiss Charlie's hand, but Charlie kept it firmly tucked behind Sophie's elbow; in her other gloved hand, she gripped her reticule.

When the baron realized that Charlie's hand wouldn't be forthcoming, he simply bowed. "Lady Charlotte, it is indeed a pleasure to make your acquaintance." His gaze transferred to Sophie again. "Your father did inform me you would be in London, but I really hadn't expected to run into you either. How fortuitous."

"Yes," said Sophie. "Quite."

Lord Buxton's gaze moved past her, and the light in his small blue eyes dimmed.

"And who might this be?" inquired a deep male voice from behind Sophie's left shoulder.

Lord Malverne. Sophie was suddenly grateful for his large, solid presence.

Lord Buxton looked a trifle uncomfortable as Sophie introduced him to Lady Chelmsford and the viscount. Indeed, perhaps she would be intimidated, too, if she were subjected to such a cool, almost disdainful perusal by a veritable Corinthian who wore his title as well and as easily as his perfectly tailored clothes.

Lady Chelmsford didn't look overly impressed by the baron either. Peering through her lorgnette, she gave him a thorough inspection as though he were a stray dog, or some other creature she didn't quite like the look of. "Lord Buxton, pray tell us how you know Miss Brightwell."

"Ah, Miss Brightwell and I are country neighbors," said the baron with a sly grin. "You might say I'm an old family friend." He winked at this last pronouncement.

"An old family friend?" repeated Lord Malverne with the quirk of an eyebrow, his expression sardonic as though he clearly doubted the veracity of the statement.

"Yes. Sophie's—I mean, Miss Brightwell's—stepfather and I have been close acquaintances for many years." Lord Buxton's gaze slid to Sophie again. "Indeed, I hope I might make a similar claim about our relationship, Miss Brightwell."

Sophie wasn't quite sure whether she wanted to laugh or cringe in horror. How was she supposed to respond to a statement like that? The man must be truly mad. He must know she barely tolerated his presence.

As she stood there gaping, trying to formulate a response that wasn't an obvious snub, Lord Buxton took the opportunity to press his suit. "Perhaps I might call on you, Miss Brightwell, while you are in town?"

Oh, dear Lord. Sophie's stomach turned. She could think of nothing worse than being courted by the baron. "Well . . . I . . ." How on earth could she say no without appearing rude?

To her relief, Lord Malverne came to her rescue. "Miss Brightwell's social calendar is quite full I'm afraid," he said in a tone that brooked no argument. His usual charming smile was replaced with a stony, forbidding expression that Sophie had never seen before.

Lord Buxton produced a small forced smile. "Well . . . no doubt I shall see you when you return home to Monkton Green, Miss Brightwell," he said in a scrupulously polite tone.

Lord Malverne answered for her again. "No doubt."

"I shall bid you all adieu then." Lord Buxton gave a stiff bow as he continued, "It was a pleasure to meet you, Lady Chelmsford, Lady Charlotte . . ." His smiled faded. "Lord Malverne." With that, the clearly disgruntled baron turned on his heel and stalked off down Conduit Street in the opposite direction from which he'd originally been heading.

"What a horrid man," remarked Charlie with a shudder as they turned onto Mill Street. Lord Malverne and Lady Chelmsford led the way again. "Does he really know your family that well?"

"It is quite true that he's been friends with my stepfather for many years," replied Sophie. "He sometimes comes to Nettlefield Grange for dinner."

"You poor thing." Charlie shuddered again. "The way he looks at women. You especially. I feel as though I need to take a bath as well when we return to Hastings House. I'm glad Nate made short shrift of him."

Sophie was rather glad too. She studied Lord Malverne's wide shoulders and his handsome profile as he leaned in closer to listen to something his aunt was saying. He'd been her unexpected champion today, and she was nothing but grateful.

It seemed quashing her foolish tendre for him was going to be much harder than she'd originally thought.

CHAPTER 9

Lord L. might have stolen her drawers, but has he
stolen this lady's heart too?

Or perhaps she has stolen his . . . In either case,
what if her husband finds out?

The Beau Monde Mirror: The Society Page

**White's Gentleman's Club, St. James's Street,
London**

April 5, 1818

"You're not *still* under the weather after last night, are
you?" Max, the Duke of Exmoor, asked with a cocky
grin when Nate waved away the footman offering him a
glass of sherry.

"Either that or he's just getting soft in his old age," Mac-
Queen remarked drily. Lounging in one of White's dark
brown leather chairs, he flicked a flake of pastry from the
sleeve of his black superfine evening coat before choosing
another bite-size venison pie from the silver tray on the low
table between them. "Come to think of it, that might prove
awkward if we pay a visit to Pandora's later this evening."

Nate scowled at them both. "I'm simply overwhelmed
by your wit and compassion."

The truth was, he was exhausted. Last night, after he'd
escorted his aunt home, and then Charlie and Miss Brightwell

back to Hastings House, he'd accompanied Max and Mac-Queen to an out-of-town boxing match. And that was followed by an all-day stint at the races.

It hadn't helped that when he *was* at home and in his own bed—he wasn't about to make the same mistake twice and enter his old room—he was plagued by thoughts of Miss Sophie Brightwell. He'd tossed and turned for hours, his head filled with visions of her: in Gunter's with her wet skirts plastered against her long, slender legs; at Madame Boucher's, modeling exquisite couture gowns with her creamy décolletage on display; in her room with the bodice of her nightgown gaping open after he'd tried to pleasure her breasts . . .

He'd eventually been so desperate to fall sleep, he succumbed to the impulse to slake his lust by his own hand. Which had helped for a while, but then he dreamed of her and had woken with another bloody cockstand. He hadn't been this consumed with desperate need since he was an adolescent. For Christ's sake, it was enough to drive a man mad.

Even more disturbing to his equilibrium was the knowledge that he'd experienced an unexpected surge of protectiveness when that slimy baron, Lord Buxton, had tried to foist his detestable company onto Sophie. Although he'd told himself he was protecting Charlie from the bastard, it was really Sophie he was defending. He'd immediately sensed how uncomfortable she was around the man, and so he thought nothing of sending the odious prat away with a flea in his ear.

Yes, the last thing he needed was to develop tender feelings for Miss Brightwell. His lustful urges had already landed him in enough trouble. Given the bargain they'd struck, before he knew it, he'd be falling in love with the chit.

He inwardly shuddered at that idea. Maybe he *did* need a drink.

"Nate. Christ, anyone would think you'd been struck by Cupid's arrow, the way you're dreaming away," prompted Max.

"My apologies, gentlemen. What did I miss?" Nate gave a contrite grimace. He really needed to pull himself together.

"Max was just asking if you know the whereabouts of Gabriel," MacQueen said. "Neither of us has seen him since we met at Limner's Hotel two nights ago."

Nate shook his head. "No . . . I suppose I'd assumed he was just spending a good deal of time with a certain countess." Although the word about town was that Lord Astley had returned to his country estate again, it always paid to err on the side of caution when discussing another gentleman's wife within the walls of White's. One never quite knew who might be listening.

"At some stage I expect he'll have to come up for air," observed Max with a wry smile. "If the countess lets him. She has quite an appetite, that woman."

Ah, so the question as to whether Max had joined the party in Lady Astley's bedroom the night of the great drawers caper had at last been answered. Nate had never asked Max or Gabriel what had transpired. And he wasn't about to now. For some reason, a story that might have once titillated suddenly didn't hold much appeal for him.

Maybe MacQueen was right after all.

He *was* going soft.

However, that didn't seem bloody likely considering he was half-hard all the time thanks to a certain black-haired, blue-eyed chit who tasted sweeter than strawberries.

Damn. His balls tightened again. Even though he didn't much feel like it, Nate waved over one of the footmen and ordered a decanter of claret to replace the one MacQueen and Max had just polished off.

Max grinned. "Now that's more like it, Malverne. There's nothing like the hair of the dog that bit you to repair a flagging constitution."

Nate reached for a pastry. "So what do you propose we do for the rest—"

At that moment, Gabriel materialized in their quiet corner of the club.

"Are you all right, man?" MacQueen asked, his one good eye darkening with concern at the sight of their friend's haggard appearance. Gabriel's hair—always a storm of black curls at the best of times—was even messier than usual, and dark stubble shadowed his jaw. His clothes were rumpled, and beneath his green eyes were smudges of fatigue.

Gabriel threw himself into a vacant leather wing chair and ran a hand down his face. "She's killing me," he said after a moment. "I can't keep up with this woman."

Max let out a loud guffaw that drew a few stares from other noblemen around the room, and Nate grinned. Even MacQueen couldn't suppress a smile.

"Maybe you should retire to your country estate for a while," suggested Nate. The Earl of Langdale's ancestral seat was in Cumberland. "I'm sure she won't follow you there."

Gabriel heaved a great sigh. He looked truly dazed. "Maybe you're right. I can now see why her husband keeps disappearing back to *his* country estate."

MacQueen offered him the platter of pastries. "Eat up, man. It looks like you need the sustenance."

Gabriel took one. "Christ, it's enough to make a man consider marriage just to have a legitimate excuse to say no." He shook his head and grimaced. "I can't believe I just said that."

"Oh, how the mighty have fallen," chuckled MacQueen.

The footman returned with the decanter of claret and fresh glasses. Once they were all armed with drinks, they settled back into their chairs.

"What say we pay a visit to Vauxhall tomorrow night, to see what delights are on offer?" suggested Max. "I think a change of scenery would do us all good."

"Now that's a capital idea," agreed Gabriel after taking a large swig of his claret. He reached for another oyster vol-au-vent. "And perhaps the following day we could plan a trip to Brighton. I could do with some fresh sea air."

Nate blew out an exasperated sigh. "I'm afraid I can't, old chaps."

MacQueen's dark brows snapped together in a suspicious frown. "Why?"

Nate shrugged. "Business." How could he admit to his friends that he'd been blackmailed into taking part in a husband hunt for his sister's best friend? They'd skewer him alive with their gibes.

Max cocked a skeptical brow. "Business? *You* have business?"

Nate refilled his claret glass. The smooth wine was blunting the sharp edges of his tension already. "Yes. I do."

Gabriel smirked. "Female business, I'd warrant."

Nate mustn't have adequately schooled his features, as MacQueen pinned him with a penetrating stare. "Out with it, Malverne. You haven't been your devil-may-care self lately, and I think we'd all like to know why."

Damn. Was he that easy to read? Nate took another sizable swig of his wine, then contemplated the toes of his boots. What could he say that wouldn't sound awful? He really didn't want to talk about Miss Brightwell. Or how his sister was involved. Or how he got caught up in the crazy scheme in the first place.

But then again, his friends were bound to notice when he began escorting both ladies around town. *All of society will be sure to notice.*

"I've been tasked with chaperoning my sister and her friend to a number of social events over the next few weeks, so I won't be free to carouse as much as usual," he said at last.

For a moment, there was deathly silence, and then his friends all burst out laughing, drawing more annoyed looks from other club members.

Max eventually wiped the tears from his eyes. "I'm sorry. Did you really just say you're going to act as a chaperone?"

Nate sighed. "Yes. I did."

"Good God, man. Why?" asked Gabriel.

"I . . . cannot say. It's a . . . delicate matter."

"Delicate matter?" repeated MacQueen, his tone incredulous. "Next you'll be telling us you're falling in love with your sister's friend. Because why else would you agree to such an arrangement? Unless you've changed your mind about seducing debutantes and you have nefarious designs on her?"

"I hardly think so," scoffed Nate. "She's Charlie's age so

practically out of the schoolroom as far as I'm concerned. In any case, my sister would have my guts for garters. And you all know how good she is with a sword."

"Ah, so she's one of the notorious girls that was expelled from your sister's ladies' academy then," surmised Max, his blue eyes still brimming with tears of laughter.

Nate sat back and studied the play of firelight in the ruby red depths of his claret. "It hardly matters. You can speculate all you like, but I won't be drawn into sharing any more details."

"Christ," Gabriel said in a low voice laced with shock, "he won't kiss and tell. Gentlemen, I think he actually does harbor a tendre for this girl."

"That's absolute rot." It wasn't a tendre. There were no *tender* feelings involved. It was lust, pure and simple. And he needed to put out the fire in his veins, straightaway.

The problem was, he didn't seem to know how.

"I think our friend doth protest too much," MacQueen said, his steel gray eye glimmering with amusement. He refilled his claret glass. "But don't worry, your secret is safe with us."

"Egad, you three can be bastards sometimes."

Gabriel gave him a good-natured slap on the shoulder. "We won't disagree with you, my friend. But look on the bright side. You're in good company because, most of the time, you behave like a bloody bastard too."

CHAPTER 10

> Promenading in Hyde Park during the fashionable
> hour isn't what it used to be.
>
> Not when a certain pair of Disreputable Debu-
> tantes venture forth . . .
>
> To what lengths will these young "ladies" go to
> catch a husband?
>
> *The Beau Monde Mirror: The Society Page*

Hyde Park, Mayfair

April 6, 1818

"Miss Brightwell, you look truly splendid today," observed Lord Malverne with a polite smile as Sophie
and Charlie descended the stairs into the vestibule of Hastings House.

Charlie had decided they should promenade around
Hyde Park this afternoon; they would be testing the ton's
waters, so to speak, before they embarked upon a journey
into London's ballrooms and salons—if they received any
invitations, of course.

Sophie tried not to blush as she met Lord Malverne's
eyes and replied sedately, "Why thank you, my lord." She
would assume his compliment was sincere as she'd donned
one of her new ensembles—a smart poke bonnet and promenade gown, which was a lovely gentian blue trimmed with
black frogging and buttons.

She'd almost observed that the viscount looked remarkably splendid as well, but that would draw attention to the fact that she'd made note of his striking appearance. Charlie would cast her a suspicious look, and Lord Malverne would undoubtedly smile in that knowing way of his. And then she would blush and, oh, she really should stop overthinking things where Lord Malverne was concerned.

Charlie arched an eyebrow. "I'm pleased to see you've decided to take your responsibilities seriously, Nate."

Lord Malverne offered an arm to both Charlie and Sophie to escort them out to the waiting barouche, a shiny black affair with an elegant pair of matched grays strapped into the traces. "Considering what's at stake for both Miss Brightwell and myself, believe me, I'm taking them *very* seriously."

Charlie inclined her head in approval. "Good to hear."

Although a liveried footman stood at the ready by the barouche's steps, Lord Malverne himself handed them into the carriage, then took the black leather seat opposite theirs. Leaning back, he canted his long legs across the space between the seats, his black Hessians brushing against Sophie's skirts.

"Is your aunt coming too?" asked Sophie as the barouche moved off.

Charlie nodded, the green feathers in her neat bonnet bobbing with the movement. "Yes, we shall drive past her residence on Park Lane on the way. Aunt Tabitha agreed that, on our first public foray, we must adhere to the etiquette rule book as much as possible. The scandalmongers can have nasty teeth, and we don't want to give them anything to feed off of. Our behavior must be beyond reproach."

Sophie pulled a face. "Heavens, you make the ton's gossips sound like sharks, Charlie."

"They can be," remarked Lord Malverne drily. "Society's hunger for scandal borders on the insatiable."

Charlie's mouth twitched with a smile. "You don't seem to mind feeding the gossipmongers on occasion though, Nate. You're quite used to it."

Lord Malverne shrugged one shoulder and grinned. "What can I say? I aim to please."

An impish twinkle appeared in Charlie's eyes. "Yes, especially the ladies of the ton. Sophie, did you know Nate was almost arrested for public indecency about a year ago? He lost a wager at White's and had to ride down Rotten Row, stark naked, during the fashionable hour. Of course, *I* wouldn't have enjoyed such a salacious spectacle, but I'm sure there were many ladies who did."

My goodness. Heat rushed over Sophie's face as a mental image of a Lord Malverne in all his naked, muscular glory atop a shining steed popped into her head. Aloud she managed to stammer, "*Al-almost* arrested?"

Charlie's smile was pure devilry. "A mounted Bow Street Runner who was on patrol gave chase, but apparently Nate's horse was faster. Although, Nate didn't get away entirely scot-free." She turned her amused gaze on her brother. "You did complain about chafing for a week or so afterward, didn't you, Nate?"

"Charlotte," Lord Malverne warned. There was a faint wash of color across his high cheekbones, and Sophie realized he was blushing too. "I'm sure Miss Brightwell does not wish to hear you recount such . . . unpleasant details."

Charlie was unrepentant. "Unpleasant for you perhaps. But it was really quite funny watching you walk around with a bow-legged gait for several days."

Sophie bit her lip to stop herself from smiling. It must be lovely to be in a position like Lord Malverne's. Not only was he rich, handsome, and titled, it seemed he could do whatever he pleased and society didn't really give a fig. Whereas she would always be watched, pointed at, and judged, rather like a pilloried prisoner, or one in the docks awaiting sentencing. Any misstep off the narrow path of decorum could end her just as effectively as the hangman's noose. To have the same amount of privilege that circumstance had bestowed upon Lord Malverne would be heady indeed.

When they reached Park Lane, Lady Chelmsford took

her place beside her nephew in a flurry of gray and lilac skirts. After she was settled and greetings were exchanged, the barouche set forth for Hyde Park.

"I've never done this before. Promenaded in Hyde Park during the fashionable hour," admitted Sophie as they rolled down one of the carriage drives. "I'm really not sure what to expect." It was actually quite crowded with other equipages; light phaetons and smaller curricles bowled merrily past, along with dashing ton bucks and ladies atop their equally dashing mounts. Other gentlemen and women strolled here and there across the manicured grounds or gathered in small groups to converse. Of course, there were no naked rakehells about, mounted or otherwise.

Lady Chelmsford offered an encouraging smile. "If you are wondering how to make a good impression, my advice to you is just sit up as straight as you can and smile serenely as though you hadn't a care in the world."

"Yes," agreed Charlie. "It's all about being noticed in the 'right' way. While we don't wish to be ignored by others, we also don't want to create a spectacle"—she shot her brother a pointed look—"that will keep us firmly imprisoned in the dungeon reserved for social pariahs."

"By 'others,' Charlie means the arbiters of society who may invite you into their homes, and to their tiresome balls, and equally tiresome soirees if they deem you worthy enough," drawled Lord Malverne. He didn't look impressed.

"Tiresome?" asked Sophie.

Charlie laughed. "Nate is worried he will be harried by all of the debutantes looking for prospective husbands. That's why he steadfastly avoids most of the regular, respectable activities and entertainments of the Season." She leaned closer and murmured in Sophie's ear, "Until now, of course. I think your little arrangement will do him a world of good. Even though he'll never admit it."

Sophie had trouble suppressing a smile as she brazenly caught Lord Malverne's gaze again. "Heavens, that does indeed sound tiresome. Being admired and sought out so much, you feel harried."

Lord Malverne's wide mouth twitched with amusement at her unexpected dig. "It's a cross I have to bear, but I am happy to suffer through any number of events for you, Miss Brightwell." He transferred his gaze to his sister. "And of course for you, Charlotte."

"Well, I, for one, am looking forward to chaperoning you gels this Season," remarked Lady Chelmsford. Her brown eyes gleamed with anticipation over the plump powdered apples of her cheeks. "After today, I'm certain we'll receive a slew of invitations."

Charlie gave a small sigh. "I hope so. Because neither Sophie nor I will find ourselves husbands sitting around at home staring at the wallpaper."

Lady Chelmsford eventually decided they should stop the barouche beneath the shade of a large willow tree by the banks of the Serpentine. "Let us see how much interest we can snare," she said as she returned a nod to an older, elegant dame in another barouche driving along Rotten Row. "One thing is certain: a dash of notoriety is better than mediocrity for drawing attention."

Sophie had begun to notice that some of the tonnish women passing by—whether on foot or in their carriages—sent curious glances their way before smiling and bending their heads together to exchange remarks that were clearly about them. It was impossible to tell whether they were talking about the fact that the scandalous Lady Charlotte Hastings had at long last made a public appearance with her aunt or if the topic of their conversation was the disreputable rake Lord Malverne.

Either way, it wasn't long before a number of ton matrons took turns to draw their barouches and phaetons alongside theirs to pay their respects to Lady Chelmsford. Charlie and Lord Malverne were greeted with polite smiles and due respect, whereas Sophie felt as though she'd turned into a cheap curio—something novel to be examined briefly and then ignored when the observer determines it is of little use or value.

Turning her gaze to the Serpentine, she watched the bright diamonds of light created by the setting sun dance across the surface of the water. At least no one had laughed at her or given her the cut direct. *Yet.*

Lord Malverne leaned closer, drawing her attention away from the lake. "So was I correct in my assessment that tonnish activities are tiresome?" he murmured in a conspiratorial fashion.

"I'm quite content to enjoy the view," remarked Sophie, trying to ignore the scent of Lord Malverne's spicy cologne as it teased her nostrils, or the bump of his pantaloon-clad knee against hers. She didn't think it would be wise to agree with him within earshot of Charlie, Lady Chelmsford, or their current conversation partners, the Countess of Poole and her decidedly spinsterish sister.

Lord Malverne smiled in such a way that Sophie's heart tripped and her cheeks heated. "So am I. The view is quite spectacular."

"You really shouldn't do that," she said, trying to adopt an expression that would pass as reproving, but wasn't *too* stern. It wouldn't do to appear waspish.

Infuriatingly, Lord Malverne's chiseled mouth simply tilted into a half smile that was even more roguish. "Do what?"

"Openly flirt with me," replied Sophie under her breath. She tried to smooth the pleats of a frown from her forehead.

"Why not?"

"Because certain people"—she shot a pointed glance toward Lady Chelmsford and her friends—"might misinterpret the nature of our relationship."

Lord Malverne removed his top hat and raked his hand through his thick chestnut locks as though taunting her. Did he know that simple action always made her chest tighten with longing? "Miss Brightwell, you are about to have your first Season," he said, his dark gaze holding hers. "You need to know how to flirt. And as I've essentially been recruited to help you, I think you should heed my advice."

Sophie knew Lord Malverne spoke perfect sense. But even though she'd privately resolved to add the skill of flirting to her rake-ensnaring arsenal as per the Society of Enlightened Young Ladies' husband-hunting plan, now that the moment was upon her, it seemed her bravado had deserted her. For heaven's sake, they were in a park in broad daylight, not in a candlelit ballroom. She firmed her gaze and her resolve in the face of such naked masculine charm. "Be that as it may, we—you and I—shouldn't flirt right under the very nose of your aunt. What on earth will she think?"

"She's busy talking with her friends and Charlotte. Besides, what my aunt thinks hardly signifies at the moment. It's the opinion of other gentlemen that matters." Lord Malverne's gaze grew darker and hotter. More intense. "You know I haven't any designs on you, Miss Brightwell, so what harm can it do? Look at it as practice. Men like it when women flirt."

Sophie arched a brow. "You mean, men like you."

Another breath-stealing smile broke across Lord Malverne's face. "You mean, you don't want a man like me?"

"Of course I do." *Oh, God, did I really just say that?* "I mean, no . . ." Her face flaming, Sophie drew a calming breath. "What I mean to say is, I want a man who wishes to marry me. A man who will care for me, perhaps even fall in love with me. So I don't think we should flirt in public like this. Onlookers might believe you and I are courting."

Lord Malverne cocked a brow and lowered his voice. "So you want to flirt privately then?"

Good heavens, the man was vexing. And too damn attractive. "I will admit I do need the practice," she replied. "But conducting a lesson in the middle of Hyde Park during the fashionable hour is one of the *least* private settings in the whole of London. I'm certain it will keep any potential suitors from approaching. It is not a sound strategy."

Lord Malverne leaned back and replaced his hat, tilting it at a rakish angle. "Well, I think you're wrong, Miss Brightwell. *I* think men will notice you more, if another man—like me—starts flirting with you in public. Men are competitive creatures, and believe me, they'll want to vie for your attention if you become the focus of someone else's. They'll want to see what all the fuss is about. You'll become the latest fashion or craze. The talk of the ton."

Sophie's eyebrows snapped together. "So you're likening me to a hat or mental mania?"

"Nathaniel, Sophie, my dear," interjected Lady Chelmsford. Lady Poole and her sister had moved off and they were alone again. "Do stop bickering. People might notice."

Lord Malverne looked completely unfazed by his aunt's admonishment. "I was simply discussing the finer points of flirting with Miss Brightwell. And it seems we have a difference of opinion."

Lady Chelmsford arched an imperious brow. "While I agree flirting has its place, scowls and frowns are not usually involved. So please stop teasing Miss Brightwell, Nathaniel." She nodded toward the near distance. "I think some eligible gentlemen might be headed our way at long last."

To Sophie's surprise and not a small degree of curiosity and amusement, Lord Malverne's brows plunged into a scowl as he caught sight of two ton bucks riding toward them. Charlie, on the other hand, was smoothing her skirts and tucking a stray curl into her bonnet.

"You know them?" asked Sophie, glancing between the viscount and Charlie.

"Yes." Lord Malverne's mouth was a tight line.

"It's Baron Edgerton and Viscount Claremont," murmured Charlie. "I've never been formally introduced to them, but their names should be at the top of our 'most eligible' list, Sophie."

Her brother's eyebrows shot upward toward his hairline. "You have a list? Of eligible bachelors? And you put these two scoundrels on it?"

"Hush, you two," warned Lady Chelmsford. "They are almost upon us. Smiles at the ready, my dear gels."

"I need to have a serious talk with you, Charlotte Hastings," growled Lord Malverne beneath his breath.

"Oh, stop acting like some old maiden aunt," countered Charlie. Turning away, her mouth lifted into a welcoming smile.

Sophie slid a pleasant smile into place too. Which wasn't hard to do, in fact, as the two gentlemen approaching them on horseback were both decidedly attractive. *Rakishly* attractive.

Greetings were exchanged and Lord Malverne—a stiff smile in place—introduced his aunt and sister. Confusion flickered as Sophie noted Lord Malverne's forbidding frown had returned when it was her turn to be introduced. Shouldn't he be pleased his tactic of flirting might very well have worked?

"I'm delighted to make your acquaintance, Miss Brightwell," declared the slender-framed Lord Edgerton. His fair hair was cropped into tight curls and his gold-flecked hazel eyes were filled with laughter. He reminded Sophie of a wicked yet charming fay-like creature who could easily enchant one with a single smile.

Lord Claremont, on the other hand, had dark brown hair and shoulders almost as wide as Lord Malverne's, and a brooding, direct gaze she found most appealing. His blue gray eyes caught Sophie's as he inclined his head in greeting. "As am I," he said in a voice that was so rich and deep, Sophie swore it vibrated right through her body to her very toes. "Have you been in town long, Miss Brightwell?"

Sophie sensed Lord Malverne's glowering stare as she answered, "Only a week, my lord."

"Well that's good to know because if it had been longer, I would have taken Lord Malverne to task for monopolizing your fair company."

Sophie felt a hot blush stealing over her cheeks. Lord Edgerton, Charlie, and Lady Chelmsford were engaged in a lively conversation, which meant Lord Claremont and Lord Malverne were both looking at her. It was difficult enough being the sole focus of one rake. But two?

She cleared her throat and made herself hold Lord Claremont's gaze. "Lord Malverne and I . . . we are just family friends," she explained. "You see, Lady Charlotte and I were at school together—"

Oh no! Why had she brought up that particular subject? In one fell swoop she'd embarrassed herself and poor Charlie.

However, Lord Claremont didn't seem perturbed. Perhaps,

by some miracle, he wasn't even aware of their past indiscretion as he smiled. "That is a relief indeed," he said softly, "because I don't particularly fancy having to compete with Lord Malverne for your lovely company."

Oh, my goodness. Lord Claremont couldn't be interested in her, could he? Or was he simply flirting because that's how rakes tended to interact with women? Sophie had no idea.

Before she could think of what to say next, Lord Claremont continued, "Are you by any chance going to attend Lord and Lady Penrith's ball next week? Because if you are, I shall be there and I would be honored if you'd reserve a dance for me."

"I . . . I'm not certain if I am." Sophie cast a look toward Charlie, who was now listening to her exchange with Lord Claremont, along with everyone else. Lord Malverne still looked like a storm cloud. "If *we* are," she amended. "Attending that is." Good heavens. Sophie inwardly cringed. Could she be any more inarticulate?

"I believe we will," declared Lady Chelmsford. "I received the invitation just this morning in fact."

"Well, I look forward to seeing you then, Lady Chelmsford, Lady Charlotte." Lord Claremont caught Sophie's gaze again. "Miss Brightwell." The glance he spared Lord Malverne was fleeting. "Malverne."

Lord Edgerton bid everyone adieu as well, and then the two men wheeled their Thoroughbred horses around. Kicking them into a canter, they headed down Rotten Row.

Charlie slid her aunt a suspicious look. "You didn't tell me you'd received such an invitation."

Lady Chelmsford waved a dismissive hand. "I haven't. But I shall soon procure one. Lady Penrith owes me a favor, and I'm not afraid to call it in. I'd warrant those two young men are *very* keen to further their acquaintance with you and Miss Brightwell. This visit to the park has been most successful, don't you think?"

"A veritable triumph," remarked Lord Malverne drily.

"Watch your tone, young man. You might be seven-and-twenty, but I wouldn't think twice about boxing your ears."

Lady Chelmsford signaled for the driver to move on and take them home.

Lord Malverne inclined his head. "My apologies, ma'am." He caught Sophie's eye. "I'm pleased for you, Miss Brightwell. A debutante could do worse than Lord Claremont, despite all of his faults. Lord Edgerton on the other hand . . ." Lord Malverne pinned his sister with a pointed stare.

"Good heavens, my lord," replied Sophie. Her forehead dipped into a confused frown. "Lord Claremont only proposed that we share a dance next week. It's not as though he proposed marriage. I imagine he was just being polite."

Charlie laughed. "And so was Lord Edgerton. Really, Nate. I hope you aren't going to behave like a fire-breathing dragon guarding its lair all Season whenever any eligible gentlemen approach us. How on earth are *we*"—she shot a meaningful glance at Sophie—"to find husbands?"

"You and I need to discuss what the definition of an 'eligible' gentleman is, dear sister. Lord Claremont fits the bill, *just*. And I very much want to see this 'list' of yours."

Charlie lifted her chin. "Well, you can't. If I have any questions about anyone in particular, I'll ask you."

Lord Malverne's brown eyes darkened to obsidian. "Are some of my friends on this list? Because if they are—"

"Goodness gracious, I think I'll need to have a sherry before I venture out anywhere with you two again. And two more when I get home," declared Lady Chelmsford.

Sophie couldn't blame her.

After this afternoon, she felt as if she needed a sherry too.

CHAPTER 11

Spring is in the air! But what of love?
    Suggestions on how to keep your morale high
when that special someone you have your eye on this
Season remains as elusive as a butterfly.

The Beau Monde Mirror:
The Essential Style and Etiquette Guide

Hastings House, Berkeley Square

April 7, 1818

The following morning was so warm and lovely, the sky
such a perfect china blue, that Charlie suggested they
take breakfast on the flagged terrace that led onto Hastings
House's small but elegant courtyard garden. The parterre
beds were brimming with bright bursts of color—daffodils,
irises, crocuses, and tulips all vied to be noticed like budding debutantes—and in one corner of the garden, a large
magnolia tree dripping with magnificent white and dark
pink blooms held court. It was quite a heavenly space and
a balm for Sophie's soul.

Last night, she'd tossed and turned into the small hours,
yet when she did fall asleep, she was plagued by odd dreams
featuring both Lord Malverne and Lord Claremont. Dreams
she couldn't quite recall that had left her feeling unsettled
and moody.

Dressed in a simple morning gown of pale pink sprigged

muslin and a snowy woolen shawl with her hair loose about her shoulders, Sophie was enjoying the relaxed pace of the morning. If she were a cat, she would curl up and go to sleep on the warm gray stones beneath the wrought iron table where their breakfast had been set out.

"Gracious, it's quiet," remarked Charlie as she poured them both a fresh cup of tea. "It's strange, but there are times when I do actually miss my younger brothers, rascals that they are."

The adolescent Hastings boys—the fourteen-year-old twins Daniel and Benjamin, and seventeen-year-old Jonathon—were currently away at Eton. Charlie had disclosed to Sophie that their father sent the unruly lads to the exclusive college "for some discipline" well over a year ago because he'd been sick and tired of trying to engage, and then retain, sufficiently skilled tutors who could keep them in check.

Indeed, the only reason Charlie had enrolled at Mrs. Rathbone's academy was that Lord Westhampton had refused to employ another governess after the last one quit in a flood of tears courtesy of the Hastings boys' antics. Knowing Charlie as she did, Sophie rather suspected her spitfire friend had not been overly kind to her governesses either.

Even though noblemen's daughters generally did not attend such establishments, Charlie had asked her father if she might attend the school anyway; she'd argued that her mother had passed away some years ago, and because she no longer had a governess, becoming a pupil at Mrs. Rathbone's was the only feasible way to acquire the attainments every young lady needed to make a successful debut.

Sophie would always be grateful for the fact that she'd crossed paths with Lady Charlotte Hastings, and her other dear friends, Olivia and Arabella, despite everything that had happened after their one night of folly.

As Sophie picked up her freshly poured cup of tea, she glanced at her friend's wistful countenance. She took a small sip, then said carefully, "In some respects it must be nice to have so much peace. But perhaps it is too quiet sometimes? I certainly found it that way in Monkton

Green." She didn't want to suggest that Charlie had been lonely during the past year, but with Lord Westhampton so involved with his parliamentary duties, which she'd heard were a passion of his, and with Lord Malverne constantly coming and going, there must have been countless times when Charlie was at loose ends. And alone. At least Sophie had the company of her mother and half sisters.

To think her bright, lively friend had suffered so made Sophie's heart ache.

Charlie reached out and squeezed Sophie's hand. "Please don't be sad for me. It hasn't been so bad," she said, a small smile tugging at the corners of her mouth. "Despite my notoriety, Aunt Tabitha and Father managed to arrange for my debut at court last year. And Aunt Tabitha endeavors to keep me busy when she is in town. She belongs to a wonderful society of bluestockings, and the ladies who are members do not seem to mind that I have a scurrilous past. Through them, I have taken up archery and fencing, and have been involved with some of their charity work in St. Giles and Whitechapel. And on the odd occasion when Arabella has visited from up north, I've accompanied her to various charitable institutions too."

"I'm glad then," Sophie said. A faint breeze lifted the loose strands of hair about her face, and a few rose petals that had fallen from the arrangement of flowers upon the table drifted toward the scattered letters and invitations lying among the teacups and plates. "Have you had any letters from your brothers lately?"

While they'd breakfasted, she and Charlie looked through a small pile of correspondence. Sophie had received a short letter from her mother and one from her half sister Alice; both did little more than assert everyone was well before fishing for details about her first week in London. Although it had only been five days since her story was submitted to Minerva Press, she was also relieved that it hadn't been rejected outright.

Charlie shook her head. "No. They are not ones to correspond. Jonathon sends Father a brief letter once a month because he is obliged to by the school, but that's all."

She flipped through the correspondence once again and sighed. "Aside from the invitation to Lady Reading's dinner party—I'm sure Aunt Tabitha had a hand in arranging that—there really isn't much of interest here. Lady Kilbride—she's one of Aunt Tabitha's bluestocking friends—is holding a *musicale* that is sure to go on for hours and hours, and then there's this invitation to a decidedly dull-sounding card party. I'm afraid the only bachelors we will encounter are long-suffering gents who've had no luck at Almack's and whose mamas badgered them into going." She sighed again and picked up the last remaining cinnamon and raisin bun before taking a small bite. "I shouldn't sound so ungrateful," she said after she'd finished chewing. "They are invitations after all. Last year I didn't receive a single one."

Sophie pushed the crumbs of her half-eaten bun around her plate. "I know the feeling," she said. "But the future is looking brighter."

Charlie smiled. "Yes, it is. I really hope Aunt Tabitha can procure an invitation to Lord and Lady Penrith's annual spring ball. It's sure to be a spectacular event." She sent Sophie a sly smile. "Especially if a certain viscount is there."

"I'm sure you mean me, don't you, sweet sister?"

Sophie's attention swung to the nearby French doors where Lord Malverne had appeared, and her breath hitched. The morning sunlight highlighted the red and gold strands in his thick chestnut hair, and as Nate strode toward them, she couldn't help but slide her gaze to the glorious vision of his muscular legs encased in formfitting buckskin riding breeches and gleaming top boots. In one hand he carried black leather gloves, and tucked beneath his other arm was a riding crop.

Nate cast aside his gloves and crop onto a chair, and his eyes danced with mischief as he plucked a fat juicy strawberry from the crystal fruit bowl and popped it in his mouth.

Sophie promptly blushed and dropped her gaze to her teacup as he chewed with relish. Had Lord Malverne picked up that strawberry on purpose to tease her? After his behavior in the park yesterday, she wouldn't put it past him.

Charlie rolled her eyes. "You know very well I'm referring

to Lord Claremont." She gestured to a small pile of letters near the fruit bowl. "Those are for you, by the way."

Lord Malverne picked them up, flicked through them quickly, and then tossed them onto the table again. "I'll deal with them later."

"There are several that probably should be sent on to your steward at Deerhurst Park." At Sophie's curious look, Charlie added, "Father gifted Nate an estate in Gloucestershire when he came of age. It's quite lovely. Right on the banks of the River Severn. Just like Elmstone Hall, our country home."

"Do you enjoy country life, my lord?" asked Sophie. Lord Malverne always seemed a little restless beneath his urbane demeanor, as if he was always seeking something to entertain him. Something to excite him. She couldn't imagine he would enjoy rusticating at his country estate for too long.

He shrugged and plucked another strawberry from the bowl, then placed his booted foot on the chair closest to her. "Some aspects of it. I particularly love riding. In fact, I was about to head out to Hyde Park to put my new gelding through his paces." His brown eyes twinkled with mischief. "Do you like to ride, Miss Brightwell?" He bit into the strawberry with his perfect white teeth.

Sophie swallowed. Why did it seem as though he were asking her something else entirely? Something that bordered on improper, perhaps even sexual. Forcing herself to hold his gaze even though she feared her face was the color of the strawberry, she replied, "Although I cannot claim to be a skilled horsewoman, yes, I do like to ride. Very much."

"When your riding habit is ready, we should go out to the park with Nate," Charlie said. "Perhaps we might catch the attention of some other 'eligible gentlemen.'"

Lord Malverne frowned at that. "I still want to know who is on that list of yours, Charlie."

"What, so you can warn them to stay away from us?" Her golden brown eyes flashed with annoyance.

"Yes. If I deem them unsuitable."

"You probably think everyone is unsuitable."

"When it comes to my little sister, why yes, they probably are. Especially *my friends.*"

"Well"—Charlie folded her arms and lifted her chin in a belligerent fashion—"you still have to help Sophie."

"I will. A promise is a promise." Lord Malverne pulled on his gloves and collected his riding crop. "I will do whatever I can to help you in your hunt for the perfect match, Miss Brightwell."

Sophie inclined her head. "Thank you, my lord."

He flashed her a dazzling smile. "You're very welcome."

"As I've said before, you mustn't mind his flirting. I don't think he can help himself," observed Charlie as they watched the viscount trot down the stairs to the gravel path that led to a garden gate, to the mews where the family kept their horses, Sophie assumed.

"Yes, I know he doesn't mean it. In fact, I suspect he was giving me a lesson. Yesterday when we were at the park, he suggested I must practice because men like it when women flirt."

Charlie nodded. "That's one thing I can agree with at least. Come." She rose and gathered up the pile of correspondence. "Let's get dressed and go for a stroll. I think it would be rather nice to call on Olivia to see how she is faring."

"I have just finished volume one of a certain set of memoirs," murmured Sophie as she picked up her own letters from home and followed her friend toward the doors into the morning room.

Charlie grinned. "Excellent. We shall have something to take to her then. And perhaps I'll purchase a box of something delicious at Gunter's to give her too. Something sweet to temper all that wicked spice."

Sophie dared not add that when it came to Lord Malverne, that particular principle didn't seem to apply.

Nate kicked his new gelding, Invictus, into a brisk canter once he reached Rotten Row. Given that it was midmorning, it was fairly quiet in the park. Most bucks of the ton chose to ride earlier in the day, and as the fashionable hour for promenading wasn't until the late afternoon, not many were out and about.

Spying a wide expanse of grass that was practically deserted, Nate decided to give Invictus his head. The black gelding exploded into a gallop, and in no time, they'd reached a shady copse of oaks on the other side. Nate wheeled Invictus around and they bolted across the heath again. He needed this hard ride. He needed to feel the wind in his hair and hear the solid beat of the horse's hooves. Feel his muscles strain and flex and his own heart pound, the race of his blood.

But most of all he needed to put Sophie Brightwell out of his mind because his mad infatuation with her was threatening to unman him.

He didn't want to admit it to himself, but he liked the girl more than he should. He liked her smile, he liked the way she blushed when he flirted with her. He especially liked the way she looked at him, as though desire warred with shyness whenever her gaze traveled over his body. When her eyes touched his mouth and she was clearly recalling what he'd done.

In the darkness of the night, in his bed, he couldn't seem to get out of his head how her satiny skin had tasted. The feel of her breast in his hand. Although he'd been drunk that night, the memory of their brief bedroom encounter had somehow seared itself into his brain.

And then, of course, he couldn't deny the uncharacteristic surge of other strong emotions over the past week: a wave of protectiveness when that odious baron had accosted her, and the stab of jealousy when Claremont had hinted at his interest.

All of these things implied he was beginning to like her *too* much.

Yes, he didn't like it one little bit.

As he drew Invictus up near the gravel bridle path, the sound of clapping and the call of *bravo* caught his attention.

Matthew Ellis, Lord Claremont, waited by a low hedgerow. His fine bay gelding tossed its head as he drew close.

Shit.

"That's a nice piece of horseflesh you have there, my friend," Claremont said by way of greeting.

Friend my arse. Nate had known Claremont in his university days at Oxford, and they were both members of White's, but he wouldn't have classed the other viscount as a friend. Nevertheless, he forced himself to don a nonchalant smile. "Thank you. I could say the same about yours."

Talk fell to their mounts and the respective horse studs they preferred and an upcoming race meet before Claremont turned the conversation in the direction he'd clearly wanted to steer it in from the start. "Your sister's friend, Miss Brightwell, she's quite a charming young woman."

Nate willed his features to retain a pleasant neutrality even as his fingers tightened about the reins. "Yes. She is."

Claremont nodded. "Although she mentioned there is no connection between you and her, other than that of 'family friend,' I just wanted to make certain it was indeed the case. I wouldn't want to encroach on another man's territory, so to speak."

Damn. Nate supposed his unexpected fit of jealousy had shown. He needed to rid the useless, aggravating emotion from his body without delay, and what better way was there to do that than by relinquishing all claim to Sophie, perceived or otherwise? Unclenching his jaw, he said smoothly, "Miss Brightwell's assessment of our relationship is accurate. She is my sister's friend, nothing more."

Claremont's mouth lifted into a self-satisfied smile, and Nate wondered if Sophie found the man attractive. She'd blushed and stammered yesterday, so perhaps she did.

She could do worse.

Indeed, even though the idea rankled, she'd be better off with someone like Claremont. He was decent enough. And the word about town was he genuinely was in the market for a wife.

Unlike himself.

Claremont patted his horse's neck. "I'm pleased to hear it. If you could pass on my regards to Miss Brightwell, I'd be most grateful."

Nate inclined his head. "Of course." *Not bloody likely.* He wouldn't stand in Claremont's way, but he wouldn't court Sophie for him.

"Until next time then." Nudging his mount's withers, Claremont moved off down Rotten Row.

It's better this way, Nathaniel Hastings. No good can come of this ridiculous infatuation you have, and you know it.

Kicking Invictus into another frenzied gallop, Nate decided he'd best spend the rest of the day engaged in as much vigorous activity as he possibly could. He'd fence, he'd box, and then later tonight, he'd visit the Pandora Club and swive himself stupid.

Then perhaps, when he fell asleep, he wouldn't dream of Sophie Brightwell.

CHAPTER 12

⊘℧

A pair of Disreputable Debutantes make their debut at the spring ball of the Season!

One wonders how on earth they procured invitations . . . and why a certain viscount paid particular attention to a young lady of no consequence with clearly no sense of decorum.

The Beau Monde Mirror: The Society Page

Penrith House, St. James's Square, London

April 14, 1818

I'm so nervous, I think I'm going to be ill."

As the Hastings carriage drew to a halt outside of Penrith House's brightly lit facade with its enormous portico and grand steps flanked by ornate Doric columns, Sophie's stomach churned so wildly, she felt as though she was being tossed about on a boat in a stormy sea.

Charlie reached out and gave her clenched hands a gentle squeeze. "You'll be fine. Just smile and nod until you feel a little better. I'm sure everyone will be so dazzled by your loveliness, they'll be rendered speechless. Wouldn't you agree, Nate? Madame Boucher has outdone herself with this gown."

Even though the light in the carriage was dim, Sophie discerned the slight movement of Nate's head and the flash of his white teeth as he transferred his gaze from the window

to her. "Yes. I would. Miss Brightwell, you are the epitome
of style and grace. Fairer than a princess."

"Thank you." Sophie did indeed feel a little like a fairy-
tale princess in her new turquoise silk gown. Molly, Charlie's maid, had also gone to a great deal of trouble to dress
her hair. While small ringlets framed her face, the rest of
her locks had been pulled up to her crown and cascaded in
long, glossy sausage curls toward her nape. Silver combs
adorned with tiny seed pearls helped keep the curls in
check and completed the elegant Grecian style. In her
gloved hands she clutched a matching reticule and fan, and
on her feet she wore a brand-new pair of silver slippers.

Lady Chelmsford, resplendent in dark green velvet,
added her compliments as well. "My dear Miss Brightwell,
both you and Charlie will be the prettiest debutantes here
tonight. You mark my words. You're sure to make a splash."

Let's hope it's for the right reasons, thought Sophie as
the footman threw open the carriage door and let down the
steps. *And not because we're those "wicked girls who were
expelled."*

Thankfully, the receiving line was relatively short, so
Sophie didn't have to wait in nervous agony for too long
before she was introduced to the ball's hosts, the Earl and
Countess of Penrith.

But she needn't have worried. Lady Chelmsford pre-
sented her and Charlie with the effortless aplomb expected
of a seasoned society noblewoman. And then of course
Lord Malverne smoothed the way. With his urbane manner
and charming smile, he brought a glow to Lady Penrith's
cheeks, and after exchanging a private word with their host,
he left the earl quietly chuckling.

"So far so good," Sophie whispered as they passed out
of earshot.

"Yes," murmured Charlie. "It would be embarrassing
indeed if the hosts gave us the cut direct at the door."

Beyond an ornate marble arch lay the massive ballroom.
Sophie's breath caught as she took in the enormous crystal
chandelier and the high domed ceiling painted with a
fresco of cherubs, half-naked nymphs, and other mythical

creatures cavorting in the clouds. In keeping with the spring theme of the ball, the window embrasures were festooned with garlands of bright blooms. The room was fit to burst with guests, and between the swelling strains of the orchestra, the buzz of incessant chatter, and the peals of laughter, Sophie wondered how she would be heard by anyone tonight unless she all but shouted at them.

Despite the crush, Lord Malverne expertly steered them through tight knots of guests and between towering arrangements of flowers and leafy ferns to a slightly less crowded section where his aunt could take a seat upon a plush settee that would also give her a relatively unobstructed view of the ballroom floor. The supper room wasn't too far away either.

Lord Malverne bent toward the marchioness. "Can I get you anything, dearest aunt?"

Lady Chelmsford murmured something into his ear, and then he wove his way through the throng, heading for the supper room. Sophie didn't fail to notice at least half a dozen pairs of female eyes following his wide shoulders encased in a perfectly cut midnight blue superfine evening coat. Her chest swelled with a deep sigh. She really must stop thinking about Lord Malverne in a romantic way. He might have attempted to seduce her when he was foxed, he might tease her and flirt with her, but he wasn't interested in her. Not really.

He was Charlie's brother and a hardened rake who didn't wish to wed.

He's not for you, Sophie Brightwell, so stop pining for the moon.

Find another who will love you as you should be loved. You deserve nothing less.

Sophie turned her attention to the dance floor, where a lively quadrille was taking place. The swirl of colors, the bob of feathers, the flashes of jewels and bright smiles were entrancing. Charlie passed her a glass of champagne that she'd taken from the tray of a passing footman. "Here's to a wonderful evening filled with fun and laughter and perhaps even a little romance," she said, touching the edge of her glass to Sophie's in a toast.

Sophie smiled back. "And here's to you, Charlotte

Hastings, for making this happen. I wouldn't be here in this beautiful gown if it weren't for you."

"Oh, stop it. Don't get all sentimental on me or I'll begin to cry." Charlie gave a mock frown. Although Sophie rather thought her friend's brown eyes shone suspiciously. "And if I have a red nose and eyes, I'll have no hope of attracting anyone."

They both sipped their champagne in companionable silence for a short while as they continued to watch the dancing—or at least pretended to; anticipation swirled through Sophie as she surreptitiously scanned the room for Lord Claremont, and she suspected Charlie was looking out for Lord Edgerton too.

It wasn't until Charlie responded to something her aunt said that Sophie noticed the whispering, sideways glances, and smirks directed their way. A group of three other debutantes who stood nearby were clearly gossiping about her and Charlie.

To Sophie's dismay, she also recognized one of them: Lady Penelope Purcell. Attired in an exquisite gown of rose-pink silk with pearls at her throat, at her ears, and laced through her pale blond hair, Lady Penelope was indeed the epitome of elegant perfection. Except for one thing: her disdainful gaze, which was directed straight at Sophie. When she caught Sophie looking at her, she arched a brow before murmuring something to her companions, which set them tittering.

It was obvious they knew of Charlie's notoriety and thus suspected she, Sophie Brightwell, was cut from the same scandalous cloth. Would they never be forgiven?

When one of the other debutante's eyes met Sophie's, the young woman all but sneered and turned her nose up in the air as if she had smelled something offensive—perhaps a sack of potatoes on the turn, or a barrel of rotting fish. She whispered something behind her fan to her friends, and then they all laughed again.

Even though there was noise all around, the derisive tone was so clear, it cut Sophie to the bone.

Blinking away a rush of stinging tears, she dropped her

gaze to her champagne glass and watched the bubbles rise to the top. She didn't want to mention the cruelty of the other women to Charlie if she hadn't noticed the exchange. She also wondered why on earth Lord Westhampton would think Lady Penelope a suitable match for his son. Did he not know the young woman was such a judgmental and spiteful creature?

"I wouldn't worry about them if I were you," murmured Lord Malverne. His shoulder gently brushed against hers. "Apart from Lady Penelope, most of those girls are from ne'er-do-well families trying to snare a rich husband with a title bigger than their papas'."

Sophie tried to smile. "They sound a lot like me then."

"They're nothing like you."

Sophie's gaze whipped up to Lord Malverne's, and the emotion she saw in his rich brown eyes made her heart stop. Made her breath quicken.

"I suppose you're right," she said in a voice that was noticeably husky. "My stepfather doesn't even have a title."

Lord Malverne's eyes grew darker, his gaze more intense. "You know that's not what I meant."

"Malverne. Good God, man. It's been an age since I've seen you at a society ball. Decided to enter the marriage mart, have you, eh what?"

Lord Malverne's mouth curved into a smile that seemed a little pained as he turned to the rotund, gray-haired gentleman standing by his other shoulder. "Lord Whitmore, it *has* been an age. But to answer your question, no. To my father's great disappointment, I'm not really in the market for a wife. I'm just fulfilling brotherly duties." He indicated Charlie, who was chatting with Lady Chelmsford, with a nod of his head.

"Pity," said Lord Whitmore. "My daughter, Emily, is here somewhere with my wife." He glanced about the room before his gaze returned to Lord Malverne. "You recall Emily, don't you? Tall gel. Strong bones. Good teeth?"

Lord Malverne shook his head, his expression even more pained. "I'm afraid not. I've not had the pleasure of an introduction."

Lord Whitmore slapped him on the shoulder. "Well, if she's anything like her mother, she's destined to be an excellent breeder. She could do with a decent chap like you for a husband. Good stock is what it's all about, after all. I'll tell my wife to keep you in mind for Emily." He raised his glass of brandy in a salute. "Tallyho then. Please pass on my regards to your father."

Sophie bit her lip to suppress a wave of laughter.

"What?" asked Lord Malverne. His expression was severe but his voice was threaded with mirth. "Are you laughing at me, Miss Brightwell?"

"A little," she admitted, her own voice bubbling with amusement too. "But heavens. I also feel rather sorry for poor Emily. Her father is quite a character, isn't he?"

"He's an old family friend of my father's. We've chatted at White's a few times."

"Ah, the old family friend story. So . . ." Sophie paused to sip her champagne. "How are you going to help me find a husband, my lord?"

Lord Malverne cocked an eyebrow. "I thought I made it clear when we promenaded in Hyde Park, Miss Brightwell. We are going to flirt, and then all the men will come running."

"Because they think I am a juicy bone and would like a bite?"

The corner of Lord Malverne's mouth twitched. "Your words, not mine, Miss Brightwell."

"I suppose formulating poetic turns of phrase is not a strong point of mine."

"Nor mine. Or most men, I expect."

This time, Sophie arched a brow. "So I shouldn't expect my suitors to be dreaming up odes praising my aspect and my eyes, like Lord Byron?"

"I'm afraid not. The truth is, Miss Brightwell, most gentlemen, especially rakes, are quite base creatures beneath their well-cut clothes and easy smiles." He leaned closer in a conspiratorial fashion and murmured, "Would you like me to be frank?"

"Yes, please do. I believe these are things I must learn

about the male of the species if I am to succeed in finding a mate."

"Well, to be *perfectly* frank, most of the time they are probably thinking about what treasures you conceal beneath your gown, Miss Brightwell. And how your lips might taste."

Oh, my goodness. Sophie swallowed and resisted the urge to lick those very same lips, because that's where the focus of Lord Malverne's gaze seemed to be right at this moment.

Was he foxed again? Because that would explain his daring behavior and his wicked words. But he hadn't a drink in his hand, and the soft, warm breath that fanned across her lips didn't smell like brandy or wine at all. She closed her eyes for a moment at an unbidden memory of how Lord Malverne's breath and his firm lips felt upon her skin. The other wicked words he'd spoken to her in the velvet darkness. Hot desire surged and made her pulse race and her head spin. Made her giddier than the champagne she'd been sipping ever could.

Perhaps it was the champagne that made her whisper when she opened her eyes, "Aside from flirting, that's another thing I don't know how to do."

Lord Malverne's mouth tilted into a half smile. "Kissing? Have you never been kissed on the mouth before?"

"No. No, I haven't." She dragged her gaze away from Lord Malverne's mouth and up to his eyes. "Is that a skill a rakehell would consider when choosing a prospective wife? Whether she can kiss well or not?" *Heavens, when did I become so brazen?*

Even though Lord Malverne wore a snowy white cravat, Sophie watched his throat move in a visible swallow. "Miss Brightwell, you seem to have mastered the art of flirting in a flash." A soft, husky note had entered his voice. "I don't doubt that you would also master kissing in an instant as well."

"Ahem . . ."

Oh no! Her face flaming, Sophie took a step away from Lord Malverne and turned to face Charlie. And then released a startled gasp when she discovered that Lord Claremont was standing right beside her friend. He cast her a small, apologetic smile before politely greeting her and Lord Malverne.

Charlie's expression, on the other hand, was as stern as a schoolmarm's. She clearly wasn't pleased to discover her brother overtly flirting with her best friend in the middle of a ballroom. "Nate, I don't fancy being a wallflower all night. Why don't you play the part of dutiful brother and ask me to dance? I believe another set is about to start at any moment."

"Of course." Lord Malverne offered his arm to his sister. "If you'll excuse us, Miss Brightwell," he said smoothly, as though they'd only been discussing something as innocuous as the weather, not kissing. His tone was flinty as he muttered, "Claremont," through gritted teeth, as though the other viscount was an annoying afterthought.

How odd. It seemed Lord Malverne was well on the way to fulfilling his part of their secret bargain, so why was he so disgruntled about it?

Smoothing the frown from her brow, Sophie turned back to Lord Claremont, who smiled warmly at her. "Miss Brightwell, I was hoping I might find you here tonight," he murmured in that lovely deep voice of his.

"That was my fond hope, too, Lord Claremont," she replied. "That you would find me. Or that I would find you. Oh, goodness . . . My apologies for blathering on so. I do that sometimes when I'm nervous." Sophie bit her lip as a blush scorched her cheeks. How was it that she could now flirt with Lord Malverne, but sounded like a henwit around the only other gentleman who'd paid her any interest since her arrival in London?

"I make you nervous?" Lord Claremont's blue gray eyes twinkled with amusement from beneath a messy wing of dark brown hair.

"A little," Sophie murmured. If her face grew any hotter, she imagined she'd burst into flames.

"Well, I also have a confession to make, Miss Brightwell. I'm a little nervous around you too."

Sophie blinked. She made this handsome rake of a viscount nervous? "Surely not."

"Ah, but it is indeed the case. I'm nervous that you might have changed your mind about permitting me a dance."

"I would love to dance. If you are asking me, that is."

"I most certainly am."

As Lord Claremont led her out into the middle of the polished parquetry dance floor where all the other couples were gathering, Sophie's eyes found Charlie and Lord Malverne. Their bright chestnut locks were easy to spot in the crowd, and then, of course, Lord Malverne stood half a head taller than most other gentlemen.

Guilt suddenly pinched Sophie's heart. Was it awful of her to be yearning to dance with Lord Malverne when she was about to dance with Lord Claremont? Lord Malverne could have asked her; she was an acquaintance of the family after all. But then again, perhaps he was keeping his distance so other gentlemen like Lord Claremont would have the opportunity to be her partner. Although, it didn't feel as if Lord Malverne had been "keeping his distance" when they were flirting. And in a most inappropriate manner.

Yes, all things considered, it was probably better that Lord Malverne didn't dance with her.

But oh, she so wanted to . . .

As Lord Claremont slid an arm about her waist and caught her right hand in a gentle grip, Sophie realized with a jolt that they were assuming the position for a waltz, the most intimate of dances.

Her alarm must have shown on her face, as Lord Claremont said gently, "By your expression, it appears I should have asked if you waltz, Miss Brightwell. If you would prefer not to . . ."

Sophie met his soft gaze and immediately felt contrite for giving him the impression that she didn't wish to dance with him. "I've had dancing instruction in the past and know how to waltz, my lord. I just never have at such a grand affair as this. This is my first ball. And my first dance."

The light in his eyes was warm. "Ah, then I am honored to be your first, Miss Brightwell."

The music swelled, and Lord Claremont began to expertly steer her about the floor. He was a gentleman in every respect. Even though the waltz required him to press her body against his during turns, he kept a respectful distance between them at all other times.

"You dance well, Miss Brightwell." Lord Claremont smiled down at her after he executed a particularly tight turn and she followed without a misstep.

"It is easy when one's partner is so skilled."

Lord Claremont's gloved hand squeezed hers gently. "Why thank you. I shall count myself a lucky man indeed, if it is the first of many dances."

"I hope so too." Again that twinge of guilt in the vicinity of her chest and the uncomfortable feeling that she might be telling an untruth returned. Lord Claremont, for all his handsome looks and smooth charm, didn't stir her as another particular viscount did.

But then, she'd only just met Lord Claremont and they barely knew anything about each other. They'd met twice, and danced once. And for some reason she couldn't fathom, he kept singling her out . . .

If he did wish to pursue her, she should at least consider his suit. She'd be foolish not to.

As they turned another corner, Sophie's gaze slid across the room and snagged on Lord Malverne as he danced with Charlie. When their eyes met, he inclined his head and cast her a smile that made her heart flip in that peculiar way it always did.

It seemed her head and heart were at complete odds, and for the moment, there was nothing she could do about it.

A h, so that's the beguiling Miss Brightwell who has you so enthralled."

Nate turned his gaze away from the dance floor where Claremont was waltzing with Sophie for the second time this evening and shot Gabriel a sardonic look. The earl's features were shadowed by a nearby velvet curtain, but he couldn't mistake the glint of mischief in his friend's eyes. "Enthralled. I hardly think so."

Gabriel snorted. "Really? You can't take your eyes off her."

Nate rolled his eyes. "I'm *supposed* to be watching her. I'm unofficially chaperoning her, remember?"

Gabriel's mouth twitched with a smirk. "Call it what you like, my friend. I *know* the truth. You're on your way to being well and truly smitten."

Nate shifted his gaze back to the dancing couples again, seeking Sophie out. She was smiling up at Claremont in a way he didn't like, but what could he do? Suddenly, bloody Langdale's observations rankled more than they should. "I'm making sure Claremont behaves. It is a waltz after all."

Gabriel shrugged. "He's not so bad." They watched in silence for a moment longer before he added, "She is fetching though. All that raven hair and big blue eyes framed by long, lush lashes. What was that poem Byron penned again? 'She Walks in Beauty' et cetera? Even though she's not my type, I'm tempted to ask her to dance."

Nate shot him a narrow-eyed look. "You keep your dirty hands off her. I know where they've been. What are you doing here anyway? This isn't your sort of party."

"Lady Astley asked me to attend. I haven't seen her for a few days, so I thought why not?"

It was Nate's turn to smirk. "And yet you suggest *I'm* the one who's smitten."

"I assure you this affair is purely carnal."

Nate dipped his head. "Well, be careful," he murmured. "Her husband is here tonight. I spied him heading for the billiard room when I was in the supper room a little earlier."

Gabriel's smile was pure devilry as he adjusted the cuffs of his black superfine evening jacket, as though he was preparing to head into battle. "What can I say? I like to live dangerously." He clapped Nate on the shoulder again. "Adieu, my friend. If you're up for it later on, Max and MacQueen are going to head to the Pandora Club around midnight."

"I'll keep it in mind."

Nate returned his attention to the dancing once more. On the other side of the dance floor, he spied Charlie talking to Lord Edgerton and another young buck he didn't know.

Now Edgerton was one he needed to watch. Charlie was wilder than most, and Edgerton had a dangerous edge to him, a bit like Gabriel. She'd be attracted to the dog, and he wouldn't think twice about taking advantage. Again, he was a lot like Gabriel.

God, he really wished his father would take a bit more of a parenting role in regard to looking out for Charlie. He should be here, sorting the wheat from the chaff.

For all his faults as a parent, Nate couldn't really blame his father for insisting he take his responsibilities as his son and heir more seriously. He had to grudgingly admit that he'd been lax in his duties as a landowner of late. But no matter how much his father wanted him to surrender to matrimony's noose sometime in the future, he just didn't know if he could.

He'd honestly rather charge headlong onto a battlefield than wed.

Guilt cramped his gut as his thoughts turned to Sophie. He'd thoroughly compromised the girl, and if he were an honorable man, he'd be engaged to her right now, not toying with her as he went through the motions of trying to help her find a husband.

You mean Miss Brightwell. He had to stop thinking of her in such familiar terms. Easier said than done when he'd already been familiar with her. Too familiar.

And she clearly couldn't forget that either. When she'd flirted with him earlier, when she'd suggested she needed tuition in kissing, his balls had tightened. In fact, they still ached now. It probably didn't help that he hadn't been anywhere near a woman in weeks. Every time he'd been to the Pandora Club, he ended up gaming and drinking. Whoring had little appeal for him at the moment. He didn't want to believe Gabriel was right—that he was smitten—but perhaps he was.

It was a sobering thought.

Christ, he needed a drink. And a woman. But not Sophie. Definitely not Sophie.

A sweet-as-strawberries young woman like Sophie deserved better than what a jaded, never-get-anything-right rake like him could ever offer.

The waltz came to an end, and Nate watched Claremont ferry Sophie back to the watchful eye of his aunt. Arming himself with a glass of champagne, he then turned in the other direction. After he'd had a word with Edgerton, he was going to have a little fun.

He certainly wasn't going to pursue Lady Penelope. His father had rocks in his head if he thought that chit was a suitable match. She might be physically appealing, but in other respects, she wasn't attractive at all. The way she'd looked at Charlie and Sophie made his blood boil. He'd rather seek an introduction to Lord Whitmore's statuesque daughter with good teeth, Lady Emily.

Although prostitutes currently had no appeal, and married women were out of bounds—the risk of causing a public scandal that would upset his father was too great—there were plenty of attractive widows here tonight . . . like the lovely and sexually adventurous Lady Taunton.

Nate was certain he'd spied the young baroness in the card room shortly after his arrival. His mouth curved into a smile as he recalled their past encounter at a house party the year before. Lady Taunton and her equally adventurous friend, Lady Seymour, had been enthusiastic participants in a game of strip vingt-et-un before they both joined him in a vigorous all-night round of bed sport.

Straightening his shoulders, Nate pushed through the crowd with determined strides.

Viscount Malverne was on the hunt.

CHAPTER 13

❧❧

Secrets. Everyone has them.
    But are your friends trustworthy enough to keep
them safe?

The Beau Monde Mirror:
The Essential Style and Etiquette Guide

Hastings House, Berkeley Square

April 15, 1818

The morning was gray and cold when Sophie left her
room in search of breakfast. Charlie's door opened as
hers clicked shut.

"Perfect timing," her friend said as she slipped her slender arm through hers. "I trust you slept well?"

"Like a proverbial log. And you?"

Charlie's topaz eyes shone brightly. "The same. There's
nothing quite like a bit of flirting and dancing to make one
both exhausted and content, wouldn't you agree?"

"Entirely." Sophie hoped Charlie would forgive her for
the little white lie. While it was true she'd been exhausted
after the Penriths' ball last night, she couldn't really claim
she felt content.

Although she'd half expected Lord Malverne to pursue
the imperious rather than "perfect" Lady Penelope to keep

in his father's good books, she was taken aback when she observed him shamelessly flirting with an older, very attractive woman for the remainder of the night; a certain widowed blond baroness by the name of Lady Taunton. Lady Chelmsford had identified her when Lord Malverne escorted the widow into supper. It shouldn't hurt, she knew she was being ridiculous, but it did all the same.

Even though Lord Claremont asked her to dance a second time, *and* joined her, Charlie, and Lady Chelmsford during supper, her gaze had inexorably strayed to Lord Malverne. Envy had pricked at her as she'd watched him talk and laugh with Lady Taunton; the stab of jealousy was especially sharp when he'd leaned close, his large hand sliding to the woman's waist as he whispered something meant only for her, in her ear.

It was silly to feel so piqued. Lord Malverne was a rakehell after all. But knowing it and observing him in action were two entirely different things.

Once they reached the gallery below, a squall of rain lashed the casement windows.

"Goodness gracious," said Charlie, gathering her paisley silk shawl more closely about her shoulders. "What an appalling day. I know we had discussed calling on Olivia, but I'm wondering if it would be best if we holed up somewhere warm, reading books and drinking hot chocolate."

"I think that sounds like an excellent idea."

As they drew closer to the morning room where breakfast was served, the sound of raised voices could be heard over the sheeting rain. Male voices. Lord Westhampton and his son were arguing.

Pausing a few feet from the door near a window embrasure, Charlie raised a finger to her lips.

"Should we go back to our rooms and order trays?" Sophie whispered. It felt wrong to be eavesdropping on such a heated moment.

Charlie shook her head. "Their disagreements never last long. And I'm starving. Ordering trays will take too long."

Sophie turned to face the window and tried to focus on

the rain-lashed pane and the view of the sodden courtyard garden beyond, instead of the snatches of angry conversation drifting out through the ajar door and along the gallery.

"It doesn't matter what you say, Father, I won't be spending the summer at Elmstone. When I'm not in town, I shall devote my energies to setting things to rights at Deerhurst Park. As we agreed."

"Your management of Deerhurst isn't the issue at the moment, Nathaniel. Your ongoing refusal to spend more than a day or two once a year at Elmstone is. Your brothers miss y—"

"Father, you know how difficult it is for me."

A razor-sharp silence extended for the space of one heartbeat, then another, before Lord Westhampton broke it. "I know. But it's been fourteen years since Thomas—"

"Just like you, I'm very well aware how long it's been." Lord Malverne's deep voice was as rough as gravel. "Not a day goes by that I don't . . ."

Another silence, marked only by the tick of a nearby longcase clock and the drumming of rain, stretched out for a full, painful minute. Assailed with awkwardness and guilt, Sophie turned to Charlie, who again put her finger to her lips.

Lord Malverne said something else, but his voice was so low, Sophie couldn't make out the words. Not that it was any of her business to begin with. She glanced at Charlie and wondered why she'd wanted to remain here in the gallery.

"Nathaniel, before you go . . ." Lord Westhampton faltered and there was another awkward interval in which Sophie would have bolted if Charlie hadn't placed a hand on her arm. "At the risk of upsetting you further, there's something else I need to bring to your attention. While I'm heartened to hear that you've been squiring your sister about town and at long last attending respectable events, I'm less than thrilled to also hear that you may be pursuing Miss Brightwell. Your aunt was so concerned, she sent a note first thing this morning. In her words, you were 'flirting up a storm.' However, I would caution you against forming an attachment with someone like her. I still firmly believe the Duke of Stafford's daughter would be a much better—"

"I know what your opinion is, Father. Rest assured, I have no desire to court Charlie's friend. Or any particular affection for her. She's a lovely girl but I agree with you. She's not right for me. And while I will keep Lady Penelope in mind, I would also like to consider other . . . options, shall we say? It's only the beginning of the Season after all."

"Quite."

Well, there it is. I'm not good enough. And Nate feels nothing for me. At least I know for sure. Tears of humiliation burning her eyes, Sophie was about to flee when Charlie gathered her into a brief, fierce hug. "Oh, Sophie. I'm so sorry you heard that. Don't think for a minute you're not welcome or wanted here. I'm sure my aunt and father are just worried that Nate is toying with your affections and will hurt you."

Sophie dashed away her tears and nodded. She hoped Charlie was right. She was just about to tell her friend exactly that when Lord Malverne spoke again. "If there's nothing else, Father . . ."

Oh heavens, he is leaving. Panic flaring, Sophie pulled away from Charlie. But before she could retreat, the viscount appeared in the doorway, his expression as dark and somber as the day.

Sophie's breath caught in her throat. She'd never seen Lord Malverne display such stark, deeply felt emotion, and it made her momentarily forget her own pain.

As his gaze touched hers and then shifted to Charlie, his manner immediately changed. A forced smile replaced his scowl. "Miss Brightwell. Charlotte. Good morning to you both." And then he continued on his way, his strides long and purposeful. Within a moment, he'd disappeared up the stairs.

"Will he be all right?" Sophie asked. Despite what he'd said to his father about his lack of affection for her, part of her yearned to go after him. To offer comfort. "He looks so . . . bereft."

"Don't worry about Nate." Charlie clasped both of Sophie's hands in hers. "He has the same argument with Father about Elmstone Hall every year. I'm sorry you had to hear it like this, but I suppose you should know . . ." She broke off and the expression in her brown eyes became so sad,

Sophie's heart cramped with emotion too. "Nate hasn't always been the oldest. We had another brother, Thomas. When Thomas was fifteen, he met with an accident at our country home, Elmstone Hall." She swallowed before whispering, "He . . . he drowned in the nearby river."

Sophie's breath hitched and tears pricked her eyes. "Oh, my Lord. I'm so sorry, Charlie. I had no idea."

"You weren't to know. It was a long time ago. I was only seven years old at the time, and I feel so dreadful as my memories of Thomas are not as strong as I'd like them to be. Nate was thirteen when it happened and he . . . he blames himself even though he's not to blame at all."

Poor Lord Malverne. Nathaniel.

Nate.

What a terrible burden for a boy to bear. It made her wonder how it had shaped the man he'd become. There were so many things she didn't know about him. Charlie had also told her he'd served in Wellington's army. That he'd been at Waterloo.

Yet he hid his pain so well.

Charlie touched her cheek. "Don't cry, my sweet friend. Nate will be all right." She took her arm again. "Come. Let us breakfast with my father. I'm sure he'll be glad to have the company."

Sophie wasn't at all sure considering what he'd just said about her to Nate. The earl had already been so very kind to sponsor her Season. She prayed he didn't regret his decision.

When they entered the morning room, they discovered Lord Westhampton had abandoned the breakfast table and was standing, cup of coffee in hand, at the window, studying the rainy aspect. Like Lord Malverne, he was tall and broad shouldered but with dark hair rather than chestnut. Although there was a touch of gray at his temples, he was clearly still a vigorous man for his age.

Sophie suddenly wondered why he'd never married again. From what Charlie had told her, her mother had died from complications following childbirth many years ago. Sadness tugged at her heart. Charlie's family had been touched by too much loss and sorrow. And it seemed they were still learning to deal with the aftermath.

At the sound of their entry, Lord Westhampton turned and greeted them with a polite smile that instantly relieved Sophie's tension to some degree. It didn't *seem* as though he was angry with her for flirting with his son.

"Good morning, Miss Brightwell. Charlotte," he said smoothly with a slight inclination of his head.

Sophie curtsied. "And a good morning to you, my lord. Although, it seems the weather is determined to make it otherwise."

Lord Westhampton's smile was genuine this time. "Yes indeed. But it seems your fair company and my daughter's has brought some of the sunshine back."

Charlie crossed the room and kissed her father on his lean cheek. "Good morning, Papa," she said warmly. "If you have the time, come and sit with us and we will tell you all about the ball at Lord and Lady Penrith's last night."

"Ah, yes. I would indeed like to hear your stories." Lord Westhampton's gaze traveled to Sophie as they approached the table. "I trust you had a good time, Miss Brightwell?"

"Yes indeed, my lord. It was most diverting. The most exciting night of my life, in fact. I am most grateful to you, and Lady Chelmsford, for making this possible."

"It's been my pleasure. And I'm sure my sister would say the same." The earl rang a bell by his place setting, and several footmen appeared to pull out his chair, hers, and Charlie's. Sophie was always astonished at the number of staff Lord Westhampton retained; she couldn't even begin to count them. At Nettlefield Grange, her stepfather only employed a housekeeper, a butler, two housemaids, a footman, and a few men who tended the stables and the grounds.

After the footmen had replenished Lord Westhampton's coffee and had served her and Charlie cups of steaming hot chocolate, Charlie proceeded to give a detailed account of everyone they'd encountered, and the gentlemen they'd both danced with.

"So it sounds as if Lord Claremont has taken an interest

in you, Miss Brightwell," remarked Lord Westhampton as he took a thick slice of ham and a poached egg from the platter offered to him by one of the footmen. "Dancing with you twice in one night, and sharing supper with you? It sounds as though he might wish to pay you formal court."

Sophie blushed and studied the toast on her plate. "I'm sure he was only being polite."

Charlie smiled. "I'm sure he wasn't."

"And what was your brother up to during all of this?" asked the earl as he sliced neatly through his ham. "I was rather hoping he might take a fancy to a suitable debutante at long last."

Clenching her napkin beneath the table, Sophie tried to ignore the small slice of pain provoked by his remark.

Charlie put down her honey-slathered crumpet. "He . . . I'm not certain."

Lord Westhampton cocked an eyebrow. "Which means he was up to no good. Chasing some widow, was he?"

Charlie replenished her hot chocolate and said carefully, "I really couldn't say."

The earl sighed. "Well, one can only hope that one day he meets such a lovely young woman that he'll fall head over heels in love before he's even had a chance to realize it. I think a bolt from Cupid's bow is the only sure remedy for Nathaniel's ennui."

When Sophie looked up from buttering her second piece of toast, Lord Westhampton was studying her with a speculative gleam in his eye. Confusion swirled through her. Surely he didn't mean her. Especially after he warned Nate not to dally with her. She might be a suitable friend for Charlie, but he didn't really think someone like her—a girl from a quiet corner of Suffolk with no connections or fortune to speak of—would be a suitable match for his son, a viscount? Would he?

But then, Lord Claremont seemed to be pursuing her . . .

Dismissing the whole idea as nonsense, Sophie took a bite of her toast. Her family might hope she'd win the hand of a viscount—and she might also secretly hope to win a particular viscount's heart—but that didn't mean it would happen. She wasn't a princess and her life wasn't going to be a fairy tale. And the sooner she embraced that harsh reality, the better.

Nate paused outside Charlie's sitting room and placed his hand on the smooth oak paneling of the door. It was slightly ajar and while all was silent save for the sound of the incessant rain, he'd heard his sister and Sophie talking and laughing only a short time ago when he was headed to his rooms to change out of his sodden clothes after his ride in Hyde Park.

It was just after three o'clock, and he'd thought about spending the rest of the afternoon and evening at White's, but suddenly the idea held little appeal. He wanted . . .

Truth to tell, he didn't know what he wanted. He felt restless. Unsettled. Even more so than usual. After his argument with his father, he'd spent the next few hours directing his pent-up energy into his favorite physical pursuits aside from bed sport—boxing, fencing, and riding.

Deep down he realized that what he really needed was a bout of good, hard swiving. However, even the prospect of bedding Lady Taunton had not been tempting enough last night. She'd certainly seemed amenable to just about anything when they'd kissed on the Penriths' terrace. And he could have taken things much further considering their past amorous exploits.

But he hadn't.

He was frustrated in the extreme, but he couldn't seem to do anything about it other than come by his own hand. And that was hardly satisfying.

And now he was hovering outside his sister's rooms, hoping Sophie might be inside. Christ, he was mooning about like a lovestruck adolescent.

No, Nathaniel Hastings. You are not *in love. You are in lust.* No matter how hard he tried to fight his base urges, he'd become obsessed with the idea of seducing Sophie. And he couldn't do that, corrupt his sister's best friend, because he had an itch he needed to scratch. An insatiable thirst he needed to quench. Perhaps his palate was jaded and he suddenly craved something different, a taste of something sweet and innocent as opposed to his usual diet of well-practiced passion that bordered on the perfunctory.

If only Sophie hadn't openly flirted with him about kissing last night. She'd admitted she'd never been kissed before, and he couldn't get the idea out of his head . . .

Yes, he really should go before he did something both stupid and unconscionable.

He pushed open the door.

Even though the day was dull, Charlie's sitting room was brightly lit by an abundance of candles, lamps, and a dancing fire. In the golden light, the gilt and polished satinwood furniture gleamed, as did the glossy raven locks of the girl his eyes immediately locked on to.

Curled up on a silk-upholstered settee with her legs tucked beneath her and her head bent over a book bound in red leather, she hadn't heard him enter. Charlie was nowhere about.

I should leave . . .

Too late. Sophie raised her head, and her beautiful blue eyes widened for a moment before she swiftly closed the book she'd been reading and put it to one side. "Lord Malverne," she said, swinging her legs to the floor and sitting up straight. "Are you looking for Charlie? She's not here."

He smiled. "Yes. I see." Approaching the settee, he continued, "I imagine she's not far though."

Sophie worried at her bottom lip as she placed her hand on top of her book. "No. No, she's not. She's taken her new kitten downstairs. It needed . . ." She blushed. "Well, it needed to go outside."

"Kitten? When did Charlie get a kitten?"

"A few days ago. After Charlie's maid heard there was a mouse in my room, I believe some of the female staff became a little nervous about the whole matter. So one thing led to another . . . and now Charlie has a kitten."

"Good God." Nate rounded the end of the settee and claimed a dainty wing chair by the fireside.

"You don't like kittens?"

"I suppose I'm more of a dog man, myself. I have several hounds at Deerhurst Park. And you? What do you prefer?"

Sophie smoothed a palm along her soft pink muslin skirts. "We have several barn cats at Nettlefield Grange. And my stepfather has a collie for rounding up the sheep, but I've never had a pet of my own."

"But if you could, what would you choose?" He supposed his questions might be about inconsequential matters, but he found he really did want to know more about this young woman. Which was strange; he normally didn't give a brass farthing about such things. He supposed it was just another peculiar quirk he could add to the growing list: *My Odd Behaviors around Miss Brightwell.*

"I think I'd rather like a horse," she replied with a decided nod. "My mother, and my two younger sisters, Alice and Jane, we all share a mare. She's really my mother's horse actually. My stepfather keeps other horses, of course. Great hulking draft horses for the farm."

"Charlie suggested we all go riding sometime. I think that would be a rather capital idea too. Would you like that, Miss Brightwell?"

She smiled and Nate's heart jolted oddly against his ribs. "Yes. I would. Very much."

"Excellent. Perhaps when the weather is better."

"Yes." Her whispered agreement was barely audible. Yet somehow Nate got the distinct impression she might be saying yes to something else . . .

His whole body tightened with acute awareness, and as he pushed his restless fingers through his still-damp hair, he noticed Sophie's eyes following the movement. Damn, he really wished she wouldn't look at him like that. It made him ache in a way he shouldn't. He'd never experienced anything quite like it before.

"Sophie." Her name escaped him without conscious thought. In the quietness of the room, he suddenly became aware of the desire humming in the air between them. Of his own heart beating much too fast and the increased pace of Sophie's breathing. His gaze drifted from her eyes to her mouth, then lower to her décolletage, where the firm ripe mounds of her small but tantalizing breasts rose and fell with each breath she took. His mouth watered and his cock twitched.

What if he stole one small kiss? It's not like he was naked and in bed with her. Undressing her . . .

Sweet Jesus. What the deuce was he doing, teasing her with his eyes and, in the process, torturing himself?

I really must *go . . .*

Instead, like a man possessed, he began to lean forward, his gaze riveted on Sophie's mouth. And that's when she broke the spell by whispering, "Do you like to read, my lord?"

He blinked and sat back. The daze of desire had turned him into a dolt in more ways than one as he said quite idiotically, "I'm sorry. What did you say?"

Sophie repeated the question, a little louder this time. "I wondered if you like to read." Beneath her breath she murmured, "I thought I heard someone outside in the hall."

"Right." Dear God, he hadn't even closed the door. And if one of the servants, or worse still, Charlie, had walked in on them, he *would* be visiting the archbishop to procure a special marriage license. Of that there was no doubt. The idea of being leg shackled was akin to someone throwing a bucket of ice water over him. His ardor began to cool.

"So do you? Like to read?"

Nate cleared his throat. "No, not particularly. I take it you do?"

"Yes. Very much so."

"Charlie does too." He glanced toward the book Sophie was reading when he'd come in, and her hand immediately slid over the cover again. "Are you reading anything good at the moment? You seemed engrossed when I entered."

Sophie's cheeks pinked to the color of her gown. "Oh . . . it's just a book from your library actually." Her hand bumped a cushion and it fell on top of it, hiding the cover. "It's not that interesting. Just something to help while away the time on a rainy afternoon."

Curiosity pricked Nate. The cushion's fall, had that been

by accident or design? Even though he hadn't glimpsed the title of the book, the distinctive dark red leather cover and the faded gold tooling seemed familiar somehow. "Oh? What's the title? It might be one of the few books I *have* read."

Sophie's whole face turned the same hue as the book she was trying to hide. "I'm sure it's not."

Nate leaned forward, intrigued. *What the devil was the minx reading?* "Well, I won't know unless you tell me."

Sophie swallowed. "It's . . . it's a set of memoirs. They're deathly boring, to be perfectly honest."

Nate cocked a brow, and amusement stirred in his chest. He suddenly had an idea of the book's title after all. "Oh, really? Your nose was practically buried in that book, Miss Brightwell. Whatever you were reading didn't look deathly boring to me. In fact, I suspect it was more than a little stimulating."

Quicker than a swooping bird of prey, Nate's hand dove beneath the cushion and snatched up the book. And then, his suspicions confirmed, he burst out laughing.

"Well, well, well, what have we here, Miss Brightwell?" he said, flipping through the dog-eared pages. "*Memoirs of a Woman of Pleasure*, volume two? Tell me, how was volume one, because I assume you read that first? Which part was your favorite?"

Sophie's expression was so stricken with mortification, Nate's heart immediately cramped with guilt for tormenting her so.

"I . . . I don't know what to say, Lord Malverne," she whispered. She dropped her gaze to her lap where her fingers twisted in her skirts. "What you must think of me . . ."

"Oh, Sophie." Nate cast the book onto the low table before the settee. "I'm sorry I teased you. A little salacious reading never hurt anyone. And it's not like I can sit in judgment considering I've read it myself. Actually, when I was younger, I read both volumes several times. Cover to cover."

Sophie's eyes widened. "You did?"

He waggled his eyebrows. "I most certainly did."

"Char—I mean, it seemed like a good idea to read them

so I would know what to expect if I ever marry. Not that a husband and wife would ever do things like . . . I mean . . . I really don't know why I'm saying all this. I only seem to be casting myself in a light that's worse than bad."

"I hardly think so, Sophie." Just knowing she enjoyed reading erotic material was making Nate's head spin and his cock twitch again, but that wasn't important right now. He needed to reassure her that he didn't think any less of her. "You are the sweetest, most lovely girl, and—"

"I'm sure you're talking about me, aren't you, Nate?" Charlie entered the room, a small tortoiseshell kitten in her arms.

"Of course." Nate sat back in his chair and crossed one ankle over his knee. "Soph—I mean, Miss Brightwell was just telling me you had procured a kitten. But I said I didn't believe her, so I decided to stay here and see for myself."

"Her name is Peridot," Charlie said.

"Peridot?"

"Yes, on account of her striking green eyes."

Charlie crossed the carpeted floor and placed the ball of black, white, and tan fuzz in his lap. "Peridot, meet Nate, and Nate, meet Peridot."

Nate lifted the kitten into the air and stared into its wide, blinking, light green eyes.

"Isn't she pretty?" said Sophie.

"Very." The kitten batted at his nose with one small paw, and Nate laughed. "Pleased to meet you, Miss Peridot."

"Will you stay for tea, Nate? While I was downstairs in the kitchen, I ordered a tray. There'll even be ginger cake."

He shook his head as he placed Peridot on his thigh and tickled the soft fur beneath her tiny chin. "Thank you, but no. I was on my way to White's when I saw your sitting room door was open and I thought I'd stop by for a chat before I headed out." He glanced at the window. The rain hadn't abated at all, and he was suddenly tempted to throw his plans aside and instead stay here with Sophie and Charlie, drinking tea and playing with the kitten.

Horror lanced through him. Dear God, what was he turning into?

His decision made, he passed the purring ball of fluff to Sophie. "I shall see you all tomorrow, I expect. And if the weather is fine, perhaps we can at last all go on that ride we've been talking about. Good afternoon, ladies."

Ignoring Charlie's quizzical stare and the errant, completely inappropriate wish that he could somehow trade places with the kitten—it was sitting on Sophie's lap and she was stroking its head with gentle fingers—he started for the door.

When Sophie called farewell in that sweet, lyrical voice of hers, he nearly turned back.

But only for a moment. He'd almost descended into madness once this afternoon, and he wasn't about to make the same mistake twice.

As soon as Lord Malverne had disappeared, Sophie buried her face in her hands. "Oh, Charlie, I'm so embarrassed. I think I might die."

"Why? What happened?" Charlie came and sat by her on the settee.

Sophie peered through her fingers and nodded at the "memoirs" on the table.

"Oh . . . ," said Charlie. "Nate caught you reading it, did he?"

Sophie dropped her hands and petted Peridot again. "Not quite, but it doesn't matter. He knows I've been reading it. He must think I'm the most awful hussy."

"I'm sure he doesn't. He didn't say that, did he?"

"No, of course not. Na—I mean, your brother is too much of a gentleman to say anything like that. But how could he *not* think I'm a flagrant hussy?"

Charlie sighed and tucked a stray strand of hair behind Sophie's ear. "You know, he's read it too."

"Yes, he said that also. Both volumes from cover to cover."

"And the reason is, those memoirs were the *only* books that could hold his attention when he was a youth. In fact, those books were the first ones Nate ever read. When he was thirteen."

Sophie gasped. "Surely not . . . Are you certain?"

Charlie turned around to make sure the door to the sitting room was closed. "Nate once confessed all to me when he came to me for help with a document his man of business had sent and he couldn't decipher a few long-winded legal terms. Apparently, when he was young, he had great difficulty learning to read and spell. Indeed, he was deemed to suffer from illiteracy."

"Goodness. What a terrible affliction." Sophie couldn't even imagine not being able to read and write. "My younger sister Jane had a similar difficulty when she was very young. I remember how frustrated she would become. And how hard she worked to overcome it. It wasn't until she was nine that she could really read on her own."

Charlie's smile was sad as she nodded. "So you understand perfectly. Nate has always felt his failure most keenly. For many years, his tutors and governesses despaired. He was wild and unruly and it didn't matter how cross anyone got with him, or how often Father took away things he loved like horse riding to punish him, he just couldn't seem to learn. Father sent both Thomas and Nate to Eton, but things only seemed to get worse. In fact, the school threatened to expel Nate during his first semester. It probably didn't help that Thomas was a gifted student. Father was always comparing them and telling Nate he was such a disappointment."

Oh, poor, poor Nate. Sophie ached for the young boy he used to be. Always in trouble. Never being able to succeed. "But he can obviously read and write adequately now."

"Yes, although I believe he only reads because he absolutely has to, not because he enjoys it. He's been to Oxford— not that he studied all that much—and has served in His Majesty's army, but he still struggles at times. But if it hadn't been for Thomas and those memoirs, I suspect he wouldn't have learned to read at all."

Understanding glimmered in Sophie's mind. "So Thomas helped him?"

Charlie nodded. "Yes. After Nate's first terrible semester at Eton, when he and Thomas returned to Elmstone Hall for the holidays, Thomas found the memoirs in the library. And considering he was fifteen and Nate was thirteen, he decided to teach Nate how to read by using a text that would spark his interest, make him motivated to succeed. And it worked."

Oh, my goodness. While Thomas's plan was both wicked and unconventional, it was also brilliant. Sophie was not familiar with the workings of an adolescent boy's mind, but if reading about the amorous adventures of Miss Fanny Hill had helped Nate to learn to read when every other method had failed, she couldn't condemn him or his brother.

As Charlie had said, it had worked.

"Thomas sounds like a very clever and caring brother. No wonder Nate feels his loss so deeply."

"Yes . . ." Charlie picked up the sleeping kitten from Sophie's lap and transferred it to her own. She stroked the soft fur between the kitten's ears with a gentle finger. She looked as though she was about to add something else, but at that moment, there was a knock on the door. Their afternoon tea had arrived.

Sophie removed the naughty memoirs from the table and tucked them beneath the cushion again as two of the housemaids entered bearing trays stacked with fine bone china teacups and saucers, a silver teapot and urn, the tea and sugar caddies, a milk jug, and the ginger cake.

As Sophie poured the tea and sliced the cake—Peridot was curled into a tight little ball on Charlie's lap—her mind kept returning to Nate. *Lord Malverne*, she reminded herself sternly.

He was a complex man, and the more she learned, the more she was intrigued by him.

Enamored of him.

No matter how she tried, she couldn't seem to rid herself of this unwise infatuation.

Her hand trembled and she almost spilled the milk as she dispensed it into the cups. If she hadn't heard that noise outside the door—whatever it was—if she hadn't said anything, would Lord Malverne have kissed her on the mouth?

She bit her lip to suppress a small smile. It suddenly occurred to her that perhaps the viscount might be a little bit infatuated with her too.

CHAPTER 14

It seems scandalous scoundrels and wanton women galore were present at a certain address in C. Square last night.

Find out what really happened at that ball . . . One wonders if the ton's most Errant Earl will ever learn his lesson?

The Beau Monde Mirror: The Society Page

Astley House, Cavendish Square, London

April 18, 1818

The next few days passed in a whirl of social activity for Sophie. Charlie had eventually accepted the invitation to Lady Kilbride's *musicale*, and Lord Westhampton had escorted her, Charlie, and Lady Chelmsford to the King's Theatre to see a vibrant production of Rossini's *The Barber of Seville*. Lady Chelmsford had also hosted a small private dinner party. At the *musicale* and dinner, Sophie had made the acquaintance of several respectable young gentlemen from her own rank, but no one had really caught her attention.

Lord Claremont had not attended the dinner party despite the fact that Lady Chelmsford had invited him. And Lord Malverne had not been present, either, much to Charlie's annoyance. Indeed, since the rainy afternoon when she and Lord Malverne almost kissed, Sophie had barely seen him. Even though it was probably for the best, it had left her with an odd feeling of dissatisfaction. Although she didn't really want to admit it to herself, she missed him.

But perhaps tonight she would have better luck in the husband hunting stakes. Perhaps tonight would be different and she'd meet the man of her dreams. A man who'd fall in love with her and she with him. That's what Sophie told herself anyway as she followed Lady Chelmsford and Charlie around the edge of the elegant ballroom in Astley House.

As they'd prepared for the evening, Charlie had reported her brother *would* be attending the Earl and Countess of Astley's ball to assist with "chaperoning" duties. Apparently she'd threatened once again to expose his bedroom faux pas to Lord Westhampton if he didn't, and so Nate had promised he would definitely be here. However, he'd told Charlie he would make his own way to Cavendish Square.

Taking up a position near the supper room again, Charlie and Sophie made sure Lady Chelmsford was settled on a comfortable shepherdess chair close to friends before they moved closer to the ballroom floor to "mingle"— although Sophie suspected it was more a case of "being seen." It also gave them the advantage of looking out for any eligible gentlemen of means. The event certainly wasn't as crowded as Lord and Lady Penrith's spring ball, so it was far easier for Sophie to scan the throng for the only gentlemen she was really interested in, Lord Malverne and Lord Claremont.

It had been five days since she'd last seen Lord Claremont at Penrith House, and although her pulse hadn't raced in the same way it did whenever she was with Lord Malverne, his apparent disinterest, after seeming so *very* interested in her, stung. It made her wonder what she'd done wrong. But then again, perhaps he'd simply learned more about her—her inferior birth and her family's lack of a fortune. That would easily account for his turnabout. She supposed she couldn't blame him if that were the case.

She blew out a sigh before she sipped her champagne.

"Why so glum, Sophie dear?" murmured Charlie in a

low voice. "Remember we must smile and look agreeable if we are to have any hope of attracting the attention of the opposite sex. Neither your gorgeous blossom-pink gown, nor the pearls in your hair, will be enough."

Sophie drew a steadying breath and curved her mouth into a smile she hoped would approach serene if not altogether inviting. "I know. But surely my gown counts for something. As does yours, Charlie. That shade of primrose yellow suits you perfectly."

Charlie slid her an arch smile. "I'm sure it's the low cut of my neckline that will sharpen the interest of the gentlemen here, rather than the color."

Sophie couldn't argue with that. It was true there was an ample amount of Charlie's bosom on show this evening, far more than she would feel comfortable displaying. But then, Charlie's bust was more eye-catching than her own, much smaller one. "Do you think Lord Claremont will put in an appearance?" she asked, scanning the room once more for the sight of the handsome dark-haired viscount.

"He'd be mad not to," said Charlie, her tone stiff with indignation. "When I next see him, I've a mind to scold him for ignoring you for so long."

"I'm sure he's had good reason."

"Be that as it may, he could have sent word, or at the very least flowers—" Charlie broke off and nodded toward the arched doorway leading into the ballroom. "Look, Nate has arrived at long last." She suddenly grasped Sophie's arm. "Oh, my word. His friend Gabriel, the Earl of Langdale, is with him."

Oh, my word was an understatement. Sophie's eyes widened at the sight of Lord Langdale. She recalled Charlie had once described the earl as magnetic, and she hadn't been wrong. Indeed, most of the women in the room seemed to have turned their attention toward him and Lord Malverne. Sophie could almost hear the collective gasp and the ripple of feminine awe that followed in the wake of their progress across the room.

Dressed in black save for his white shirt and cravat, with a tumble of black unruly curls framing his face, Lord Langdale reminded Sophie of a beautiful fallen angel as he prowled toward them. Lord Malverne in his perfectly tailored navy blue evening coat and matching breeches looked equally handsome. However, for all the Earl of Langdale's beauty, it was Lord Malverne who never failed to make her breath catch.

Sophie swore all eyes were on them as Lord Malverne and Lord Langdale stopped before her and Charlie.

Lord Malverne bowed as they both bobbed polite curtsies. "Good evening, sister dearest. You look well. And Miss Brightwell, you are just as lovely as always." He inclined his head toward the earl and continued, "May I introduce my friend, Lord Langdale?"

"Of course." Sophie held out her hand, and the charismatic earl bent over it, brushing her gloved knuckles with a gentlemanly kiss.

"It's a pleasure to meet you at last, Miss Brightwell. I've heard a lot about you." His startling green eyes sparkled with mischief. "All good of course."

Sophie blushed but managed to reply, "I'm pleased to hear it." Casting Lord Malverne a glance, she noted his shoulders had tightened and his smile had slipped a fraction. He looked as though he wanted to hit Lord Langdale. What had he said about her to his friends? But perhaps Lord Langdale was only teasing her.

"Lord Langdale, it's been far too long," declared Charlie.

"Indeed it has, Lady Charlotte." Lord Langdale bent over her hand as well. "I'm not sure why your brother keeps you hidden away. It is most unfair of him to deprive the world of your fair company."

"It's to keep curs like you from sniffing about her, that's why," said Lord Malverne with a smile that wasn't unfriendly.

Lord Langdale placed a hand on his chest. "You wound me, Nate. You know I would never act with dishonor when it comes to your sister. Or indeed, the fair Miss Brightwell."

Lord Malverne cocked a brow. "Good to hear it."

The country-dance came to an end, and Lord Langdale smiled at Charlie. "Lady Charlotte, would you care to dance?"

Ignoring her brother's scowl, Charlie smiled back brightly.

"I would love to, my lord." She passed her champagne flute to her brother and took the earl's proffered arm.

Lord Malverne tossed back Charlie's discarded drink. "Would *you* care to dance, Miss Brightwell?" he asked in a low velvet voice that made her shiver and her toes curl.

Sophie glanced at the other couples. It appeared a waltz was about to start. She didn't hesitate. "Yes, please. I would like that. Very much."

Lord Malverne took her champagne and handed it and Charlie's empty glass to a nearby footman before tucking her hand into the crook of his arm.

I'm going to waltz with Lord Malverne. Nate. Even though her heart had begun dancing, Sophie nevertheless tried to affect a calm demeanor as Lord Malverne placed one large hand at her back and then, clasping her right hand, gathered her closer. Much closer than Lord Claremont had.

How could it be that only this man's touch set her pulse racing and her skin tingling with delicious sensation? His hands seemed to sear her, even through her clothes. When she looked up at his face, his gaze was so hot, she thought she might melt. "Are you ready, Miss Brightwell?" he murmured.

She swallowed and licked her lips, not altogether certain his question pertained to the waltz. "Yes."

His smile made her breath catch. "Good."

The orchestra began to play and Lord Malverne swept her into the dance. For such a large man, his movements were light and graceful, and Sophie found she didn't have to concentrate on the steps at all. He made waltzing seem effortless.

After they'd covered half the floor, when she'd started to become slightly accustomed to the novel sensation of having Lord Malverne's lean hips pressed against hers, she ventured a comment. "You've been busy, my lord. I've barely seen you these past few days. But I'm glad you're here tonight."

"So am I," he said, his dark eyes caressing her face in a way that made her already flushed cheeks heat all the more. "I've been remiss in my chaperoning duties. It's time to whet the appetites of the other gentlemen here so they'll come flocking."

Sophie glanced away, confused. His eyes said one thing, but his words made it clear that he still wasn't interested in her.

"What's wrong?" he asked softly.

She forced herself to smile and met his gaze. *Just flirt. Keep the tone light. Don't let him see how you really feel.* "Nothing at all, my lord. It would appear that you're the dog and I'm the juicy bone again. Is that right?"

He must have believed she wasn't upset as his smile relaxed and his gaze grew warmer. "Perhaps this time I'm the cat and you're the mouse."

She arched an eyebrow. "Oh, so you're going to pounce on me?"

Mischief sparked in his eyes. "Either way, I have a mind to devour you. You look particularly delicious tonight."

Sophie affected a pout, even as heat scorched her cheeks. "For shame, you put me to the blush with your wicked banter."

He laughed, a wonderful, deep chuckle that curled around her. Through her. "I do love that about you, Miss Brightwell. That you are so easy to tease stirs me no end."

"You are cruel indeed, my lord."

"Unfortunately, I am."

They danced for a little while more in silence. Sophie decided to just enjoy the moment, to memorize the details of this encounter so she could take them out and treasure them later when she was alone: the way Lord Malverne's leg scandalously slid between hers during a particularly tight turn, the flex and ripple of his hard upper arm and shoulder muscles beneath her hand, the spicy musk of his cologne and the man himself. It was bittersweet dancing with him thus. He was everything she wanted, but any interest or desire he demonstrated was clearly all for show.

"I haven't had the opportunity to thank you for arranging invitations to Lord and Lady Astley's ball, my lord," Sophie said as they waltzed past a laughing Charlie and Lord Langdale. The invitations to such events had been few and far between, and Sophie wondered if both she and

Charlie were still deemed as unsuitable by most arbiters of the ton's ballrooms. It wouldn't surprise her if that were indeed the case.

Lord Malverne shrugged a wide shoulder, his eyes on his sister and his friend. No doubt he was double-checking that the earl was behaving himself as he'd promised. "It's Lord Langdale you should really be thanking. He was the one who arranged it after I called in a favor."

"Charlie tells me he's a good friend. That you both served in Wellington's army together."

"Yes. We did."

Oh dear. Such a clipped reply. The lines bracketing Lord Malverne's chiseled mouth had grown deeper, and the warmth in his eyes faded as he looked past her again. Sophie's heart plummeted. "My apologies, my lord. I shouldn't have said anything," she murmured. "You must think me dreadful to fish so. About your time in the military."

His gaze returned to her face, and the smile that curved his mouth was tinged with melancholy. "No. It's all right. It's true Lord Langdale and I served together. Along with two other very good friends. We won the war, but not all of our friends were so lucky to be there at the end. It was both the best and worst of times. But when all is said and done, it was an honor to serve."

"You are a brave and good man, Lord Malverne."

The viscount's eyes glinted with an emotion Sophie didn't dare to name. "You wouldn't say that if you knew what I was thinking most of the time, Miss Brightwell."

The waltz came to an end with a great orchestral flourish, and Lord Malverne escorted her back to the edge of the dance floor.

"Thank you again for the waltz, my lord," Sophie murmured as he began to relinquish his hold on her.

He squeezed her fingers gently before he let go. "It was my pleasure, Sophie."

Oh. What did that mean? He'd used her first name. Just as he'd done the other day when he tried to make amends for teasing her about her salacious reading habits. Just as he'd done when she thought he was going to kiss her . . .

"Sophie. Wasn't that wonderful?" Charlie's eyes glowed and her cheeks were flushed as she returned to Sophie's side. "It's such a shame Nate has forbidden Lord Langdale to court either of us, don't you think? I swear that man is too divine."

"Yes. It is a shame," Sophie agreed as she watched Lord Langdale head toward Lord Malverne, who was now waiting by the billiard room door. "He's very handsome."

Charlie had forbidden her brother to court her too. But what if Lord Malverne was beginning to change his mind? He'd flirted with her shamelessly after all. He liked teasing her. He'd almost kissed her on the lips . . .

As she watched him disappear into the billiard room, Charlie gently tugged at her arm. "Come. Let's go and sit near Aunt Tabitha to see if any men of her acquaintance would like an introduction or, indeed, a dance."

Sophie had the sinking feeling it wouldn't matter how many gentlemen she danced with tonight, she would only be thinking of one and how much she wanted him.

But the wanting isn't one-sided . . . More than ever, she was certain of it.

She suddenly had an idea, an idea so mad and bold, it made her stomach flutter and her fingers tremble. Dare she carry out her plan?

On the way back to Aunt Tabitha, she helped herself to another glass of champagne to bolster her courage. And if she needed it, she'd have another.

The time had come for her to take charge.

Nate lounged against the door leading to the billiard room, champagne in hand, watching a laughing Sophie being swept around the dance floor by Timothy, Lord Edgerton. *Cheeky bastard.* Trust him to have asked her for a waltz. And unlike Claremont, he was holding her much too close.

Claremont. The man's apparent lack of follow-through with Sophie confused him. He'd appeared keen enough, especially after their private conversation in Hyde Park. He wondered if Sophie's feelings were hurt by the man's obvious snub. Like most young women, she'd have been right to assume the viscount's attention last week meant something. While he felt bad for her, the other, ungracious part of him was also relieved that Claremont had turned out to be a bit of a bounder after all.

But then, remember he asked you to pass on his regards to Sophie. But you didn't.

Guilt pinched and he took a swig of champagne. Claremont could go to hell. If the viscount were serious, the least he could have done was send Sophie flowers or even a note if he hadn't time to make a call or turn up anywhere else.

He was heartily sick of all this business, watching his sister and Sophie being wooed and courted by a pack of ne'er-do-wells or, worse, rakes that were so dissolute, they could only ever be described as blackguards. He'd already had to chase Rollo Kingsley, Baron Rochfort, away from Charlie and Sophie. From what Nate knew of the man, his tastes were dark, and a violent temper lurked beneath his smooth facade.

He wondered if there weren't more scoundrels here tonight than usual simply because Lady Astley would have sent out most of the invitations.

Egad, the woman was brazen. But then, so was Gabriel. While they'd played a game of billiards, Lady Astley had made come-hither eyes at his friend from across the room. And now Gabriel had disappeared . . .

Considering the woman's husband was here tonight, Gabriel was going to get himself killed if he wasn't careful. Nate couldn't imagine the Earl of Astley would take kindly to being cuckolded beneath his own roof during a ball he and his wife were hosting.

The waltz came to an end, and Nate spent a moment deciding whether he wanted something stronger to drink like brandy or another dance with Sophie.

He really should stick with the brandy. It was far less addictive.

Turning toward the billiard room again—earlier on he'd spied a footman lurking in a corner with a tray of brandy-filled glasses—his attention was caught by the sound of a violent commotion; the orchestra screeched to a halt as an angry male voice rent the merry atmosphere of the ball to shreds.

"You filthy bastard!"

Hell, bloody hell. Gabriel had been caught. He just knew it.

Several women screamed and another man shouted as Nate swung around just in time to see Lord Astley plant a punch in Gabriel's face. His friend reeled backward and hit the floor.

Shit. Dropping his champagne glass, Nate darted around clusters of gaping guests until he reached the dance floor. Gabriel was already climbing to his feet.

Skidding to a halt on the parquetry tiles, Nate put his hands up in a placatory gesture. "Astley. Let's take this outside. Your guests don't need—"

"Don't you tell me what to do in my own home," the earl shot back, shoulders heaving. His gaze darted past Nate to his wife, Lady Astley, who stood white-faced and shaking a few feet away, and then back to Gabriel. His eyes narrowed to slits. "It's you, isn't it, Langdale? Don't deny it. I should call you out."

Gabriel straightened and, with barely a grimace, used his sleeve to wipe away the blood dripping from his split lip. "Yes. I'm afraid so, old chap," he said in a tone as dry as ashes.

Astley's face turned crimson. His eyes bulged. "Why you—" He launched himself toward Gabriel, but Nate, anticipating his attack, stepped between them. Catching the enraged earl by the shoulders, he used his weight to stop the forward momentum of the charge.

"Not here, Astley. Not here," he gritted out, struggling to contain the earl. "There are better ways to handle this." Turning his head slightly, he called out to Gabriel. "Go. Now."

Gabriel didn't need to be told twice. With a toss of his black curls, the Earl of Langdale stalked across the floor into the nearby drawing room, and then out through a set of French doors leading onto the back terrace.

"I'm going to kill him," growled Astley as Nate released him. The earl flexed the bleeding knuckles of his hand.

"That's your business entirely." Nate made a small gesture, indicating the guests around them. Whispers behind hands and fans had started up. "Shall we call it a night?"

The earl shook his head. "No need for that. I'll be stuck with too much champagne and lobster." He tugged at the lapels and the cuffs of his evening jacket, lifted his chin, and then strode over to his trembling wife.

"Madam." He offered Lady Astley his arm, and after a moment in which she studied his face with suspiciously bright eyes, she slid her hand into the crook of his elbow. To the room in general he called, "Carry on."

Once the earl and countess had left the ballroom, it seemed the assembled guests all heaved a collective sigh of relief.

Nate did too. Christ, he really needed that brandy. But first he needed to check on his aunt, Charlie, and Sophie.

And then on Gabriel.

Five minutes later, he found Gabriel in the darkest corner of the deserted, rain-washed garden, smoking a cheroot by an ivy-clad wall and a dripping oak tree.

"I know I'm bloody mad," he said in a low voice as Nate approached.

"We're all a bit mad, my friend."

Gabriel tipped his head back and blew smoke into the damp, cool night air. "True. Although some of us might be a *bit* more mad than others."

"Do you love her?"

Gabriel ran a hand down his face. "This is going to sound bad, but no. No, I don't."

"Astley wants to gut and castrate you. I'm not sure in which order."

"I know. The problem is, you and I both know that if he calls me out, he's the one who'll end up dead."

Gabriel wasn't boasting. It was true. He'd been one of the surest shots in Wellington's army. He wouldn't miss.

He drew on his cigar again and continued, "Call me a

coward, call me lazy, call me callous, or simply a man with no honor, but I don't fancy being arrested and hauled in front of the courts for killing a man in a duel. Especially when I feel nothing for his wife. I just couldn't be bothered."

Nate nodded. There was sense in what Gabriel had just said. Most duelists slipped the noose even in cases where one party had been killed. But there would still be a court case. Nate could understand why Gabriel wanted to avoid all that. "What will you do?"

Gabriel dropped his cheroot and ground it into the rain damp lawn with the toe of his shoe. "I think a trip to the Continent is well overdue," he said. "Perhaps I'll rent a villa on Lake Geneva like Byron and write poetry or paint. Drink copious amounts of claret or become addicted to an entirely healthy pursuit like basking in the sunshine." He shrugged. "You know me. It's always too much or too little."

Nate gripped his shoulder. "I do, and I understand completely. Whatever you do, make sure you take a trunkful of prophylactic sheaths with you."

Gabriel's teeth flashed white in the darkness. "Don't worry, I will. I might even write a letter or two."

"God, I wouldn't bother. You know I won't read them."

Gabriel laughed and pulled him in for a brief hug. "I'll be back. When things have settled down."

"Safe travels, my friend. And for my peace of mind, do try to stay out of trouble."

"I'll try but I can't promise anything. No matter what I do, trouble always has a knack for finding me."

Nate watched Gabriel disappear into the inky shadows at the side of the house. He trusted his friend would be all right. He'd been through much darker times, battled all sorts of demons in the past, and he'd always overcome them.

Gabriel was strong.

Much stronger than he was.

He sighed and raked a hand through his hair. He was tired. So tired.

"Lord Malverne?"

"Sophie." Nate turned and frowned into the darkness.

There she stood, only a few yards away, a pale slender wraith with a cloud of night black hair silhouetted against the brightness spilling from the doors and windows of Astley House. *She walks in beauty like the night . . .*

Nate swallowed, and when he spoke, his tone was harsher than he intended. "What are you doing here? It's been raining. Your silk slippers will get wet. And your gown."

"I don't mind. I wanted to make sure you—I mean things—were all right."

"Yes. Yes they are."

Both propriety and common sense dictated he and Sophie should go back inside. That they shouldn't be out here in a wet garden all alone. But Nate's feet refused to move. His tongue refused to say the words that would turn her away.

Words that would save her from him.

She moved closer, the gravel on the path barely crunching beneath her careful, light footfalls. "Lord Langdale—"

"He's gone. He'll be fine. He always is." *Four yards . . .*

"Thanks to you. You were very brave."

"I'm no hero, Sophie. Just a man helping out his friend." *Two yards . . .*

"Yet not everyone would."

Nate blew out a sigh. "I suppose not."

She was at his side now. Much too close. He could feel the warmth of her. It beckoned to him. He wanted to reach out, gather her close, bury his face in her hair. Savor her sweetness . . . devour her . . .

He clenched his fists.

"We need to go back inside." There, he'd said it. The right thing. He could push down all of his base impulses. Ignore the tightening of his loins. The temptation heating his blood. The ravenous hunger . . . It wasn't so hard.

But then she brushed against him, and her naked fingers—she'd discarded her white silk gloves—threaded through his.

Her voice was the merest whisper, barely discernible above the patter of raindrops from the oak tree, the sound of music and voices emanating from the house. Yet he couldn't mistake the blatant invitation, the insistent plea in her tone. "Lord Malverne . . . Nate."

In that moment, he knew he was lost. "Oh, hell."

"Oh, hell." Nate groaned the curse as he slid a large hand to the small of her back and pulled her hard against his lean, muscular body. "We shouldn't be doing this."

"I, for one, can't think of a reason why we shouldn't," Sophie murmured, boldly sliding her hands beneath the smooth velvet lapels of his evening jacket. When he'd followed Lord Langdale out here, she'd slipped outside, too, hiding in the shadows, keeping her distance until the earl left.

What she was doing, it was wicked. It was unwise. But she was so tired of being teased, so tired of waiting for Nate to put his scruples aside, for him to take what she wanted to give.

She wasn't quite sure how far either of them was willing to go, but they could at least begin with a kiss.

It was so dark in this far corner of the garden, Sophie could barely discern Nate's features. The sharp lines and angles of his cheekbones, his determined chin and jaw, the fine cut of his chiseled mouth, the glimmer of his dark, fathomless brown eyes, all were hidden in the shadows. But she could feel so much. The furnace-like heat of his body. The movement of sleek, hard muscle as he raised a hand to ever so gently push a tendril of her hair behind her ear. His potent male scent and the faint touch of his breath. The heavy thud of his heart . . .

Arousal shivered over her skin and the want, *the ache*, deep inside her grew more insistent. It was a pulse that seemed to have a rhythm all of its own, separate from that of her own madly beating heart.

She parted her lips. Leaned closer. Nate hadn't pushed her away, and she sensed the shift in power, slipping away from him and into her hands. The feeling was heady, like she'd just swallowed a shot of strong brandy. It gave her courage. It made her brazen. Still, a voice inside her head cautioned, *Keep the tone light. Don't let him see how you really feel . . .*

Her tongue darted over her lips, then she whispered so very close to his mouth, "I know you've taught me how to flirt, but I think it's about time I learned how to kiss, Lord Malverne. Properly. If I am to catch a wicked rake—"

He lost control. With a groan, he caught her face between his hands and kissed her.

His mouth pressed against hers, his lips firm yet soft as they slid and brushed. Coaxed and teased. It was a gentle wooing, yet something powerful, something hungry, something wild, unfurled inside her.

Plunging her fingers into his thick silky hair, she pushed herself closer, mimicking the movement of his lips, wanting to learn what would please him, what would make him groan again. To make him want her as much as she wanted him.

When his hot tongue swept against the seam of her lips, she gasped and drew back.

"I'm sorry, I've shocked you," Nate murmured against her lips, his breath teasing her just as much as his touch. "We can stop the lesson here."

"No . . . I just wasn't expecting . . . I've read of such things . . ." Sophie feathered her fingers over his jaw; it was tight with tension. If they stopped now, she'd die. "I want you to do it again. Taste me with your tongue."

"Christ, I'm going to burn in hell for this."

Again, Nate captured her face and claimed her mouth. This time when his tongue pressed against her lips, she opened for him, letting him slide inside to taste her, just as she'd demanded.

The sensation, the whole experience of being invaded so intimately, was so, so wicked. And utterly addictive. Nate's tongue as it explored her mouth was hot and wet; a velvet rasp, both rough and smooth. Commanding yet gentle.

Sophie loved everything about it.

Nate pulled back, drawing a breath, and Sophie chased

him for more. She glanced a kiss across his jaw, the corner of his mouth. Her fingers curled around his lapels. "Don't stop."

"I won't."

He leaned back, lounging against the wet, ivy-covered wall and drew her into the space between his muscular thighs. His arms circled her, lashing her body to his again as he plundered her mouth like a starving man.

Sophie kissed him back with equal ardor and desperation, her tongue tangling with his. Even through the layers of her clothes, and his, she could feel the rigid length of his manhood pushing against her belly. She should be shocked but she wasn't. No, not at all.

The strange pulse of desire between her thighs became even stronger and she shamelessly rubbed herself against Nate like a cat in heat. Nate's mouth grazed along her jaw, then down her neck, and the memory of him ravaging her with hot kisses when he was naked in her bed made her moan. She grasped one of his wrists and placed his hand on her breast.

"Sophie. Sweet Sophie." Nate seized her mouth again and responded to her unspoken, blatant demand, his fingers gently kneading her breast, teasing her tight, aching nipple.

It wasn't enough. She wanted more. She wanted his mouth there. His lips suckling, his tongue flicking—

It started to rain. Heavily.

"Damn." Nate shrugged out of his jacket and cast it over her head. "Come." Catching her hand, he led the way as they dashed up the gravel path, back to the terrace. Breathless from kissing, the cold shock of the rain, and laughter, they took shelter in the shadows, away from the windows and doors.

"Do you think anyone saw us?" Sophie whispered as she handed Nate's jacket back.

He shrugged it on. "I'm not sure. I don't think so . . ." He paused and cupped her cheek ever so gently. "Sophie . . ." Beneath his rain-damp hair, his brow furrowed and his wide chest expanded as he drew a deep breath.

He was about to tell her he shouldn't have kissed her. Taken such liberties.

He was afraid he'd compromised her again. And that there might be consequences.

The knowledge stung but what had she expected? *Don't let him see how you really feel. Don't scare him away.*

Sophie put a finger to his lips. "You are a very good teacher, Lord Malverne. And everything we just did, I wanted. But the lesson is over. I don't want you to worry or start thinking you've taken advantage of me. We both know that's not true. And I also want you to know I don't expect anything else."

He clasped her hand and kissed her fingers. And nodded.

That simple action nearly broke her heart. Somehow she kept her smile in place.

"I think it's best we go home," he said. "I know it's cold out here, but if you can bear it for just a minute longer, I'll fetch your redingote and order the carriage. Then I'll escort you around the side of the house to the front."

"What will you tell your aunt and Charlie?"

He grimaced. "I'm hoping they'll believe you came looking for me but that I'd already returned to the house. And because you've been caught in the rain, we need to go home." His shoulder lifted in a shrug. "It's the best I can do."

She crossed her arms, grateful it was so dark in the shadows; he wouldn't be able to see how brittle her smile had become. "I concur."

Nate rubbed her chill bare arms. "I'd leave you my coat but then . . . Oh, sod it." He slid it off again and draped it around her shoulders. "After what happened earlier in the ballroom, I don't care what anyone thinks."

"Thank you."

He touched her cheek, a brief caress. And then he was gone.

Sophie sighed and leaned back against the whitewashed wall of the house, clasping Nate's jacket about herself, savoring the warmth and his scent. It was still raining and a wind had risen. A sudden squall blasted her with icy drops and she shivered.

Closing her eyes, she touched her fingers to her lips; they felt tender and slightly swollen. *Kiss bruised.* She would never forget this night and Nate's ardent kisses and caresses. He might not care for her, but he desired her. And she never, ever thought a man like Nathaniel Hastings—a viscount and renowned rakehell—would ever want someone like her, Miss Sophie Brightwell, a shy, quiet girl from the country.

Whatever happened in the future, she wouldn't regret a single thing.

CHAPTER 15

What a to-do at London's most fashionable tea shop!

Tonnish misses trade vicious barbs while patrons take tea. Read on to discover what the notorious Miss S. B.—one of the Disreputable Debutantes thrown out of a certain "ladies' academy" three years ago—said to a less than perfectly poised Lady P. . . .

The Beau Monde Mirror: The Society Page

Hastings House, Berkeley Square, Mayfair

April 23, 1818

I'm sorry I'm such miserable company," Charlie croaked, wiping her bright red nose with a kerchief before adjusting her shawl about her flannel night rail. "Especially when you need cheering up."

"You're not miserable at all." Sophie joined her friend and a snoozing Peridot on the window seat in Charlie's sitting room. Although disappointment weighed heavily upon her heart, she managed a smile as she stroked the kitten's soft fur. "And I'll be all right. I think rejections are fairly commonplace in the business of publishing. It just means I'll need to submit my book elsewhere."

During breakfast, the correspondence had arrived, and to Sophie's dismay there'd been a sizable package among all the other letters; Mr. A. K. Newman from Minerva Press had returned her manuscript along with a very brief but polite letter of rejection. It appeared *The Diary of a Determined Young Country Miss* was not quite right for the publishing house at this particular point in time.

And she would indeed try elsewhere. If she didn't find a suitable match by Season's end, her family would definitely need the extra income. The prospect of having to marry Lord Buxton loomed like an ever-present ominous cloud on the horizon of her life.

Perhaps detecting her despondency, Charlie gave her arm a quick squeeze. "I'm certain you'll find someone who'll be mad for your book. Just you wait and see." She twitched back the blond lace curtains from the casement window and examined the pale blue sky and scudding gray clouds. "At least the weather isn't so miserable today. It might be a bit windy but the rain has stopped at last."

The rain that had begun the night of the Astleys' ball had continued on and off for the last four days. Even though Sophie had feared she might catch a chill after being caught in the downpour with Nate, it was poor Charlie who'd come down with a terrible head cold the very next day.

"Would you like me to order a nice hot bath for you?" Sophie stroked her friend's undressed hair. The bright chestnut curls cascaded across her shoulders and down her back. "Or more hot chocolate?"

Charlie coughed into her kerchief and shook her head. "No to the hot chocolate. But perhaps a pot of tea and a bath. That would be lovely."

"I'll ring for Molly."

After she'd issued her requests to Charlie's lady's maid, Sophie took a seat at a small table beside the fire with her writing slope and began to pen a new query letter to another publisher, a certain Mr. John Murray. The task would help to occupy her mind and keep her from dwelling on Minerva Press's rejection.

And Nate's.

Ever since the ball at Astley House, Nate had been avoiding her, she was sure of it. The morning following the ball, when Charlie had first announced she was beginning to get sick, Lord Westhampton informed them over break-fast that his son had departed for Suffolk of all places, with his friend the Duke of Exmoor, to investigate the latest in prize horseflesh for the duke's stables.

It stung that Nate hadn't said goodbye. And worse still, he hadn't let anyone know when he would be back.

Sophie supposed she only had herself to blame if Nate had decided to keep his distance. She'd taken things too far, too fast. She had made him feel guilty and scared him away. It seemed he didn't mind flirting with her, but tutor-ing her in the art of kissing was another thing entirely.

Yet, Nate was the one who'd joked about "devouring" her on two occasions. He was the one who'd nearly kissed her in Charlie's sitting room, but she had stopped it when she heard a noise in the hall.

It was too confusing, too frustrating, and thinking about it all—on top of the rejection letter—was putting her in a bad mood. Which was a shame considering the day was going to be fine for once.

Inspiration struck Sophie like the sudden wash of sunlight that touched Charlie's bent head, burnishing her curls to a bright coppery gold. She wouldn't be defeated. Yes, she'd stop by Mr. Murray's office on Albemarle Street this very morning and submit her story straightaway. There was no chance whatsoever that it would get published if it simply sat around here, its brown paper packaging gathering dust.

And as Albemarle Street was only a short walk from here, she'd then visit Olivia and find out if she'd had any luck in the husband hunting stakes. And, of course, she'd fill her friend in on all the latest gossip—although she would have to leave out the part about her first kiss. If Charlie found out . . .

Sophie shuddered. If Charlie found out, she'd tell her father, then Nate would be obliged to marry her. And he clearly didn't want to. Caring for him the way she did, her heart would be in danger of being irrevocably broken if she were to end up married to a man who didn't reciprocate her love. It would be the most intolerable of tortures.

Yes, she was warming to the idea of setting out on a

purposeful walk with each passing minute. She walked two miles or more every day when she was home at Nettlefield—weather permitting—so it was no wonder she was beginning to feel restless. It was a shame Charlie was too unwell to come, but on the way back, she'd stop by Gunter's and pick up something delicious for her to eat. Some of her favorite toffees perhaps.

Her letter to Mr. Murray complete, Sophie announced her intentions to Charlie, then changed into one of her new walking gowns, a deep rose red affair with smart black frogging. Within fifteen minutes she was venturing forth onto London's busy streets, one of the Hastingses' young housemaids sullenly trailing behind her; Sophie didn't think she appreciated the wind tearing at her bonnet and skirts while she carried Sophie's manuscript.

Once her story was delivered into the care of Mr. Murray's secretary, Sophie set out for Grosvenor Square with a much lighter heart. Despite the feistiness of the wind, she was enjoying the fresh air and the sight of the rain-washed blue sky. However, her spirits flagged again when she knocked on the door of Olivia's town house and was told by the arrogant butler that Miss de Vere and her guardians were presently "out" and he couldn't give her any indication whatsoever when they would be returning. He disdainfully accepted her hastily scrawled note to Olivia as though she'd just handed him a soiled kerchief—unlike Charlie, she didn't own smart calling cards—and then she took her leave.

For want of something else to do, she strolled along Upper Brook Street toward Park Lane and Hyde Park. Of course, she could always go for a walk through the park, but the maid was a slight creature—indeed she looked as though a good gust might blow her right off her tiny feet—and although it wasn't likely she'd encounter pickpockets, she'd rather have a footman accompany her all the same. She could always call on Lady Chelmsford, whose town house was not far away. But then she remembered the marchioness was also out of town for a few days. She'd gone to Bath to visit a friend who'd taken ill.

Her bright mood dispelling into gloom with each passing

moment, Sophie turned around and headed for Hastings House again. She dared not think of it as home, even though Charlie loved her dearly and welcomed her with open arms.

Home. Despite everything, part of Sophie was a little homesick. She missed the peace and quiet of the countryside and the company of her gentle half sisters and mother. She couldn't really say the same about her stepfather. He was a hardworking, austere man, taciturn most of the time, and when he did speak, his manner was gruff. She wasn't sure what her mother saw in him, other than the fact that he'd always been a good provider. They'd married when Sophie was still very young after her own father had died at sea, fighting the French.

The only other thing Sophie knew about her real father was that she'd received her distinctive dark hair color from him. Her mother, Alice, and Jane were all fair-haired, and sometimes she wondered if that was the reason why her stepfather had never warmed to her; she clearly was another man's child.

It didn't take long to reach Berkeley Square again, and after Sophie dismissed the maid—she'd caught the girl glancing longingly at Hastings House as they walked by— she crossed over to Gunter's. As usual, it was quite crowded. While she perused the counter, the display cases, and shelves, she became conscious of several other young women to her right, whispering and giggling like a gaggle of geese.

As Sophie pretended to study a plate of tiny petit fours, her stomach twisted into knots of anguish. They were making fun of her. She just knew it.

Lifting her gaze, she gave a startled gasp. Lady Penelope Purcell stood nearby, and the contemptuous expression in her ice blue eyes was so hard and cold, Sophie shivered.

"You're one of those awful girls who was thrown out of the ladies' academy a few years ago, aren't you?" Lady Penelope declared in such a precise, cut-crystal voice, half the tea shop turned to look at them.

At me. Sophie swallowed to moisten her dry mouth. She

fought to keep her voice steady as she said, "I beg your pardon. I don't know what you mean."

"Goodness gracious." Lady Penelope arched a flaxen brow. "It seems you are also a practiced liar. I *saw* you, Miss Sophie Brightwell, at Lord and Lady Penrith's spring ball. How you, or your equally scandalous friend, Lady Charlotte Hastings, ever received an invitation, I'll never know."

"How do you know my name?"

The young women around Lady Penelope tittered, and their ringleader answered Sophie with a smirk. "Oh, heavens, you are precious. You were announced, Miss Brightwell. The whole gathering knew who you were. I'm surprised Lord Claremont asked you to dance." Her gaze turned sly. "I'm sure he hasn't called on you since, has he? But that's hardly surprising given your reputation."

Even as a great wave of humiliation crashed over Sophie, she suddenly heard Lord Malverne's voice in her head. *I wouldn't worry about them if I were you. Apart from Lady Penelope, most of those girls are from ne'er-do-well families trying to snare a rich husband with a title bigger than their papas'.*

The thought of Lord Malverne, her own private champion, dismissing them, lent her strength. Raising her chin, she looked this far-from-perfect young woman in the eye. "I might have a besmirched reputation but at least I'm not a cruel, heartless bully."

Lady Penelope's mouth dropped open and her friends gasped.

"Well, I never." The duke's daughter was clearly fuming as her face turned the same shade of red as Sophie's gown.

One of Lady Penelope's friends stepped forward and jabbed a finger in Sophie's direction. "The whole ton shall learn that you are nothing but a rude, social-climbing, lying hussy."

"It takes one to know one. And by the way, what was your name, Miss . . . ?" Sophie arched a brow.

The girl sniffed and tossed her curls over one shoulder. "None of your business."

Sophie inclined her head. "Good day to you then, Miss None of Your Business." Her gaze shifted to the duke's daughter. "Lady Penelope. Yes, I know who you are too. I trust I shan't be seeing any of you, ever again."

"Trust me. You won't." Lady Penelope turned on her heel and stalked from Gunter's, Miss None of Your Business and the two other tonnish misses following in her wake.

Sophie turned back to face the astonished attendant behind the counter. "What do you recommend, sir?" she said in a surprisingly calm voice.

"The . . . the ah, the chocolate, walnut, and fig tarts are very nice today, miss. And we have a new type of petit four. It has a lovely center of raspberry cream."

"Wonderful. I'll have half a dozen of each, thank you."

Once the tarts and petit fours were packaged into small boxes, Sophie carefully picked them up and turned back to face the room. At least a dozen pairs of eyes swung back to their cups of tea and plates of decadent treats. Head held high, she marched from the tea shop, an obliging waiter opening the door for her on the way out.

It wasn't until she'd begun to skirt the park in the center of Berkeley Square that Sophie was hit by the enormity of what she'd just done. Stopping beneath a shady plane tree, she grasped the park's iron railing and dragged in several deep breaths, waiting for the bout of dizziness and shaking to pass.

Had she really set down a duke's daughter in front of so many people? What on earth had possessed her? As the glow of victory dissipated, the remnants of mortification and hot indignation swirled around inside her. But beneath it all was regret and smothering apprehension. There was sure to be some mention of the incident in at least one of the newspapers. What would poor Charlie say? None of this was her fault. They'd only just started to receive a few more invitations to more prestigious functions, and now she'd gone and lost her temper. She'd probably just reinforced everyone's poor opinion of her, that she really was a trollop with the manners of a harridan.

"Miss Brightwell . . . Sophie?"

Sophie closed her eyes again, praying for strength. Could this day get any worse? She knew that male voice. And it was a voice that belonged to someone she dreaded and despised.

Lord Buxton.

Perhaps she could pretend she hadn't heard him. That the wind had tossed his voice away. She started forward again—Hastings House wasn't that far off—but Lord Buxton could apparently walk with a swiftness that belied his portly frame.

"I say, Miss Brightwell." Lord Buxton stepped directly in front of her, forcing her to stop. Due to his exertion, his florid face had turned an even brighter shade of red and his breath sawed in and out, gusting over her face.

Sophie tried not to wrinkle her nose as she smelled sour coffee. Nevertheless, she took a step backward. The baron was standing much too close.

"Lord Buxton," she said, aiming for a polite tone, but missing the mark. She sounded exactly how she felt— impatient and more than a little annoyed. "I'm afraid I'm in a hurry."

She made to move past him but he put up a hand and stepped closer again. "Please wait. I witnessed what happened in Gunter's just now and I wanted to say, *brava*, Miss Brightwell. I was most impressed by your show of pluck."

"Thank you, my lord, but I really must go—"

He suddenly reached forward and grasped one of her upper arms, preventing her escape. "Miss Brightwell. Sophie," he said in a low voice. "Why are you determined to avoid me? For the past few days I've waited very patiently at Gunter's to catch a glimpse of you—"

Nausea roiled as shock hit Sophie like a punch to the stomach. Lord Buxton had been stalking her, watching and waiting for the right moment to pounce? "Why on earth would you do such a thing?" she gasped, trying but failing to shake off his hand.

He drew himself up and looked down his large, bulbous nose at her. "Because I wish to pay you court, Miss Brightwell," he said stiffly. "And that blackguard of a viscount you were with the other day chased me off like I was some sort of mongrel dog. Which I am not, as you very well know."

Sophie's stomach pitched again. "Have you made your intentions known to my stepfather and mother?" she demanded in a voice that shook with the force of her emotions. "Have you sought their permission to pay your addresses?"

Lord Buxton's small blue eyes narrowed to slits. "Your stepfather knows I have a keen interest in you, Sophie—"

"Do not use my first name, my lord. You presume far too much." She pulled her arm free from his hold and nearly dropped the boxes containing the treats from Gunter's. "I do not wish to slight you, but please, leave me be. Your attentions are not wel—"

With the speed of a striking viper, the baron gripped both of her arms with bruising force, pulling her closer. "Now listen here, you little upstart—"

"Take your hands off Miss Brightwell this instant or I will remove your hands from your wrists," rumbled a low voice laced with cold menace.

Lord Malverne. Oh, thank God.

As Nate advanced toward them with long, sure strides, his expression as dark as thunder, his chestnut hair billowing wildly in the wind, he looked like a vengeful warrior on the charge.

In the face of such ire, Lord Buxton let Sophie go. He stepped back several paces, adjusting his cuffs as if checking that his hands *were* still actually attached. "We were just . . . reminiscing about—"

"One more word and I'll knock your teeth out," growled Nate as he stopped by her side. "And if I ever see you in Berkeley Square again, or anywhere near Miss Brightwell for that matter while she is under my care and my father's, you can expect the repercussions to be ten times worse."

Lord Buxton gasped like a landed carp. "Well, I never."

Sophie almost smiled. It was the second time within the space of ten minutes that she'd heard that phrase.

Nate's lip curled into an aristocratic snarl. "Just stop. Just go."

Lord Buxton raised his chin and addressed Sophie. He

quivered with so much indignant anger, she could almost see his graying side-whiskers bristling. "Your stepfather will be hearing about this. You mark my words." Then he turned on his heel and stormed off, his coattails whipping between his legs like the tail of a scolded dog.

Nate touched her arm gently. His brown eyes were soft with concern. "Are you all right?"

Sophie nodded. "A little shaken, but other than that, I'm fine." She glanced down at the slightly crumpled boxes in her hands. "I'm hoping these treats from Gunter's survived."

Nate gave a mock frown. "Well, that does it. If that excuse for a baron has ruined anything from Gunter's, I'm going to have to call him out." He took the boxes from Sophie, tucked them beneath one arm, and then offered the other to her. "Come, Miss Brightwell, the time is ripe for us to feast."

"If I'd known you were returning, I would have purchased more." Oh, how she'd missed him. Sophie tried not to lean too far into him as they continued across the square toward Hastings House.

Nate's eyebrows rose. "Are you accusing me of gluttony, Miss Brightwell?"

"I've seen the way you eat, Lord Malverne," she countered.

Sophie couldn't be sure, but she thought she heard Nate mumble something like *minx* beneath his breath as they climbed the stairs to the town house, and she laughed.

Suddenly everything seemed right with the world. Sophie would enjoy this moment, no matter how brief, then tuck it away in her heart along with all her other treasured memories of Nate. Because how could she not?

She couldn't deny the truth anymore.

She loved him.

CHAPTER 16

What are you reading this Season?

For a comprehensive list of the latest titles one must simply have on one's shelf, look no further than our literature review section.

The Beau Monde Mirror

Sleep eluded Nate like a siren eluded a sailor. It beckoned, he wanted it with a passion, but he couldn't reach its shores. His attempts kept getting dashed on the rocks of bad dreams and unfulfilled desire. Try as he might, he couldn't stop thinking about Sophie and the kiss they'd shared. The kiss she'd initiated.

He wanted her so desperately, he'd forced himself to leave Hastings House the morning after the Astleys' ball, hoping that time and distance would ease his physical ache for her.

Apparently it hadn't.

Neither had other, more disturbing emotions than lust lessened with his time away. When he'd arrived home and had witnessed that cur of a baron accosting Sophie—handling her roughly—and her subsequent fear and disgust, he wanted to cleave the dog in two. The wave of protectiveness he'd felt shocked him to his core. He'd tried to tell himself he was just behaving as any gentleman would, but for the most part, he wasn't a gentleman. His violent reaction suggested that he was starting to care for Sophie. And he couldn't. He *wouldn't.*

He really should put more effort into helping her find a decent husband. If she belonged to someone else, then surely all of these budding emotions, both tender and violent, would wither and die.

With a heavy sigh, Nate rose from his twisted bedsheets and glanced at the Boulle mantel clock. It was almost midnight. He needed a drink and something to take his mind off Sophie. God knows what that could possibly be.

After spending a delightful afternoon with his sister and Sophie in Charlie's sitting room, he'd ignored his better judgment and elected to stay in for dinner for once; he thought if he spent time with Sophie, conversing and taking part in mundane activities such as playing cards and chess, his unhealthy fascination would fade. But everything she did, everything she said, only seemed to sharpen his appetite all the more. He was like an opium addict. He'd had a taste of something that had taken him to heaven and he couldn't get enough of it.

After pulling on a shirt, loose trousers, and one of his silk banyans, he slid on a pair of leather slippers and quit his room. There was a particularly good cognac in the library. His smile was somewhere between a self-derisive smirk and a grimace as he descended the stairs. At least that was one craving he could satisfy.

His father frequently worked into the early hours of the morning on parliamentary or personal business matters. However, tonight, when Nate pushed open the library door, he found the room was dark and deserted. Which was a relief indeed. He knew his father cared about him, but every time they interacted, something invariably went awry. And he was too weary to clash with him tonight.

Hopefully it wouldn't be too long before he could move back to Malverne House. The family home was both a solace and a source of torment for him. A bed of thorns. And thus it had always been.

Rather than call one of the servants, Nate spent a few minutes restoking the banked fire and lighting a lamp and a few candles. Once the golden light danced over the book-shelves and green velvet curtains, he poured himself a large tumbler of cognac, then claimed one of the brown leather wing chairs before the hearth. The potent brandy seared a warm path down his throat as he took a sizable sip. Almost immediately, the coil of tension inside him began to ease; his muscles loosened and his jaw unclenched. Although the dull ache in his groin continued, because he couldn't stop picturing Sophie in his arms, moaning into his mouth. Chasing him for kisses. Reaching for his hand and placing it on her breast . . .

He rubbed a hand through his hair. He needed some-thing else to distract him. Not for the first time in his life, he wished he enjoyed reading. But he could never lose him-self in the pages of a good book when he constantly stum-bled over unfamiliar words and had to reread passages to make sure he'd correctly interpreted the meaning. It was akin to translating ancient Greek at times. He needed to be motivated indeed to persist with the task. It was a chore. Not a pleasure at all.

He sighed and his attention was caught by a slim volume on the dainty occasional table beside him. The russet brown leather cover was embossed with gold motifs. Pick-ing it up, he studied the spine and deciphered the gold let-tering: *Hebrew Melodies*. Byron.

He'd heard of Lord Byron's lauded book of poetry but he'd never had the inclination to actually try reading it. Flipping open the volume, he glanced at the table of con-tents and one title in particular jumped out at him: "She Walks in Beauty."

Lord Byron could have written the poem about Sophie. Even though Nate had never actually read it, he knew some of the lines because they were oft quoted. Struck with an uncharacteristic surge of sharp interest, he located the page where the poem began and started to work out the words, his lips moving as he read:

She walks in beauty, like the night
Of cloudless climes and starry skies;
And all that's best of dark and bright
Meet in her aspect and her eyes:
Thus mellow'd to that tender light—

The door to the library clicked open and Nate turned in his seat.

Sophie.

It was as though Byron's lyrical poem was an incantation, and upon reading it aloud, Nate had summoned her, the beautiful girl who haunted his dreams and made him yearn for things he shouldn't.

She gasped when she saw him rising to his feet, and a bright pink blush washed over her cheeks. "Oh, Lord Malverne. I'm so sorry. I had no idea . . ."

She started to back out and close the door, but Nate called, "Wait. Don't leave on my account." He held up the volume of poetry. "I couldn't sleep so I thought I'd try to read."

"It seems we both suffer from the same affliction." Sophie stepped into the room again and closed the door with a soft click. "Would you mind terribly if I looked for a book too?"

"No. Of course not." Book still in hand, Nate gestured about the room. "Take your pick. That's what they're here for after all."

Sophie smiled softly. "Yes."

She traversed the richly hued Persian rug on slipper-shod feet and stopped before one of the towering bookcases. Nate lounged back in his seat again, and as he sipped his cognac, he couldn't resist the urge to drink in the sight of Sophie Brightwell in her night attire. Over her white cotton night rail, she wore a dressing gown of dusky blue velvet, and her glorious raven black hair was unbound; it cascaded in waves down her back, almost to her waist, like a black silk waterfall. His fingers itched to run through it. To arrange it about her when she was naked.

Jesus Christ, he needed to stop his thoughts right there.

He didn't want to sport an erection in front of the poor girl. She'd come in search of something to read, nothing more.

To his surprise, she joined him at the fireside with her chosen book, claiming the wing chair on the other side of the occasional table. The sweet floral scent of her that reminded him of roses—whether it was the soap or perfume she used, he wasn't sure—teased him and made his loins tighten with longing. He took a larger sip of the cognac, praying it would douse the desire stirring in his veins.

Clearly oblivious to his internal struggle and the potential danger she was in, Sophie leaned closer. "Do you mind if I ask what you're reading?" she asked, nodding at his book.

He closed the volume and turned the spine away so Sophie wouldn't see it. Perhaps it was cowardly, but he was reluctant to admit he'd been reading a poem that reminded him of her. "Poetry."

He also wanted to change the subject in case Sophie asked him something about the book and he inadvertently revealed too much about his inadequacy, so he added, "What have you chosen?"

She smiled and showed him the cover. "*Sense and Sensibility.* It's the loveliest novel. One of my favorites. The author, Miss Jane Austen, has a wonderful way with dialogue. She's penned the wittiest lines. And the reader is always assured of a happily ever after."

He cocked an eyebrow, amused by how passionate she was about her topic. "Oh, really?"

"Yes. The stories are actually quite entertaining commentaries about society, but what I love most is how the hero and heroine always find their perfect match. Some might say they are silly, romantic books, but I would counter, what is wrong with romance? Isn't that something each of us yearns for? To have romance in our lives?"

"Perhaps. But real life isn't like a book."

"No. But that doesn't mean we shouldn't wish for happiness and love. Life would be rather dismal and lonely without them, don't you think?"

"Touché." Nate didn't wish to state that he didn't believe

in happily-ever-afters anymore. Her enthusiasm shone in her beautiful blue eyes and in her smile, and he didn't want to be responsible for smothering it with his cynicism. Not tonight at least.

Sophie continued, "When you're finished with your book of poetry, perhaps you might like to try reading my favorite novel by Miss Austen, *Pride and Prejudice*. I've heard that even the Prince Regent is a great admirer of the author's work."

Nate inclined his head. "I believe I've heard that too."

"Well . . ." She shifted to the edge of her seat as though she were about to rise.

"Would you like a sherry? Or something else?" Nate gestured toward the cabinet near his father's desk that contained various bottles and decanters of alcohol. He raised his own tumbler. "I sometimes find a small nip helps me to sleep."

Sophie bit her bottom lip. "I really shouldn't."

"Of course." Disappointment settled like a stone in Nate's stomach. He'd been foolish to even suggest such an improper thing. "It was wrong of me—"

"But yes." Sophie smiled at him shyly from beneath her long, dark lashes. "A sherry would be lovely."

"Oh. Of course." He smiled back. "I'll get you one."

When he returned to the fireside with the sherry and another decent nip of cognac for himself, Sophie had picked up the copy of *Hebrew Melodies* and was looking through it.

"Have you a favorite poem?" she asked as he handed her a small crystal glass.

Nate winced as he took his seat. He didn't want to lie to her, so he said, "To be perfectly honest, I've never read it, or indeed any other book of poetry. I only just picked it up because it was lying on the table."

Sophie looked at him, her expression soft. "The other week you mentioned you're not fond of reading. Charlie mentioned it to me too."

"Did she?" Oh, hell. He gulped down a mouthful of his drink. What else had his blasted sister said? Did Sophie know how much of a struggle it was for him? His lackluster academic performance at school? He'd never shared such a detail with a woman before. Only his family and closest friends knew of his problem.

Sophie nodded and sipped her sherry before adding gently, "She also said it was your older brother, Thomas, who taught you to read a certain set of memoirs when you were thirteen. The ones you've read from cover to cover . . ."

Heat crept up Nate's face, and he swallowed back more cognac, almost draining the glass.

A small crease appeared between Sophie's delicately drawn eyebrows. "I'm sorry. I've upset you. I shouldn't have said anything. But I just thought you should know that I knew."

"No. It's all right, Sophie," Nate said with a sigh. "Everything Charlie said is true. Reading, and indeed writing, can be a struggle for me." He shrugged and offered a weak smile. "I suppose not everyone can be good at everything."

"Yes." Sophie sat forward, her glass of sherry clasped tightly in her elegant fingers. "For instance, I'm hopeless at playing the pianoforte. I'm all thumbs. And I cannot draw to save myself. When I was at Mrs. Rathbone's academy, the drawing master used to cringe in horror whenever he saw my feeble attempts. He once likened one of my still life drawings of a bowl of figs and grapes to a bowl full of squashed dead toads. Apparently it was an abomination to the eyes."

Nate appreciated her attempt at levity, and his smile grew wider. The funny thing was, now that he knew Sophie was aware of his "secret," and she didn't seem at all perturbed, it didn't feel quite so burdensome. He was actually relieved.

He suddenly wondered how he would feel if she knew more about the things he kept hidden. She was already curious about his time in the military. And she must have questions about Thomas. The longcase clock in the hall outside chimed the half hour.

Sophie took another sip of her sherry and then set the half-drunk glass down on the table beside Byron's book of poetry. "It's growing late. I'd probably best retire," she said softly. She pressed her book to her chest but then she suddenly reached across the table and laid a small hand on his arm. "Lord Malverne, I just wanted to say, if you ever needed . . . I mean, if you ever wanted help . . . while I'm here . . . you see, I helped my sister Jane learn to read when she was younger. She had terrible trouble for many years too."

"Thank you." Nate squeezed her hand. "You're very kind. And sweet."

Oh, damn. Why had he used that word? His gaze met Sophie's, and that was a mistake too. For in her wide blue eyes he saw a reflection of how he'd been feeling for days, if not the past few weeks. Hell, if he were honest with himself, he'd felt like this ever since she first arrived at Hastings House.

There was heat and longing. Anticipation and hesitation. And another emotion he dared not name because men like him didn't believe in it.

Couldn't believe in it.

He swallowed and his gaze dropped to Sophie's mouth. Was she remembering every single detail about their tryst the other night in the garden? And what he'd done and said to her in her room?

So fucking sweet.

"You should go," he murmured huskily, desperately trying not to think about Sophie Brightwell naked and willing in her bed. Or his. Or anyplace, including this damn library. But yet again, just like in the garden at Astley House, his body wouldn't cooperate. His hand wouldn't release hers. Indeed, he felt Sophie's fingers curl around his forearm a little bit more as though she didn't want to let go of him either.

Her chest rose as she drew a shaky breath, and above the neckline of her night rail, he could see her pulse fluttering like a trapped butterfly beneath the satiny skin of her neck.

"Yes, I should," she whispered. And then, before he could summon the will to say good night, Sophie slid from her seat and into his lap, and her mouth covered his.

Yes. Oh, sweet Jesus, yes. Nate dropped his tumbler of

cognac onto the floor, and his hands came up to cradle Sophie's beautiful face. She kissed him with wild abandon,
her tongue slipping boldly between his lips, her fingers
spearing through his hair. It seemed she'd been craving him
with a burning intensity that matched his own.

Somehow, shy, sweet Sophie Brightwell had transformed
into a passionate seductress who wasn't afraid to take what
she wanted.

And it was clear she wanted him.

Her hands slid to his shoulders, then beneath his banyan.
Her fingers kneaded his pectoral muscles through the thin
cambric of his shirt, and his need escalated. Spiraled out of
control like she'd sparked a wildfire inside him. Could she
feel his cock hardening, pushing into her thigh?

Cradling the back of her head, he dragged his mouth
from hers and she whimpered.

"Sophie . . ." She'd rendered him breathless, and he
needed to draw much-needed air into his lungs before continuing. "My sweet Sophie, we should stop before we go
too far. Before *I* go too far."

"I trust that you won't," she whispered, touching her
forehead to his. She shifted on his lap, and his cock
throbbed. "I know you want me. Please don't send me
away." Her fingertips feathered along his jaw and down his
throat where his own pulse beat like a bass drum, hot and
heavy. "Just think of this as another lesson you're giving me.
An advanced lesson in passion. All the skills I'll need to
tame a rake. I know there are things we can do. Things you
can show me. I will still be a maid and no one will ever
know." She kissed his jaw, then flicked his earlobe with her
hot tongue. "Please, Nate."

God help him. How could he say no to such a proposition?

She might be young, she might be his sister's friend, she
might believe in fanciful notions such as true love and
romance—there were so many reasons howling at him to
say no to her—but right here, right now, he just couldn't
summon the will to refuse her.

He slid an arm beneath her legs and one behind her

back, and with a low growl, he swept her up and then placed her gently onto a nearby chaise longue. Her beautiful black hair fanned out on the red silk damask cushions at her back, and he had the overwhelming urge to bury his face in the fragrant waves.

There were so many other things he wanted to do. *To show her*, just like she'd asked.

He sat down beside her, and his heart pounded a wild tattoo as he began to loosen her blue velvet robe. For so long he'd dreamed about what her breasts would look like, how they'd taste. He'd already caressed them in the dark, and through her clothes. He'd touched his tongue to her nipple. But it wasn't enough. Nowhere *near* enough.

As the ribbon tie securing her night rail slipped free, Sophie's kiss-swollen lips parted and her breath quickened. Her blue eyes, as dark and fathomless as the sea, were heavy-lidded with desire; she watched his face, perhaps waiting for his reaction when he pulled the neckline of her night rail lower.

He wasn't disappointed. Not at all. Hot lust arrowed through him, heating his blood, as he absorbed the glorious sight of Sophie Brightwell's perfect, pert breasts. High and proud and as round as apples, the ivory mounds were topped with deep red raspberry nipples.

Nate's mouth watered as he cupped each globe reverently and grazed the pads of his thumbs over the tightly furled peaks. His voice was husky as he murmured, "You're beautiful, Sophie." He teased her nipples again, and she pushed herself into his hands.

"Please," she whispered, "taste me."

Nate didn't need any more urging. Bending his head, he sucked one succulent bud between his lips, then flicked it rapidly with his tongue. All the while, his fingers plucked and tortured the other nipple. Whimpering, Sophie threaded her fingers through his hair, and her whole body arched.

"Oh, sweet heaven," she panted. "Nate . . . that feels . . . oh."

He smiled as he transferred his mouth to her other breast. He loved that the usually well-spoken, prim and proper Miss Sophie Brightwell was inarticulate with desire.

But he wouldn't be satisfied until she was speechless.

He slid his hand to the hem of her night rail. It was already rucked up to her knees.

She'd said she wanted an advanced lesson in passion. The question was, did she really want to go this far?

Although she'd been rendered all but mindless with desire because of the exquisite yet torturous attentions Nate was lavishing upon her breasts, Sophie also became aware of his hand on her leg—the hot, heavy weight, the teasing caress of his fingers as they made small circles on the inside of her lower thigh. Was he going to touch her *between* her thighs?

She prayed that he would.

Before she came down to the library, she tossed and turned for several hours, thinking of Nate and how much she burned for him. The fact that he'd spent the entire afternoon and evening with her and Charlie only served to inflame the banked fire within her, so as she'd lain in her bed recalling Nate's kisses and caresses, she'd tentatively touched her own nipples and the black curls hiding her feminine folds; they were damp, and she was so shocked at her wantonness, at the evidence of her desire, that she hadn't been willing to touch herself any further.

But now, as Nate's fingers continued to stroke the tingling flesh just inside her knee, she knew she wanted him to touch her in her most secret place.

Her sex *ached* for him.

With trembling fingers, she inched her night rail higher, hoping Nate understood what she wanted. Although she'd brazenly asked him to teach her more about passion, her courage failed her at the thought of actually putting her wicked request into words.

He must have noticed what she was doing as he raised his head from her breast and locked his dark, smoldering gaze with hers. "Are you sure about this, Sophie? Do you really want me to pleasure your quim?"

"Yes," she whispered. A fiery blush scorched her cheeks

at hearing him say such a thing, but that's exactly what she wanted. "Very much. I know it's wrong and perhaps even depraved, but I want to know how it feels to . . ." She bit her lip, unable to say more.

Nate slid his hand farther up her thigh until his fingers rested just below her mound. "To come?"

"Yes."

His smile was pure sin and the most beautiful thing she'd ever seen. "It's not depraved at all. It's wonderful."

Sophie let her legs fall open for him. "Show me then."

"With pleasure."

Quivering with anticipation and acute need, Sophie closed her eyes, and when Nate's fingers drifted through her curls, she gasped. How would it feel when he—

Her thoughts scattered as Nate slid one, then two of his long fingers between her slick folds, stroking up and down, up and down in a maddening rhythm. At the same time, he suckled at her breast.

Oh, my Lord. Sophie clutched Nate's head. The sensations engulfing her were indescribable. Overwhelming. And then he touched an excruciatingly sensitive spot at the top of her sex and she bucked and cried out.

Nate immediately covered her mouth with his, absorbing the sound. "Hush, sweetheart," he whispered as he continued to rub and torture that little nub of pleasure with the pad of one clever finger. "We don't want anyone to hear."

Sophie whimpered by way of reply, and then Nate was kissing her again, his tongue tenderly ravaging her mouth as his wicked fingertips teased her quim without mercy. A powerful, irresistible force was building, tugging her toward something she wanted so very badly. A hot, mounting pressure that was almost too much to bear. She hovered on the edge of agony and ecstasy . . . and then, without warning, a bright burst of pleasure rushed through her. Consumed her.

Nate drank in her hoarse cry of elation as she shuddered and quaked, racked by wave after wave of bliss until, at last, she subsided into a helpless yet completely satisfied puddle on the chaise longue.

When some semblance of clarity returned to her, she

found Nate looking down at her, a soft smile curving his mouth. "At the risk of sounding cocky, I think you enjoyed the lesson, sweet Sophie."

"You know I did," she murmured, barely able to speak or even smile. Her limbs felt languid and heavy as though her bones had melted. The aftermath of such blinding pleasure reminded her of basking in the warm golden glow of the summer sun. "For my first time, it was . . . momentous. An occasion to remember. Thank you, Lord Malverne."

"You're more than welcome, Miss Brightwell."

As he brushed soft kisses on her forehead, the tip of her nose, her cheek, and at last, her lips, he began to adjust her night attire.

Was the lesson over? It appeared so as Nate tied the ribbon securing her night rail and the sash of her robe once more.

Nate had spoiled her, well and truly, but she couldn't help feeling things were incomplete. She'd achieved satisfaction. But Nate hadn't. When she sat up and dropped her gaze to his lap, she could clearly see his manhood tenting his shirt and trousers.

She reached out a hand and grazed her fingertips over his marble-hard chest, then rested her palm against it. His heart was thudding, galloping, and she could feel the rough rise and fall of his rib cage as he drew breath. Dare she ask him for a little more instruction?

"I don't think we're finished yet," she murmured in a velvet-soft voice. "I think there are other things I need tuition in." She glanced meaningfully at his groin. "How am I to ensnare a rake if I don't know how to please him?"

Nate swallowed hard, the sound audible in the quiet room. A wry smile played around his lips. "I'm sure he'd be happy to show you himself at this particular point."

She smiled and skated her fingers lower until they rested on his rigid abdomen. The edge of her wrist brushed the top of his jutting member, and he hissed through his teeth. "Perhaps. But I want *you* to show me, Nate. I won't tell anyone if you don't. What harm can it do?"

She lifted up the edge of his shirt and studied the shape

of him. Goodness gracious he was large. "I can see that at least part of you wants me to help you 'come,' as you put it."

Nate hadn't pulled away and his eyes had darkened to a rich, molten chocolate brown. Emboldened, she gently cupped his length. "Tell me what to do," she whispered. "I want to give you pleasure too."

H e was definitely going to hell if he let Sophie do this. But when all was said and done, Nate couldn't resist her. After pleasuring her delicious breasts and sweet, wet quim, after witnessing her first ever orgasm, he was on fire; his cock was hot and throbbing and his balls were tight and heavy, fit to burst.

As Sophie studied him from beneath her long black lashes, another surge of lust and some other potent emotion he didn't wish to identify swept over him. He caressed her flushed cheek with the back of his fingers. "All right, sweetheart."

The smile she gave him was so seductive, it nearly had him spending right then and there. "What should I do? May I undo your trousers?"

"Be my guest." Even though Sophie was gentle, Nate's cock was so primed, he found the process almost painful as she opened the fall front.

When he sprang forth, her eyes widened and she gasped.

"You can change your mind." Nate's voice was threaded with strain as he grasped his shaft at the base. "I know it's probably quite a shock to see a male of the species in full rut."

"Yes. It is. But it's also a fine sight." Her blue eyes danced with mischief. "I now understand all of the amusing euphemisms in those naughty memoirs we've both read. I'm not sure which one suits you best. 'Truncheon,' perhaps? Or 'maypole'?"

Nate *almost* laughed. The most he could manage was a crooked smile. "Maypole would do," he said. He wasn't going to claim a descriptor denoting something smaller.

"Well . . ." Sophie lifted her hand but then dropped it to

her lap. Her fingers pleated her robe. "Perhaps . . . would you mind demonstrating a little first?"

Sweet Lord. Just the suggestion of stroking himself as Sophie watched caused a drop of his seed to leak from the ruddy, engorged head.

Sophie's gaze was riveted to the sight.

"I'm very . . . aroused," Nate gritted out from between clenched teeth as he slid his fisted hand up and then down. "It won't take much to send me over the edge, Sophie. Are you prepared for that?"

She swallowed then nodded. "Yes. I want to do this."

As Sophie wrapped her cool, slender fingers around him, Nate relinquished his hold.

"Oh . . . you're so hard and soft at the same time." Her voice was laced with quiet awe. "Like forged iron wrapped in silk."

Good God. Her words made everything in Nate tighten. Did she know what she was doing to him? He leaned back on stiff arms and watched with avid fascination as Sophie mimicked his movements, sliding up and down, up and down.

He'd never seen anything quite so erotic in his life.

"Am I doing it the right way?" she whispered, glancing up at him as she continued her slow, sensual torture, squeezing him gently as her hand slid from root to tip and back again.

Nate gave a curt nod. "Yes. But don't be afraid to squeeze harder. And faster. Work me hard, sweetheart."

She bit her lip and nodded. "Very well." Her grip grew tighter, and the pace of her small pumping fist accelerated. It wasn't long before Nate could feel his climax gathering at the base of his spine, the tension building, winding tighter. The simmering pressure, the heat in his blood, was climbing, escalating to the boiling point. To the point of no return.

He couldn't hold back.

"I'm going to . . . Here it comes, sweetheart." Nate's balls contracted, and as exquisite pleasure hit him, his whole body stiffened. Eyes closed, he threw his head back, and a deep groan spilled from his throat. As his seed erupted, he was swept away on a hot, pulsating tide of release.

When he opened his eyes, he discovered Sophie was

smiling at him with open satisfaction. Even though her fingers were covered in his seed, she didn't look perturbed at all. She was triumphant.

"I'm so sorry about the mess," Nate murmured as he sat up. He lifted her hand away from his sticky groin, and with the hem of his cambric shirt, he began to wipe her fingers.

"Don't apologize, Nate." Sophie's eyes glowed with a happiness that seemed to match the warm hum of contentment in his own veins. "I wanted this. I wanted to please you. To return the favor. Don't ever doubt that."

Nate nodded as he continued to wipe them both clean. He knew Sophie had chosen to do this, but that didn't mean he should have gone along with her proposition, no matter how damn tempting. He hadn't acted with honor and it bothered him. Which was ironic, really, considering what a scoundrel he was.

Sophie might pretend this encounter, this "lesson," didn't mean anything to her, but he rather suspected it did. He'd seen it in her eyes. Her smile. Felt it in her touch. If she began to think this relationship—if one could even call it that—would turn into a love match, a "happily ever after," she was sorely mistaken.

He didn't want love. He didn't *need* love. He'd experienced and seen firsthand the devastating aftermath when tragedy struck and a loved one died, and to him, the pain of loss was intolerable.

Of course, what was done was done, but Nate didn't want to see Sophie hurt. Somehow, he had to crush down his infatuation—nay, obsession—with Sophie. Even better, rip it from his chest.

And most important, he could never let something like this happen again.

Ever.

CHAPTER 17

Unlucky in love? Is your Season not turning out the way you envisioned it?

Why not try one of our reliable remedies for bolstering those flagging spirits that many a budding debutante suffers from mid-Season?

You are not alone.

The Beau Monde Mirror:
The Essential Style and Etiquette Guide

Hastings House, Berkeley Square, Mayfair

April 24, 1818

What a to-do at London's most fashionable tea shop!

Tonnish misses trade vicious barbs while patrons take tea . . .

The horrid words glared at Sophie from the *Beau Monde Mirror*, the infamous newspaper that was really more of a scandal rag. How could she have been so stupid to let down her guard yesterday? She blinked away tears as she sipped her cup of breakfast hot chocolate.

"Oh, Sophie. Please don't blame yourself. Everything will be all right." Charlie put down the newspaper on the dining table. The soft expression in her brown eyes suddenly changed, grew hard, the golden flecks sparking with righteous anger. "If I'd been there, you know things would have been much worse. Lady Penelope Purcell would've ended up wearing at least *one* of Gunter's pies or cakes. I've long suspected she has a nasty streak. I'm proud of you for standing up to her."

Sophie *almost* laughed at that. She picked at her barely nibbled piece of toast, then pushed her plate away. "I don't know what possessed me. Honestly I don't. Lady Penelope was just so rude. And when she mentioned your name, too"—at least the *Beau Monde Mirror* hadn't reported *that* particular detail—"it seemed my anger got the better of me. I'm so sorry. I worry the invitations will be few and far between again. And your father will undoubtedly be livid too." She dropped her voice. "I know he'd hoped your brother would court the duke's daughter."

"Oh, don't worry about all that. Father will think *much* less of her when he hears what she's truly like. So you do *not* need to apologize. But did you really call Lady Penelope"— Charlie grinned as she picked up the paper again and read—"a cruel, heartless bully, and one of her cronies Miss None of Your Business?"

Sophie's mouth did twitch with a smile this time. "Yes."

"Just brilliant."

"What's brilliant, sister dearest?"

Sophie's breath caught as Nate sauntered into the morning room dressed for riding. She didn't mean to, but she blushed at the sight of him wearing his tight buckskin breeches—because now she knew all about the mysterious bulge hiding behind the fall front. She clutched her wicked hands together beneath the cover of the table at the memory of what she'd done to him. And how much he'd enjoyed it.

Thank heavens Nate hadn't noticed her self-conscious reaction. Charlie also seemed oblivious to her discomfiture as she pointed at the paper to answer Nate's question. "This. Well, not the *Beau Monde Mirror* itself, but Sophie's inspired setdown of that conceited cow, Lady Penelope Purcell and her equally vile friends at Gunter's. It's all there in the article."

Nate cocked an eyebrow as he picked up the paper and

glanced at it. "Ah, it seems yesterday was eventful in more ways than one, Miss Brightwell."

Even though she willed herself not to react, Sophie's blush grew hotter because she knew he was really alluding to what they'd done in the library last night. *Curse him.*

Charlie's gaze narrowed with suspicion as she glanced between her brother and Sophie. "Why, what else happened?"

Sophie cleared her throat but it was Nate who spoke. "You know. How after Sophie left Gunter's, that prat, Lord Buxton, accosted her in Berkeley Square?"

Charlie shuddered. "Ah, yes. At least *that* isn't in the paper."

Sophie released a small sigh of relief. She'd related slightly "edited" versions of both incidents as they all shared the slightly squashed treats from Gunter's in Charlie's sitting room. She was very careful to leave out the part where Nate had come to her rescue, and Nate hadn't corrected her—she hadn't trusted herself not to gush too much about his heroics, thus giving away how much she cared for him. Thankfully, it appeared Charlie didn't suspect anything *else* of significance had occurred between her and Nate yesterday. Or to be perfectly accurate, earlier this morning . . .

Nate snatched up a pastry and bit into it with relish.

Charlie frowned. "Aren't you going to take a seat, Nate?"

He finished chewing, then shrugged. "My valet already brought me coffee, and now I'm about to go riding."

Charlie lifted her chin. "You should take Sophie with you."

Sophie shook her head. "Oh, no. I don't think so," she said at the same moment Nate added, "I'm sure she wouldn't want to."

Charlie frowned at them both. "What rot, Nate. Of course Sophie would want to. And Sophie, whyever wouldn't you want to go? *I* can't go because I'm still not well. But you certainly don't need me to chaperone. And you both know it's perfectly acceptable for two close family friends to be seen together in public."

Nate's gaze caught Sophie's. "Well, what do say you, Miss Brightwell? Would you like to come?"

"You can ride my bay mare, Aurora," added Charlie. "She's very sweet and well behaved. You'll love her."

What could she say? Of course, part of Sophie's heart thrilled to the idea of being alone in Nate's company again. After her "lesson" last night, after he tidied them both up, he kissed her forehead and she departed the library with *Sense and Sensibility* in hand. Initially, she'd been abuzz with satisfaction, but once she reached her room, she realized Nate had barely said a word to her after he "finished." Not that she'd expected him to converse with her at great length. It had been very late after all. But still . . .

Yes, it would be worthwhile seeing Nate privately, as it would give them the opportunity to discuss how their unconventional relationship would proceed. Even though she'd told him their wicked midnight encounter wouldn't mean anything, her heart truly wished it did. And she wouldn't know how Nate was really feeling about the situation unless they had uninterrupted time to speak about it.

So she inclined her head and said, "Yes. All right. That would be lovely, my lord."

"Wonderful. It's all decided then." Charlie rose from her seat and gathered her shawl about her shoulders. "I'll ring for Molly, and she can help Sophie change into her riding habit."

Nate's gaze settled on Sophie. "I will meet you in the vestibule then, in say, fifteen minutes, Miss Brightwell?"

"Yes. Of course." Sophie stood as well. "I will be as quick as I can."

Nate's expression was friendly. His tone agreeable. Although there didn't seem to be anything overtly amiss about the manner in which he'd just addressed her, she began to get the impression that he was being guarded.

It wasn't until they were both heading toward Hyde Park on their mounts a half hour later that it struck Sophie—Nate's teasing tone and the amused twinkle in his eyes were gone.

He *was* wearing a mask. He was hiding from her.

Even though the sky was a clear bright blue and the spring sun shone warmly through the leafy branches of the lime trees lining the road, Sophie suddenly felt chilled to the bone.

She'd done exactly what she'd tried very hard not to do.

She'd gone too far and she'd scared him away.

She glanced over at Nate as he expertly steered his fine black gelding, Invictus, between two hackney cabs and onto the main bridle path in Hyde Park. Even though he sat tall with a relaxed hold on the reins, there was tension in his handsome face—she could see it in the lines bracketing his wide mouth, and in the distant expression in his brown eyes whenever he gave her a completely cordial smile. Any words he spoke were entirely pleasant and entirely inconsequential. It made Sophie want to scream at him.

But she didn't. She held her head high, and any smile she returned was equally bland and amiable.

Don't let him see that you care. Don't let him see you are hurt.

Don't make matters worse.

She smiled ruefully, even as frustrated tears pricked. How much worse could it be than this? She'd thrown herself at Nate, and now he was actively distancing himself from her. And her foolish, wayward heart was beginning to ache.

By the time they reached Rotten Row, Sophie had changed her mind again; resentment had started to simmer, and her tongue burned with the need to say something to Nate about last night. At least he could acknowledge what had passed between them. Even if he didn't want anything more to happen, she wanted some sort of reassurance that he didn't think any less of her.

But what if he did?

Sophie lifted her chin. It would be exceedingly hypocritical of him to judge her considering the scandalous things rakehells got up to. It wasn't fair that society had one set of strict rules controlling the behavior of young women, and none at all for men.

And if Nate did think less of her because of what she'd done, well, she'd rather know that too. One thing she was certain of, being treated like a polite stranger was wearing thin, and quickly.

Nate reined in Invictus by the banks of the Serpentine, and following his lead, Sophie halted Aurora alongside him.

"You ride well, Miss Brightwell," said Nate in that impeccably polite tone of his that rankled so much.

Before she could stop herself, Sophie blurted out, "Nate, why are you being such an ass?"

Nate's eyebrows shot up. "I don't know what you mean—"

"Of course you do. I told you last night that what we did was nothing more than a lesson. And I meant it. Yet this morning . . ." She drew a steadying breath. "This morning you are behaving as though we are little more than casual acquaintances. I never expected undying protestations of love from you, but neither did I expect you to keep me at such a distance. You're being perfectly civil yet perfectly annoying at the same time."

Nate swallowed. "Sophie, I do not mean to hurt you—"

"Well, you are," she flashed. "I don't understand why you should treat me so coldly. Unless you think it's because my wanton behavior last night was so shocking that you cannot bear to interact with me."

"No. No of course not. It's not that . . ."

"Then what's wrong? Please tell me."

Nate's eyes darkened as his gaze locked with hers. "Do you want me to be frank with you? Because I will be if that's what you really want."

Nate's expression was so intense and somber, Sophie's heart began to race in a most uncomfortable way. *Oh, dear.* She licked dry lips. "Yes. Yes I do."

Nate inhaled deeply as though bracing himself to deliver devastating news. "Sophie, this infatuation I have with you . . . it's fast becoming an obsession. A sexual obsession. And while I desire you a great deal, and yes, I care about you, I'm afraid I do not care *for* you. It's just not in my nature. To that end, it is essential I distance myself from you, because if I don't, I'll ruin you completely. I may be a scoundrel, but I could never do that to someone as lovely and sweet as you. You deserve someone better. A man who will love you the way you want to be, and *ought* to be loved. And that man isn't me."

Sophie's breath caught. It felt as though Nate had just pulled out her heart and stomped all over it with his shiny black Hessians. But what had she expected? Hadn't both he and Charlie warned her from the start that he was incapable of love? Still, she whispered, "There's no hope then, is there?"

Compassion flickered in Nate's eyes. "I'm afraid not."

She nodded even as despair began to clog her throat and a strange viselike pressure squeezed her chest. Her lungs burned. Where had all the air gone? The bright waters of the Serpentine blurred before her eyes. "I'm such a fool," she whispered.

Nate extended his gloved hand, as though he was about to touch her. "Sophie, I—"

"Lord Malverne!"

Nate glanced past her shoulder and smiled. "Lady Astley," he called, lifting the hand he'd been about to touch her with in a waved greeting. "Good morning to you."

Sophie attempted to blink away her tears but it didn't really matter. When the beautiful blond countess stopped her horse by Nate's, she only had eyes for him.

"You remember Miss Sophie Brightwell, don't you, Lady Astley?" prompted Nate.

Lady Astley barely turned her head toward Sophie. "Yes, of course. Good morning, Miss Brightwell," she said before immediately returning her attention back to Nate. "Lord Malverne, could you spare a moment to talk privately?"

Nate frowned. "My apologies, Lady Astley, but I don't think—"

"It's all right, Lord Malverne." Sophie was surprised that her voice sounded relatively normal. "I shall take Aurora for a short ride, just to that copse and back. I'd like to put her through her paces." Without giving him the chance to respond, she nudged the mare's sides and moved away toward the grassy expanse on the other side of Rotten Row. Some time alone, away from Nate, would be welcome right now. She was already humiliated enough. She didn't want him, or Lady Astley for that matter, to see her cry.

"Sophie," he called, but she ignored him and urged Aurora into a smart trot, then a canter.

Aurora's gait was smooth and swift, and in no time at all, Sophie had reached the copse of oaks and maple trees on the other side. She turned Aurora around but then reined her in. She wasn't ready to go back. Even though she was some distance away, she could easily see Lady Astley in her smart hunter green riding habit; her head was bent toward Nate, and Sophie thought she might even be touching his arm.

She wondered what they were speaking about. Lord Langdale perhaps and where he'd gone? Or was Lady Astley in the market for a new lover? A man she presumed to be the countess's groom waited a discreet distance away on his own horse.

Either way, it was none of her business what the woman wanted. Lord Malverne had made his position abundantly clear. He felt no more for little Sophie Brightwell than the passing lust he'd feel for a mistress. He didn't really care about her. His regard was superficial. She was merely his sister's friend. An acquaintance.

She had no claim on him. None at all. Which meant that, somehow, she needed to ignore the stab of jealousy that pierced her heart when Lady Astley laid her hand on Nate again. *Lord Malverne*, she mentally amended. She must not think of him in such familiar terms anymore.

Dashing away a fresh rush of tears with a gloved hand, Sophie decided she didn't want to watch the intimate exchange a moment longer. There was a well-worn path running through the thick copse, and bluebells nodded along the edge. If she took Aurora that way, she could then circle the trees before heading back to Lord Malverne. Perhaps Lady Astley would have moved on by then. As much as she wanted to be by herself, she wasn't silly enough to ride all the way back to Berkeley Square on her own.

She steered Aurora into the trees. Save for the warbling of a blackbird, it was very quiet in the shade. And cool. A shiver ran over Sophie, raising the hair at her nape at the exact same moment that Aurora's ears flicked back and forth. Shying to one side of the path, the mare tossed her head, her nostrils flaring. And then a low growl suddenly emanated from the bushes.

Aurora reared and screamed as two mongrel dogs hurtled onto the path. Barking, their teeth bared and their eyes wild, they lunged.

Oh, God! Somehow, Sophie held on as the mare bolted, the dogs snapping at her hooves. A man shouted, perhaps at the dogs, but it was impossible to tell as Aurora was flying down the path and then across the grass, straight toward a hedgerow.

Oh no! It is too high.

Her heart in her mouth, Sophie leaned low, preparing herself for the jump. She closed her eyes as Aurora cleared the hedge, but as the mare landed heavily, Sophie lost her seat and hit the ground hard on her rump.

All the air was knocked out of her in a huge whoosh, and when she tried to lift her head, the world spun. Black spots danced before her eyes, and she gasped for air like she was drowning.

"Miss Brightwell!"

Nate? Is Nate here already? Sophie shook her head, trying to clear it, but it was to no avail. She couldn't see straight.

"Miss Brightwell, here, duck your head down," the man urged gently, a hand at her back. His deep voice was vaguely familiar, but right at this moment, Sophie couldn't place it. "It will help you to catch your breath."

Sophie did as he suggested, and very soon, the gasping and wheezing subsided and she felt as if she could actually breathe properly again.

"That's it," murmured the man, and when Sophie looked up, it was into the soft blue gray eyes of Lord Claremont.

"My lord . . . ," she whispered. "What . . . what are you doing here?"

Lord Claremont smiled. "At the moment, rescuing a pretty dark-haired damsel in distress. But before, I was doing much the same as you, I expect—enjoying the lovely morning by taking a jaunt around Hyde Park."

Sophie frowned and pushed her hair out of her eyes. Somewhere along the way, she'd lost her hat. "Is my horse all right? She was startled by some dreadful dogs."

The viscount gestured toward the bridle path. Aurora was standing beneath an oak tree by a smart-looking phaeton. "She seems fine," he said. "But when I saw your fall, I must confess, I was more worried about *you*, Miss Brightwell."

Sophie attempted a smile. "Thank you." She really didn't know what else to say. She was too light-headed and heartsore from Nate's rejection to really think about the significance, or otherwise, of Lord Claremont's unanticipated intervention.

"Well," said Lord Claremont, sitting back on his heels. "Perhaps we should get you up." He placed a hand beneath one of her elbows. "Do you think you can sta—"

"Sophie. Sweet Jesus!" Nate was sliding off a still-moving Invictus when she looked up. Within a flash, he was on his knees, at her side, tilting her chin up, examining her face. "Are you all right? I heard those dogs and Aurora."

"I'm . . . I'm fine," she murmured, turning her head away. She couldn't deal with Nate's concern right now. Now that she knew she didn't mean anything to him. Not really.

He put an arm around her back. "Here, lean on me—"

"No," she said firmly. "I can manage." She attempted to push herself up without help from either Nate or Lord Claremont, but as she put her weight on her left wrist, she cried out in pain.

"You're hurt," declared Nate, lifting her left arm with great care.

"It would seem so," added Claremont wryly.

Nate shot him a narrow-eyed look. "I haven't seen you around town in a while, Claremont."

"No. But I'm here now."

"Gentlemen, my apologies for interrupting, but might I stand? I should like to go home."

"Of course," said Lord Claremont.

Both he and Nate helped her to her feet, and then Nate gently pushed up the sleeve of her azure blue riding habit. He frowned. "I think your wrist is beginning to swell a little. I hope there are no broken bones."

Before Sophie could protest, Nate had loosened his cravat and tugged it from his neck. The fabric was still warm from his body heat as he began to wrap it gently around her wrist. "When we get back to Hastings House, I'll send for the physician." He raised his eyes to her face. "Do you think you can ride?"

Sophie bit her lip to stifle a whimper of pain as Nate continued to bind her wrist. "I'm not sure. I still feel a little dizzy . . ."

Lord Claremont cleared his throat. "Perhaps I could be of assistance. My phaeton is just over there. I would be more than happy to take you."

Sophie smiled. "That would be greatly appreciated."

"That's good of you, Claremont."

Ignoring Nate, the viscount inclined his head to Sophie. "It's the least I can do, Miss Brightwell." He raised an eyebrow as Nate tied off the makeshift bandage. "If you're done, Malverne . . ."

Nate tilted his head and took a small step away. His gaze touched Sophie's. "I am. I'll take care of Aurora. I'll see you at home." And with that, he turned on his heel, mounted Invictus, and then went to retrieve Aurora, who was now quietly cropping the grass.

Lord Claremont settled Sophie in his phaeton, and after claiming the seat beside her, he flicked the reins, and the horses were off at a gentle trot.

"I've been meaning to talk to you, Miss Brightwell. About the Penriths' spring ball and . . . and my absence from town. I only returned yesterday."

Sophie's wrist was now throbbing, and she had to hold on to one side of the phaeton with her good arm to help maintain her perch, but nevertheless, she cast Lord Claremont a look of interest. "To be honest, I didn't know you'd been away."

"You must have thought me terribly rude then. And I do apologize for not sending word, but I'd only just met you . . ." Lord Claremont's thigh brushed against hers as they rounded a gentle corner. "You see, my poor mother took ill. In fact she's been gravely unwell. After I bade you farewell at Penrith House, I returned home to find a courier had arrived with a letter, informing me of my mother's decline and the urgent need for me to return to my estate in Hertfordshire."

"I'm so sorry, my lord." Sophie's heart clenched. "I can't even imagine how awful that must have been for you. May I ask how your mother fares now?"

"I'm pleased to say she is much improved and well on the way to making a full recovery."

"Oh, I'm so glad to hear that."

Lord Claremont's gaze caught hers. "You see, the thing is, Miss Brightwell, I had wanted to send you flowers the day after the ball, and to begin calling on you. But fate conspired against me. And now I wonder if I'm too late . . ."

"What do you mean?" Sophie breathed.

Lord Claremont paused as he concentrated on steering his phaeton into the traffic on Park Lane. "Well, after witnessing Lord Malverne's deep concern for you just before, I rather wondered if I might have a rival for your affections after all?"

Sophie's heart did a strange little somersault. What should she say? From what she'd seen, she *liked* Lord Claremont, but her heart belonged to Nate.

Only he didn't want it . . .

"I . . . I do believe Lord Malverne has no interest in courting me," she said at last.

Lord Claremont's grin was brighter than the spring sunshine glancing off his silver waistcoat buttons. "So there's hope for me yet, Miss Brightwell?"

Sophie blushed. Lord Claremont was not only a lovely man, he was titled, wealthy, and handsome. He clearly cared about others, especially his mother. And despite his rakish reputation, he'd always behaved as a gentleman ought to in her company. Indeed, he met every criterion on

the list the Society for Enlightened Young Women had created. So she would be foolish to discourage his suit,
wouldn't she?

If Nate was not for her, then she really should give
someone else a chance to win her heart. She returned his
smile. "Yes, there's hope."

"Then I am a happy man indeed."

Sophie blushed again and turned her gaze to the passing
traffic and town houses. She should feel abuzz with happiness but she didn't. Perhaps it was the pain of her injured
wrist, or perhaps it was the pain of her wounded heart and
her dented pride that was dampening her spirits.

But beneath all that, Sophie had the awful feeling there
was more than a little bit of guilt pinching at her. Should
she really be encouraging Lord Claremont if her heart
wasn't truly free to give?

*Goodness, Sophie. You barely know the man. Surely
there's no harm in giving him a chance. And there's no
sense in pining away for Nate. You've given him ample op-
portunities to stake a claim. But he doesn't want to. You will
not be a victim of unrequited love for the rest of your days.*

CHAPTER 18

❧

The Beau Monde Mirror has it on good authority
that a certain viscount—one who has only recently
returned to the capital—might have his sights set
on one of the infamous Disreputable Debutantes!

It seems there is no accounting for taste. Perhaps
love is blind after all . . .

The Beau Monde Mirror: The Society Page

Hastings House, Berkeley Square, Mayfair

April 25, 1818

Malverne, do you mind if I have a word?
Nate scowled as he recalled the conversation he'd
had with Lord Bloody Claremont not more than five minutes ago in this very room. The viscount had gone, but
Nate's foul mood remained. He poured himself another
glass of whisky, downed it in one gulp as he'd done with the
first, and then poured a third.

Throwing himself into the leather wing chair before the
drawing room fire, he then loosened his damnably tight
cravat.

God, he was still acting like a lovesick schoolboy. No,
not lovesick, because he wasn't *in* love. He was in lust with
Sophie Brightwell and, like the dog that he was, he simply
didn't want another man sniffing around the female he
wanted to bed.

Malverne, do you mind if I have a word? What a completely innocuous way to begin a conversation about whether
he would oppose Claremont's pursuit of Sophie.

Of course, for all his misplaced rancor, he wasn't going to.

Nate sighed and placed the cool crystal glass against his
hot forehead. The light was fading and he probably should
go upstairs, ring for his valet, and then head out to White's
or Boodle's or even some back-alley gaming hell. He was
in a filthy, reckless mood, and drinking, heavy gambling,
and fucking would be the only remedy to rid himself of it,
of that he was certain.

"Lord Malverne?"

Shit. Sophie.

Nate straightened and stood. "Miss Brightwell."

"I'm sorry to disturb you, my lord. I just came to
retrieve . . . my book," she said with a weak smile. Her fingers pleated the sprigged muslin of her skirts, and she
wouldn't meet his eyes. She looked uncomfortable. Uncertain. He didn't blame her one bit for being hesitant.

He'd rejected her yesterday. For her own good, he'd told
himself. While he still firmly believed that he was doing
the "right and honorable thing," it didn't make him feel any
better.

He was sure his foul mood radiated from him like heat
radiated from hell.

As his inner demons continued to wage war, he dredged
up an equable voice and said, "You're not disturbing me."

But that was a lie. He was a mess. He'd never felt more
disturbed in his life.

Sophie nodded and crossed to the other side of the
hearth and picked up her book, *Sense and Sensibility*. It lay
beside an enormous arrangement of pale pink roses framed
by soft green feathery ferns; Claremont had sent the flowers
this morning along with a card that still lay nestled in between the blooms. Nate took another sip of his drink to
conceal a snarl. The courtship had begun before Claremont
had even spoken to him.

"How is your wrist?" he asked when Sophie didn't

immediately quit the room. She hovered by the flowers, trailing her fingertips through the ferns. The white bandage was bright against the dark gleaming mahogany of the tabletop.

"Sore," she replied. "But improving."

"I'm glad." The physician had diagnosed a simple sprain, which he predicted would be completely healed within a few weeks.

"Thank you." Sophie stroked a soft pink petal and Nate swallowed. Bloody hell, he really shouldn't focus on her fingers or what she could do with them. Or her lips. She was currently abusing the plump, delectable flesh with her teeth. He was bound to become aroused. Again.

He dragged his gaze from her mouth, and at the same moment, she looked up too. Their eyes locked. For one long moment they stared at each other, the air crackling with tension, but it was Sophie who was brave enough to break the silence.

"Lord Claremont has asked me if he might pay court. He's writing to my stepfather to seek his permission, and I understand he's spoken to your father as well."

"Yes. I know. He spoke with me too."

Sophie nodded and dropped her gaze back to her book. Her fingers curled around the leather cover. "I told him that he might."

"I'm glad." It was a lie this time, but he couldn't think of anything else to say.

"Well then." Sophie took her book and tucked it beneath her slender arm. "I shall leave you to . . ." She glanced at his drink. "I shall leave you. Good evening, my lord."

She bobbed a curtsy as if she were a stranger and turned to go.

She was at the door when something inside him made him call out, "Sophie, wait."

She stopped and turned, a question in her beautiful blue eyes. It hurt to see there was no hope. Bastard that he was, he'd clearly done a wonderful job at killing that.

"I feel as though . . . At the risk of creating further discord . . ." He ran a hand through his hair in frustration.

What was it that he wanted to say to her? Why was he pro-
longing this agonizing interaction? It wouldn't do either of
them any good. He certainly didn't want to give Sophie false
hope. But she needed to forget him and move on. And he
should at least explain why. Surely he owed her that much.

Yes, he needed to make her understand why there was
no hope for him.

For them.

"Please. Won't you come back? We need to talk."

Sophie studied Nate—she'd given up trying to think of
him as Lord Malverne anymore—and considered his
request. She was trying so very hard to distance herself
from him just as he'd been doing with her.

But there was something about his manner tonight that
gave her pause to reject him outright. He seemed on edge.
His waistcoat was rumpled, he wasn't wearing a coat, and
his cravat was loose. His chestnut hair was more than artfully tousled; it was messy as though he'd raked frustrated
fingers through it too many times.

And then there were the dark shadows of fatigue beneath his equally dark, somber eyes.

She nodded and closed the door. "Very well."

She returned to the fireside and selected a bergère with
gilt legs that was directly opposite Nate's wing chair. Only
a hearthrug separated them, but to Sophie, it may as well
have been a vast, stormy sea.

She placed her book very carefully on the side table by
her elbow and nursed her sore wrist in her right hand. And
she waited.

Nate reclaimed his wing chair and studied the contents
of his tumbler for a long moment. "Can I get you anything,
Sophie?" he asked, raising his glass.

She shook her head. "No. Thank you."

He nodded, sipped his drink, and then placed it on the
table by his elbow. Then his eyes met hers. "I want to explain
to you why I am the way I am. I thought if you understood,
then perhaps it might be easier . . . for you."

Sophie's grip tightened on her sore wrist. Of course she had a million questions about why he thought he was incapable of feeling love for a woman. It was evident that he loved Charlie and his aunt. She was certain he loved his younger brothers. She even suspected he loved his father, although the relationship oftentimes appeared strained—from what she'd observed at any rate.

There was some kind of impenetrable barrier inside him. A fortification around his heart. And in his mind.

Perhaps he might inadvertently give her a clue that would help her to knock it down. Or at least expose a crack that would allow her to sneak inside.

Stop, Sophie. Don't you dare hope. You've shed too many tears over Lord Malverne already.

But she could at least hear him out.

She raised her chin. "All right. I will listen."

Nate winced at her cool manner, but she couldn't help the way she felt.

From now on, she needed to guard her heart too.

He picked up his drink again and took another sip, as though fortifying himself. "You already know about my illiteracy," he began. "And how my older brother Thomas helped me to overcome it to some extent."

Sophie nodded. "Yes."

He sighed and ran a hand down his face. "You see, I firmly believe there is only so much pain a heart can bear. And my heart"—he placed a large hand, fingers splayed, against his chest—"cannot take any more, Sophie. It's wounded beyond repair."

He took another swig of the spirit he was drinking and bared his teeth in a grimace. "Has Charlie told you about our older brother Thomas? How he died?"

She nodded. "A little. She said . . . she said he drowned. When you were thirteen."

Nate's face twisted for a moment before he raised his glass again. When he spoke, his voice was thick with emotion. With grief. "When Thomas died, I thought I might die. I *wished* I had died. Because it was my fault he drowned. And everything that occurred after that was my fault too."

Sophie's heart cramped at witnessing Nate's pain. "What happened?" she whispered. "If you can bear to tell me."

Nate leaned forward, his forearms resting on his muscular thighs, and he turned his glass back and forth, back and forth between his palms, watching the golden brown liquid swill and splash. "Even though Thomas died fourteen years ago, to me it feels as if it happened only yesterday. At the end of that summer, before we were due to go back to Eton, there was a spell of terrible weather. It had been raining for days and days, and the river that ran beside Elmstone Hall, the Severn, was swollen, fit to burst."

Nate paused, staring into the fire, and Sophie waited. She didn't want to rush him. Not when the haunted look in his eyes made her heart weep and she hadn't even heard the worst.

"I've mentioned before I've always been restless, not one to sit still for long," he said at last, "and I was much worse as a youth. I hated being confined indoors, so as soon as the rain stopped, I persuaded Thomas to accompany me on a ride. Fool that I was, despite Thomas's warnings, I got too close to the edge of the bank—it had been weakened by all the rain—and it broke. Disintegrated. My horse and I both went in and . . ." Nate swallowed and pinched the bridge of his nose. "My horse got swept away but I managed to grab hold of a tree that had been uprooted and had fallen in the river a little farther downstream. I begged Thomas to go and get help. But he refused to. He told me it would be too late. The current was so swift. Deadly. And I was barely holding on to a branch that was threatening to break."

Sophie blinked away tears but again didn't say a word. She didn't want to interrupt.

Nate shook his head and he drained the rest of his drink. "Thomas dismounted and crawled along the log. Reached out and pulled me to safety. But as I clambered up higher . . ." He shook his head again. "I don't quite know what happened, whether I bumped him, or he overbalanced, I just don't know. But Thomas fell in. And when I realized and tried to grab his hand, it was too late. He was gone. He went under. I couldn't see him. He was dragged away."

"Oh, Nate. I am so, so sorry." Sophie wanted to reach out her hand to him, but she feared he would reject her touch. Instead she nursed her sore wrist and tried to swallow back her own tears.

Nate sighed and wiped a shaking hand across his mouth. "They found Thomas a day later. He'd been washed three miles downstream. Along with my horse." He raised his stark gaze to Sophie. "Everyone insisted it was an accident. That it wasn't my fault. But it was. If I had listened to Thomas . . . He was my brother and I loved him. But it was his love for me that ended him."

"I can't even imagine what you've lived through, Nate," Sophie whispered.

He gave her a wry smile. "I'm afraid my sad tale doesn't end there. Nor for the rest of my family."

She didn't want to see Nate suffer any more, but she sensed he needed to share his burden. "I'll listen to whatever you wish to tell me."

He nodded and his chest swelled before he released a shaky sigh. "When our mother found out what had happened—she was pregnant with the twins, Daniel and Benjamin—she went into labor. It was the shock, I expect, of losing Thomas. And . . . the labor did not go well for her. A month after the birth, she died of a terrible fever. The doctor explained it was a relatively common complication. But I can't help but think . . ." He swallowed and shook his head, unable to go on.

Oh no. Sophie bit her lip to stop a sob from escaping.

Several minutes passed and then Nate spoke in a voice so low, Sophie had to lean forward to catch his words. "My father, he loved my mother, deeply. Although he's never blamed me for what happened to her, either, I cannot help but feel responsible. She died of a broken heart, *because* of me. And my father has never been the same since."

"What do you mean?"

"Since her passing, he works himself to the bone. Whether it's managing his estates, his business ventures, or parliamentary affairs, it doesn't matter. As far as I'm aware, he doesn't keep a mistress. And he's never courted another woman. He's a shell of a man. His heart is broken. And witnessing his sorrow, his pain, has made me realize that I could not endure the loss of the woman I loved. The cost is too high. I've already lost so much and witnessed the people I care about suffer great loss too." Nate caught her gaze. "I would understand if you think me a coward, Sophie, but I cannot afford to fall in love. The loss of it would surely destroy me."

Sophie didn't know what to say. Words seemed so inadequate to express how she was feeling, and what she was thinking. She wanted to offer Nate comfort. She wanted to persuade him that the tragedies that had befallen his family really weren't his fault. He clearly held a deeply ingrained belief that denying himself love was the only way he could survive. It was a bizarre form of self-preservation.

But love could also heal, couldn't it?

She cleared her throat and said the only thing she could think of that wouldn't result in a vehement denial. "Nate, there's one thing I know to be true about you. You are not a coward. You are fiercely loyal to those you care about, and I could never judge you for your past, or your choices." She drew a breath and continued before she lost her nerve. "And I also firmly believe you are a good man, despite what you think about yourself."

Nate gave her a sad smile. "We both know I'm not good, Sophie. I try to be, but I'm not. I'm a walking disaster. I drink too much to help me sleep at night. I live the life of an abandoned rakehell. And I have taken advantage of you, but you are too good and sweet to admit it."

"I suppose we must agree to disagree on that score then," Sophie said gently.

Nate inclined his head. A smile tugged at the corner of his mouth. "Yes. At least we can agree on that."

"Good." Sophie didn't know what else to say, so she rose and tucked her book under her arm. "Thank you, Nate, for confiding in me to help me understand. I can see how much such disclosures pain you, and I'm deeply honored that you trust me. I promise not to share your secrets with anyone else."

"Thank you." Nate rose too. "I do trust you, Sophie. And I wish you well."

"And I, you."

It wasn't until Sophie closed the drawing room door behind her that she let the tears flow unheeded. Tears for Nate and everything that he'd lost. And tears for her own loss too.

As soon as the door closed, Nate poured himself another whisky with shaking hands. He couldn't recall the last time he'd ever bared his soul like that to anyone. It was terrifying to revisit such devastation. Harrowing.

He felt as if he'd been keelhauled.

But at least Sophie had been able to catch a glimpse of how damaged he was. Hopefully now she would be able to forget him and start anew with Claremont.

It was only when he'd returned to his seat that another thought occurred to him as his gaze snagged on the roses Lord Claremont had sent. Sophie hadn't asked the staff to place them in her room. And she hadn't taken the card Claremont had written just for her either . . .

Nate smirked. Yesterday, Sophie had accused him of being an ass, and perhaps he was. Not only that, he was undoubtedly a perverse prick, because the fact that Sophie had left Claremont's roses and his love note here made him smile.

CHAPTER 19

The perennial question on every debutante's mind is how does one ensure one is the epitome of grace, style, and propriety at all times during the Season? Whatever the occasion—morning calls, dinner parties, an evening at the theater, balls, or the gayest of soirees—rest assured you will only be noticed for the *right* reasons if you adhere to our recommendations on fashion, deportment, and manners.

The Beau Monde Mirror:
The Essential Style and Etiquette Guide

Hastings House, Berkeley Square, Mayfair

May 9, 1818

"Oh, Miss Brightwell, aren't these blooms gorgeous?" declared Lady Chelmsford as she swept into the drawing room. Her eyes glowed with appreciation as she took in the huge bunch of yellow roses gracing one of the mahogany tables. "Your Lord Claremont is quite the charmer, isn't he?"

"Yes, he certainly is," agreed Charlie, looking up from the game of loo she and Sophie were playing. "Since he's begun unabashedly courting Sophie, he sends a new arrangement every few days. I'm expecting some exciting news any day now." She threw Sophie a knowing smile, which, much like the roses, Sophie tried to ignore.

Sophie simply smiled in agreement at Lady Chelmsford's pronouncement about the flowers and Lord Claremont's charm; the marchioness had arrived earlier, and while they waited for the tea trolley to arrive, she'd paid a visit to see her brother, Lord Westhampton, who was ensconced in the library, working on a new bill for Parliament. Nate, as usual, was "out" somewhere.

In fact, since the evening he shared his harrowing past with her, she'd barely seen him. Which was all for the best, really. The less she saw him, the easier it would be to forget him. *Such a pity it isn't working.*

She sighed as she halfheartedly played her cards. Not for the first time over the last fortnight, guilt pricked at Sophie's conscience. Lord Claremont—Matthew—was lovely. Wonderful. She should be thinking only of him and giddy with excitement when she did. But she wasn't giddy, and her thoughts kept straying to another viscount. And therein lay the source of her disquiet and her moral dilemma.

Of course, she couldn't fault Lord Claremont's behavior or the manner of his gentle wooing. Since he'd openly declared his intentions to court her, he'd been very attentive. The perfect gentlemanly suitor.

Nearly every day for the past two weeks, she'd seen him. There were numerous chaperoned walks and carriage rides, as well as afternoon teas with Lady Chelmsford at her house, here at Hastings House, and at Gunter's, and he'd spent a delightful evening with her, Lord Westhampton, and Charlie at the theater. Indeed, today was the first day that they hadn't made any plans to see each other, and if Sophie was honest with herself, she was more than a little relieved. She very much needed time to herself to reflect upon recent events. A quiet interlude to examine her feelings.

As the days passed, she knew it wouldn't be long before Lord Claremont tried to kiss her, and then he might even offer for her hand. But the problem was, instead of feeling a thrill of anticipation, she was beset by an attack of jangled nerves.

Closing her eyes, Sophie touched one of her playing

cards to her lips as an unbidden memory of Nate's kisses surfaced. Of the exhilaration that had flooded her. The all-consuming intoxication. Would it feel like that when Lord Claremont pressed his mouth to hers? Dear Lord, she hoped so. She kept telling herself that, in time, love and desire would grow, that when her bruised heart healed, she might begin to feel differently.

But what if she was wrong?

The thought weighed heavily, hanging over her like a dark storm cloud threatening rain on a summer's day.

The morning tea trolley arrived, and after Lady Chelmsford took charge and dispensed everyone's tea according to their specifications, talk turned to the latest gossip about town—rumor had it that Lady Astley had taken another lover, but no one knew who it was. Sophie prayed it wasn't Nate. Not that she could complain. He had the right to see whomever he wanted, precisely as she was doing.

Sophie had just politely declined another piece of cinnamon tea cake—she'd lost her appetite of late—when the butler arrived with the morning's post and a neat bundle of papers.

"Oh, here's something from Arabella," declared Charlie. She cracked the wax seal on the travel-stained parchment and opened the letter. "'My dearest Charlie, Sophie, and Olivia,'" she read, "'I trust you are all well and, by now, I'm sure each of you has more than one eligible (perhaps even rakish) gentleman well and truly wound around your finger.'" Charlie threw Sophie a mischievous look over the top of the page. "Well, in your case, my friend, she's quite correct."

Because Lady Chelmsford was now busily sorting through the correspondence, Sophie poked her tongue out at Charlie. "What else does she say?"

"It seems she's having a marvelous time. She writes, 'I must confess, despite my reluctance to embark on this grand tour, I have been enjoying myself more than I thought I would. Of course, my cousin Lilias and Aunt Flora are their usual exacting selves. But aside from their myriad complaints about the lumpy inn beds and poorly sprung carriages, they certainly haven't been stingy when it comes to experiencing the cultural delights on offer in Paris. I absolutely adored the Louvre Museum and Aunt Flora even let me visit the much lauded foundling hospital, l'Hôpital des Enfants-Trouvés; wonders will never cease! Although the Place de la Concorde and our tour of the Conciergerie made me shiver with horror . . . '" Charlie turned the page. "Oh, it seems they'll be making their way to Switzerland very soon. Once there, they have plans to visit Montreux on Lake Geneva to see Château de Chillon and its famous dungeon too. I am so envious."

Sophie was a little envious too. Ever since she'd read Lord Byron's poem about the lakeside medieval castle, she'd wanted to see it. "Does she give her direction so we might send her our latest news?"

"Yes she does. And yes, we should." Charlie sent her a smile. "I certainly think she'd be thrilled to hear Lord Claremont is courting you in earnest. And that our plan for catching rakes is at least working for you."

Sophie shrugged a shoulder. "I think a healthy dose of luck has come into play in my case."

"Oh, pooh. That's nonsense." Charlie passed her Arabella's letter. "We should call on Olivia so she can read this. And, Aunt Tabitha, if you could spare the time to come along, too, we might even be able to persuade the de Veres to let her out of her gilded Grosvenor Square cage for an excursion."

Lady Chelmsford put down a gilt-edged invitation and peered at her niece over her silver lorgnette. "That sounds like an excellent idea." She sorted through a few more letters, then held one out to Sophie. "Miss Brightwell, there seems to be a missive here for you."

Sophie's heart leapt. Was it a reply from the publisher Mr. Murray? However, as soon as she caught sight of the neatly written script, she knew it was another letter from home. There seemed to be one every second day, saying the same things. Asking the same questions. Sophie winced as she read her mother's effusive words about Lord Claremont again. Ever since the viscount had sought her stepfather's permission to court her, her mother had been over the moon. Sophie supposed she couldn't blame her for being excited at the thought that her lowly born daughter—one who'd been stained with notoriety—might become a viscountess. Her elevation in fortunes would help the whole family. Apparently, Lord Buxton's demands for payment of the money her stepfather owed had become more insistent of late. So her mother was no doubt hoping Lord Claremont would be able to help out in that regard.

Sophie grimaced. Poor Matthew. He was courting a girl with no dowry whose family was in debt.

"Bad news?" asked Charlie. She must have noticed Sophie's pained expression.

"Only the usual. Lord Buxton keeps hounding my stepfather to settle his debt."

Charlie frowned. "You've never mentioned how much your stepfather actually *does* owe him."

Sophie winced. "I believe it's two thousand pounds."

Charlie's frown deepened. "I thought they were friends."

"They are. However, I suppose even a friend couldn't easily overlook *that* amount."

"Yes . . ."

Charlie glanced at her aunt, who now seemed engrossed in the *Times*. "You know, I'm sure my father, and perhaps even Aunt Tabitha, could assist if needed," she murmured.

"No. No you mustn't say anything. Your family has already been more than generous, having me here and paying for my debut."

Charlie nodded, the expression in her eyes earnest. "All right then. But please know we are always here to help."

"Thank you."

"And who knows"—Charlie's eyes danced with mischief—"perhaps there is a certain viscount who might be able to lend a hand too."

Again that unmistakable pinch in the vicinity of her chest. "Yes."

Sophie bent her head to read Arabella's letter but she could barely focus on the words. It seemed the mantle of guilt shrouding her was growing heavier by the day.

The Mayfair Bluestocking Society, Park Lane

May 11, 1818

Dust motes drifted in the sunlit air filtering through the wide casement windows into the upper-floor studio of Fifty-five Park Lane, the graciously appointed rooms rented by the Mayfair Bluestocking Society.

Seated beside Lady Chelmsford on a plush velvet settee, Sophie—still mindful of her healing wrist—watched with avid fascination as Charlie and Olivia danced back and forth across the polished beechwood floor with light-footed grace, their white calf-length skirts flaring with their movements, the blades of their silver foils flashing. All was quiet save for their soft pants of exertion, the slide of supple kid leather half boots on the floorboards, and the synchronous rasp of colliding blades.

"Olivia is doing very well, isn't she?" Sophie whispered to Lady Chelmsford. She didn't wish to spoil her friends' concentration midround, nor provoke a censorious glare from the steely-eyed fencing master, Signor Santoro, who stood by one of the windows as straight as a soldier with his hands behind his back. Charlie had warned her that he could be quite the martinet.

"Yes, she certainly is," the marchioness replied, sotto voce, behind her purple silk fan. "I'm so pleased her dragon of an aunt acquiesced to the outing. I know I stretched the truth a little when I told Mrs. de Vere you would all be helping me to put parcels of clothing and blankets together for the poor. But considering poor Olivia is a veritable prisoner in her own home, I think she deserves a jolly good dose of fun instead."

Sophie nodded. "I do not know how she abides such an existence."

"Neither do I, my dear Miss Brightwell. Neither do I."

They watched Charlie expertly dodge an aggressive thrust by Olivia before she elegantly lunged forward in a neat countermove. The blossom-tipped end of Charlie's foil touched her friend's quilted satin waistcoat, and Olivia froze.

"Touché. The point goes to Lady Charlotte," declared Signor Santoro with an emphatic nod of his head. "And thus she wins the match."

Sophie and Lady Chelmsford applauded as the middle-aged Italian fencing master indicated that Charlie and Olivia should salute each other with their swords.

"And may I say, *brava*, Miss de Vere." Signor Santoro's mouth lifted into an unexpected smile beneath his curling waxed moustache as Olivia and Charlie shook hands. "Lady Charlotte is one of my best female students, and you held your own for a good deal of the match."

Olivia pushed a dark lock away from her flushed cheek. "Th-thank you, signore. But I'm sure Charlie was just being kind."

"Pfft. I assure you I wasn't." Charlie's forehead creased into a frown as she tugged off one of her white kid gloves. "But tell me, who were you thinking of skewering in the second round? That was a rather impressive thrust. I didn't even have time to think about parrying it."

"Yes," agreed Sophie, rising to her feet and crossing the floor to her friends. "You were lightning quick, Olivia. I'm glad I wasn't facing you. I'm sure I would have lost a limb."

Olivia's blush deepened. "I was thinking about my horrid cousin F-Felix," she murmured. "He's down from Cambridge at the moment. He's just so . . . temperamental. And trying. I wish he would leave." She shuddered, then reached out to touch Charlie's arm. "I apologize if I hurt you."

Charlie hugged her. "Don't be a peagoose. Of course you didn't."

Signor Santoro twirled the end of his moustache while giving Olivia a thoughtful look. "Miss de Vere, you must have received some instruction before, no? You are too skilled to be a complete novice."

Olivia smiled shyly. "Yes, I have, signore. But it's been quite a while since I trained, so I'm afraid I'm rather rusty."

"Aha, I knew it," exclaimed Charlie, tugging off her other glove. "Who taught you? Confess."

"My f-father. He served in the military before I was

born." Olivia dropped her gaze and poked the toe of her boot with her foil before she added softly, "He believed all young women should learn to fence to improve their flexibility and posture. My mama used to fence too. I was twelve when I had my first lesson."

"Your parents were very wise, my dear Miss de Vere," said Lady Chelmsford gently. She rose from the settee and thanked Signor Santoro for his time. "Now, I suggest you two gels change into your day gowns and then we shall all repair to Gunter's for tea and cakes. Ordinarily I'd suggest we take tea at Chelmsford House, but I'm afraid Cook is in a dither about tonight's dinner party." She gave Sophie a little nudge. "I'm pleased to say your Lord Claremont is coming."

Sophie wanted to say that he wasn't really *her* Lord Claremont. But since he'd begun courting her in earnest, she supposed that, in a way, he really was.

As she trailed after Charlie and Olivia into the nearby changing rooms, her thoughts strayed to the evening ahead. Lady Chelmsford had invited Nate to her dinner party, but she doubted he would come.

Indeed, she had no idea what Nate really thought about Lord Claremont's pursuit. Or if he even cared. He'd told her he was glad the viscount was courting her when she'd first mentioned it to him, and she had no reason to believe he'd changed his mind.

None at all. His ongoing indifference hurt more than it should.

Why was her silly heart so, so stubborn? If only she could skewer her feelings for Nate. Excise every thought of him from her mind.

Sophie gave herself a mental shake as she helped Olivia with the ties at the back of her day gown. She really needed to stop thinking about Nate. But perhaps tonight, Lord Claremont would kiss her and sweep her off her feet, and she would never think of Nate again.

A small, melancholy sigh escaped her. *If only that were so.*

Chelmsford House, Park Lane, Mayfair

"Miss Brightwell, I've been meaning to tell you how lovely you look this evening. The blue of your gown suits you very well."

Warmth flooded Sophie's cheeks as Lord Claremont's gaze drifted over her with frank admiration. Beneath the mahogany card table, his muscular leg brushed against hers, and her blush deepened.

"Thank you, my lord," she murmured. Seated in a quiet corner of Lady Chelmsford's drawing room, they were playing a postprandial game of piquet while their hostess and the other dinner party guests—twelve in total including Charlie and Lord Westhampton—lingered over their tea, sherry, and port by the fireside, or gathered around the pianoforte, where Lady Penrith played a delicate minuet.

But not Nate.

He'd sent his apologies to his aunt sometime during the afternoon. In Sophie's opinion his excuse was quite feeble. He'd apparently only just recalled a prior engagement with the Duke of Exmoor—a night at the theater—but Aunt Tabitha had accepted it with good grace.

Sophie had tried very hard to ignore the dip of disappointment deep inside her when she learned that, yet again, she wouldn't be seeing him. But as soon as she arrived at Chelmsford House, she decided she would have a marvelous time anyway. When Lord Claremont greeted her with enthusiasm, and smiled in that disarming way of his as he chatted to her during dinner, she did begin to relax and enjoy herself. Perhaps a little too much.

She dropped a card onto the table and frowned. How much champagne had she drunk tonight? Four glasses or three? Surely not five . . .

Squinting at her cards, Sophie tried to decide which ones to keep and which to discard. Indeed, she was finding it a challenge to focus on the game right at this moment, and she couldn't quite recall whether she was the younger or elder hand.

Younger. You are the younger hand, Sophie. You need to pick up the cards left in the talon. Blast this befuddlement assailing her. How would she ever keep track of her points when she couldn't even recall how many glasses of champagne she'd had? To make matters worse, she'd quite foolishly accepted a glass of sherry from Lord Claremont when they sat down to play. She really should have asked for tea.

"Sophie—you don't mind if I use your first name, do you?—have you finished choosing?"

Sophie glanced at Lord Claremont over the top of her cards, and he smiled so warmly at her, it was clear he didn't seem to mind that she was as soused as a tipsy cake. "Um . . . not quite."

She hastily picked up several cards from the talon and sighed—all useless spades and no additional face cards; she probably should have called carte blanche. And then Lord Claremont's knee pressed against hers again and she smiled to herself. Perhaps her considerate suitor wasn't going to be *quite* the perfect gentleman tonight. If only he would take her out to the terrace and push her up against the wall and ravish her until she couldn't think straight . . . And make her forget all about Nate.

Ugh. Nate.

Her frustration must have shown on her face because when she discarded her final card, the knave of hearts, Lord Claremont reached out and covered her bare hand with his. She smiled as she examined his long, well-shaped fingers. She liked it whenever he discreetly touched her elbow, her waist, or her hand. Indeed, she'd felt a glimmer of *something* when his fingers had brushed hers as he'd passed her a glass of sherry earlier.

Sliding her hand from Lord Claremont's, she took another sip of the smooth wine. No doubt the alcohol was helping her to relax. To let her guard down. Strange how the warm, fuzzy feeling suffusing her body right now was akin to the sensation of falling in love.

Perhaps I am . . .

Oh, she really wanted to fall in love with Lord Claremont. She stared into his blue gray eyes, trying to focus on what he was saying. Something about going outside to take a turn about the terrace. The need to take the air?

"Yesssh. I mean, yes." Sophie put down her cards with deliberate care. "That sounds like a wonderful idea, Lord Claremont."

The viscount stood and offered his arm. "You know, I would be most honored if you called me Matthew, dear Sophie," he murmured by her ear as she rose.

"Of course." Everything was a little out of kilter for a brief moment, and Sophie was grateful for Lord Claremont's support as she slipped her hand into the crook of his strong arm. She tipped her head back and smiled. "Matthew."

He patted her hand and led her on a sedate progress across the room until they reached the open French doors leading out to the terrace. When Sophie glanced back to the group about the fireside, Lady Chelmsford inclined her head and Charlie gave her a most unladylike wink. Lord Westhampton, who was deep in conversation with Lord Penrith, hadn't noticed where Lord Claremont was taking her.

Oh, well. She had the consent of one of her chaperones. And really, how much mischief could Lord Claremont really get up to when the doors were wide open and everyone was only a few feet away?

Well, hopefully he'd be game enough to try something . . .

They wandered over to the sturdy gray stone balustrade to look out upon the walled garden. Chinese lanterns lit the meandering gravel paths, and the delicate scent of peonies and dew-damp grass hung in the cool night air. "Is this far enough, or would you care to make a circuit of the garden with me?" murmured Lord Claremont. He moved closer, and Sophie found herself pressed against the stone railing.

It seemed mischief making of the amorous kind was definitely on Lord Claremont's mind.

"I . . ." Sophie swallowed, and her pulse fluttered oddly. Did she really want to do this? Take things further? Now that the moment was upon her, apprehension coursed through her veins. "I'm not sure."

Lord Claremont's warm breath coasted along her ear. "I understand completely, and I hope you'll forgive my presumption. You are such a sweet thing and I wouldn't want to press you for certain, shall we say, favors if you are not ready."

A small sigh of relief escaped Sophie. "Thank you, Matthew," she whispered. She looked up through her lashes at Lord Claremont, and he made an odd sound deep in his throat as though he was biting back a groan.

"I have to tell you something," he said softly. "I need to go away for a couple of days, and I wanted to make sure . . ." He trailed off and swallowed. "Well, I wanted to make sure you wouldn't think my interest had waned. Because if you did, I would be utterly miserable if you looked elsewhere."

Sophie's breath caught as guilt wrapped tight tendrils about her chest. "Why . . . ? Why would you think that?"

Lord Claremont touched her cheek. "I've seen the way Lord Malverne looks at you, Sophie. Even though he assured me he doesn't harbor a tendre for you, I believe his denial was false."

Surely not. Sophie shook her head. She couldn't believe that. Mustn't believe that. Because if Nate cared for her . . . even loved her . . .

Irritation flared. *No, Sophie. He doesn't. If he did, he'd be here with you right now. Not at the theater with the Duke of Exmoor. Lord Claremont is simply feeling insecure because he probably senses* your *hesitation. And you must end this foolishness at once.*

She boldly laid a hand on Lord Claremont's satin-smooth lapel, steeling herself for what would come next. One thing was clear, Lord Claremont *had* to kiss her so she'd know how she truly felt, once and for all. "Matthew, I'm certain you are mistaken about Lord Malverne. Even though I'm staying at Hastings House, I barely see him. And because you are going away"—she slid her fingers up to his wide shoulder and met his gaze—"I don't want to think about him. I'd rather think about you."

Oh, my goodness. What had she done? Something hot and dark flared in Lord Claremont's eyes. He raised a hand

and tipped her chin up with gentle fingers. "Sophie, may I kiss you?" he murmured.

She nodded. She *had* to do this. "Yes." And then she closed her eyes.

Lord Claremont's kiss was as sweet and light as the peony-scented air, a brush of warm lips followed by a firmer press with the subtlest promise of more lingering behind it. Lord Claremont's tongue touched the seam of her lips, but instead of yielding to his invitation to deepen the kiss, Sophie drew back.

Damn and damn again. Disappointment gripped her heart and she had to keep her eyes closed to hide a rush of stinging tears.

She'd felt nothing. Nothing at all. She hadn't been tempted to part her lips. She hadn't wanted to taste Lord Claremont back. She didn't want to grasp his shoulders and sink into him. Or wrap herself around him and never let him go.

Why couldn't she fall in love? It wasn't fair. Not for her. And certainly not for Lord Claremont.

He dropped a gentle kiss on her forehead. "I'm sorry if I pressed you for too much too quickly—"

"No. Not at all." Sophie forced a smile even as her face burned with shame. "It was . . . lovely." Lord Claremont had no idea how wicked she really was. There seemed to be only one particular man who aroused such extreme passions in her. *And love.*

Inconvenient, unrequited, undeniable love.

"Yes." Lord Claremont touched her hot cheek. "It was perfect. Just like you. I shall miss you while I am away. And I will think of our kiss often."

Oh, no. She wasn't perfect. Far from it. Her heart and head awhirl with a storm of conflicting emotions, Sophie simply nodded before stammering, "I . . . I will think of you. And of our kiss too." Because what else *could* she say that wouldn't sound dreadful?

Her response appeared to satisfy Lord Claremont as he smiled and pressed a chaste kiss to her hand before leading her back inside.

Besides, perhaps she *would* miss Lord Claremont. After

all, she liked him. Very much. She might even go so far as to say she was deeply fond of him. And didn't absence heighten affection?

Stepping inside, Sophie darted a glance toward the fireside to see if anyone had noticed how long she and Lord Claremont had been gone, and her gaze collided with a dark, smoldering stare.

Nate.

Sophie's heart stopped for an instant before taking off at a wild pace. *What on earth is* he *doing here?*

And why did he look so . . . disreputable? He seemed on edge, perhaps even dangerous, as he stood brooding by the fire, a glass of brandy in one hand. His strong jaw was shadowed with stubble, there was a purple bruise on one of his cheekbones, his hair was messy rather than artfully tousled, and his cravat was a disaster.

And his eyes . . . she felt trapped yet she couldn't look away. Didn't want to look away.

Resisting the urge to check her hair and her gown, Sophie remained motionless as Nate's burning gaze raked over her, lingering on her lips. Did he suspect Lord Claremont had kissed her? And if he did, did it matter to him? However, expecting him to open his heart to her was beyond foolish.

She might as well ask for the moon.

As soon as Nate spied Lord Claremont escorting Sophie back into his aunt's drawing room, he scowled. According to Charlie, Sophie had been out on the terrace "taking the air" with Claremont.

With a snort, he threw back the brandy his father had just given him, in one bitter gulp. Not bloody likely.

But as Sophie drew closer and he ran a practiced eye over her, he couldn't detect any overt signs that she'd been ravished. Even though her cheeks were slightly flushed, her glossy raven curls were perfectly arranged, and her blue silk gown wasn't disheveled in any way. Her lips weren't kiss swollen.

God, why had he come? Watching Sophie with Claremont was akin to poking at a barely healed wound. He
shouldn't do it, but he couldn't resist the urge. For the most
part, he'd managed to avoid seeing them together. Indeed,
for the last two weeks, he'd been purposely evading Sophie
for her own sake as much as his own.

And it wasn't as though he was short of entertainment
options this evening. After the play—a rather mediocre production of *As You Like It* at the Haymarket Theatre—Max
had suggested they visit a new Roman-themed brothel complete with spectacular baths not far from Pall Mall. Apparently one could be plied with grapes and wine while being
massaged in exotic oils by a bevy of nubile, semiclad cyprians. As appealing as the prospect was—Nate had spent several hours bare-knuckle boxing at Gentleman Jackson's
during the afternoon, and a massage would have eased his
aches and pains—he'd declined. He'd told his friend he felt
obligated to put in an appearance at Chelmsford House to
pay his respects to his aunt Tabitha. Of course *that* was a lie;
he'd wanted to spy on Sophie.

So now, here he was, a veritable dog in the manger, glowering at the only woman he wanted but that his battered
heart wouldn't let him or anyone else have.

One thing was certain, he damn well wasn't going to sit
here and watch Claremont flirt with Sophie under his very
nose. Depositing his brandy glass on the marble mantelpiece, aware that all eyes including Sophie's were on him,
he addressed the lucky bastard. "Good evening, Claremont.
Are you up for a game of billiards? My aunt informs me her
staff have finished ironing the baize." His gaze touched Sophie's. "Of course, only if you don't mind, Miss Brightwell."

Sophie's cheeks grew bright with color. "Why would I
mind?" She removed her hand from Claremont's arm and
murmured in a low voice that was far too intimate for Nate's
liking, "My lord, go ahead. I was about to take tea with the
ladies."

Claremont inclined his head. "As you wish, my dear
Miss Brightwell."

Nate ground his teeth as he stalked across the plush

oriental carpet, heading for the billiard room. *My dear Miss Brightwell.* What would Claremont call her next? Sweetheart? My love?

My lady wife?

He yanked two billiard cues out of their oak stand, and as he passed one to Claremont, he congratulated himself for not whacking his opponent over the head with it. "The usual rules?"

Perhaps sensing the tension crackling in the air between them, Claremont simply inclined his head before retreating to the other end of the table. Without a word, Nate set up the ivory balls on the dark green baize. Then both of them leaned forward to take their opening shots to see who would begin the game.

Nate struck his billiard ball with a resounding crack. And then, all at once, his ire rushed out of him . . . only to be replaced by the crushing weight of inevitability.

It wouldn't be long before Claremont proposed to Sophie, and there was no reason in the world for her to refuse him.

Christ, the bastard had better make her happy. Because if he didn't, Nate wouldn't just strike him with a billiard cue, he'd tear him apart.

CHAPTER 20

A certain captivated viscount pursues his Disreputable Debutante in earnest . . .

Speculation is rife. Wagers are even being laid at White's.

Will there be an announcement of impending nuptials soon?

The Beau Monde Mirror: The Society Page

May 13, 1818

"Oh, my goodness. Lord Claremont has returned, Sophie," said Charlie, peeking down to the square below from behind the drawing room's green velvet curtains. "I wonder where he's been."

Sophie smoothed her damp palms down her white muslin skirts. Since Lady Chelmsford's dinner party, Charlie kept speculating that the viscount might have gone to Suffolk to "meet" with her stepfather, but Sophie kept refusing to believe it, instead suggesting he'd probably gone to check on his Hertfordshire estate and his mother.

Of course, neither of them *really* knew. But Sophie rather suspected she was about to find out.

"Let me look at you." Charlie abandoned her position by the window and arranged the curls about Sophie's face and tweaked the sky blue sash beneath her bust. "There's no need to pinch your cheeks as they are flushed already." She stepped back and clasped her hands together beneath her chin. Her topaz eyes glowed. "You look lovely. And I'm so excited for you. Where would you like to meet with him? Here or in the garden?"

"Charlie . . . ," Sophie warned. "I think it's a little premature to speculate about the nature of Lord Claremont's visit. I don't see why this one would be different from any of the others."

"Nonsense. I have a feeling this visit is going to be significant indeed. And I'm rarely wrong."

"Well, I, for one, would beg to differ," drawled Nate as he entered the room. His gaze touched Sophie briefly before returning to his sister. His mouth twitched with a sardonic smile. "But indulge me, what is it that you think you are so right about, Charlotte?"

"Lord Claremont is here," replied Charlie with an arch smile. "And *I* think he will seek a private audience with Sophie."

Was it just Sophie's imagination, or did the lines around Nate's eyes tighten imperceptibly?

"However, I don't think he will," added Sophie.

"He'd be mad if he doesn't," replied Nate.

Did he really mean that? The tension in Nate's shoulders, the flicker of some strong emotion in his eyes—was it jealousy?—seemed to belie his flippant tone. Sophie lifted her chin. "So, on the off chance that Lord Claremont proposes to me today, would I have your blessing, my lord?"

A muscle twitched in Nate's lean jaw but as he opened his mouth to reply, there was a knock on the door.

It was the butler, announcing that Lord Claremont was here to see her. And that he wished to speak with her privately.

Charlie grinned and clapped her hands. "See, I *was* right. Where will you meet him? We can leave. Although it's a lovely afternoon so perhaps outside . . . ?"

Sophie glanced at Nate. He'd gone very still and seemed to be markedly interested in the toes of his top boots. That muscle was working in his jaw again. He hadn't answered her question, curse him.

She addressed the butler. "Outside in the courtyard

garden, I think. Please tell Lord Claremont I shall join him shortly."

"Very well, Miss Brightwell."

Charlie kissed her cheek. "I'll wait here," she whispered. "I promise I won't peek."

Sophie squeezed her friend's hands. Her own were shaking. "Wish me luck," she whispered back.

Charlie drew away a little and touched her cheek. "Darling Sophie, you will *not* need luck. This was clearly destined to be."

Sophie nodded. Nate still hadn't said anything, and his silence was killing her. However, as she passed by him on her way out, he said in a soft, low voice, "I wish you nothing but happiness, Miss Brightwell."

As she closed the door on him, Sophie wished she could be happy too.

She found Lord Claremont by the small fountain at the back of the garden. He rose from the stone bench positioned beneath an ancient beech tree, and even though his face was in shade, Sophie couldn't fail to see the warm glow in his eyes as she approached.

She forced a smile. She was so nervous, it felt as though a hummingbird had taken up residence in her chest. "Lord Claremont, welcome back to town."

He cocked a dark eyebrow. "So formal, my dear Sophie?" He bowed over her hand, his eyes holding hers, and feathered a kiss over her knuckles. "Last time I saw you, you called me Matthew. I would be overjoyed if you used my first name again."

She attempted another smile, hoping it reached her eyes. "Of course. Matthew."

"Will you join me?" Lord Claremont gestured to the stone bench. "I must confess, I was most pleased to hear you agreed to meet with me in the garden."

Sophie smoothed her skirts over her lap as she sat. White rose petals drifted across the gravel path at her feet. "It's a lovely day."

"Yes." Lord Claremont's gaze caressed her face. "And it

is my sincere hope that it will soon become even more wonderful."

Sophie's breath quickened. *Oh no.* Lord Claremont was going to propose marriage to her; she was certain of it now.

But she wasn't ready. She really wasn't.

Guilt pressed so heavily on her chest, she almost couldn't breathe. Guilt for pretending an affection she didn't feel these past few weeks. Guilt for *not* being able to feel it and the worry she might never learn to love this man. Guilt for hurting Lord Claremont if she refused him.

And then there was the guilt she would feel for disappointing her family in the event she said no.

"Sophie, are you all right, my love?" Lord Claremont picked up her hand, then his brow creased with a frown. "Why, you're shaking."

"I . . . I'm a little nervous," she said in a voice that shook too. Oh, why had he called her *my love*? Surely he didn't love her.

Lord Claremont's wide mouth lifted into a smile. "I will confess, I am a little nervous too. And I suspect you might know why."

"Lord Clare—I mean, Matthew."

Lord Claremont's smile slipped. "I also must confess, I'm now a trifle worried because you keep calling me Lord Claremont. What's wrong, dear Sophie?"

Sophie swallowed. Her mouth was so dry, and her tongue felt as if it were tied in knots. "I . . . I don't wish to disappoint you, my lord, but perhaps I should also confess that I had not expected . . . I mean, you are a viscount and I . . . my family . . ." She stopped and bit her lip. Oh, this was so hard. Why hadn't she put a stop to this madness sooner?

"Hush." Lord Claremont placed a long finger against her mouth. "While I was away, I visited your stepfather. And he has given his blessing to what I am about to do."

To her horror, Lord Claremont hopped off the bench and knelt before her on bended knee. "Sophie dearest. You are the sweetest, most delightful young woman I have ever met, and from the moment I saw you in Hyde Park, I knew I wanted to make you mine. You've stolen my heart and I pray I've stolen yours." Lord Claremont clasped both of her hands in his. "Sophie Elizabeth Brightwell, will you do me the inestimable honor of consenting to be my wife?"

"Oh, Matthew." Tears flooded Sophie's vision. "I don't know what to say. Believe me, I want to say yes. Truly I do . . ."

The hope in Lord Claremont's eyes faded and his frown was back. "But . . ."

"But . . . while I esteem you highly and regard you with a great deal of fondness, my heart isn't . . . our courtship has progressed at such a rapid pace . . . I do not wish to hurt you, but . . ."

Lord Claremont's smile was sad. "You do not love me."

She shook her head. "I'm afraid not."

"Perhaps in time?"

Sophie tried to smile but managed no more than a tremble of her lips. "Perhaps. I could not say."

Lord Claremont reclaimed his seat next to her. He hadn't relinquished her hands, and he kissed them before he spoke. "I will take heart in the knowledge you have not rejected me outright then, sweet Sophie. Might I ask you to do one thing though? Will you think on my proposal? If you need time, I am more than willing to give it to you." He touched her cheek. "Because I firmly believe you are worth waiting for."

Sophie's vision blurred again. If only she *could* love him. But that depended on her overcoming her love for Nate. And so far, that had proved an impossible feat. "You are too kind, Matthew."

"I'm afraid it has nothing to do with kindness."

He kissed each of her hands again, then rose. "I will wait until I hear from you before I call again."

She nodded and wiped away a tear that had slipped onto her cheek. "I will let you know my answer soon."

He gave her an elegant bow. "I look forward to it."

Sophie sat in the garden for long minutes, watching the play of light and shadow on the path as the beech tree's branches waved gently in a light breeze. Flowers nodded and a fat bumblebee buzzed about the nearby rose arbor.

When her tears had dried and her head felt clearer, she got to her feet and raised her chin. She was so very sick and tired of feeling like a petal tossed about in the wind.

The time for plain speaking had arrived.

"My lord, which waistcoat would you like to wear this evening? The black satin with the paisley pattern or the midnight blue silk? My lord?"

Nate dragged his gaze away from the square below and turned to his valet. Claremont had left a little sooner than he'd expected, but of course, it really wasn't any of his business. "I don't mind, Davenport. Whatever you think matches."

As soon as Sophie quit the library, Nate had decided he'd best make himself scarce. He'd pass by Grosvenor Square to see what MacQueen and Max were up to. Hopefully, within the space of an hour, he would be drinking and laughing at White's and planning how to spend the rest of his night. Gambling and whoring seemed like appealing options right about now. Dwelling on what might have been didn't.

"The midnight blue silk then it is, my lord."

"Wonderful."

"Your bath is ready, too, my lord."

"Excellent." Nate began to remove his neck cloth.

"And the decanter of brandy has been refilled as well. I took the liberty of pouring you a glass. It's on the wash-stand by the bath."

"You know me too well, Davenport." Nate began to work at the buttons on his pinstriped waistcoat.

"I'm here to serve, my lord."

"I shall ring for you when I'm ready to dress."

"Of course, my lord."

The door to his room clicked shut, and Nate shed his shirt. Even though it was only midafternoon, he really did need that brandy; Davenport certainly knew him and his moods too well.

He crossed to the bath and took a swig of his drink. And

then another. He decided he could probably drink a whole bottle right now and it still wouldn't be enough to quell the fire in his soul.

Sophie would belong to another man. He might wish her well, but that didn't mean he wished the same for Claremont.

Christ, he was a contrary bastard.

The door latch snicked again. "Forget something, Davenport?"

"It's not Davenport. It's me."

Sophie? What the—?

Nate swung around and sure enough, there she was. She leaned against the closed oak door, studying him with solemn blue eyes.

"What are you doing here?" In his confusion, his tone was harsher than he meant it to be. *Why aren't you with Claremont . . . ?*

Her gaze was steady as she drew a deep breath. "I need to speak with you, Nate. To tell you something . . . Lord Claremont has indeed asked me to marry him. However, I have yet to give him a definite answer. But since his departure, I've decided I'm going to say no."

She is going to say no? Nate's heart leapt and despaired at the same time. He did indeed want Sophie to be happy, to have whatever her heart desired.

As long as it wasn't him.

But he couldn't say any of that. Instead he said the most obvious thing that sprang to mind. "Sophie, you shouldn't be here. If you are discovered . . . You need to be more careful about your reputation."

Her heated, adoring gaze raked over him, taking in his half-naked state. Lust speared though him and he swallowed, his throat tight with longing. He should really throw on a shirt. A banyan. Tell her again to leave his bedroom. But he didn't.

Sophie's eyes met his again and she shrugged. "At this point, I really don't care. In most of society's eyes, I'm regarded as fast anyway. And what I've come here to say *must* be said."

She crossed the room and to Nate's astonishment, she took the glass of brandy from his hand and took a large sip; it was as though she was fortifying herself for what she was going to say next. "The reason I'm going to say no to Lord Claremont," she said in a low voice, "is my heart isn't free. It belongs to you, Nathaniel Hastings. You, and only you." She raised her chin and looked him straight in the eye. "I love you. I've tried not to. But I do. And that's never going to change."

Oh no. No, no, no. He had known this to be true, for weeks now, but hearing it from Sophie's sweet lips, seeing the determined light in her eyes, was another thing entirely. Because he couldn't say it back. Nate rubbed his fingers through his hair. "Sophie . . . I . . ."

Her mouth curved into a sad smile. "It's all right, Nate. You don't have to say anything. I know you cannot," she said softly. "I don't expect anything from you. Nothing at all. But I'm tired of pretending I don't feel anything for you." She discarded his brandy and placed her hand against his naked chest. Her cool fingers flexed against the rigid plane of muscle, yet somehow her touch burned. Seared straight through him to his wildly thudding heart. Branding him in some elemental way.

"I know you want me, even though you do not love me," she murmured. "So I wondered if I might be so bold as to ask you for one last kiss before I go."

Nate frowned. His thoughts were addled. His brain was not working. "Go?"

"Yes. After I send word to Lord Claremont, I'm going to return home to Nettlefield Grange. Tomorrow, if your father can spare a carriage. Or I shall take a mail coach. Lord Claremont's courtship has certainly been public knowledge, and there's sure to be talk about the fact that I've turned him down. My London Season will be well and truly over."

Sophie is going to leave . . . Nate's heart stopped as though he'd just been kicked before it lurched into an unsteady gallop again. It was inevitable, of course. He'd anticipated it as soon as he realized Claremont would propose.

But fool that he was, he hadn't expected her departure to be so soon. *Tomorrow* . . .

Sophie's hand slid to his bare shoulder. Did she know her touch was the most exquisite of tortures? And how much danger she was in? Hot lust pounded through his veins once more, loosening the tight reins on his control.

Perhaps she did know all of these things but didn't care. Her blue eyes were dark with desire as she murmured, "So I ask you for this one last favor, Nate. One last kiss that I shall keep as a cherished memory, close to my foolish heart."

Nate closed his eyes for a brief moment. This was madness. He sucked in an unsteady breath and forced himself to say, "We shouldn't."

"Probably not." Her fingers traced over his jaw. His lips. "But let's do it anyway. Kiss me goodbye, Nate. I'll never ask you for anything else ever again."

God help him, he couldn't resist the naked need in her gaze. The beckoning fire of her touch. They pulled at him like the moon pulled at the tide. A better man would turn her away.

But today, right here, right now, he wasn't that man.

"Sophie," he whispered, touching her delicate cheek, and before he could draw another breath, she pressed her mouth to his and kissed him.

Fire roaring through him, Nate caught her slender, pliant body against his and kissed her back with unrestrained abandon. Angling her head with his hands, he plundered her mouth with lips and tongue. Devoured her. She tasted so damn good. Like the sweetest honey or the most sublime wine.

How could he possibly give her up? His body craved her like an addict craved opium, and it seemed no one else would do. Since he'd first tasted her, he hadn't bedded a single woman. Hadn't desired another woman.

All rational thought splintered when Sophie slid her hand between their bodies and cupped his straining member through his buckskin breeches. He groaned and rocked his hips into her. Backed her up against the wall beside the window and palmed her small breast. She filled his hand and he squeezed gently, relishing the moan that spilled from her lips into his mouth, the press of her impudent nipple into his palm.

Panting, she dragged her mouth from his, but he was a man possessed, and he needed the taste of her more than he needed air. And any part of her was fair game. He grazed his mouth along her jaw and ravished her neck as she continued to stroke him. If she kept this up, he was sure to come in his breeches.

This was more than a single kiss, but for the life of him, he couldn't seem to stop himself.

"Nate," she breathed as he pushed her gown aside and lavished her shoulder with desperate kisses. "Touch me. Love me."

Nate growled and tugged down her bodice and underclothes. The sound of fabric tearing rent the air, but he didn't care. He bent his head and sucked her rosy puckered nipple into his mouth. Tugged on it gently with his teeth, then soothed the sting with his tongue.

Sophie fumbled with the buttons at the fall front of his breeches, then slipped her hand inside. Her fingers curled around his shaft, and when her thumb swiped through the seed leaking from him, he sucked in a breath.

"We need to stop," he groaned, burying his face in her neck. "I don't want to ruin you, Sophie." Deflowering her was *not* something he could live with.

She tugged at his hair until he looked up and met her passion-glazed eyes. All the while her wicked fingers worked him, sliding up and down, up and down. Squeezing. Pumping. Driving him insane. "You know as well as I that we can both seek satisfaction in other ways. Like we did before. But if you want me to stop . . ." Her fingers stilled, and Nate thought he might die.

"No. I don't want you to stop. Here . . ." He led her to his bed and lay down on the claret red counterpane, his weight on his elbows. His throbbing cock jutted straight up, demanding attention. "Climb on top of me, Sophie. Slide your quim back and forth along my length. Ride me."

Had he shocked her with his wicked invitation? For one long moment Sophie stared at his manhood, her teeth pressing into her swollen lower lip. Then she hoisted up her snow white muslin skirts and straddled his hips. He felt her soft curls brush his shaft, and then, when she lowered herself, he was enveloped by hot, wet heat.

Fuck. He closed his eyes and hissed at the sheer, overwhelming pleasure of feeling her slick furrow against his naked flesh.

"Are you all right?" she whispered. "Am I hurting you?"

Nate attempted a smile even though he thought he might explode at any moment. "No. Not at all. It's just that you feel so god damn wonderful, Sophie."

She nodded and leaned forward, bracing herself on her arms before sliding herself along his throbbing length. Her naked breast bobbed like a cherry-tipped blancmange, and Nate swallowed as moisture flooded his mouth. "That's it, keep going, sweetheart."

At his words of encouragement, Sophie smiled and set up a slow, measured pace, undulating back and forth, gliding over him, torturing him yet pleasuring him at the same time. When she leaned down and kissed his chest, her tongue flickering against one of his nipples, he bucked and grasped her hips. More than anything he wanted to bury himself inside her, balls deep, but he couldn't, *wouldn't* betray her in that way.

"Go faster, sweetheart. Grind yourself against me if you want to. I won't break."

She rocked faster, pressed harder, and his orgasm began to build. Sophie panted and circled her hips, and Nate couldn't resist the urge to help push her over the edge into pleasure too. He slipped a hand beneath her skirts and pressed his thumb against her core, circling and rubbing the dew-slick flesh, increasing the friction.

"Oh . . . oh my . . . oh . . ." Sophie's thighs squeezed his hips, and then her whole body spasmed. Throwing her head back, she let out a ragged cry before collapsing forward.

Nate hugged her against him, and as he buried his face in her deliciously fragrant neck, he rolled his hips, grinding himself against the fresh flood of moisture bathing his rigid length. The hot wet friction was enough to send him plunging headlong into bliss as well.

"Sophie," he groaned. His balls tightened and his seed fountained from his cock in hot spurts, coating his belly and Sophie's mound and slender thighs.

For long minutes they lay that way, Sophie lashed against him, both of them catching their breath. How odd that he suddenly didn't want to let her go.

But he must.

He slid his hands to her slender waist, and as Sophie pushed herself up, she smiled softly. "Thank you, Nate," she murmured. She dropped a swift kiss on his lips, then slid from the bed.

Nate's gut twisted with guilt as he sat up and clumsily refastened his breeches. He wanted to say something but what? *Stay? Don't go?*

But that would imply he wanted Sophie to stay forever. And they both knew that such an eventuality would only end in disaster. She wanted a happily ever after with a husband who loved her. And he was only bound to disappoint her.

Turning away from him, Sophie adjusted her clothing in silence.

"Sophie . . ."

She glanced over her shoulder. "You don't need to say anything, Nate. You gave me what I wanted and I'm grateful."

Grateful. Nate frowned and scrubbed his hand down his face before he got to his feet. For some reason it bothered him that Sophie should feel this way. As though he'd just thrown her the scraps from his table, nothing more. He wanted more from her than gratitude. He wanted . . . The truth was, he didn't know what he wanted anymore.

As he approached her, she turned around. "I expect I'll leave early in the morning, so I may not see you for some time . . ." She trailed off and bit her lip. "And who knows, perhaps when I do see you again, my heart will be healed."

Nate itched to touch Sophie's face, to cradle her cheek,

but he didn't. His fingers curled into a fist instead. "I expressed the sentiment earlier today, but I will say it again because it's true. I wish you nothing but happiness, Sophie."

She nodded, and even though her blue eyes were bright with tears, she smiled. "I believe you. Goodbye, Nate."

It wasn't until the door shut that Nate realized he had tears in his eyes too.

May 14, 1818

"Oh, Sophie. I will miss you so." Charlie hugged her so tight, Sophie thought she might never let her go. "You must promise to write. And often."

"I will." Tears misted Sophie's vision as her friend released her. Through the open front door, she could see a mizzling rain was falling on the square and on Lord Westhampton's carriage. He'd been quite happy to lend it to her, even at such short notice. It would be a far more comfortable journey compared to the one she would have if she took a public coach.

"I've said it already, but you do not have to leave on my account, my dear friend. We've already endured half a Season of stares and whispers, and I am happy to continue to do so."

Sophie shook her head. "You are too generous and kindhearted for your own good, Charlie. You will fare much better in the husband hunting stakes without me. I'm expecting some good news from you by the end of the Season."

Charlie snorted. "I wouldn't hold your breath."

"And please do say farewell to your aunt and Olivia for me if you see her."

"I will."

Sophie didn't ask her to say the same to Nate. She'd already said her heartfelt goodbye yesterday when she'd visited his room. She hadn't seen him since, and she expected it would be a long time before she ever did again. Which was all for the best, she decided.

She hugged Charlie again to hide the fact that her eyes

were brimming once more. Then she hurried down the stairs and into the waiting carriage.

As the carriage pulled away, she settled back against the squabs and closed her eyes. Her throat ached as she tried to crush back a fresh wave of burning tears. She didn't want to look back at Hastings House. She only wanted to look toward the future. One in which she was whole and happy and not pining after a wicked viscount with rich brown eyes and a heart-melting smile.

She'd taken a chance and had declared her feelings, but still Nate had remained silent . . . even though she was certain she'd seen deeper emotions like tenderness and yearning in his eyes as they'd shared their bodies so intimately. And then a flicker of regret when she'd said goodbye. But perhaps she'd only imagined all of it because she wanted him to reciprocate her love so badly.

Well, she wouldn't beg. And if Nathaniel Hastings had a change of heart, he knew where to find her.

CHAPTER 21

❧

The Disgraced Debutante, Miss S. B. of M. G.,
returns home amid a cloud of rumors about her time
in the capital . . .

Perhaps one purportedly smitten viscount came
to his senses?

The Suffolk County Chronicle:
Vignettes of Village Life

Nettlefield Grange, Monkton Green, Suffolk

May 15, 1818

Sophie, I cannot believe you turned down Lord Claremont. A viscount! What on earth were you thinking?"

Sophie sighed and closed her eyes for a moment, praying
for patience. She had expected her mother to be upset and
angry. But facing it was another thing entirely. Especially
when this was the third time she'd heard the same argument—
and she'd only arrived home yesterday. "As I explained before, Mama, I esteem Lord Claremont greatly, but I'm afraid
I do not care for him."

Her mother fixed her with an exasperated look. Her face,
pinched with strain, was almost as pale as the lace cap she
wore. "I truly wonder what is wrong with you sometimes.
Why wouldn't you care for him? I met the man when he
came to speak with Mr. Debenham. Lord Claremont is

handsome, and charming, and rich . . . and he's a viscount, for goodness' sake!"

"I agree he is all those things, Mama. But I will not marry unless it's for love."

Her mother shook her head, and her eyes filled with tears. "Sophie Elizabeth Brightwell. Where did I go wrong? I had such high hopes for you when Lord Westhampton wrote, inviting you to stay. But now you've gone and ruined everything again."

Sophie's heart twisted with guilt but she said nothing, because what else *could* she say? She couldn't admit that she'd fallen in love with her best friend's brother, a wicked rake whom she loved to distraction. A man who was averse to both marriage and love.

Instead, she looked out of the drawing room window to the garden where their geese pecked for grubs in the grass. Alice's cat sat on the stone wall, watching them, her tail twitching. It was such a shame that she hadn't heard anything from the publisher about her children's novel yet. She fervently prayed that at least one of her dreams would come true. If only there was some way for her to earn at least a little money to help out her family . . .

Her mother's exaggerated sigh pulled her from her maudlin musings. "I expect Mr. Debenham will be able to talk some sense into you when he returns from his call with Lord Buxton. Everyone in the village believes you are to become a viscountess. Oh, the shame if you don't, Sophie. The shame." Her mother subsided onto the chintz-covered settee and pressed a crumpled linen handkerchief to her eyes. "Poor Alice and Jane will be heartbroken too. Crushed. They were so excited when they found out their sister was going to become Lady Claremont."

"I'm sorry, Mama. I truly am. But I cannot help the way I feel."

"And then of course there is this awful matter with Lord Buxton." Her mother dabbed at her tears. "Mr. Debenham was so relieved when Lord Claremont asked for your hand. He was sure the viscount would clear the debt."

Sophie frowned. "I don't understand why Father cannot work out some sort of arrangement with Lord Buxton. They are friends, after all."

"I do not know either. And I worry . . ." Her mother trailed off and bit her quivering lower lip.

"You worry about what, Mama?"

"You probably think I haven't noticed, but I've seen the way Lord Buxton looks at you, Sophie. He fancies himself in love with you, even though he's old enough to be your father. I know he followed you to London. At any rate, because you are not promised to Lord Claremont, I wonder if he will now try to pressure Mr. Debenham into making another sort of arrangement to settle the debt."

Sophie's mouth grew drier than the Sahara. "What do you mean?"

A shadow of apprehension flickered across her mother's face. "I fear Lord Buxton will promise to clear the debt in exchange for your hand in marriage."

Oh no. Sophie shook her head. She could never marry Lord Buxton. "I won't do it. I simply cannot."

Her mother sighed. "I understand. I do. Lord Buxton is too old for you, and your personalities will not suit. But if you refuse him, I also worry that he will turn his attentions to Alice. She is seventeen now . . ."

Sophie's stomach roiled so much, she thought she might be sick. "Surely Father would never agree to such an arrangement."

Her mother shrugged. "I cannot be sure."

"Well, Lord Buxton cannot make anyone wed him if she does not wish it. Me or Alice."

Her mother's eyes swam with tears again. "But what if Lord Buxton calls in the debt, Sophie? Mr. Debenham cannot pay it. I fear we may lose the house."

Sophie's heart plummeted to the worn Aubusson carpet at her feet. The situation was dire indeed. Charlie had once suggested her father, Lord Westhampton, or Lady Chelmsford could assist if need be, but would her stepfather actually accept their help? He was a proud man.

She could well imagine he'd rather sell off his step-daughter than accept financial assistance from virtual strangers.

Sophie closed her eyes and shuddered at the memory of Lord Buxton accosting her in Berkeley Square. But this time, Nate wouldn't be here to save her.

Nate. Tears scalded Sophie's eyes at the thought of him. She missed him desperately.

His smile. His handsome brown eyes. His teasing manner. *His kisses.*

On the long carriage journey home, she'd resolved not to think about him. But it was a battle she didn't seem to be winning at the moment.

"Sophie, I can see how upset you are. Try not to fret." Her mother reached out and squeezed her hand. "I'm sure something can be worked out."

But Sophie could tell that her mother was just saying that to comfort her. Her tone and the worry lines around her eyes belied her words.

She supposed the coming days would reveal Lord Buxton's intentions. And if she had to, she would swallow her pride and go to Charlie for help. Because there was no way on heaven or earth that she would marry Lord Buxton to alleviate her stepfather's financial troubles. And she wouldn't stand by and watch poor Alice be a sacrificial lamb either.

Hastings House, Berkeley Square, Mayfair

May 30, 1818

"Goodness, Nate. You look . . ."

Nate drained the last mouthful of his bitter black coffee, then poured himself another cup. "A mess? Shocking?" *Like I just crawled out of the farthest, darkest reaches of hell?*

"Well, yes . . . ," said Charlie as she took a seat at the mahogany breakfast table. She poured herself a cup of tea, then dispensed sugar and milk before adding, "I probably wouldn't have put it that way exactly. But yes, you do look a mess." Her brown eyes lifted to his in a penetrating stare. "I would venture to say you should still be abed."

Nate sighed and ran a hand down his face. He wished he were still abed too. He had a monumental headache and an unsettled stomach courtesy of spending too many nights out with Max and MacQueen, carousing and gambling over the past fortnight. But not whoring.

No, it didn't matter how tempting the demirep, widow, or bored nobleman's wife—he'd been propositioned more than once by the insatiable Lady Astley over the last few days—he felt nothing, not even a fleeting stirring of lust.

The only time he experienced true desire was when he dreamed or fantasized about Sophie. Indeed, it was a wonder his palm wasn't sporting blisters considering how many times he'd made himself come by his own hand since she'd departed.

Had it really only been two weeks since she left?

In some ways if felt like forever. Could it be that Nathaniel Hastings, Lord Malverne, a confirmed bachelor, actually missed the company of a particular woman? And not just because he was lusting after her?

He'd never experienced a malaise like it. It was . . . a novel experience. Bloody annoying too. It seemed he'd become a pathetic shadow of his former self. Why, last night he'd even stayed home and had begun reading *Pride and Prejudice*. This morning he was particularly exhausted because he'd stayed up until the early hours, plowing his way through chapter after chapter of the witty, entertaining tale. He could certainly see why Sophie loved Miss Austen's works.

He grimaced as he threw back another mouthful of coffee. Hopefully the malaise—whatever it was—would pass soon. Maybe he should think about following in Gabriel's footsteps and take a jaunt to the Continent. Yes, perhaps he just needed a change of scenery . . .

"Nate, you haven't heard a word I said, have you?"

Nate shook his head. "My apologies, dear sister. No, I haven't."

Charlie sighed and put down her jam-laden toast. "You know what's wrong with you, don't you?"

Nate narrowed his gaze. "I beg your pardon?" He wasn't sure he wanted to hear his sister's opinion on what ailed him.

"You miss her."

Nate felt his cheeks grow uncharacteristically hot. Christ, was he blushing? He flipped open the *Times*. "I don't know what you mean."

Charlie snorted. "Don't pick up that paper to avoid me. I know you're not really reading it." She reached out and pushed the pages down, catching his eye again. "Just look at you. You don't eat properly. Your sleeping habits are even worse than usual—and don't shake your head at me—you think I haven't heard you prowling the hallways at all ungodly hours of the night? You have shadows beneath your eyes and you've lost weight. I've never seen you so miserable."

"You think I'm miserable?"

"Well, aren't you?"

If he admitted that, it meant he would be admitting to Charlie's first point—that he missed Sophie. He might be prepared to admit it to himself, but he certainly wasn't going to say it aloud. Because if he truly did miss Sophie, it might mean that the tendre he'd harbored for her had evolved into something much, much worse.

Charlie was right. He was a mess.

When he didn't respond to her question, Charlie sighed. "Nate, it's not a sign of weakness to admit you care for someone. Even Father has noticed the cloud of gloom over your head. And he agrees with me. You're not yourself because you're in love with Sophie."

Nate ground his teeth. "I'm not . . . Men like me don't—"

"Fall in love? Yes, yes. I've heard you say it all before. That doesn't make it true. And I know you just use it as an excuse to protect yourself from ever being hurt again. You cannot deny it."

Good God, when did Charlie become so perceptive? Out

loud he said, "No matter how much you wish it to be otherwise, you are very mistaken about how I feel."

Charlie scowled at him. "Well, let me ask you this, Nate: why wouldn't you fall in love with Sophie? For heaven's sake, she's perfect for you. And she loves you. Everyone knows it. I suspect even poor Lord Claremont knows it. Indeed, I knew from the very first time you two met in Hyde Park three years ago that you and Sophie were meant for each other. You might pretend otherwise, but I saw how she caught your eye. Why, when we were at Mrs. Rathbone's academy, I even introduced her to all the things you like because I hoped that one day—"

Nate frowned. "What do you mean? What things?"

Charlie lifted her chin. "You know, the brandy, and tobacco, and a particular set of memoirs . . . I wanted Sophie to appreciate some of the things you like. So that when you had the opportunity to meet again, she wouldn't be so shocked by some of your rakish appetites."

Nate couldn't keep the incredulous tone from his voice. "Good God, Charlie. Is that the real reason you smuggled all of those items into that girl's school?"

The light in Charlie's eyes was militant. "It was part of the reason. I still maintain young women would benefit from learning about such taboo topics. We are all expected to lead such cosseted lives. To never put a foot wrong. To be seen and not heard on matters of importance. To acquire useless attainments such as drawing and how to sing like an angel and sit properly when most of the time men are just thinking about what's beneath our skirts. Now, don't look at me like that, Nate. You know it's true. It infuriates me no end."

She sighed and her expression softened. "But this isn't about me, Nate. When you accidentally invaded Sophie's room that night, I could have gone to Father, of course, who would have insisted that you marry her straightaway. But I didn't want you to resent Sophie because you'd been forced to marry her out of obligation. I wanted you to fall in love with her by getting to know her as a person. Hence, I blackmailed you into becoming her chaperone. I knew if you spent a good deal of time together—especially if you saw her being courted by others—you'd soon realize what a prize she is."

Horror shot through Nate. "Good Lord, your machinations are simply diabolical."

Charlie arched a fine brow. "I like to think of my plotting as . . . clever."

Nate shook his head. "Be that as it may, I'm a blackguard, Charlie. Fit for nothing other than wasting my days away at this club or that. Sophie deserves better. A man who adores her."

"And that man *is* you, why can't you see it? You *are* good enough, Nathaniel Hastings. Your life doesn't have to be so empty and hedonistic. Your arguments are flawed and weak, and you know it."

Charlie paused to pour herself another cup of tea. "There's something else I think you should know about . . . about Sophie's current situation . . ."

"What do you mean?" Nate held his breath as Charlie again fussed about with sugar and milk and stirred her tea with a silver teaspoon far too many times. He wouldn't put it past her to be torturing him on purpose.

"I'm worried now that Sophie has returned home, that odious man, Lord Buxton, will continue to pursue her. She hinted as much in the letter I received yesterday."

Nate's hands curled into fists at the thought of the middle-aged baron going anywhere near her. He'd been so focused on trying to alleviate his own misery, he hadn't even considered Sophie's circumstances. What a prat he was.

Charlie fiddled with the handle of her teacup. "But I fear it's worse than Sophie has let on."

Alarm spiked, making Nate sound terser than he wanted to. "Stop mincing words, Charlie. Out with it."

"It seems Sophie's stepfather, Mr. Debenham, owes Lord Buxton a substantial amount of money. Quite frankly, I'm concerned Sophie will be pressured into wedding the baron. I cannot be sure, but perhaps Lord Buxton will waive the debt if she agrees to marry him." She shrugged.

"You saw the lascivious look in that man's gaze too. It just seems like something he would do."

Nate clenched his teeth so hard, his jaw cracked. Christ. Sophie wasn't a commodity to be traded like a sack of grain or a prize heifer. "Did Sophie ever disclose to you how much her stepfather owes Lord Buxton?"

Charlie nodded. "Two thousand pounds. In her letter she mentioned her stepfather recently attempted to secure a loan from his bank in Bury St. Edmonds, but unfortunately his request was rejected."

Nate leaned back and breathed a sigh of relief. It was a significant sum but not a king's ransom by any means. He'd occasionally gambled away more than that at the gaming tables in the space of a night. "Thank you for telling me that, Charlie. I won't have that man hounding Sophie."

Charlie's smile was bright. "So you are going to declare your undying love for Sophie and offer for her hand?"

Nate gave his sister a wry smile. "I admire your tireless optimism, Charlie. But no."

"So what do you plan to do?" Charlie gave him a curious look from beneath her lashes.

He hadn't been able to save Thomas. He was responsible for his mother's death too. He might not be able to offer Sophie the love she deserved, but that didn't mean he would stand idly by and see her suffer. "I think it's time my man of business paid a visit to Suffolk."

CHAPTER 22

Has a stroke of good luck at last reversed the fortunes
of a particular well-known family of M. G.?
   The question on the tips of everyone's tongues
is, does this family have a secret benefactor?

The Suffolk County Chronicle:
Vignettes of Village Life

Nettlefield Grange, Monkton Green, Suffolk

June 1, 1818

Sophie's hands shook as she tore open the letter from
Mr. John Murray, publisher, that had just arrived in
this morning's post. Anticipation warring with anxiety,
she didn't even make it inside the house before she'd perused the opening words, then perused them again to make
absolutely sure she'd understood correctly. The shifting
dappled light cast by the oak tree above her head wasn't
helping matters. Nevertheless, she drew a deep breath
and forced herself to read the words at a slower pace for a
third time.

> Dear Miss Brightwell,
>   I am pleased to offer you a contract of publication for
> your delightful children's novel The Diary of a Determined
> Young Country Miss; or, a Young Lady of Consequence . . .

Joy surged and Sophie's heart sang. It was true. She'd done it. Accomplished a cherished goal. Not only was she going to be a published author, she would earn some sorely needed income at long last. She didn't know how long she could continue to fend off Lord Buxton—

"Sophie, Sophie, come quickly. You'll never believe what's happened."

What on earth? Her heart bolting into a gallop, Sophie thrust her letter into the pocket of her pinafore, picked up her skirts, and then raced across the lawn, past the rose garden, and up the stairs leading to the front door of the grange. Her mother stood on the threshold, her cheeks flushed and her lace cap askew, waving a sheet of paper. Another letter?

Alice and Jane hovered behind her in the narrow hall. Relief surged when Sophie saw both of her sisters were smiling. Fifteen-year-old Jane's hands were clasped beneath her chin and as she bounced up and down on her toes, her blond curls bobbed too.

More good news then, thank heavens.

"What is it, Mama?" Sophie asked as she was tugged inside by three pairs of hands and led into the stone-flagged kitchen, where her mother had been making strawberry jam with Mrs. Peel, the cook. The mouthwatering smell of bread baking greeted her, and she felt her own mouth curving into a smile.

"Oh, my goodness." Her mother fanned her face with her cap. "Such wonderful news."

"Yes?" Sophie prompted. Exasperation began to blend with the buzz of excitement fizzing through her veins. "Don't leave me in suspense."

It was Alice who spoke. Her fair cheeks were flushed pink too. "Papa just sent word that the debt to Lord Buxton has been cleared. We won't lose Nettlefield. And you won't have to marry him."

Thank you, God. Thank you. Sophie pressed a hand to her chest as another wave of blessed relief washed over her. "That is indeed wonderful. But how? Where did the money come from?"

Her mother shrugged. "Mr. Debenham did not say. Perhaps he will tell us more when he arrives home. He was at the bank at Bury St. Edmunds when he found out, but he was so excited, he sent a message." Her gaze shifted to Mrs. Peel, who stood by the stove, quietly beaming as she stirred a large pot of the bubbling jam. "Do we have any bottles of the elderflower or bramble wine in the larder? I think we should all have a small glass when Mr. Debenham arrives home."

Sophie sank onto one of the wooden chairs and placed her trembling hands on the cool scrubbed oak tabletop. Her mind was awhirl with questions and possibilities. It was unlikely Lord Buxton had decided to waive the two-thousand-pound debt; he'd been holding it over her stepfather's head like the sword of Damocles for over three years.

As far as she was aware, the only other person who knew of the debt outside of their family circle was Charlie.

Had Charlie had something to do with this? She'd recently sent her friend a letter disclosing some of her worries about the future—namely her mother's hints that Lord Buxton *still* intended to pursue her, and that her family was still in debt to him, despite her stepfather's best efforts.

Had Charlie shared the information with someone else? Like her aunt Tabitha, or her father, Lord Westhampton?

Sophie's gaze fell on the enormous bowl of hulled strawberries in front of her.

What if Charlie had told Nate? Nate had sought to protect her from Lord Buxton on two occasions. If he knew of her precarious situation, would he have been moved to help her?

She had no idea. It really was just wild speculation on her part at this point.

The main thing was, she was safe, and indeed her whole family was safe from Lord Buxton. And that was definitely a cause for celebration.

Pushing her hand into her pinafore's pocket, Sophie withdrew Mr. Murray's letter. "Mama, I have something else to share with you . . ." She swallowed, hoping with all her heart that her mother would be excited for her too. "Some months ago, I wrote a book. A children's book. And a publisher from London has made me an offer." With trembling fingers she passed her mother the slightly crumpled page.

"Sophie. That's brilliant," cried Alice, and Jane squealed. Sophie suddenly found herself crushed in a tight embrace by two pairs of warm arms.

"Is it the stories you wrote for me?" asked Jane. Her blue eyes shone with tears.

"Yes indeed." Sophie pushed a strand of her sister's hair away from her flushed cheek. "Mr. Murray, the publisher, thinks they're delightful."

"Oh, Sophie." Lydia Debenham sank onto the neighboring oak chair. Her eyes were suspiciously bright too. "I never thought . . . I honestly didn't believe you could . . . You're so very clever." She dabbed at the fat tear rolling down her cheek. "Will you ever be able to forgive me? For dismissing your writing? And doubting you?"

"Oh, Mama. Of course I will." Sophie rose from her seat and hugged her mother tightly. Her cheeks were suddenly wet too. "There's nothing to forgive."

Several hours later, Sophie's stepfather arrived home; her mother, still as giddy with joy as a schoolgirl, greeted him by throwing her arms about his tall, almost gaunt form and, to Sophie's surprise, her stepfather kissed her on the mouth. In all her life, she'd *never* seen him demonstrate physical affection for her mother in that way.

She was also dragged into a hug with Mr. Debenham when her mother announced her publication news.

It truly was a day of miracles.

Everyone gathered in the drawing room, including Mrs. Peel and Mr. and Mrs. Hawley, Nettlefield's butler and housekeeper. The elderflower wine was served and a toast was made to the family and good fortune. After the servants had quit the room, Sophie at last ventured the question that was burning the tip of her tongue. "Father, do you know the identity of our mysterious benefactor?"

"Yes, I believe it was Lord Westhampton's son, Lord Malverne," he said. His pale gray eyes regarded Sophie with a narrow-eyed speculative look. "The bank manager reported it was the viscount's man of business who arranged for the deposit of monies into my account earlier this morning. Lord Malverne had written a personal banknote to the sum of two thousand pounds."

All eyes turned to Sophie and her mother said, "Do you know why Lord Malverne would do such a thing, Sophie? I mean, how on earth did he know about the debt? He is Lady Charlotte's older brother, is he not? Lord Westhampton's heir?"

Sophie tried but failed to suppress a blush. Trying to ignore the sensation of heat flooding her entire face, she said, "Yes, he is Lord Westhampton's oldest son. And as to why he has done this, I have no idea. And as to how he knows . . . I must confess, I did confide in Lady Charlotte about my concerns. I was frustrated that we were so beholden to Lord Buxton. And I was worried he would press his suit even though I was not receptive to it. I certainly didn't expect her to share such information with her brother. But it appears that she did."

"Lord Malverne is a most generous man," her stepfather remarked, his gaze still considering. "And such a grand gesture is not one I'd expect from a young ton buck. How old is he again?"

"I . . . I could not say really." Sophie's face was burning. "Less than thirty perhaps . . ." Of course, she knew Nate was seven-and-twenty but she thought it best to prevaricate; it wouldn't do to divulge how well she actually *did* know him.

"And he's not yet married, is he?"

"No. But he's very much a bachelor."

"Well," added her mother, "whether he's a bachelor or not, we will be forever grateful to him, won't we, Mr. Debenham?"

Her stepfather nodded. "Yes, we will. I shall write to him and thank him."

Sophie remained silent, her cheeks still aflame, and sipped her wine. She would write to Nate, too, expressing her heartfelt thanks. But nothing more. He knew how she felt about him. There was no need to belabor the point.

She might be a lonely spinster for the rest of her days,

but at least she had her writing career. And she wouldn't have Lord Buxton breathing down her neck anymore.

And that was something to be grateful for indeed.

Brookfield Park, Suffolk

June 6, 1818

Nate watched Max, the Duke of Exmoor, putting one of Brookfield Park's prize Thoroughbreds through its paces around the training track. His friend was in the market for a stallion for his own stables in Devonshire. While Nate enjoyed riding and racing, horse breeding wasn't a passion of his. But it certainly was for Max.

The early morning mist wreathed a distant stand of trees in a soft golden glow, and on high, a hawk wheeled in the clear blue sky. It was going to be a beautiful day. Nate inhaled a deep breath of the cool, clean air and realized this was the best he'd felt in an age. Deep down he knew it wasn't just the change of scenery that was doing him a world of good. Or the fact that his father had recently recognized that he'd mended his ways, and decreed he could move back to Malverne House if he wanted to.

It was because *he'd* done something worthwhile. Something that had helped someone he cared about in a most tangible, fundamental way.

Sophie Brightwell. Sophie was safe.

And he was nothing but relieved.

She'd written to him, thanking him for his intervention. Even though it was a short letter, it was nonetheless warm and sincere. And she'd signed it: *Yours, Sophie.*

Not *yours sincerely.* Or *yours faithfully.*

Just *yours.*

Yours . . . such a small simple word, yet one that spoke volumes. Because he knew exactly what she meant. She was his.

She loved him.

And he'd been such an idiot not to embrace her and never let her go.

He crossed his arms and felt the crinkle of paper. Sophie's letter was folded and tucked neatly into his coat's breast pocket, and Nate fancied he could feel it against his chest . . . as soft and featherlight as Sophie's touch. Since he'd received her letter three days ago, he'd painstakingly deciphered every word and had read them over and over again until he'd learned it all by heart. Traced the neatly formed script with a fingertip, recalling the times he was privileged enough to actually touch her beautiful body.

Sweet Sophie. She'd never asked him for more than he was willing to give. Yet she'd also given of herself so freely, despite the fact that she was always the one who had the *most* to lose: her reputation, her virtue, her home. Everything.

Every single thing Charlie had said about him was true. He recalled the exact moment he'd laid eyes upon Sophie all those years ago. It was an icy December day in Hyde Park and she was wearing a plain dark blue pelisse. But nothing else about her had been plain. When she'd lifted her beautiful blue eyes to his face and gave him a shy smile, she took his breath away. He'd wanted her. Badly. But she was only eighteen then and she was Charlie's best friend. So he'd tried to forget about her. But then she'd come to stay at Hastings House . . .

Nate sighed. He knew he was a coward at heart. He might have fought in His Majesty's army and faced down Frenchmen on the battlefield, but for years he'd lived with a heart fortified against feeling any tender emotion for the fairer sex. And he'd furnished that cold, impenetrable stronghold in his chest with lies. Lies he told himself every single day. Love makes you weak. Love is your enemy. Love wounds far too much. You are a base creature incapable of love, and you are not worthy of it either.

Well, he was finished with lying to himself. And to Sophie.

Sophie was brave and loyal. Loving and giving. Everything that he wasn't. But that was about to change.

He was going to change. Because Sophie was worth it.

He just prayed she would forgive him for being such a selfish, foolish ass for so long.

Max reined in the sweating gray stallion in front of him. "Well, what do you think?"

Nate reached out and stroked the horse's muscular neck. "He's a fine beast. I'm envious."

"I'd warrant he'd even give Invictus a run for his money."

"I don't doubt it for a moment."

Max slid off the horse. "Once I've settled making the arrangements to purchase Ghost here, why don't we stop by that inn a few miles back at the last village?" He rubbed his flat torso. "I'm in the mood for lashings of something hot and filling."

Nate shook his head. After he'd received Sophie's letter, even before Max had announced he was journeying to Suffolk, he'd decided he needed to pay a visit to the county too. "I'm afraid I might have to leave you to it, old chap. I have another . . . appointment, you could say."

Max threw him a quizzical look. "Has this been your plan all along, Malverne? I was beginning to think you had suddenly taken issue with my personal hygiene when you insisted we take separate carriages."

Nate cocked an eyebrow. "Well, now that you mention it—"

Max gave him a friendly shot to the shoulder. "Whatever it is you're up to, I wish you good fortune, my friend." He frowned. "Now, just wait a moment. Doesn't your sister's friend, that chit you've been mooning over, hail from Suffolk? Is this most important matter related to an affair of the heart, Lord Malverne?"

Nate snorted. "It's none of your business, Your Grace."

Max grinned. "Ha! I'm right then. At long last, one of the mighty *has* fallen. I can't say I'm surprised."

"How's that?"

"You've been bloody miserable for weeks. A right royal pain in the arse. I look forward to seeing you when you've got something to smile about again."

Nate grinned back. "All going well, hopefully that will be within the next few hours."

CHAPTER 23

⁓⁓

Summer is upon us at last and with it comes the promise of long, warm halcyon days.

Garden parties and dining al fresco are clearly all the rage for Suffolk's most discerning hostesses, but is your country garden ready to impress?

The Suffolk County Chronicle:
The English Country Garden Horticultural Column

Nettlefield Grange, Monkton Green, Suffolk

June 6, 1818

Sophie scowled and then sucked at the drop of blood welling from her fingertip. A nasty thorn had just pricked her as she'd snipped off a yellow rose from the gnarled, ancient bush in Nettlefield's front garden. Her mother had asked her to pick a basketful of blooms for an arrangement that would decorate the dining room table because—Sophie shuddered—Lord Buxton was coming to share their Saturday luncheon. Mrs. Peel had been roasting a joint of lamb for several hours, and there would be bowls of honeyed carrots, minted peas, and roasted potatoes, all followed by strawberry fool for dessert.

Sophie had been looking forward to it all until she heard Lord Buxton had been invited. Now she'd all but lost her appetite, despite the wonderful aromas emanating from the kitchen.

Her stepfather had proclaimed this to be a "reconciliation luncheon." Why he'd forgiven the horrid man, given all the stress he'd put their family through, Sophie would never know.

With a sigh, she looked over the bunch of white, yellow, and apricot roses in the wicker basket on the grass at her feet; she needed a few more of the yellow blooms, otherwise the arrangement would look unbalanced. Reaching forward, she gingerly pushed aside one of the rosebush's branches, then readied her pruning shears to cut another flower—

"Miss Brightwell! What a delight for the senses. A feast for the eyes. Fancy finding a rose among the roses."

Blast and damn! It was Lord Buxton. How had he sneaked up on her like that? She hadn't heard a horse or a gig on the laneway. He must have come on foot.

Odious man.

Sophie lowered her pruning shears, but as she turned, she let go of the branch she'd been holding much too quickly and it whipped back into place, scratching her upper arm and ruining the sleeve of her white muslin gown.

Double damn!

This morning was turning out to be vexing in more ways than one.

"Oh no, Sophie. Look at your gown. And your arm." Lord Buxton stepped forward, one pudgy hand outstretched, and with prickly rosebushes at her back, Sophie had nowhere to go.

Even though her arm was starting to sting, she replied, "It's all right. 'Tis but a scratch. And I'm sure my sleeve can be repaired." She glanced meaningfully toward the house. "I'm sure Father is in. He would be most pleased to see you."

"All in good time." Lord Buxton smiled, exposing his yellowing, misshapen teeth. "I actually came a little earlier in the hope I might speak with you alone, Sophie." He touched her forearm, and Sophie shivered as unease snaked down her spine. "And here you are . . ."

Unfortunately, a tall rhododendron bush obstructed her

view of the drawing room window where Alice and Jane were currently ensconced. Which meant neither of them could see her either. Or the fact that she was trapped.

Sophie swallowed and tried to step sideways to maneuver around the baron. "Yes. But I must go back in. Mama is expecting me to arrange—"

"Tsk, tsk. Why are you always in such a hurry to get away from me, Sophie? We've known each other for so long. Years. Indeed, it seems like I've been waiting forever for you to come of age." One fat finger slid along her arm toward the crook of her elbow. "What harm can it do if you and I linger a little longer here in the garden? It is such a lovely day after all."

Ugh! Sophie almost lost the coddled egg she'd eaten for breakfast all over Lord Buxton's Prussian blue waistcoat. "Lord Buxton, I do not wish to hurt your feelings, but I did try to tell you once before in London that your attentions are not welcome. At all. I could not be clearer or more certain."

"Ah, but that was about the time you were being courted by Lord Claremont, was it not? And you turned him down. And I cannot help but wonder if that's because your heart belongs to another." Lord Buxton suddenly grasped both of her upper arms so tightly, Sophie gasped. His fingers pressed into the scratch, making it burn. "Someone like me, Sophie dearest? I've seen the way you look at me."

With revulsion! "Lord Buxton, please step aside. At once." Sophie still had the pruning shears in her hand, and while she did not wish to inflict bodily harm on the baron, she would defend herself if she absolutely had to.

"I know I was a little abrupt in London when I last saw you, but my passion for you runs so very deep," murmured Lord Buxton, pushing closer. His large belly pressed against her, and she had the awful feeling that he was beginning to sport an erection in his too-tight pantaloons. His hot, stale breath wafted over her face, making her stomach pitch and roll in earnest. "Pray, do not be shy, darling Sophie. You have a scandalous past after all. I sometimes dream about all of the wicked things you must have got up to in London. Besides, what harm could one little kiss do? You know I'll offer for you, despite your ruined reputation."

The gall of the man! Anger sharpened Sophie's voice as she spoke with every ounce of vehemence she could muster. "Lord Buxton, I wouldn't accept a proposal from you if you were the last man on earth! Now, let go of me this instant, or so help me, I'll—"

She got no further as all of a sudden Lord Buxton was yanked backward, away from her.

"You heard Miss Brightwell, you dog. Leave her alone."

Nate! Before she could even think to say another word, he threw his fist, striking the baron's jaw, and Lord Buxton's head snapped to the side. He hit the ground in an inelegant heap.

"You bastard," Lord Buxton groaned, spitting blood onto the grass. His lip was split and his small beady eyes were wild. "You'll pay for this . . . this outrage."

"I already have paid," snarled Nate, flexing his fingers. "Two thousand pounds. This family owes you nothing. Miss Brightwell owes you nothing."

Lord Buxton scrambled to his feet. "So it was you." He swayed for a moment, then pulled a handkerchief from his coat pocket and held it to his mouth. His gaze darted to Sophie. "Have you been doing the viscount special favors in return for—"

Nate stepped forward and threw another swift punch. This time it landed squarely in the middle of Lord Buxton's ample belly. The baron doubled over, wheezing. "Might I suggest you keep your mouth shut, Lord Buxton?" growled Nate. "I don't take kindly to those who hurl insults at my future wife."

Wife? Sophie gasped. Surely she was dreaming. Had Nate really come all the way to Nettlefield to ask her to marry him?

Lord Buxton straightened, clutching his middle. "You, sir . . . have gone too far. I should call you out."

Nate shook his head. "I served as an infantry captain in His Majesty's army under Wellington. Do you really think you could best me in a duel, Lord Buxton?"

The baron's fleshy face paled to the same shade as his white linen neck cloth. His gaze skittered to Sophie. "Please pass on my apologies to your stepfather, Miss Brightwell. I will not be sharing lunch with your family today. Or any day henceforth."

With that, he turned around and walked a little unsteadily across the lawn, toward the path leading to the front garden gate.

Sophie released a shaky sigh of relief and dropped the pruning shears by the discarded basket of roses. "Thank you, Nate," she said softly. "Thank you for everything."

Her heart fluttered oddly in her chest. She was shaking and too nervous to turn around to look at him directly. The leaves of the old oak by the gate fluttered gently in the light breeze. Nate's spicy cologne mingled with the scent of the roses, and she had to fight the urge to bury her face in his wide chest.

I don't take kindly to those who hurl insults at my future wife. Did Nate really just say that, or did she imagine it? It was only the insistent sting of the scratch on her arm that convinced her that she wasn't actually dreaming.

She could feel Nate's gaze on her face, drifting over her body like a whisper-soft caress.

"Sophie," he murmured, stepping closer. The heat of his large body seared her. Made her tremble all the more. "Why won't you look at me?"

"I'm afraid to," she admitted. Her voice was little more than a husky whisper. "I've tried so very hard to stop loving you. If I look at you, and I don't see in your eyes what I've always longed to see . . ." She closed her eyes and shook her head. "I don't think I could bear it."

"Oh, sweetheart." Nate's fingers were gentle beneath her chin. "What an absolute mess I've made of things. I've been such a fool. The king of fools. You have good reason to doubt me. When I think of how much I've hurt you . . ." His breath caught, and Sophie opened her eyes.

And her heart tripped. Nate was looking at her with such naked adoration, she had to remind herself to breathe too. Reaching out, she touched his hard chest with trembling fingers. Was that his heartbeat she could feel, crashing against his ribs? Was this wicked, rakish, never-fall-in-love viscount nervous? "Tell me why you are here, Nate. I need to hear you say it."

He swallowed, and the expression in his brown eyes firmed. "Sophie, ever since you said goodbye, I feel as though I've been living in a desolate wasteland. A place bereft of sunlight, and beauty, and hope. A hell of my own making. And it's all because I've been too blind, nay too stubborn to admit to myself that I've fallen hopelessly, irrevocably, and passionately in love with you. Sophie, you are everything I want. Everything I dream of. And I would humbly beg your forgiveness." He caressed her cheek with the back of his fingers as he whispered, "And if perchance, you still loved me, too, I would be a happy man indeed."

Oh, my goodness. Sophie drew a shaky breath as joy flooded her heart. Nate had just told her that he loved her in the most beautiful, heartfelt way. She could scarcely fathom it. "Of course I forgive you, Nate." She traced the shape of his lips. His dark eyebrows. His strong, lean jaw. Yes, he was real. *This* was real. "And yes, I love you. With all my heart. I've never stopped loving you. And I know I'll love you forever and always."

Nate's mouth tipped into a crooked smile. "Forever and always. I adore the sound of that, my sweet Sophie."

All at once, Nate sank to a bended knee before her. Clasping both her hands in his, he raised them to his lips, then his gaze caught and held hers. "Sophie Brightwell, you've captured my heart and captivated my soul. I cannot bear the thought of living without you a moment longer. Will you do me the untold honor of consenting to be my wife?"

Sophie's vision blurred with tears of pure bliss. Her heart sang with joy. "Yes, Nathaniel Hastings," she whispered, "unequivocally, undeniably, wholeheartedly yes."

"Oh, God, Sophie." Nate surged to his feet and caught her to his chest. He spun her around, and when he put her down, he cradled her face. "I never thought I could be so happy. I love you so much." He slanted his mouth over hers and kissed her gently, his lips sliding over hers with such tenderness, Sophie's breath caught. "I love you." Nate's next kiss was deeper, the press of his lips firmer. His fingers slid into her hair, and his tongue slipped into her mouth.

"I love you." His words were almost a groan when he pulled back to draw breath. And then he kissed her again, his mouth ravishing, his tongue plundering. And she kissed him back with equal fervor. His hands skimmed across her shoulders, down her arms, over her body until they cupped her bottom and pulled her firmly against him. She could already feel the press of his hard manhood against the softness of her belly. Oh, how she wanted him. She wanted—

"Sophie?"

Oh, God. Sophie gasped and Nate dragged his mouth away. She looked up to discover her mother staring at her in openmouthed horror.

She swallowed. "Mama," she said in a voice that was noticeably husky with emotion and desire. "Mama, this is Lord Malverne. He and I . . . we are to be married. Nate just proposed. And I've said yes. We are in love."

Her mother blinked. "M-married? But . . ." Her forehead creased into a perplexed frown. "Married, you say? You are going to marry Lord Malverne?"

"Yes, Mama," Sophie said with a smile. "I am."

Nate, who'd been standing behind her all this time, probably to conceal the suspicious bulge at the front of his breeches, at last stepped forward and bowed. "Mrs. Debenham. How do you do? It is indeed a pleasure to finally meet you. Sophie has told me so much about you."

Her mother blushed and bobbed a curtsy. "Lord Malverne. It is an honor to meet you. Our family owes you so much . . ." Her forehead knitted into a frown again. "But is it true? What Sophie just said? Have you proposed marriage to my daughter?"

Nate's mouth curved into a smile that was pure, unadulterated charm. "I have indeed, Mrs. Debenham. And I count myself the luckiest man alive right at this moment because Sophie consented. I love her and I'm overjoyed that her affections are returned with the same degree of ardor."

"Well, I never!" Her mother's hands flew to her cheeks. "I cannot believe it. That's wonderful news." Her gaze shifted to Sophie. "I think I understand why you turned down Lord Claremont now."

Before Sophie could respond, her mother exclaimed again, "Sophie! What on earth has happened to your arm? And your sleeve."

She winced. "Ah, the yellow rosebush attacked me."

Nate frowned when he examined the scratch too. "You should get this attended to, my love," he said gently.

"And you should have your knuckles seen to as well."

"My word, are they bleeding too?" asked her mother. "What happened?"

Sophie traded glances with Nate. She supposed she would need to explain the situation to her mother and step-father at some stage anyway. "Ah, Lord Buxton was here a short time ago. And he and Nate had a disagreement . . . about me. Lord Buxton won't be coming for lunch today."

"Good heavens, Sophie. You've got three men fighting over you? And you thought you were going to be an old maid."

She took Sophie by the arm and continued to prattle away as she ushered her toward the front stairs of the house. "Now come, you two. Let's go inside. Lord Malverne, I take it you will join us all for luncheon? Mr. Debenham would love to meet you, of course, and I'm sure you would like to discuss your, er, intentions in regard to Sophie with him. And then when you are done, I daresay, luncheon will be on the table. And what a feast it will be! Mrs. Peel— she's our cook—has baked the most wonderful roast lamb. And then there's strawberry fool for dessert. If you don't mind my saying so, you look like you need a bit of fattening up, my lord."

"Mother!" exclaimed Sophie but Nate laughed.

"I would love to join you for luncheon, Mrs. Debenham. I especially can't wait for dessert." He cast Sophie a heated look that made her blush to the roots of her hair. "I particularly love strawberries. The sweeter, the better."

* * *

Nate stayed for lunch and, to his surprise, had a most enjoyable time. The company was convivial. Sophie's stepfather, Mr. Debenham, might have a laconic manner, but he also had a dry wit that brought a smile to Nate's face on more than one occasion during the simple but delicious meal. Mrs. Debenham was a trifle flighty but undoubtedly of a sweet temperament. And Sophie's two younger half sisters, Alice and Jane, were both well-spoken, intelligent girls. When they eventually had their Seasons, he didn't think it would take long at all for them to find suitable matches.

However, by the time dessert arrived, Nate was champing at the bit to leave. To have Sophie all to himself. *To make love to her.*

Perhaps it was the nature of the strawberry-laden dessert that started to get him all hot and bothered beneath his cravat. Perhaps it was the fact that he hadn't seen Sophie for over three weeks. Or perhaps it was simply the case that whenever he looked at his beautiful *fiancée*, she took his breath away. Her cheeks were flushed and her blue eyes glowed with joy as she chatted and laughed. And then there was the distraction of her glossy black hair; errant, curling strands kept slipping from the loose coil at the back of her head and caressing her face. His fingers twitched with the urge to either brush the stray locks behind her ears or pull the pins out so her hair tumbled about her slender shoulders and the rest of her preferably naked body.

Yes . . . they needed to leave, and soon, before he embarrassed himself by growing an erection at the dinner table.

Decision made, Nate put down his silver spoon and rose from his chair. "Mr. and Mrs. Debenham, would you mind terribly if I took a turn about the garden with your daughter? It's such a lovely afternoon."

"Of course not. By all means," replied Sophie's stepfather.

"Yes, do take a walk," added Mrs. Debenham. "Take as long as you like."

Sophie blushed as she stood. "Thank you, Father. Mama."

When they reached the front garden, Sophie gave Nate a curious look as he steered her down the path and out the gate. "This isn't the garden," she remarked as they followed the lane meandering between the hedgerows. "Are we going to the village instead? And, by the way, how did you get here? You seemed to appear from nowhere. I didn't hear a horse or a carriage."

Nate grinned. "To answer your first question, yes we are going to the village. And to answer your second, I came in my carriage. I left it at the inn so the horses could be watered, and then I walked here. It's less than a mile so I thought, why not?"

"Oh. I really should be wearing my bonnet, spencer, and gloves if we are walking to the village. People will talk."

"Let them. And besides, you won't need them," said Nate.

"Won't need them?"

Nate cast her a sinful smile. "No. In fact, considering what I have planned for the rest of the afternoon and evening, you won't need any clothes at all, Miss Brightwell."

Sophie blushed a delicious shade of pink. "But . . . I can't. We shouldn't do anything that would raise eyebrows. Not here in Monkton Green at least."

"Ah, you see we won't be staying here. My carriage shall take us to Saxbridge. I've already hired a room for the night—the bridal suite—at the Rose and Crown under the name of Mr. and Mrs. Hastings."

Sophie gasped and stopped in the middle of the lane. "You did?"

"I can see you are shocked, but please don't worry, darling Sophie. When we arrive in Monkton Green, I shall send a message to Nettlefield to let your parents know there's been a change of plans to allay any fears. Something along the lines of Charlie and Aunt Tabitha traveling with us so everything appears aboveboard. And then, tomorrow, we shall repair to London. Your family will be more than welcome to follow, of course. There are more than enough rooms at Hastings House or even Chelmsford House for that matter. If that's all right with you, my love?"

Sophie looked as though she couldn't quite decide if she wanted to hug him or berate him. "But . . . but what if they find out none of it's true?"

Nate cocked a brow. "What can your parents really do? Demand that I marry you?"

Sophie laughed then kissed him. "You are an incorrigible rogue, Lord Malverne. But I've always loved that about you. All right, we shall run away to Saxbridge together and you can have your wicked way with me."

"I'm pleased to hear it," he murmured in a low velvet voice that he knew would make her shiver with anticipation. "Because before the night is through, I intend to be very wicked indeed."

CHAPTER 24

❧

Scandal in Saxbridge!

You might need to have the smelling salts at hand before reading further . . .

The Disgraceful Debutante, Miss S. B. from M. G., was sighted in the company of a well-known, thoroughly wicked rakehell . . . at a coaching inn . . .

All alone! The mind boggles!

The Suffolk County Chronicle:
Vignettes of Village Life

The Rose and Crown Inn, Saxbridge, Suffolk

June 6, 1818

The five-mile carriage ride to Saxbridge really took no time at all, yet to Nate, it was absolute torture. He was torn between his desire to strip Sophie naked in the carriage so he could make mad passionate love to her then and there, and his desire to treat her with all the tender reverence she should be accorded, this wonderful woman who would soon be his wife. She should be undressed slowly and with care, and he should worship her as she should be worshipped. It was her first time, and he wanted the experience to be beautiful for her.

In the end, he tried to satisfy himself, and her, by kissing her senseless and fondling her delectable breasts through the layers of her clothing. By the time the carriage drew into the yard of the inn, both of them were disheveled and panting with need.

After Sophie had hastily repinned her hair and he'd retied his cravat and buttoned up his waistcoat, he handed her down from the carriage himself, then escorted her inside.

The inn was small, but when he'd inspected it earlier in the day, it looked to be of a superior standard. It was a Tudor-style building with low-beamed ceilings and slightly uneven wooden floors, but all the woodwork gleamed with polish, and the furnishings were of good quality. And the bridal suite—while not fit for a king exactly—was lavish enough, with a large tester bed swathed in rich blue damask curtains, a matching counterpane, and an abundance of fat pillows.

As Nate waited for the innkeeper to check that the room was ready, he noticed Sophie was biting her kiss-bruised lower lip. "Are you nervous, my love?" he murmured in a low voice meant only for her. "We don't have to do this. We can wait until after we are wed. I've just been missing you so desperately, I suppose I'm not acting with the gentlemanly restraint I probably should."

Sophie shook her head and smiled. "I am a little nervous. But no, I don't want to wait. I'm desperate for you too."

He kissed her hand, his tongue touching her satiny skin, and she blushed.

"Miss Brightwell. Goodness gracious me."

Nate turned his attention to the plump, well-dressed woman bustling into the inn with a bespectacled female companion, possibly her daughter, and a sad-eyed spaniel following in their wake.

A flicker of apprehension crossed Sophie's face. "Mrs. Danvers. Miss Danvers. Good . . . good afternoon. I did not expect to see you here . . . Are you on your way to London?"

"No. I'm on my way to Bury St. Edmunds, but I shall be returning home tomorrow. I must say, I certainly never expected to see you in Saxbridge, either, with . . ." Mrs. Danvers examined Nate through her gold-rimmed quizzing glass. "I don't know you. What are you doing with Miss Brightwell?"

Nate summoned a charming smile and bent over the woman's hand. "Allow me to introduce myself, Mrs. Danvers. Miss Danvers. I am Nathaniel Hastings, Lord Malverne. And Miss Brightwell's *fiancé*."

Mrs. Danvers's sparse gray eyebrows shot up. "What? You're engaged to our Miss Brightwell?" The woman blinked at Sophie. "Is this true, Miss Brightwell? Do your parents know?"

"Of course it's true. And yes, my parents know. They have given us their blessing."

Mrs. Danvers's disbelieving gaze traveled over Nate again. "Well, I never . . ."

At that moment, the innkeeper returned. "Mr. Hastings. I'm so sorry to keep you waiting. Here is the key to your room. I trust you and your charming new wife will enjoy your stay in our bridal suite. Please do not hesitate to ring for anything that you might need during the course of your stay."

Nate took the brass key and inclined his head. "Thank you." When he turned around, he wasn't surprised at all to see Sophie had turned bright red and that Mrs. Danvers was gasping for air. Miss Danvers's eyes were as round as the lenses of her spectacles. The dog was the only one who looked disinterested.

Not wishing to prolong the awkward encounter, Nate bowed. "Mrs. Danvers. Miss Danvers. It was a pleasure to make your acquaintance. I hope you'll forgive me, but I have other pressing business to attend to. Good day."

With that, he took Sophie's arm, and with key in hand, he escorted his betrothed up the wooden staircase to the upper floor where the bridal suite lay.

As soon as they were inside, Sophie clapped her hand over her mouth. Nate wasn't sure if she was trying to suppress a scream or a fit of giggles.

Unfortunately, her reaction was one of pure horror. "Nate! Oh, my goodness. That was Mrs. Danvers, one of Monkton Green's worst gossips. The scandal will be all over the village by tomorrow evening. And what will my parents think? When they find out we pretended to be new-lyweds, they'll suspect your aunt and Charlie weren't here to act as chaperones either."

Nate shrugged and began tugging at his neck cloth. "Scandal be damned, my darling Sophie. I love you and you love me. Nothing else matters."

She shook her head as though he were an errant child who'd exasperated her and she didn't quite know what to do about it. But at least she was smiling. "Oh, Nate. I suppose you are right."

"About this I am." Nate grinned and threw his neck cloth over a nearby wing chair. "Now come here, my love. Let's do something that's *really* scandalous."

S ophie laughed as delicious anticipation unfurled low in her belly. She was about to make love with her husband-to-be and now, thanks to him, she didn't give a fig about what anyone else thought.

However, a knock on the door to their room had her jumping.

Nate shrugged out of his swallowtail coat. "It's all right. I expect it's our luggage." He tossed the garment aside as he crossed to the door. "Ah, Nichols, my good man. Just deposit everything on the chest by the foot of the bed, if you'd be so kind."

Our luggage? Sophie blinked. Sure enough, Nate's footman carried in two leather valises, a hatbox, and several large parcels tied up with string. When the door clicked shut after the departing servant, Sophie raised a quizzical brow. "What else have you been up to today, Lord Malverne?"

Nate shrugged as he sat down in the bedside wing chair before tugging off one of his boots. "I hope you don't mind, but I took it upon myself to do a little shopping on your behalf on the way here. Bury St. Edmunds's shops aren't a patch on Bond Street's, but I hope you like the clothes and undergarments I chose for you. I even remembered to purchase a bonnet, gloves, and a hairbrush."

"Of course I don't mind. That's so very sweet of you." Sophie crossed to the end of the bed and unwrapped one of the parcels. Inside lay a fine linen chemise trimmed with exquisite lace and a pair of gossamer silk stockings. "*You* chose these undergarments for me? They're divine"—she threw him a mock frown—"even if they're shockingly sheer."

Nate waggled his eyebrows as he tugged off his other boot. "I know. Positively indecent, aren't they? I had such fun picking them out." His boots and stockings removed, Nate stood and pulled off his shirt in one smooth movement. "Now, Sophie, my love," he said as he dropped the garment onto the chair. "As much as I'd love to continue chatting with you about my shopping expedition, I think the time has come for you to start removing *your* clothes."

Oh. Sophie swallowed. She'd done all kinds of scandalous things with Nate, but she'd never been completely naked in front of him, in broad daylight. Her body might be thrumming with desire and her mouth watering at the sight of Nate's bare, heavily muscled upper body, but her stomach was aflutter with butterflies. What would he think of her?

He was a rake and he'd bedded so many women.

But she didn't want to think about them. And right at this moment, Nate only had eyes for her. Indeed, his hot gaze was so intense as she began to pull the pins from her hair, she thought she might catch alight.

He moved closer. "Would you like me to help?" he asked in a low voice that seemed to stroke over her like a velvet-soft caress.

She swallowed and nodded. "Yes." Trying to smile with a confidence she didn't feel, she added, "For some strange reason, I seem to have gone all shy."

"Don't be. I love you, Sophie. And you're beautiful." He seemed transfixed by the sight of her hair, tumbling about her shoulders. Lifting one of the tresses, he rubbed it between his fingers. "It feels just like silk."

She smiled. His soft, reverent words gave her confidence. "Would you help me undo my gown?"

"Gladly." Nate stepped behind her and swept her hair to one side. As he undid the laces of her gown, stays, and shift, he dropped a trail of featherlight kisses upon her nape and down the length of her spine, making her tremble with delight. "Your skin feels like satin beneath my lips," he whispered as he gently cradled her jaw with one large hand. Burying his face in her neck, he inhaled and the gentle current of his breath stirred her desire all the more. "I've always loved how you smell . . ." He laved her shoulder with a hot, openmouthed kiss. "And taste."

When her garments had pooled on the floor at her feet and she stood naked but for her stockings and slippers, Nate drew her against him, her back to his front. His large hands rose to cup her breasts. "You have such pretty breasts, my love." His thumbs circled her nipples, and liquid heat flooded her sex. "So perfectly round and perfectly delicious. My mouth waters at the sight of them."

"It does?"

"Oh, yes. And I'd warrant your sweet cunny is just as lovely."

Sophie bit her lip and dropped her head back against Nate's shoulder. The folds of her quim were now heavy and throbbing with need. Any lingering shyness had at last fled. "How can you say such wanton things?" she whispered. Nate's member was a hard rod against her bottom, and she had the urge to rub herself against it.

He scraped his cheek against hers, the gentle rasp of his stubble making her shiver. "I intend to *do* wanton things with you, my love. Climb upon the bed."

Sophie kicked off her slippers and did as he asked. Lying on her back, reclining against the plump pillows, she felt both desirable and beautiful as Nate's fevered gaze drifted over her. She reached for the ribbon garter of one of her white silk stockings, but he stayed her hand. "Leave them on, my sweet. Seeing you almost, but not quite, naked stirs me like nothing else."

"Very well. But while *I* am almost completely naked, you are far from it. Remove your breeches, Lord Malverne. Your bride-to-be wants to see *you* in all your naked glory."

Nate grinned. "I'm more than happy to oblige."

Within moments, Nate had whipped off his formfitting breeches, revealing his thick, muscular thighs, firmly rounded buttocks, and proudly jutting manhood. Sophie bit her lip as a fresh wave of desire washed through her.

"Do you like what you see?" he asked as he slid onto the bed beside her.

She nodded. "Yes. You take my breath away, Nate." She touched his warm chest and ran her fingertips through the dark hair dusting his pectoral muscles. "You are beautiful too."

He smiled. "Thank you. Now . . ." He kissed her mouth, then her shoulder. "It's time for this viscount to be truly wicked."

"What we're doing isn't wicked enough?" asked Sophie as Nate lowered his head and drew one of her nipples into his mouth and suckled.

Nate raised his head and flicked his tongue against her other nipple. "Not anywhere near it."

His fingers skimmed over her ribs, across her belly, then down to the black curls at the apex of her thighs. One long finger brushed the wet seam before he pushed between the folds.

Oh, it feels so good.

Closing her eyes, Sophie threaded her fingers into Nate's thick silken hair and gave herself over to the desire flowing through her veins like molten honey. Nate began to circle the small sensitive bud at the top of her quim, and she moaned, spreading her legs wider. Arching into his touch.

All of a sudden, Nate skated down the bed and gently pushed her thighs even farther apart until his shoulders fit between them. Her sex was completely exposed, and he was studying her most private parts with an expression that could only be described as rapt.

"What are you doing?" she gasped. She'd read about all sorts of sexual practices in *Memoirs of a Woman of Pleasure*, but she never thought Nate might actually do some of them. With her.

"Being wicked." He looked up the length of her body, his dark gaze hot and hungry. "I want to taste your cunny, my love, and I'd wager it's just as sweet as the rest of you."

He ran one long finger up one slippery fold, then down the other, before sliding it into her tight, virginal entrance. Sophie sucked in a breath at the novel sensation of being invaded in such an intimate place. But she rather thought she liked it, especially when Nate began working his finger in and out of her, mimicking the act of love.

"So . . ." He cocked an eyebrow. "You haven't answered me, Sophie. Will you let me use my mouth on you? To pleasure you?"

"Mm-hmm. If you want to." Her shock and any lingering inhibitions had been washed away by delicious sensation. Everything Nate did to her always felt wonderful. He loved her and she trusted him. "Do whatever you like. I'm yours."

"Sweet Jesus, Sophie," Nate groaned. His breath was hot against her dew-drenched folds. "If *you* say wicked things like that, I'll come before I even get inside you."

Sophie smiled but then all coherent thought fled when the tip of Nate's tongue delicately lapped at her sex.

Oh, my God. Wicked didn't even begin to describe the sensation. Could something be divinely wicked? If it could, it was this. Her breath quickened as Nate's tongue flickered over and around the tiny throbbing nub where her pleasure was centered. Her insides tightened and rippled as her orgasm began to build, the familiar tension growing. Swelling. It felt as if a beautiful budding thing was about to bloom just like a flower bursting open in bright sunlight.

Nate slid another finger inside her and increased the pace of his thrusting. The exquisite friction increased, and she rolled her hips and gripped the silk counterpane beneath her. Pleasure beckoned. She could feel it pulling, tugging, but just out of reach. She moaned in frustration, and then Nate captured her nub with his lips and suckled. And that was enough to throw her heavenward into ecstasy. Scintillating bliss radiated through her and she cried out, twisting and writhing, holding on to Nate's head as he continued to pump his clever fingers while ravishing her pulsating core with his mouth.

When she could stand the pleasure no more, she curled her fingers into his hair, trying to lift his head. "Nate . . ."

"Yes, my love?" The evidence of her arousal shone on Nate's lips and chin. Heavens, she was wet. She supposed she should be embarrassed, but she felt so drugged with satisfaction and wonder, she wasn't. And Nate certainly wasn't bothered. Not judging by the sinful, satisfied twinkle in his dark eyes.

"Thank you. That was truly amazing. Indescribable, really. Indeed, you've loved me so well, I'm certain I won't be able to move for a week."

"Surely not." Nate crawled up the bed until he hovered over her, his hot, hard body close to but not quite touching hers. He bestowed a gentle kiss on her lips. "We've only just begun."

He buried his face in her neck and devoured her throat and jaw, and very soon, Sophie felt desire stirring deep inside her lower belly again. How was it possible? Nate was turning her into a wanton creature with an insatiable appetite for all things carnal.

She suddenly wanted the man she loved with all her heart to truly make her his. Her hand slid between their bodies, and she brushed her fingers along Nate's rigid shaft.

He immediately jerked. "Sweetheart," he groaned. "I so want to be inside you. Will you let me?"

She kissed him. "Of course. I want that, too, darling Nate." She wrapped her fingers about him and gently squeezed. "I've been waiting so long for this moment. I cannot wait to be yours."

Nate's forehead creased with a concerned frown. "It will hurt at first. Or so I've been led to believe. I must confess"—he stroked her face as he looked deeply into her eyes—"this is a first for me too."

"What do you mean?"

"Well, not only am I making love to the one and only woman I've ever fallen in love with, this is the very first time I've bedded a virgin."

Sophie arched an eyebrow. "Surely not. You must be teasing me."

Nate's gaze was serious again. "Not at all."

"Goodness, I hope I measure up then."

"Sophie Brightwell, to me, you are incomparable in every single way imaginable. And I consider myself blessed indeed that you have consented to be mine." Nate dipped his head and caught her mouth in another lingering kiss that made Sophie's toes curl and desire pulse with an insistence that could not be denied.

"Nate," she murmured when he released her mouth, "I cannot wait a moment longer. I love you, and more than anything, I want this, for us to be joined as one flesh."

"God, I love you, Sophie." The flames of desire behind Nate's eyes were tempered by the soft conviction of his words. And in that moment, Sophie truly believed him. Any doubts she'd had that Nate really loved her were utterly chased away.

Nate gently nudged her thighs apart with his legs and positioned himself at her entrance. The head of his member parted her folds. "You're still very slick, my love. That should help ease my way." His gaze locked with hers. "Are you ready?"

She laced her fingers around the back of his strong neck. "With my whole heart, I say yes."

Nate began to thrust his hips in a series of gentle pulses. Even though Sophie was ready and willing, his penetration burned and brought tears to her eyes.

"I'm sorry, my heart," he whispered. "You are so very tight."

Despite the pain, Sophie couldn't help but tease him. "And you are so very large."

"You are doing wonders for my self-esteem, darling girl."

Sophie closed her eyes and swallowed a whimper as Nate pushed farther in. Surely he must be *all* the way in by now. "As if your self-esteem needs stroking, Lord Malverne," she murmured when she was able to catch her breath again.

"By you it does." Nate pressed forward again. "I need constant reassurance that you consider me worthy."

"Of course you are. And you always will be."

"Almost there." As Nate surged forward one last time, Sophie gasped, but the worst of the pain seemed to have passed.

"My brave girl," he whispered before feathering tender kisses across her cheeks, forehead, and then her mouth. "Are you all right?"

Sophie attempted to smile but she suspected it was more of a grimace. "Apart from the fact that I feel as though I've been impaled by a maypole, I'm perfectly fine."

"It will get better . . ." Nate's face showed signs of strain as well; his brow was beaded with perspiration, and the skin over his cheekbones was stretched tight. His substantial biceps muscles were bunched with tension as he held himself perfectly still. "If you can stand it, I'd very much like to move, my love."

"Of course." Sophie curled her fingers around his wide shoulders. "You've given me so much pleasure, my darling Nate. Take yours."

Nate stared down at the beautiful woman in his arms, and thanked heaven for the gift of her. He didn't deserve Sophie, but he was thankful all the same.

He bent his head and captured her mouth as he began to move, each glide long, slow, and measured at first; he knew Sophie was putting on a brave face for him. She enveloped him so tightly, it was as if he were gripped by a silken fist. The pressure, the friction, the wet heat were overwhelming in their intensity; it wouldn't be long until he achieved his own climax.

But he wanted Sophie to be with him when he tumbled into bliss as well.

He worshipped her lips, her neck, her breasts, anywhere he could reach with his mouth as he gradually began to increase the pace of their coupling. And by degrees he felt Sophie relax; her fingernails no longer dug into the flesh of his shoulders and she started to move her own hips, her pelvic thrusts perfectly timed with his.

When she moaned and wrapped her legs about his buttocks, he thrust harder, faster. Deeper. His blood pounded; his heart raced at breakneck speed. He could feel his orgasm gathering pace, gathering power like a storm; the pressure was building, coiling around his spine, drawing his balls up tight, making his hammering cock throb with the need to let go. To surrender to the irresistible urge to pour everything he had into Sophie.

Christ, he needed to come but Sophie wasn't on the brink yet. She panted beneath him, her eyes squeezed shut. He thrust his fingers into the tumbling black mass of her hair.

"Sophie . . . come with me, sweetheart . . . look at me."

Her blue eyes met his, and then her whole body arched. Her fingernails scored his back and she screamed his name. Her core spasmed with such force, it sent him over the edge as well.

Groaning, shuddering, he was engulfed by a great pulsating rush of pure ecstasy. Stars exploded behind his closed eyelids. All the while, Sophie's rippling sex squeezed him, milked him until he had nothing left to give.

Sweet Jesus. He'd never had a more profound sexual experience in his life.

When he at last emerged from the sublime haze of deep satisfaction clouding his senses, he discovered Sophie's mouth had curved into the most beautiful smile he'd ever seen. It was a smile he'd never forget until his dying day.

"I love you, Nathaniel," she whispered, her blue eyes shining with tears, and with such adoration that Nate's thundering heart almost stopped.

"And I love you, too, my sweet Sophie. Now, forever, and always." And then he pressed his mouth to hers, sealing his promise with a kiss.

EPILOGUE

❧

Wedding bells are ringing in Gloucestershire!

The word is out . . . Nathaniel Hastings, Viscount Malverne, is to wed Miss Sophie Brightwell of Monkton Green, Suffolk, at his country estate.

Felicitations to Lord Malverne and his new viscountess!

The Beau Monde Mirror: The Society Page

Deerhurst Park, Gloucestershire

June 20, 1818

Sophie still couldn't quite believe it. But every time she glanced at the shining diamond-encrusted gold wedding band on her ring finger, she knew it must be true; she and Nate had indeed been married by special license in Deerhurst's private chapel only a few short hours ago.

She never thought she could be so happy. She was awash with it. And she couldn't stop smiling.

Sipping champagne with Charlie and Olivia, the late afternoon sunshine bathed the flower-filled gardens of Deerhurst Park in soft golden light. Could she actually be in heaven? From her position on a stone bench by a fragrant rose arbor, she was afforded a glorious view of her breathtakingly handsome husband; attired in a perfectly cut swallowtail coat of dove gray and ivory trousers, with the gentle early evening breeze coming off the River Severn ruffling his chestnut hair, he was a striking sight. He was currently conversing with his father, Lord Westhampton, the devilishly handsome Duke of Exmoor, and her stepfather. When Nate threw his head back, laughing at something the duke said, her smile widened. Yes, she couldn't quite believe it.

"Quick, pinch me, Charlie," she said, reaching for her friend's hand. "I want to make sure this is real and I'm not dreaming."

Charlie laughed. "You will have bruises all over you at this rate, Lady Malverne. How many times have you asked me to do that today?"

"Too many, I expect," said Olivia. "She's asked me too."

Sophie was thrilled Olivia was here sans her guardians. Somehow, Lady Chelmsford had managed to persuade her friend's aunt and uncle that she would be able to provide suitable chaperonage during her stay at Deerhurst.

Charlie's aunt was presently chatting to Alice, Jane, and her own mother, who was glowing with champagne and good cheer. Sophie had never seen her mama so happy. And she could certainly understand why. All her daughters' futures would be secure. Not only was her oldest daughter now Sophie Hastings, Viscountess Malverne, both Alice and Jane would have spectacular debuts when their time came.

The sound of male laughter again drew Sophie's attention to the group gathered by the river. It was wonderful that the Duke of Exmoor had been able to attend considering Nate's other two good friends hadn't. Lord Langdale was still on the Continent, and Hamish MacQueen, the Marquess of Sleat, had been called away to attend to business on his remote estate on the Isle of Skye. It appeared Lord Sleat was a magnanimous man indeed, as not only had he sent his sincerest apologies, he'd gifted her and Nate a whole crate of fine French champagne for everyone to enjoy at the wedding breakfast.

Sophie couldn't wait to meet the mysterious marquess. Not for the first time, she wondered if Olivia had taken a fancy to him.

Charlie's thoughts must have been in concert with hers as she remarked, "It's a pity Lord Sleat isn't here, Olivia."

Olivia promptly blushed. "J-just because I'm his temporary neighbor, it doesn't mean I'm going to develop a tendre for him," she said with a proud lift of her chin. "And even if I did, I'm sure he'd never notice me. He's hardly ever at home anyway. And when he is, he keeps to himself. As do I."

Charlie threw her an arch smile. "So you've noticed his comings and goings then, have you?"

"Hardly."

"I should bring my kitten Peridot over when the marquess returns from Scotland so she can 'get lost' in his garden."

Olivia rolled her eyes, clearly exasperated.

Sophie laughed. "The plan has some merit, Olivia. You should consider it."

That elicited a most unladylike tongue poke from Olivia, which sent them all into fits of laughter.

The men all cast curious glances their way, and when Nate caught her eye, Sophie smiled back, and he grinned and raised his glass to her.

When she turned back to her friends, she noticed the direction of Charlie's gaze; she was staring wistfully at Maximilian Devereux, the Duke of Exmoor.

Sophie gave her a quizzical look. "Wasn't the Duke of Exmoor on the top of our list of eligible rakes, Charlie?"

Charlie shrugged and blushed at the same time; and it wasn't like her to blush at all. She was clearly pretending a nonchalance she didn't feel. "Yes, he's still there," she remarked drily. "But I've decided he's not fun enough. A stiff duke is not for me."

Sophie couldn't resist teasing her. She arched a brow. "What's wrong with a stiff duke?"

Charlie burst out laughing. "Oh, Sophie! What have I done to you? I've corrupted you." She wiped her eyes and added in a quieter voice, "On second thought, it's probably my brother."

Now it was Sophie's turn to blush. Considering what she and Nate had been up to whenever they had the chance to be alone, she had good reason to. She decided to change the subject. "My dear friends, I will do whatever I can to help you find your perfect matches. Indeed, it seems to be the case that one really *doesn't* need Almack's to catch a husband."

Charlie's eyes twinkled with mischief as she remarked, "You'll be in the family way by next Season. You won't be any help at all."

Sophie opened her mouth to protest, but Charlie held up a finger. "Well, you cannot deny that it will be a definite possibility given the man you're now married to. I'm surprised Nate didn't whisk you away to the bedroom straight after the ceremony. Unless . . ." Charlie gave her a sly look, and heat seared Sophie's cheeks.

"Ha! Confess now, Sophie dearest," crowed Charlie, a triumphant gleam in her eye. "My wicked brother has already had his wicked way with you, hasn't he?" She lowered her voice and added, "What is it like? In general terms. I don't want to know *all* the details because we *are* talking about my brother."

Even though Olivia's cheeks were pink with embarrassment, she leaned forward to listen also.

Sophie lifted her chin in mock indignation. "I will not divulge *any* details." She sipped her champagne before whispering, "But it *is* wonderful. It's much better than reading about it."

"Well, so it should be," said Charlie with a mischievous smile. Then she sighed wistfully. "One day I hope to experience such a marvelous thing, to be truly loved and cherished."

Sophie squeezed her arm. "I'm absolutely certain that one day you will."

Nate's gaze drifted to Sophie and he wondered if she would be amenable to sneaking away from everyone very soon. Of course, she looked nothing but divine in her ivory and silver silk gown, but he rather fancied getting her out of the ensemble as soon as possible. His mind's eye was suddenly filled with the image of her sprawled naked across the enormous four-poster bed in the master suite. He would let down her glossy black hair from its elaborate arrangement of curls threaded with silver ribbon and pearls and slide off all of her undergarments, perhaps except for her stockings. Oh, and she could also leave on her necklace of pearls and sapphires, his wedding gift to her.

Yes, he rather liked the idea of pleasuring her while she was not quite naked . . .

Good God, he needed to change the direction of his thoughts, at once, or before long he'd be sporting an erection. And that really wasn't done when one's sister, aunt, and mother-in-law and her young daughters were only a few yards away. He didn't think his father-in-law, Edward Debenham, and his own father would appreciate such a spectacle either; they might be deep in conversation about crop rotation and irrigation at the present moment, but they weren't blind.

Nate drained his champagne, hoping that would quell the fire in his loins, then turned to Max . . . and noticed the cad was surreptitiously inspecting his sister. Charlie was openly laughing, her head tipped back, her riotous curls gleaming like burnished copper and gold in the light of the setting sun. Nate knew she was beautiful, in the way one knew a painting or sculpture was beautiful. But that didn't give his friend the right to ogle his baby sister.

"You dog, Devereux." Nate's tone was laced with exasperation. "Stop eyeing Charlie like she's a potential conquest. If you go anywhere near her, you know I'll have no choice but to kill you. And I'd rather not."

Max snorted, his aristocratic nostrils flaring. "I'm not like you, old chap. I'm not likely to get smitten by a fine pair of eyes."

"Oh, from where I'm standing, it didn't look like you were admiring my sister's eyes."

"I cannot help it if she draws *everyone's* eye. Miss de Vere is quite fetching as well."

"Stay the hell away from my wife's friend and my sister."

Max inclined his head. "Trust me, I will. I'm not in the market for a wife."

"And that's exactly my point." Nate clapped him on the back, then grinned. "On that note, if you'll excuse me, I'd like to go and speak with mine."

Night had descended by the time Nate finally did have the chance to spirit his new wife away to Deerhurst's master bedroom to do exactly all the things he'd been fantasizing about all afternoon.

Velvet darkness cloaked the grounds beyond the open casement window; the air was cool but not unpleasantly so, and a light breeze stirred the lace curtains as he sipped a glass of brandy in the window seat. Nestled against his banyan-clad shoulder was Sophie. Her gauzy white robe gaped open, providing him with a tantalizing glimpse of her rosy red nipples. About her slender neck was the pearl and sapphire necklace. She'd kept it and her stockings on during their vigorous bout of lovemaking.

He thought he was sated, but when his gaze drifted lower to the dark shadow of her sex and her long slender legs, he swallowed. He no longer had a taste for just brandy . . .

Sophie was reading aloud to him from Hastings House's copy of *Pride and Prejudice*. He'd been doggedly reading it for weeks, and while he found it entertaining, it was also hard work. On more than one occasion he'd been tempted to abandon it. But Sophie had insisted he reach the hard-fought happily ever after between Elizabeth Bennet and Mr. Darcy.

"I do love this next part, when Elizabeth asks Darcy to describe how he came to fall in love with her because what he says reminds me of you: 'I cannot fix on the hour, or the spot, or the look, or the words, which laid the foundation. It is too long ago. I was in the middle before I knew that I *had* begun.'" Sophie closed the book with a sigh. "I so adore Mr. Darcy."

"Really?" Nate fondled a lock of her black-as-midnight hair. "I think I might be jealous."

"Surely not. I might adore Mr. Darcy but my heart belongs to you, Nate. You and only you."

"I'm afraid I am not as noble as Mr. Darcy. From what I recall, he never tried to seduce Elizabeth in a dark garden or the library."

Sophie lifted her head, her blue eyes twinkling with mischief. "From what *I* recall, I was the one who tried to seduce you, Lord Malverne."

"That's what I love about you, my Lady Malverne. You have a wicked streak, too, which I plan to capitalize on right now."

"Really?"

"Mm-hmm . . ." Nate set aside his brandy glass and bent his head to catch his beautiful wife's mouth in a rapturous kiss. His hand slid inside the sheer robe and found one of her breasts. "Let's see how wicked we can both be right now."

The copy of *Pride and Prejudice* slid to the floor as Sophie turned in his arms. Her smile was deliciously seductive and, just like her invitation, impossible to resist. "Make love to me, my wicked viscount."

And, of course, that's exactly what Nate did.

TURN THE PAGE FOR A LOOK AT
AMY ROSE BENNETT'S NEXT BOOK . . .

HOW TO CATCH AN ERRANT EARL

DUE OUT IN SPRING 2020.

It's oft quoted that charity begins at home. But any well-bred lady or gentleman with a truly benevolent disposition must devote some time and energy to worthy causes, especially those philanthropic endeavors which better the lot of the deserving poor.

This Season, do consider attending a ball, a public assembly, or perhaps even a *musicale* in aid of charity. Visit our Society Advertisements section to find a comprehensive list of upcoming events . . .

The Beau Monde Mirror: The Society Page

Gunter's Tea Shop, Berkeley Square, London

April 2, 1818

Thank goodness it is raining.

At least that's what Miss Arabella Jardine told herself as she stepped out from the puddles beneath the portico of Gunter's and caught the attention of a jarvey on the other side of Berkeley Square. As the hackney coach splashed its way toward the tea shop, she could pretend she was only dashing away raindrops, not tears, from beneath her spectacles as she turned back to face her three dearest friends in the entire world. Friends she'd bonded with three years ago at Mrs. Rathbone's Academy for Young Ladies before they were all unceremoniously expelled amid a cloud of scandal for 'conduct unbecoming.'

Friends she'd only just been reunited with at Gunter's. As they'd taken tea and indulged in all manner of gastronomical delights, they'd also shared their hopes and dreams. Made plans for the future. Just as they'd done at Mrs. Rathbone's when they'd formed the Society for Enlightened Young Women. But now, due to circumstances beyond her control, Arabella was obliged to say farewell to her friends yet again.

Blast her family and their inconvenient plans to embark on a frivolous Grand Tour. Arabella endeavored to suppress a scowl as she fiddled with the buttons on her fawn kid gloves. She wanted to stay here in London with Charlie, Sophie, and dear Olivia. Being dragged across Europe to gawk at endless musty cathedrals and crumbling castle ruins was surely a waste of time and money. Money she could put to good use elsewhere given half the chance . . .

Lady Charlotte Hastings—or Charlie to her friends—pulled Arabella away from her disgruntled thoughts by enveloping her in a warm hug. "My darling Arabella, you must hold to your promise to write to us while you are gadding about the Continent." Charlie's unruly auburn curls tickled Arabella's cheek. "I don't care where you are—even if you're atop Mont Blanc or exploring the depths of the Black Forest—I will pay for the postage."

"Aye, as long as you all write back to me too." Arabella adjusted the shoulder strap of her leather satchel as Charlie released her. The hack had drawn up beside them. "I want to hear all about how your husband-hunting goes this Season." Her gaze met the eyes of each of her friends in turn. "Each and every one of you."

"Of course," said Sophie with a shy smile. A bright blush suffused her cheeks and Arabella rather suspected she was thinking about Charlie's very dashing, very eligible brother, Nathaniel, Lord Malverne. He'd joined them at Gunter's for a little while and Arabella was certain she'd detected a spark of interest in the wicked viscount's eyes as he'd conversed with Sophie. Even though Sophie's reputation was tarnished by the academy scandal—and her family was most decidedly 'lower gentry'—he should still be interested. Shy yet sweet Sophie, with her glossy black hair and enormous blue eyes, was breathtakingly beautiful. Indeed, all Arabella's friends were fair of face and disposition, and accomplished in all the ways that mattered in the eyes of Society.

Unlike herself. Arabella swallowed a sigh. Not only was she a Scottish orphan with dubious parentage and 'unnatural bluestocking tendencies'—at least according to her aunt Flora—she possessed a gap-toothed smile and was so longsighted she had to wear glasses most of the time. Even if she did make a debut this Season alongside her friends, she was certain she'd never receive anything more than a passing glance from most gentlemen of the ton. It was a good thing she had other plans for her future. *Secret plans.* As soon as she bid her friends goodbye, she was going to put them in motion this afternoon. All going well.

Her resolve to succeed in her mission reaffirmed, Arabella pushed her spectacles firmly back into place upon the bridge of her nose; Charlie's exuberant hug had dislodged them a little. "Are you ready to leave too, Olivia?" The jarvey was scowling at them from beneath the hood of his dripping oilskin. They really should go.

Olivia sighed heavily. "Y-y-yes," she replied, gathering up the skirts of her fashionable gown and matching pelisse so the fine fabric wouldn't trail through the muddy puddle directly in front of her. Her mouth twisted—Olivia's stammer always got worse when she was anxious—before her next words emerged in a bumpy rush. "As m-much as I hate to bid you all adieu as well, I m-must. Aunt Edith will undoubtedly be w-watching the clock."

Final hugs were exchanged, and once Arabella and Olivia were safely installed in the damp and dim interior of the hackney, it pulled away, barreling across the sodden square.

Olivia de Vere currently resided in a rented Grosvenor Square town house with her horribly strict guardians. Even though it was only a relatively short distance from Berkeley Square, Arabella had made arrangements to share a hack with her friend to not only avoid being soaked in the rain,

but to help Olivia escape her gilded cage for the outing to
Gunter's.

A wee bit of subterfuge had been involved; Olivia's ter-
magant of an aunt believed Arabella's aunt Flora had accompanied them on their excursion—which wasn't the case
at all. Even though Gunter's was a respectable establishment, there would be hell to pay if Olivia's aunt learned her
niece had visited the tea shop without a suitable chaperone.

"I really w-won't see you again before you depart for the
Continent, will I?" The expression in Olivia's dark brown
eyes was so forlorn, Arabella's heart cramped with sadness.
She suspected Olivia was often as lonely as she was.

"I'm afraid not," she replied softly. "Bertie, my cousin's
husband, has booked us all on the Dover Packet and we're
due to set sail for France in three days' time."

Olivia's mouth twitched with a smile. "I'm rather
tempted to stow myself away in your trunk. I won't take up
much room."

Arabella laughed, pleased to see her friend's spirits returning. "Believe me, I would take you if I could. Aunt
Flora and my cousin Lilias are sure to be exacting in the
extreme during the journey. Your company would be most
welcome."

Olivia reached out and squeezed her hand. Despite the
sheeting rain and the traffic snarls, they were fast approaching Grosvenor Square. "I have a feeling you are going to
have a m-marvelous time, despite your misgivings. And
who knows, perhaps you might meet a charming Italian
prince or handsome Swiss nobleman who'll sweep you off
your feet." Olivia's eyes glowed. "Just imagine it."

Arabella very much doubted that would be the case.
And unlike Olivia, Charlie, and Sophie, she didn't possess
a romantic bone in her body; love matches weren't for
plain, practical women like her. However, she dredged up a
smile in an effort to appear lighthearted. "Well, unless his
name is on the list of eligible gentlemen we just devised at
Gunter's, I don't see how I can seriously consider his suit."
She lowered her voice even though no one else was in earshot and rain was drumming on the roof of the hackney. "I

mean, with no one of our acquaintance to vouch for him, what if he's really a dastardly rogue with a skeleton or two in the closet—literally—like a murdered first wife? Or as Charlie mentioned earlier today, what if he's afflicted with the pox?"

Olivia giggled and gave a theatrical shudder. "Perish the thought."

"At least your broodingly handsome neighbor, Lord Sleat, is on the list." Charlie had mentioned the Scottish marquess was a friend of her brother's and a highly suitable candidate for a husband. Even though he'd been terribly wounded at Waterloo and now sported an eye patch, apparently he was quite the gentleman beneath his rugged exterior. And *very* popular with the ladies of the ton.

"Yes." Olivia sighed and tucked a lock of dark brown hair back into the confines of her fine straw bonnet. The hackney coach had stopped before her town house and she threw a wistful glance at the adjacent residence with its ornate pillars and shiny black double doors. "But I don't see how I shall ever cross paths with him. He very much keeps to himself." Her mouth curved into a wry smile. "I think I shall secretly dub him the mysterious marquess."

The front door to her own house cracked open and Olivia grimaced. Gathering up her reticule, she hugged Arabella one last time. "Take care, my lovely friend. I must go before my aunt sends one of her horrid footmen out to haul me inside. Have a wonderful trip."

After waving Olivia off and issuing new instructions to the taciturn jarvey, Arabella hastily closed the hack's door against a sudden squall of icy rain which snatched at her sage green skirts and her leghorn bonnet. Settling into the battered leather seat once more, she removed her glasses to wipe off the rain spots with a lawn handkerchief, then checked her hem and brown kid boots for splashes of mud. For the most part, she wasn't fussy about her appearance, but she wanted to make a good impression at her next appointment. The matron at London's Foundling Hospital was expecting her . . . and so was Dr. Graham Radcliff.

She hadn't added the physician's name to the Society for

Enlightened Young Women's list of eligible gentlemen. Her association with this particular man was her very own closely guarded secret, one she didn't feel ready to share with her friends quite yet.

Arabella's stomach tumbled oddly and she frowned at her reflection in the hack's rain-lashed window. She was nervous and she did not want to be. Was the rising feeling of anticipation and trepidation in her heart related to the fact she was about to tour an establishment which would surely bring back certain memories she'd rather not revisit? Or was it because she was going to meet the clever and engaging Dr. Radcliff once again? He'd suggested her visit coincide with the hospital board's meeting today. As well as providing medical expertise to the institution, the physician was also one of the directors.

She fiddled with the worn pewter buckle of her grandfather's old leather satchel. The good doctor's letter of introduction to the Foundling Hospital's matron lay safely within. It had been just over a year since she'd last encountered the gentleman—a former medical colleague of her dearly departed grandfather, Dr. Iain Burnett. Arabella sometimes suspected her grandfather had been not-so-subtly trying to play matchmaker when he'd first introduced her to the widowed physician at a charity *musicale* in London in aid of the Foundling Hospital.

A smile trembled about Arabella's lips at the bittersweet memory. That had been in the winter before her grandfather had passed away. And a year and a half after the academy scandal had erupted and Arabella's name had become mud in polite society—both in London and in Edinburgh, where she now lived with Aunt Flora, Lilias, and her husband, Albert Arbuthnott. There was one unpalatable truth Arabella had already learned in life: the stain of scandal was not easily removed; it tended to cling to one's person wherever one went.

If tonnish society—here or in Edinburgh—ever learned of the real scandal attached to her past, she'd surely be banished forevermore.

At least Dr. Radcliff didn't know anything about *that*.

What he did know of her—that she was a bluestocking who'd rather attend a public lecture on vaccination than an assembly or ton ball—hadn't shocked him in the slightest. Indeed, on the two occasions they'd met, Dr. Radcliff had always treated her with the utmost respect. And over the past year, they'd corresponded regularly about all manner of medical and social welfare topics—from the latest recommendations in treating infant colic, to the pressing need to expand access to universal dispensaries, and the case for improving nutrition for the inmates of charity poorhouses.

It seemed Dr. Radcliff truly understood her desire to advocate for public health programs, just like her grandfather had done. In her opinion, improving the wellbeing of infants and children in institutionalized care was of paramount importance. Hence her visit to the Foundling Hospital. She wanted to learn as much as she could about the famous institution's practices because one day—if she ever had the means and social connections—she dreamed of opening a similar hospital in Edinburgh.

An impossible dream, perhaps, but Arabella was committed to making it a reality. One thing she didn't lack was determination.

The Foundling Hospital, 40 Brunswick Square, London

"I'm afraid the matron cannot see you this afternoon, Miss . . ." The plump, middle-aged housekeeper of the Foundling Hospital squinted down at Dr. Radcliff's letter. The hospital's entry hall was not only chilly and damp but poorly lit, and it took her a moment to find Arabella's name again. "Miss Jardine, is it?"

"Yes, that's right." Beneath her disheveled blond curls, Arabella's forehead knitted into a frown. This wouldn't do at all. Out of the corner of her eye, she noticed the hall porter reaching for the handle of the front door. A large-boned, heavily browed man, he looked like he wouldn't hesitate to eject her at a moment's notice. Turning her attention back to the housekeeper, Arabella decided to argue her case. "But I have an appointment. Dr. Radcliff arranged it. He's on the hospital board, I believe."

The woman sniffed haughtily as her gaze flicked over Arabella. She clearly wasn't impressed by Arabella's person. Given her plain attire and the fact she was unchaperoned, it was obvious she wasn't well connected or from a family of means. It didn't appear to matter that she knew the physician either. "Yes, I know Dr. Radcliff," she said, handing back the letter. "Fine gentleman he is. And ordinarily Matron would be happy to show you about. But not today. Perhaps you could come back next week when we run our public tour."

A knot of frustration tightened inside Arabella's chest. "Unfortunately that won't suit as I'm leaving town the day after tomorrow for an extended period of time. Is there anyone else who might be amenable to showing me around? One of the other staff members perhaps? A nurse or teacher? Dr. Radcliff mentioned he would be attending a board meeting this afternoon. Is there somewhere I could wait for him?" It suddenly occurred to her that she was more disappointed about the prospect of not seeing Dr. Radcliff than missing out on a guided tour. And she hadn't expected that.

The housekeeper sighed heavily, her ample bosom straining the seams of her plain black gown and white cotton pinafore. "I really don't think so, Miss Jardine," she said in a clipped tone. "Besides, I'm sure the good doctor has better things to do with his time. Just like our matron. With a number of children falling ill overnight—" The woman clamped her lips together as if she'd said the wrong thing. "Everyone is just too busy."

Alarm spiked through Arabella. "Oh, dear. I hope whatever it is, it isn't too serious." No wonder the matron was busy. Illness could spread like wildfire through an institution like this with devastating consequences. She'd once witnessed a measles outbreak in Edinburgh's North Bridge Orphanage, an institution she'd visited with her grandfather on many occasions. "Is there anything I can do to help? I've a good deal of nursing experience myself."

The housekeeper arched a thin eyebrow, clearly unconvinced by Arabella's claim. "I don't think so. Matron has everything well in hand, miss." Her gaze skipped to the porter's and Arabella felt a cold draught wash over her back and eddy about her ankles as he opened the door.

Taking a step closer to the housekeeper, Arabella slipped her hand through the slit in her gown's woolen skirts and pulled her coin purse from her pocket. The woman's eyes gleamed when she heard the coins chink together. "Miss . . ."

"Mrs. Bradley."

"Mrs. Bradley." Arabella opened her purse and removed one of her precious sovereigns. She'd intended to purchase a few bits and pieces on Bond Street before she returned to the Arbuthnott's rented town house on Half-Moon Street, but she was willing to make a small sacrifice if it meant she could stay. "Would it help if I offered you a wee donation as a token of my appreciation for your trouble?" she said in a low voice. "If you could spare a little time to take me through the girls' wing. And then as I suggested, I could wait somewhere for Dr. Radcliff. I hear there's a picture gallery . . ."

Mrs. Bradley snatched up the proffered coin and tucked it into the pocket of her pinafore faster than an alley cat pouncing on a rat. She gestured at the porter to shut the door. "Very well, Miss Jardine." Turning on her heel, she strode across the hall toward another door. "Follow me."

As soon as Arabella entered the girls' dormitory, with its endless rows of narrow beds covered in stiff white sheets and rough, dun, woolen blankets, an icy shiver skated down her spine and her stomach clenched. Her breath caught and her pulse fluttered wildly like a trapped moth beneath her skin. She had to curl her gloved hands into fists to hide her trembling fingers.

It was always this way. It didn't matter that she'd visited similar places countless times with her grandfather. No amount of rational thought could overcome her body's visceral response, the immediate instinct to turn and run, run, run out the door and back into the street into the fresh air and light.

Perhaps it was the absence of curtains at the high, barred windows, or the echo of footsteps on cold, bare floorboards that caused such a reaction. Then again, it could have been the sharp scent of laundry starch and lye soap that transported her back to another time and place. Another orphanage she'd rather not remember, with its mean-spirited nurses and their harsh orders. Their hard eyes and even harder hands that pushed and slapped and pinched.

But it was those very memories that drove her ambition. Her desire to make things better for other abandoned or orphaned children. Fifteen years might have passed since she'd last been an inmate of Glasgow's Great Clyde Hospital and Poorhouse, but she would never, ever forget how it felt to be a small, desperate child rendered mute with crushing fear and despair. The terrible, smothering sense of being completely alone and unloved.

Unwanted.

If Mrs. Bradley noticed Arabella's odd demeanor, she didn't remark upon it. She simply delivered what appeared to be a well-practiced speech about the children's routines: when they rose and when they slept, how a cleanliness inspection was always conducted after morning prayers, the nature of the children's personal chores and domestic "employments," based upon age, and the amount of time allocated to academic studies such as arithmetic and literacy lessons.

All the while, Arabella strove to listen and make mental notes of details such as how many children were accommodated within the hospital. The budget allocated for uniforms. The number of teaching and nursing staff employed by the board. This was what she needed to know in order to begin making her own plans to establish a foundling home and orphanage.

But right now she couldn't seem to focus, even when she endeavored to jot down pertinent information in a notebook she retrieved from her satchel. It seemed she would have to come back another time to gain a better understanding of the running costs that would be involved.

Unless Dr. Radcliff would be willing to share such details. He was on the board after all. But that would require

Arabella to summon the courage to tell him about her ambitious plans. And she didn't know him well enough for that. Well, not yet . . .

By the time Mrs. Bradley had shown Arabella through the refectory, one of the classrooms, and the laundry, she was feeling almost like herself again. Seeing the children—who all appeared to be sufficiently nourished and adequately clothed in gowns of brown serge, crisp white pinafores, and matching bonnets—had helped to reassure her that the Foundling Hospital took better care of its inmates than the Great Clyde Hospital had. Some of the younger girls had even traded shy smiles with her.

Mrs. Bradley gave the hospital's sick ward a wide berth—as was to be expected given an outbreak of illness—so the last point of call was the kitchen.

The familiar smells of boiled beef and baking bread hit Arabella as soon as they crossed the threshold into a cavernous room. Like the laundry, the kitchen was abuzz with activity. Older girls who appeared to be aged between nine and perhaps fourteen diligently peeled and chopped potatoes, kneaded bread, or stood by the fireside tending to whatever bubbled in the enormous cast-iron pots. Arabella also spied a much younger child, who couldn't have been more than five, huddled on a low stool by the fireside half-heartedly working a small pair of bellows; a totally unnecessary activity in Arabella's opinion, considering the fire was already burning brightly.

Indeed, the kitchen was a good deal warmer than any of the other rooms she'd visited so far. Condensation clung to the windows and it wasn't long before Arabella felt sweat prickling down her back and along her hairline.

The fearsome cook—Mrs. Humbert—was a stout, florid-faced woman with work-roughened hands, a caustic tone, and a scalding glare. When her gaze scoured over Arabella, she tried not to flinch. She'd just mustered the courage to ask Mrs. Humbert if the children were ever provided with any other types of vegetable besides potatoes when all hell broke loose.

The young girl by the fire tumbled off her stool onto the

flagged hearth, her body jerking oddly. The other girls who'd stood nearby screamed and jumped back. Ladles and spoons went flying and a pot of rice pudding overturned.

"What the 'ell is goin' on?" screeched Mrs. Humbert, advancing toward the commotion.

"Sally's choking." A tall redheaded girl pointed at the little one on the floor. "She must've nicked a piece of carrot out of the boiled beef pot again."

"Li'l toad. Serves 'er right." Mrs. Humbert elbowed several gawking girls out of the way. "After I've finished fumping 'er on the back, I'll box 'er ears."

Arabella rushed to the fireside too; the little girl's eyes had rolled back in her head and her mouth had twisted. Her body was rigid and her muscles twitched.

"She's not choking. And you'll do no such thing, Mrs. Humbert." Arabella dropped to her knees beside the child and glared back at the fuming cook. "She's having a seizure."

Planting her fisted hands on her ample hips, Mrs. Humbert towered over Arabella. "An' 'ow would you know, Miss 'igh-and-mighty?" she demanded.

Arabella narrowed her gaze as she tugged off her gloves. "I know." Ignoring the cook's thunderous scowl and Mrs. Bradley's protests, she turned the girl, Sally, gently onto her side and placed a hand on her forehead. The child's skin was burning hot and her cheeks bright red, but Arabella didn't think the heat of the fire was to blame. "Does Sally have a history of epilepsy?" The cook and housekeeper stared at her blankly. "You know, the falling sickness?"

"'Ow would I know?" huffed Mrs. Humbert.

Mrs. Bradley shook her head. "Not that I know of, Miss Jardine."

"She has a fever. A high one. It can trigger fitting in babies and young children." Arabella began loosening the child's pinafore and gown. "We need to cool her down. Can someone please fetch a cloth soaked in cold water? The seizure will soon pass."

Sure enough, within a minute, Sally regained consciousness. She moaned and blinked a few times before tears welled in her large, pansy brown eyes. Eyes that seemed too large for her small, flushed face. "My head hurts," she whispered.

"You had a wee fall," said Arabella gently, stroking her hot cheek. "Do you think you can sit?"

Sally nodded and Arabella helped her up. The child whimpered and buried her face in Arabella's shoulder. "She needs to be taken to the sick ward and assessed by a doctor."

Mrs. Bradley nodded. There seemed to be a newfound respect in her eyes. "Of course. Up you get, Sally."

But little Sally was still shaking and crying. Standing up seemed quite beyond her, so Arabella picked her up. Her body was so slight, she barely weighed a thing. "I'll carry her."

"Very well." For the second time that afternoon, the housekeeper bade Arabella to follow her.

A short time later, Sally had been installed in a cot in the sick ward and the hospital's matron was thanking Arabella for her quick thinking and care.

"Dr. Radcliff mentioned you were coming today, Miss Jardine," she said, ushering Arabella outside and down the corridor. They paused by a large window which overlooked a sodden garden featuring a bed of drooping daffodils. A slender woman who was perhaps in her thirties, the matron had a calm yet efficient manner about her. "I apologize for not being able to show you around the hospital myself."

"I understand completely," said Arabella. "I can see how busy you are." There were half a dozen other children occupying beds in the ward and Arabella suspected they were all suffering from the same ailment. "Measles is a terrible illness so I truly hope you can contain the outbreak."

Beneath her starched-white cap, the matron's brow plunged into a deep frown. "How did you know?" she asked in hushed tones. "Did Mrs. Bradley say anything? I asked her not to. We don't want to alarm the public unnecessarily. Or the board, especially when the children have yet to be seen by a doctor. I hope I can count on your discretion."

"Yes, of course," replied Arabella. "And to answer your questions, no, Mrs. Bradley didn't mention it was measles.

But when I loosened little Sally's uniform, I noticed the rash on her neck and shoulders. And on her face. It's quite distinctive."

"Yes . . ." The matron gave her a considering look. "You've had medical training."

"My grandfather was a physician. I used to assist him in his practice."

"Ah." The matron nodded. "And you know Dr. Radcliff as well, I hear."

Arabella felt her own cheeks grow hot. "Yes."

"Did someone mention my name?"

Arabella turned at the sound of a pleasantly deep male voice behind her. It was indeed Dr. Radcliff. Arabella's blush deepened as her gaze met the doctor's and she nervously adjusted her glasses, hoping the action would help hide the fact that her face was so red.

The doctor was just as amiable as she recalled. A trim gentleman of middling height and age—his brown hair was shot with silver at the temples—he wasn't particularly handsome, but he possessed a charming manner and kind brown eyes. Eyes that held hers for a moment longer than was perhaps necessary before he bowed over her hand.

"Miss Jardine," he said, a genuine smile playing about his lips. While his gaze held a warm light, his long fingers were cool against her skin. "It has been far too long."

"Yes, it has," Arabella replied, dismayed that she sounded a little breathless. "It's lovely to see you again." The doctor released her hand and she curled her fingers into her palm; she fancied that she still felt his touch. Giving herself a mental shake for being such a goose, she added, "And before I forget, I must thank you for arranging a tour for me. It's been most enlightening."

"I'm pleased to hear it. And you're most welcome, Miss Jardine. I know you have a passionate interest in facilities such as this one." The doctor turned his attention back to the matron who was observing them both with a quizzical expression. "Good afternoon, Matron. I understand you have need of me."

"Yes." The young woman gave a succinct recount of the situation, even describing Arabella's intervention when Sally had taken ill. "So unfortunately, it seems we might have a measles outbreak on our hands," she concluded gravely.

Concern shadowed Dr. Radcliff's eyes. "Would that you and Miss Jardine were wrong, Matron. But I rather suspect you're not." He caught her gaze again. "If circumstances were different, I'd suggest we take a turn about the picture gallery and then ask Mrs. Bradley to arrange tea for us all"—he nodded at the matron—"in one of the parlors. But I'm afraid it will have to be another time. I hope you understand, Miss Jardine."

"Yes, of course." Even though disappointment tugged at her heart, Arabella summoned a smile. "I look forward to it."

"Perhaps when you return from the Continent?" Dr. Radcliff was following the matron toward the ward. "How long will you be away? I don't recall you mentioning that in your last letter."

"Four months at this stage."

The doctor paused on the threshold. "Be sure to send me your direction. I want to tell you all about my plans for a new clinic at Seven Dials. I'm modeling it on the Universal Dispensary for Children. Oh, and be sure to squeeze in a visit to the Enfants-Trouvés and the Enfants-Malades in Paris if you have the chance. They're both wonderful hospitals."

Arabella inclined her head. "I will. Goodbye, Dr. Radcliff. Matron." But Matron was asking the doctor if he had any Godfrey's Cordial on hand as he stepped into the room. And then the door closed behind him.

Arabella sighed as she retraced her steps along the corridor, heading toward the hospital's main entrance. It was such a shame that fate had conspired against her this afternoon. She'd been so looking forward to spending a little more time with Dr. Radcliff. Of course, their encounter had been so brief she couldn't be sure if he looked upon her as anything more than a friend. They were certainly

like-minded individuals. And from what she'd seen of him
on the three occasions they'd met, he was a most congenial,
even-tempered man. He would make some lucky woman a
lovely husband. If he wished to marry again of course . . .

Arabella had no idea what his wishes were in that regard. But after today, it had become abundantly clear to her
that she wouldn't mind at all if Dr. Graham Radcliff began
to view her as a prospective spouse. As a doctor's wife—
particularly as the wife of someone with Dr. Radcliff's social connections—it would be much easier for her to realize
her goal. To make a real difference to all those children
who were forced to endure inferior conditions in poorly
funded and poorly managed institutions up north. For now
though, she could at least take heart in the fact Dr. Radcliff
wanted to continue corresponding with her. And dare she
believe he wanted to see her again when she returned to
London? Why else would he ask how long she would be
away?

It might still be raining, but Arabella's spirits weren't the
least bit dampened as she hailed another hackney coach.
Hopefully this Grand Tour she was about to embark upon
would be over with before she knew it. And then she could
get on with the life she truly wanted.

Ready to find
your next great read?

Let us help.

Visit prh.com/nextread

Penguin
Random
House